D1482012

WITHDRAWN

THE WESLEYAN EDITION OF THE
WORKS OF HENRY FIELDING

MISCELLANIES

HENRY FIELDING

Miscellanies by Henry Fielding, Esq;

Volume One

EDITED BY

HENRY KNIGHT MILLER

WESLEYAN UNIVERSITY PRESS

1972

PRINTED IN GREAT BRITAIN
AT THE UNIVERSITY PRESS, OXFORD
BY VIVIAN RIDLER
PRINTER TO THE UNIVERSITY

TO THE HOUSES OF
DEGRAW AND MEARS

Rami felicia poma ferentes

PREFACE

THE Wesleyan edition of Henry Fielding's *Miscellanies* will occupy two volumes, of which this is the first. This edition seeks to provide for the modern reader an accurate text and an adequate historical annotation of that text. The General Introduction offers comment upon Fielding's situation in the years leading up to the *Miscellanies* (published in 1743), discusses briefly the background and significance of the major items in Volume One, and gives a chronological survey of the conjectural dates of composition for these pieces. The history of publication and the (rather meagre) response are briefly summarized. The Textual Introduction explains the principles upon which the present text is based.

It is a pleasure to acknowledge various kindnesses that the editor has enjoyed at the libraries of Princeton, Yale, and Harvard universities, the Folger Shakespeare Library, the Library of Congress, the New York Public Library, the library of the University of London, and the British Museum. I must signalize a special debt to Louis A. Landa and the late George Sherburn. Other good friends upon whom I have drawn for learning and comfort are Martin C. Battestin, William B. Coley, the late Charles B. Woods, C. J. Rawson, Sheridan Baker, Edgar V. Roberts, James Thorpe, Robert Taylor, D. W. Robertson, Jr., Maurice Kelley, and—quite beyond the call of duty—Fredson Bowers. The members of the Advisory Board of the Wesleyan Fielding have contributed, individually, useful criticism and generous encouragement; and I must express individually my gratitude to each of these distinguished scholars: James L. Clifford, Arthur Friedman, Richard L. Greene, Allen T. Hazen, Maynard Mack, Alan D. McKillop, James M. Osborn, and James Sutherland.

My profoundest obligation, as ever, is to my wife.

LIST OF CONTENTS

GENERAL INTRODUCTION   xi

   1. Circumstances of Composition   xi

   2. Contents   xvii

   3. Date of Composition   xlii

   4. History of Publication   xlvi

TEXTUAL INTRODUCTION   l

   1. The Copy-Text and its Treatment   l

   2. The Early Editions   liv

   3. The Apparatus   lv

   4. Collation   lv

MISCELLANIES, BY HENRY FIELDING, ESQ;
(VOLUME ONE)   1

   Preface   3

   [Contents]   17

   Text   19

APPENDICES   245

   A. Preface to *Of True Greatness*, 1741   247

   B. 'To Sir R. W—le,' from *The Gentleman's Magazine*, 1738   249

   C. Verses from *The Champion*, 1740   251

   D. From the *Philosophical Transactions* of the Royal Society, 1743   253

TEXTUAL APPENDICES   261

   I. List of Substantive Emendations   263

   II. List of Accidentals Emendations   264

   III. Word Division   265

   IV. Historical Collation   266

   V. Bibliographical Description   267

INDEX   271

GENERAL INTRODUCTION

In April 1743, a little more than a year after the appearance of *Joseph Andrews* (February 1742), the three-volume set of *Miscellanies, by Henry Fielding, Esq;* was published by subscription. The first volume of this substantial undertaking included most of Fielding's short poems and verse-essays, several formal essays in prose, a translation from Demosthenes, and some brief satires and Lucianic sketches. This volume is here reprinted as an entity for the first time since 1743. The second volume presented an incomplete work of prose-fiction, *A Journey from This World to the Next*, and two plays, possibly added to fill out the volume, *Eurydice* and *The Wedding Day*.[1] The third volume was given over to *The Life of Mr. Jonathan Wild the Great*.

I. CIRCUMSTANCES OF COMPOSITION

There is little satisfactory evidence concerning the genesis of this large enterprise of Fielding's middle life. Publication by subscription was at this time a well-established and often highly rewarding activity: Prior and Pope and Gay had profited by it and—perhaps more to the point—political loyalties had assured John Gay's *Polly* and Henry Brooke's *Gustavus Vasa*, both suppressed by Sir Robert Walpole's ministry, a most remunerative subscription sale in the ranks of the Opposition. As a well-known, not to say notorious, member of the anti-ministerial faction in the late 1730s, Fielding must have visualized ready profit in a set of volumes to be issued under his name—particularly if it were known that the crowning volume drew many satisfactory parallels between the career of a 'truly great' criminal, Jonathan Wild, and that of another 'Great Man' in the public eye. Moreover, publication by subscription offered the conspicuous advantage that half the purchase price was paid down

---

[1] Neither of the plays included in the *Miscellanies* was mentioned in the 'Proposals' of 5 June 1742 (see below, p. xlvi); the original plan would thus seem to have been that the *Journey* would occupy the whole of the second volume.

at the time of subscribing.¹ This was no minor consideration, for from the time that the Licensing Act ended his dramatic career in 1737, Henry Fielding found himself urgently in need of fresh sources of income.

After that blow, he had struggled to carry on two careers at once, the study of law and prolific hack-writing (for so even the brilliantly conducted *Champion* would have been characterized). He entered the Middle Temple in November 1737, was called to the bar in June 1740, and, according to his biographer Arthur Murphy, immediately began riding the Western Circuit in search of briefs during the Vacations and dancing attendance at Westminster Hall in term time.² Concurrently, from November 1739 until some time in 1741,³ he was writing essays for, and editing, the most important Opposition periodical, the *Champion*. Moreover, when he launched the *Champion*, he was apparently already involved in translating anonymously for a booksellers' conger Adlerfeld's *Military History of Charles XII*, which ultimately appeared in October 1740.⁴ Other products of Fielding's pen in these years may yet be identified.⁵

---

¹ A manuscript poem by Horace Walpole, called 'The Praises of a Poet's Life', has a probable reference to solicitations for the *Miscellanies*:

> Thus Fielding spoke, & most devoutly bless'd
> The gracious Muse, not fruitlessly caress'd:
> A whole Half-Guinea, a Subscription Fee
> That very Morn had set his Snuffbox free,
> Pledg'd to a Broker; which so late withdrawn,
> In Two Day's Time He seeks again to Pawn.

(Cited by W. B. Coley, from the collection of Mr. Wilmarth S. Lewis, in 'Henry Fielding and the Two Walpoles', *PQ*, xlv [1966], 169; Coley dates the poem *c.* March 1742, and points out its appropriateness to the *Miscellanies*.)

² 'An Essay on the Life and Genius of Henry Fielding,' in *The Works*, 2nd edn., 1762, i. 55. See also Wilbur L. Cross, *The History of Henry Fielding* (New Haven, 1918), i. 258–9. Place of publication in subsequent references is London, unless otherwise indicated.

³ Fielding said in the preface to the *Miscellanies* (see below, p. 14): 'I take this Opportunity to declare in the most solemn Manner, I have long since (as long as from *June* 1741) desisted from writing one Syllable in the *Champion*, or any other public Paper'; but the partners in the paper said in March 1742 that he had 'withdrawn himself from that Service for above Twelve Months past' (G. M. Godden, *Henry Fielding: A Memoir*, 1910, p. 139).

⁴ The evidence is an apparently genuine receipt, dated 10 March 1739, given by Fielding to the bookseller John Nourse for advance payment on his translation of the history. See W. L. Cross, i. 284.

⁵ Cf. Arthur Murphy on (vaguely) this period of Fielding's life: 'A large number of fugitive political tracts, which had their value when the incidents were actually passing on the great scene of business, came from his pen' ('Life', in *The Works*, 2nd edn., 1762, i. 56).

In January 1741, he published (with a preface defending Bubb Dodington, and incidentally himself, against the attacks of the ministerial press) a poetic essay, *Of True Greatness*, which was later reprinted without the preface in the *Miscellanies*. In the same month appeared *The Vernoniad*, his vigorous attack upon Walpole and praise of the current hero of the Opposition, Admiral Vernon.[1] In April was published the political sermon often attributed to him, *The Crisis*, and his wicked parody of Richardson, *An Apology for the Life of Mrs. Shamela Andrews*. At the end of the year, just as the new Parliament assembled, that curious political tract, *The Opposition*—which Fielding owns as his, in the preface to the *Miscellanies*—came out in apparent praise of Walpole and dispraise of his enemies.

Whether this pamphlet represented a flirtation with (or alignment with) the administration, or whether its celebration of Sir Robert was ironic,[2] disillusionment with certain self-seeking 'Patriots' of the Opposition is patent.[3] The jockeyings for position and the shifts in political loyalties of the period immediately before and after the fall of Walpole make for a confused picture; but, whatever the arcane meaning of *The Opposition*, Fielding obviously continued to maintain his cordial relationship with such 'anti-Walpole' friends and patrons as Chesterfield and Dodington and Lyttelton, and he openly expressed his admiration of the 'heroic' leader, Argyle.[4] This wing of the Opposition had

[1] The two long poems are mentioned together in a note from Fielding's hand in April 1741 (see Cross, i. 288).

[2] See Cross, i. 298–301, for the conventional view that *The Opposition* was ironic. Martin C. Battestin has argued that Fielding broke with the Opposition sometime in 1741, and that this pamphlet represented a declaration of his commitment to the Walpole cause (see 'Fielding's Changing Politics and *Joseph Andrews*', PQ, xxxix [1960], 39–55). For a different interpretation, see W. B. Coley, 'Henry Fielding and the Two Walpoles', PQ, xlv (1966), 157–78.

[3] This note is sounded throughout 1742 and 1743. For *Joseph Andrews*, see the Introduction by Martin C. Battestin in the Wesleyan edition. In the notes to the translation of Aristophanes' *Plutus* (May 1742), capitals emphasize the point: 'TO MAKE USE OF POPULAR INTEREST, AND the CHARACTER OF PATRIOTISM, IN ORDER TO BETRAY ONE'S COUNTRY, is perhaps the most flagitious of all Crimes' (p. 57 n.). See also *A Journey from This World to the Next* (esp. I. iii, vii, xxiii); *Jonathan Wild* (IV. iii *et passim*); and Volume One of the *Miscellanies*, below, pp. 53, 176, 190, and 204.

[4] The Duke of Argyle's vigorous and successful campaign to seat Opposition candidates from Scotland in the general election of 1741 gave new lustre to his reputation, and he continued to lead the anti-Hanoverians after Walpole's fall, though after his own resignation in March 1742, his influence gradually began to diminish (see John B. Owen, *The Rise of the Pelhams*, 1957, pp. 92, 97, 101–2, 110).

become reasonably suspicious concerning the motives of its erstwhile leaders, Carteret and Pulteney;[1] and, despite Fielding's praise of Carteret in one poem of the *Miscellanies*,[2] his various bitter reflections upon false Patriots in this period would seem to have been directed primarily at those who made their peace with the Hanoverian court. After Sir Robert's fall, the watchword for the *new* Opposition was anti-Hanoverianism;[3] and until the installation of the 'Broad-Bottom' Pelham administration in November 1744 (in which Lyttelton and Dodington found places), Fielding's writings reflect the bias of the political out-group against the house of Hanover and its spokesmen.

In February 1742, shortly after Walpole's resignation, came the important publication of *Joseph Andrews*. Though its success was surely pleasing, there is no evidence that it resolved Fielding's financial problems; and he continued to throw off a variety of miscellaneous compositions. In April he tried a pamphlet defending the wealthy old Dowager Duchess of Marlborough—apparently without response from that mainstay of the old Opposition, despite a tickling allusion to Walpole as 'the Corrupter'.[4] In May he entered the theatre once more with a little play in which he claimed to have had 'a very small Share', *Miss Lucy in Town*, a sequel to his popular farce of the 1735 season, *An Old Man Taught Wisdom*.[5] Also in May appeared the first sample of a projected translation with William Young of the entire corpus of Aristophanes' work, *Plutus, the God of Riches*. The reaction must have been disappointing: we hear no more of this most desirable project.

[1] Lyttelton (?) later observed of this period: ''Tis Evident now to all Mankind . . . that when the Leaders of the [Opposition] Party had fully matured their Scheme, by long Labour, great Art, and infinite Assiduity, the Farce concluded very differently from the sanguine Expectations of most People. . . . a kind of Coalition was framed between the Court and Anti-court-Chiefs; and all the Minister's Crimes and Errors, as we were before taught to call them, on a sudden buried in Oblivion' (*A Modest Apology for My Own Conduct*, 1748, pp. 6–7).

[2] *Of True Greatness*, l. 259.

[3] As Richard Grenville wrote to his brother George in November 1742, concerning the ministry's plan to hire 16,000 Hanoverian mercenaries: 'We shall have a glorious day about the 16,000. We shall see then who are Hanoverians and who Englishmen' (cited in Lewis M. Wiggin, *The Faction of Cousins*, New Haven, 1958, p. 102). Fielding glanced at the flow of money to Hanover in his *Some Papers* of February 1743 (see below, p. 193).

[4] *A Full Vindication of the Dutchess Dowager of Marlborough* (1742), p. 38.

[5] See below, *Preface*, p. 15.

In January and February of 1743, at the very time when the *Miscellanies* must have been in the last stages, we find Fielding desperately at work trying to finish a play, *The Good-Natured Man*, that at David Garrick's particular request he had brought out from his papers and revised. But, with visions perhaps of a genuine return to the theatre, Fielding could not be satisfied with this work and substituted for it the revamping of another early play, *The Wedding Day*, which was duly—but not very success-fully—performed in February.[1] Published in the same month, it was soon reprinted in the *Miscellanies*. A burlesque piece that he also included in the collection, *Some Papers Proper to be Read before the R—l Society*, was dashed off in less than two weeks in February, and printed in that month.[2]

This flood of miscellaneous writing and abortive projects might alone lead us to suppose that Fielding's circumstances during these years were less than satisfactory; but there is more personal evidence as well. The allusion in the subscription pro-posals of June 1742[3] to 'a Train of melancholy Accidents scarce to be parallell'd [*sic*]', and that, in the preface to the *Miscellanies*, to 'the Accidents which have befallen me, and the Distresses I have waded through whilst I have been engaged in these Works', as well as to 'that Degree of Heart-ach [*sic*] which hath often discomposed me in the writing them', offer somewhat vague but nonetheless poignant commentary on Fielding's affairs. He had sold his interest in the family lands at East Stour in 1738, and though the death of his uncle George Fielding in that year brought a fair legacy, litigation over the will was not resolved until 1745.[4] When in 1739 he planned to bring his family up to London, he wrote to the bookseller John Nourse to ask his help in finding a house near the Middle Temple, and began: 'Dis-appointments have hitherto prevented my paying y^r Bill. . . .'[5] When he was called to the bar in 1740, he was granted chambers in Pump Court; but, perhaps again for economic reasons, he surrendered them in November.[6]

In June 1741, his father, General Edmund Fielding, died, and the following March his first-born child Charlotte died just short

---

[1] See below, *Preface*, p. 7 and notes.   [2] See below, p. 193 n.
[3] See below, p. xlvi.   [4] See Cross, i. 241–2 and n.   [5] Cross, i. 248.
[6] See B. M. Jones, *Henry Fielding, Novelist and Magistrate* (1933), pp. 71–2; and F. Homes Dudden, *Henry Fielding* (Oxford, 1952), i. 243.

of her sixth birthday, perhaps a victim of the great epidemic fever of 1741–2.[1] A series of tormentingly severe winters followed the famous one of 1739–40, and the desperate cold undoubtedly struck most heavily those living in reduced circumstances. More-over, it seems to have been at about this time that Fielding began to suffer from that recurrent scourge of his life, the gout. The preface to the *Miscellanies* paints a stabbing picture of his affairs in the winter of 1741–2: 'I was last Winter laid up in the Gout, with a favourite Child dying in one Bed, and my Wife in a Condition very little better, on another, attended with other Circumstances, which served as very proper Decorations to such a Scene. . . .' Fielding spoke from the heart when he had Billy Booth demand, in *Amelia* (III. vii): 'For what can be more miserable than to see any thing necessary to the Preservation of a beloved Creature, and not be able to supply it?'

He had borrowed some £197 from one Joseph King in March 1741, and in July 1742 King sued for payment, while Fielding was at the same time prosecuting a 'judgment for debt' against a certain Randolph Seagrim.[2] Clearly, Fielding had both a borrower and a lender been, and neither wisely. Though he apparently made the acquaintance of his generous benefactor Ralph Allen at about this time (perhaps the autumn or winter of 1741)[3] and received some aid from him, Fielding's personal affairs were not such as to provoke merriment.

Thus it is far less surprising that the *Miscellanies* should exhibit, on the whole, an intense moral seriousness, than that the record of adversity just rehearsed should prove a prelude to the appearance within a year's breadth of two of the enduring comic masterpieces of western literature: *Joseph Andrews* and *Jonathan Wild*. If the first volume of the *Miscellanies* offers only hints of their noble zest, it reminds us nevertheless that the mind which conceived an absurd *Essay on Nothing* was the same mind that could soberly contemplate the *Remedy of Affliction for the Loss of Our Friends*—and that both are genuine aspects of a complex man, who could find in folly's cup the bubble joy, but who also knew the taste of wormwood. There is a reasonable quiet pride in the observation

---

[1] See Charles Creighton, *History of Epidemics in Great Britain* (Cambridge, 1891–4), ii. 78–83.   [2] See Cross, i. 376 and n.

[3] The evidence is surveyed by Benjamin Boyce, *The Benevolent Man: A Life of Ralph Allen of Bath* (Cambridge, Mass., 1967), pp. 125–9.

made as he looked back over the several years in which he had been assembling his *Miscellanies*, that 'I could almost challenge some Philosophy to myself, for having been able to finish them as I have. . . .'[1]

2. CONTENTS

Henry Fielding's high reputation rests upon the solid ground that he is the first and, to many, the greatest of the English comic novelists. But the low esteem in which comedy has always been held by the enduring puritan personality must provoke the constant reminder that comedy is, in truth, a most serious business. Only a trifling judgement would presume to deny that the greatest comic authors—the exalted roll of Aristophanes, Terence, Lucian, Chaucer, Rabelais, Cervantes, Swift—have been profoundly earnest moralists; and Fielding, as every honest assessment of his work has recognized, cannot be excluded from this company. One ambiguous virtue of the first volume of the *Miscellanies* is that the urgent moral and social concern which informs his comic works is here more nakedly exhibited. That this emphasis is less beguiling, less delightful, and ultimately less personally significant for most readers than his comic mastery, should go without saying; but that it serves to underscore a genuinely vital dimension of Fielding's work should be no less obvious.[2] Even the satires and humorous sketches of this volume reflect the unfailing regard for sound and viable human values that was, for Fielding, at the heart of his labours in whatever literary vineyard. It is no anomaly that an author should win fame for reasons that overlook his own professed motives: but Fielding clearly thought of himself as intrinsically a moralist and would have scorned any conception of art that ignored this primary dimension of literature. And if, as Coleridge tells us, 'the true comic is the blossom of the nettle', it may well be that we must seize the nettle before we can apprehend the bloom. The manifestly serious verse-essays and prose-essays of the *Miscellanies* present us with a body of

---

[1] See below, *Preface*, pp. 13–14.

[2] A full description and critical analysis is offered in Henry Knight Miller, *Essays on Fielding's Miscellanies: A Commentary on Volume One* (Princeton, 1961). This view of the moral-intellectual Fielding must, of course, be balanced by the needful emphasis upon the 'festive' element in such studies as Andrew Wright, *Henry Fielding, Mask and Feast* (Berkeley, 1965), and W. B. Coley, 'The Background of Fielding's Laughter', *ELH*, xxvi (1959), 229–52.

concerns that could appropriately be called, by analogy with Cicero's *De officiis*, Henry Fielding's 'Offices'.

That this is no casual analogy but an expressive emblem of Fielding's classical morality may be suggested by a brief summary; for there is scarcely a topic in the first volume of the *Miscellanies* that is not anticipated in the *De officiis*.[1] No more than Fielding was Cicero a systematic philosopher; both were practical moralists whose crucial focus was the constitution of the good society, the *bona civitas*—for both considered man to be, by his very nature, a social animal who could realize his full potential only in community with others (*De officiis*, I. v–v).[2] And this dependence of man upon man demanded 'a certain Respect and Reverence for all Men, and desire to be approved not only by the best, but by all the World' (I. xxviii. 99; Cockman trans., p. 92). Though both Cicero and Fielding considered virtue to be natural to man and based upon the essential goodness of natural impulses,[3] neither failed to confront the inescapable evidence that not all men were, in fact, good,[4] and that not all men showed themselves adequately informed of the true character of moral

---

[1] The analogy is not intended to suggest that Fielding's topics necessarily derive from Cicero: Fielding, who could house now with Cicero or now with St. Paul, obviously had many sources of moral wisdom. But the *De officiis*, as its translator Thomas Cockman declared, contained 'so many excellent Rules of Life, with reference to our Duty either to God or Men, and to those in their several Capacities and Relations, whether of Kindred, Friends, or Benefactors, as have justly recommended it to the Esteem of all the World, and given it the first Place among the eminent and most celebrated Writings of this kind' (*Tully's Three Books of Offices in English*, 1699; 6th edn., 1739, p. vii; italics reversed. Subsequent quotations are from this edition.) The many Augustan divines who insistently quoted Cicero or turned his precepts into Christian admonition might well have cried, remembering the famous tribute of Erasmus to Socrates, 'Sancte Tulli, ora pro nobis!'

[2] 'Man is generally represented as an Animal formed for and delighting in Society: In this State alone, it is said, his various Talents can be exerted . . .' (*Essay on Conversation*, below, p. 119).

[3] See *De officiis*, I. iv. 11–14, and *De finibus*, V. xv. 43 (after Antiochus). Fielding usually presented the case in negative terms, by attacking those like Hobbes and Mandeville who implied that human nature was inherently 'evil', e.g. in the *Champion*, 11 December 1739.

[4] As Cicero said (in Cockman's language): 'We don't live amongst such as are perfectly and fully wise, but such as are thought to have done very well, if they are but, as 'twere, the rough Draughts of Virtue' (I. xv. 46; Cockman trans., p. 46; cf. also III. xv. 64); so Fielding sadly asked, 'Who wonders that Good-nature in so few, / Can Anger, Lust, or Avarice subdue?' (*Of Good-Nature*, ll. 92–3). Cicero and Fielding share the conflicting pulls of a deep-felt *wish* to believe that virtue is in some way natural to man and a grim practical conviction of man's self-regarding nature. One cannot say that either satisfactorily resolved this dilemma, which is perhaps inherent in any attempt to derive a 'natural' ethics. Both fall back, for purposes of exhortation to virtue, upon the appeal to a transcendent Common Good or to religious imperatives of duty—or, contrariwise, to 'true self-interest'.

goodness (*honestum*): 'And as *Men* thus receive most extraordinary Benefits, from agreeing and conspiring to lend mutual
Assistance; so we shall find, upon changing the Scene, that
there are no Misfortunes or Calamities so great, as those which
they bring upon one another' (II. v. 16; Cockman trans., p.
155).[1]

Hence they saw an important part of their task as responsible
writers adequately to define the Good Man, the *vir bonus* (or what
is the same thing for both, the *bonus civis*), and to distinguish him
from the Great Man, the *vir fortis et magnanimus* (I. xix. 63), who
in his highest manifestation was indeed the 'True Sublime' of
human nature,[2] but whose very qualities of mind and soul could
make him dangerous to the state and to humankind: 'But here
'tis one very unhappy Thing, that most times these great and
exalted Minds are naturally ungovernable and desirous of Rule'
(I. xix. 64; Cockman trans., p. 60).[3] The lust of power or the lust
for wealth (I. xx. 68) could turn the Great Man to that 'Bombast
Greatness'[4] which threatened the liberty and well being of all
men; whereas freedom and liberty were precisely the goals
'which generous Spirits ought of all Things in the World to
maintain and contend for' (I. xx. 68; Cockman trans., p. 65).[5]
Though tyrants by their very nature were wretched and could not
truly enjoy the fruits of their 'greatness',[6] this was small consolation to those who suffered under tyranny; and the duty of the
good citizen was to recognize in its early stages, before liberty
was subverted, the marks of false greatness and of that knavery
in the mask of wisdom (III. xvii. 72) which Cicero called the most

---

[1] Cf. Fielding: 'Man feels no Ill, but what to Man he owes' (*Of Good-Nature*, l. 66).

[2] Fielding's phrase; see the preface to the *Miscellanies*, below, p. 12. Cf. *De officiis*, II. x. 37.

[3] See *Of True Greatness*, below. In the *Preface* Fielding makes a significant distinction between the characters of Goodness, True Greatness, and False Greatness. Mere goodness, though amiable and marked by 'Benevolence, Honour, Honesty, and Charity', lacks the 'parts' or genius to be truly great; false greatness, though often thought 'heroic' by 'the ignorant and ill-judging Vulgar', is a mere compound of 'Pride, Ostentation, Insolence, Cruelty, and every Kind of Villany'; whereas true greatness is that union of genius and virtue that appeared in Socrates and Brutus 'and perhaps in some among us'. This high ideal, though it lies behind the ethical structure of Fielding's novels, is never actually exemplified in his fiction—not even in Allworthy or Dr. Harrison—doubtless for the very good reason that there is no place there for the Statesman–Sage.

[4] *Preface*, p. 13.   [5] See Fielding's poem *Liberty* below.

[6] *De officiis*, II. vii. 25; III. viii. 36; III. xxi. 84. Cf. Fielding: 'It is, I believe, impossible to give Vice a true Relish of Honour and Glory' (*Preface*, p. 13; see also p. 10).

pernicious thing in life.[1] Moreover, in a society that saw 'Honour'
and the praise of one's fellow-men as primary motivations to
worthy achievement (a major concern in Book II of the *De
officiis*), praise mistakenly accorded by the public to spurious
characters was an offence against society itself and robbed the
worthy of their proper reward.[2]

Both Cicero and Fielding, then, approached the problem,
not only of educating their public in the abstract norms
of the good society, but of pressing the argument in terms of
personal responsibility, by (1) attempting to define and exemplify
(through 'characters' and allusion) the cardinal virtues, which
arose from the very nature of man and upon which social community rested; and (2) seeking to set down practical rules,
officiorum praecepta, for the guidance of the average man. The
average man: for only the sage[3] could encompass perfection of
duties (*perfecta officia*)—others could find the moral life only
through a secondary but essential morality of ordinary human
relationships (*media officia*). Hence, so far as the 'offices' of normal
mankind were concerned, practical knowledge of the duties

---

[1] 'Just as we cut off those Members of the Body, which have got no longer either Blood
or Spirits in them, and serve but to infect and corrupt the rest; so should those Monsters,
which under the Shape and Outside of Men, conceal all the Savageness and Cruelty of
Beasts, be cut off, as it were, and separated from the Body and Society of Mankind' (*De
officiis*, III. vi. 32; Cockman trans., p. 242). 'This Bombast Greatness then is the Character
I intend to expose; and . . . to strip the Monster of these false Colours, and shew it in its
native Deformity; for . . . it contaminates the Food it can't taste, and sullies the Robe which
neither fits nor becomes it, 'till Virtue disdains them both' (*Preface*, pp. 12–13; see also *Of
True Greatness*, the *Dialogue between Alexander and Diogenes*, and Fielding's character of
the sanctified hypocrite in the *Essay on the Knowledge of the Characters of Men*).

[2] Justifying his severe treatment of 'Greatness' in the *Preface*, Fielding said: 'Now if the
Fact be, that the Greatness which is commonly worshipped is really of that Kind which
I have here represented, the Fault seems rather to lie in those who have ascribed to it those
Honours, to which it hath not in Reality the least Claim' (below, p. 11). Consider also the
complaint that opens his poem *Of True Greatness* that 'So few should know the Goddess
they obey' (line 2); and, among other passages, the diatribe of Mercury in Fielding's
Interlude, against mercenary dedications: 'These Fellows prevent the very Use of Praise,
which while only the Reward of Virtue, will always invite Men to it; but when it is to be
bought, will be despised by the True Deserving . . .' (p. 241). See also the *Champion*, 4 and 6
March 1740. The genuine importance of reputation and of public opinion, however subject to confusion, abuse, and misdirection, is of no small concern in *Tom Jones* and *Amelia*;
and it lies behind Fielding's numerous bitter reflections on slander (see the *Essay on the
Knowledge of the Characters of Men*, below, pp. 167 ff., and, among many other attacks,
that upon 'Libellers' in *A Charge to the Grand Jury*).

[3] Cf. Fielding on 'the Shields of Wisdom and Philosophy, which God knows are in the
Possession of very few' (*Essay on Conversation*, pp. 125–6); and also *Of the Remedy of
Affliction*, pp. 213 ff.

prescribed by justice was superior to purely theoretical knowledge or inactive contemplation of nature.[1] The 'mean duties' of normal life could, in fact, often be known through mere natural goodness of heart, 'quae . . . ingenii bonitate multi assequuntur' (III. iii. 14); indeed, the civil law itself was based upon a natural feeling for the right, 'ductum a natura' (III. xvii. 71). But, despite this natural feeling in men for virtue, the knavery and hypocrisy of all too many, the moral confusions engendered by the corruption of language (e.g., the mistaken significance of 'expedience', *utilitas*),[2] and the temptations that every man faced in his daily life, all made it necessary that imperfect man frequently have his natural duties called to mind and dramatized.[3] Hence the duty of those blessed with a superior eloquence (II. xix. 66) was precisely to fill this office of reminding the ordinary man what kind of being he was (I. xxviii. 97),[4] how different from the beasts (I. xxx. 105–6),[5] and what, therefore, this *human* status demanded of him. The practical task was to help him to distinguish true moral utility or expedience, which should not conflict with moral rectitude (*honestas*), from the apparent good that seduced ordinary men away from virtue. This was something that the sage perfectly understood; but the average citizen required the assistance of advice and exhortation

[1] 'Quibus rebus intellegitur studiis officiisque scientiae praeponenda esse officia iustitiae, quae pertinent ad hominum utilitatem, qua nihil homini esse debet antiquius' (*De officiis*, I. xliii. 155). Argument of this order lay behind the scorn that Swift and Fielding and other Augustans expressed for the experiments of the Royal Society; see below, *Some Papers Proper to be Read before the R—l Society*. Neither Cicero nor Fielding means to call in question that higher contemplation of nature and of God that is the supreme wisdom (*sapientia*).

[2] *De officiis*, II. iii. 9. See Fielding on the word 'Good-Breeding', which he says is 'so horribly and barbarously corrupted, that it contains at present scarce a simple Ingredient of what it seems originally to have been designed to express' (*Essay on Conversation*, p. 123).

[3] As Fielding says: 'Neither will the Reader, I hope, be offended if he should here find no Observations entirely new to him. Nothing can be plainer, or more known, than the general Rules of Morality, and yet thousands of Men are thought well employed in reviving our Remembrance, and enforcing our Practice of them' (*Essay on the Knowledge of the Characters of Men*, p. 156).

[4] 'Nature has given every one of us a Character, by endowing us with that Nobleness and Excellence of Being, whereby we are set above all other Creatures' (Cockman trans., pp. 90–1).

[5] Cf. Fielding on Conversation: 'In this Respect Man stands, I conceive, distinguished from and superior to all other Earthly Creatures' (*Essay on Conversation*, p. 120). See *De officiis*, I. xvi. 50.

and example.¹ If virtue could actually be seen in her full beauty
with the physical eye, she 'would make the whole World (as
Plato has said) be in love with Wisdom' (1. v. 15; Cockman
trans., p. 16);² but, as things are, the connection and interweaving
of the virtues can only be seized by the moral intelligence. The
cardinal virtues, Justice, Fortitude, Temperance, and Prudence
demand a practical and functional definition; for Virtue lies in
activity: 'Virtutis enim laus omnis in actione consistit' (1. vi. 19).³

Justice and Charity are nearly one for Cicero (1. vii. 30) and
override all other virtues (1. vii. 20, 111. vi. 28).⁴ Charity (*beneficentia*) has two dimensions: Kindness (*benignitas*) and pecuniary
charity (*liberalitas*);⁵ and both, as Cicero and Fielding alike
insist, require an element of judgement, a weighing of the worth
of the recipient, to be genuine beneficence and not mere self-
inflating sentimentalism (1. xiv. 42, 1. xv. 49).⁶ The negative of
this virtue, Injustice, whether encompassed by fraud or force
(1. xiii. 41),⁷ represents the most general and disturbing threat
to society's welfare—particularly in the forms of Avarice and
Ambition (1. xx. 68 *et passim*), the most patent marks of false

¹ Without adequate moral discrimination, Fielding argued, even Good-Nature could
not be properly recognized: 'Yet in itself howe'er unmix'd and pure, / No Virtue from
Mistakes is less secure' (*Of Good-Nature*, ll. 15–16).
² Cited also by Fielding: 'It is truly said of Virtue, that could Men behold her naked,
they would be all in Love with her' (*Essay on the Knowledge of the Characters of Men*, p. 173
and n.).
³ Fielding's best-known argument of this point is in *Tom Jones*, xv. i. Cf. the portrait in
Of Good-Nature of the man 'Who to make all and each Man truly blest, / Doth all he can,
and wishes all the rest' (ll. 31–2).
⁴ Fielding, of course, would consider Charity as a 'theological virtue', along with Faith
and Hope; but his actual delineation of its operations has much in common with Cicero's
beneficentia.
⁵ The same division is implicit in Fielding's poem *Of Good-Nature*, which begins with
that virtue under the aspect of *liberalitas* and concludes with the extension to a broader
benignitas.
⁶ Fielding denies, in the poem *Of Good-Nature*, that this virtue is merely 'a foolish
Weakness in the Breast' (l. 3), as in a *Champion* essay (27 March 1740) he had insisted that it
maintains a constant regard to desert. See also the *Champion*, 16 February 1740; the *True
Patriot*, 8 (24 December 1745); *Tom Jones*, IV. vi; and the *Covent-Garden Journal*, 44.
⁷ Fraud was the central concern; cf. Fielding: 'It is not against Force, but Deceit,
which I am here seeking for Armour; against those who can injure us only by obtaining
our good Opinion. If therefore I can instruct my Reader from what sort of Persons he is to
with-hold this Opinion, and inform him of all, or at least the principal Arts by which
Deceit proceeds to ingratiate itself with us, by which he will be effectually enabled to defeat
its Purpose, I shall have sufficiently satisfied the Design of this Essay' (*Essay on the Knowledge of the Characters of Men*, p. 164).

greatness.[1] And since ordinary men tend to confuse wisdom with mere craftiness, *malitia* (ii. iii. 10),[2] the most unjust man of all is the Hypocrite, who exploits this common inability to make adequate moral distinctions: 'But of all Injustice, theirs is certainly of the deepest Dye, who make it their Business to appear honest Men, even whilst they are practising the greatest of Villanies' (i. xiii. 41; Cockman trans., p. 43).[3]

The virtue of Fortitude, in its social manifestation, properly results in the championing of the right: 'The first Thing therefore I would have in a truly couragious Man is, that he be a Follower of Goodness and fair Dealing, of Truth and Sincerity; which are the principal and constituent Parts of Justice' (i. xix. 63; Cockman trans., p. 60). Corrupted, however, fortitude merely produces once again that dangerous Greatness 'very little better than Savageness and Barbarity' (i. xliv. 157; Cockman trans., p. 140).[4] In the individual's own life, fortitude is more than mere 'courage'; it is a largeness of soul (*magnitudo animi*) that enables a man to confront fortune with dignity and indifference (i. xx. 66).[5]

Temperance is a virtue perhaps less commonly associated with Fielding; and yet he often celebrated it.[6] If Cicero and he do indeed part company on the Stoic demand for the absolute

---

[1] See Fielding's demonstration that 'our two greatest and noblest Pursuits [i.e. Ambition and Avarice], one or other of which engages almost every Individual of the busy Part of Mankind', both end in nothing (*Essay on Nothing*, below, p. 189). On ambition, see also *Of True Greatness* and the *Dialogue between Alexander and Diogenes*. On avarice, see *Some Papers Proper to be Read before the R—l Society*.

[2] Cf. Fielding on 'the deceived Multitude' which gives the name of Greatness to 'a Composition of Cruelty, Lust, Avarice, Rapine, Insolence, Hypocrisy, Fraud and Treachery' (*Preface*, p. 10).

[3] 'In my *Essay on the Knowledge of the Characters of Men*, I have endeavoured to expose a second great Evil, namely, Hypocrisy; the Bane of all Virtue, Morality, and Goodness; and to arm, as well as I can, the honest, undesigning, open-hearted Man, who is generally the Prey of this Monster, against it' (*Preface*, p. 4).

[4] Fielding echoes this observation in the *Champion*, 3 January 1740, commenting upon 'Valour'.

[5] See Fielding's essay *Of the Remedy of Affliction*, which distinguishes, once again, between the high virtue of the sage and the remedies accessible to ordinary men. Though Fielding's attitude toward Stoicism has customarily been misrepresented in accordance with Romantic canons of philosophy to which he did not subscribe, it is true that he found the sage (like the saint) irrelevant to practical morality, however worthy as an ideal. Fielding's stoicism, like Shaftesbury's, has a benevolist tinge: he argued that it was a 'sanguine Disposition of Mind' that put one 'out of the Reach of Fortune' (*Tom Jones*, XIII. vi).

[6] See, for example, the *Champion*, 24 January 1740; the *True Patriot*, 7 (17 November 1745); and *Tom Jones*, VI. iii.

subjection of the passions (1. xxvii. 93),[1] yet he no less than the Roman believed in the conquest of one's self and the *control* of the unruly passions.[2] Moreover, temperance was by Cicero associated with virtues of prime importance to Fielding: that considerateness for others (*verecundia*) that marked the truly good man and that served 'to set off and adorn our Lives' (1. xxvii. 93; Cockman trans., p. 87);[3] and the comprehensive virtue of *decorum*, which was an aspect of all the other virtues as well (1. xxvii. 95) and which, most broadly defined, meant 'that which is congruous or agreeable to that excellent Part of the Nature of Man, by which he is distinguish'd from the rest of the Creation' (1. xxvii. 96; Cockman trans., p. 89), i.e. the distinctively human in man. More narrowly, it was conceived as the social virtue 'agreeable to the Nature of Man, as withal to shew something of Temper and Moderation, with a certain sweet Air of Gentility and good Manners' ('cum specie quadam liberali', 1. xxvii. 96; Cockman trans., p. 89).[4] At its heart was that quality so much admired by both the 'classical' ages, consistency of behaviour: 'a constant Uniformity in our whole Lives and particular Actions' (1. xxxi. 111; Cockman trans., p. 103).[5] Decorum meant a consistency of character that was essential to all the virtues because, in its fullest sense, it included not merely the graceful concerns of beauty, tact, and taste, 'formositate, ordine, ornatu ad actionem apto' (1. xxxv. 126), but the harmonious and appropriate integration of a man's whole faculties and the realization of his own peculiar identity.[6]

---

[1] An ideal preached, however, by that good Ciceronian, Parson Adams (*Joseph Andrews*, IV. viii).

[2] See, for example, *The Temple Beau*, IV. x; *The Coffee-House Politician*, II. xii; the *Champion*, 2 February 1740. Squire Western is, of course, the very type of the man who has no command over his passions.

[3] Cf. *Of Good-Nature*, below; and Fielding's declaration, 'As this Good Breeding is the Art of pleasing, it will be first necessary, with the utmost Caution, to avoid hurting or giving any Offence to those with whom we converse' (*Essay on Conversation*, p. 125).

[4] Italics reversed in the last two citations. 'Good-Breeding', in its proper sense, was, for Fielding, the equivalent of Cicero's *decorum*, a moral as well as social quality.

[5] Cicero moves easily from a consideration of *decorum* as a desideratum in literary characters to its function in the life of the balanced soul in society (*De officiis*, I. xxviii. 97 ff.); both principles also obtain in Fielding's notion of 'conservation of character'. See John S. Coolidge, 'Fielding and "Conservation of Character"', *MP*, lvii (1960), 245–59; and Marvin T. Herrick, *Comic Theory in the Sixteenth Century* (Urbana, Ill., 1950), pp. 130 ff. This classical tenet, however, interacts with the equally ancient doctrine of the mixed nature of individual men (see below, p. xxxiii).

[6] Thus also, for Fielding, Good-Nature is not merely a social virtue but 'the mighty whole / Full Composition of a virtuous Soul' (*Of Good-Nature*, ll. 5–6).

Finally, of the cardinal virtues, Prudence (*prudentia*) was un-
questionably the central virtue in a scheme of practical morality;
for its very function was to discriminate, in the affairs of life,
between moral good and moral evil: 'Prudentia est enim locata in
dilectu bonorum et malorum' (III. xvii. 71). It was distinguished
from *sapientia*, that higher wisdom which the Greeks called *sophia*,
by its concern with the world as it is rather than as it ought to be:
its province was *scientia*, true worldly wisdom: 'rerum expeten-
darum fugiendarumque scientia' (I. xliii. 153). And Fielding's
concern, like Cicero's, was to distinguish for his readers, by
definition and example, that Prudence which was not inconsistent
with true *utilitas* from that 'which a knavish Sort of Cunning
endeavours to imitate', under the mask of a false expediency (III.
xxv. 95; Cockman trans., p. 295).[1] For to separate 'profit'
(*utilitas*) from 'honesty' (*honestas*) was to 'wholly pervert the first
Principles of Nature' (III. xxviii. 101; Cockman trans., pp. 299–
300). Self-interest had somehow, as a prime essential, to be recon-
ciled with the common bonds of society (III. vi. 26), for the sole
alternatives were savagery or tyranny; and since man can truly
realize himself only in society, his own prudence dictates that his
interests and those of society must be one.[2]

Man as a social animal, therefore, could not be defined merely
in terms of his individual qualities—difficult in any case, because
of the varied nature of man (I. xxx. 107 ff.)[3]—but necessarily in
the more universal terms of his social instinct (*communitas*) and
his relationship to his fellows and to the common good (I. vii.
22).[4] Hence the 'relative duties' of man to others, deriving from

[1] Cf. Fielding's design in the *Essay on the Knowledge of the Characters of Men* to school
good men in a knowledge of the systems by which 'the artful and cunning Part of Mankind' seek to impose on the rest of the world (below, p. 153).

[2] 'Again; if Society requires that its Members should be inoffensive, so the more useful
and beneficial they are to each other, the more suitable are they to the social Nature, and
more perfectly adapted to its Institution: for all Creatures seek their own Happiness, and
Society is therefore natural to any, because it is naturally productive of this Happiness'
(*Essay on Conversation*, p. 122).

[3] See Fielding's poem *To John Hayes*, below; and the *Essay on the Knowledge of the
Characters of Men*, which remarks upon 'that very early and strong Inclination to Good or
Evil, which distinguishes different Dispositions in Children, in their first Infancy', and
observes that 'there subsists . . . so manifest and extreme a Difference of Inclination or
Character, that almost obliges us, I think, to acknowledge some unacquired original
Distinction, in the Nature or Soul of one Man, from that of another' (below, p. 154).

[4] Cf. Fielding's attack upon instruction in mere self-interest, in the *Essay on the Knowledge of the Characters of Men*: 'This *Art of thriving* being the very Reverse of **that**

the cardinal virtues, were of first importance;[1] and both Cicero and Fielding endeavoured 'to lay down some Rules' (*quaedam praecepta*)[2] for man's conduct in these relationships.

Two social topics of major concern to Fielding—marriage and the proper evaluation of hereditary titles—are mentioned only in passing in the *De officiis*, though they were far from unimportant to Cicero. He assumed marriage to be 'the primary bond of union' in society (i. xvii. 54);[3] and, like Fielding, took nobility of birth to be essentially a matter of chance, as opposed to the character that a man could create of his own free choice (i. xxxii. 115).[4] Both Cicero and Fielding gave high prominence to the social art of conversation, Cicero as a subdivision of *decorum* and Fielding as an aspect of 'Good-Breeding'; for conversation as social talk (*sermo*) was an emblem of conversation in its broadest sense, the relationship of man to man.[5] As Cicero argued that the private citizen's duty was to live on terms of equal esteem with his fellows, 'aequo et pari cum civibus iure vivere', neither basely submissive and abject nor yet puffed up, 'neque summissum et abiectum neque se efferentem' (i. xxxiv. 124), so Fielding celebrated 'that golden Mean, which declares a Man ready to acquiesce in allowing the Respect due to a Title by the Laws and Customs of his Country, but impatient of any Insult, and disdaining to purchase the Intimacy with, and Favour of a Superior, at the Expence of Conscience or Honour'.[6] And, to conclude this brief comparison of two serious moralists, both Cicero and Fielding strongly and sincerely hoped through their writings to have

Doctrine of the Stoics; by which Men were taught to consider themselves as Fellow-Citizens of the World, and to labour jointly for the common Good' (below, p. 154).

[1] 'Trace then the Man proposed to your Trust, into his private Family and nearest Intimacies. See whether he hath acted the Part of a good Son, Brother, Husband, Father, Friend, Master, Servant, &c. if he hath discharged these Duties well, your Confidence will have a good Foundation; but if he hath behaved himself in these Offices with Tyranny, with Cruelty, with Infidelity, with Inconstancy, you may be assured he will take the first Opportunity his Interest points out to him, of exercising the same ill Talents at your Expence' (*Essay on the Knowledge of the Characters of Men*, p. 175).

[2] *De officiis*, II. xiii. 44. Paralleled in Fielding's 'I . . . shall endeavour to lay down some Rules' (p. 142), 'I shall venture to set down some few Rules' (p. 155), and so on.

[3] See the verse-essay, *To a Friend on the Choice of a Wife*, below.

[4] Fielding treats the ancient theme, *generositas virtus, non sanguis*, in the *Essay on Nothing*, pp. 186 ff.

[5] See the *Essay on Conversation*; and cf. *De officiis*, I. xxix. 103–4 (on raillery) and I. xxxvii. 132 ff.

[6] *Essay on Conversation*, p. 132.

been of service to their fellows in the community of man: 'Whoever observes these Measures laid down, (let his way of Life be either publick or private) may perform all the Duties of Magnanimity, Constancy, and Greatness of Soul, as well as of Sincerity, Fidelity, and doing Good to Mankind.'[1]

To consider briefly now the individual items that appear in the first volume: the POEMS of the *Miscellanies* represent the bulk of Fielding's effort in a mode essentially alien to him.[2] Their importance is clearly less literary than personal and intellectual, as an index to Fielding's early interests and to some of the sources (or reinforcements) of his ideas and his wit. The light verse includes several verse-epistles (two addressed to Sir Robert Walpole), a number of epigrams, a pair of mock-epitaphs, a rebus, a diatribe against London, a pair of songs, a brief and unsavoury travesty of Virgil, a fragment from Silius Italicus, and a lively burlesque in hudibrastic couplets of the first half of Juvenal's *Sixth Satire*. The greater part of the collection, however, is made up of amorous complaints and compliments, most of them addressed to 'Celia', Fielding's poetic name for Charlotte Cradock, whom he married in 1734. These poetic trifles offer a most pleasant glimpse of Fielding as an exuberant young man, dancing at the Salisbury assemblies, surveying London with cool arrogance, and turning casual events into matter for taffeta phrases. And an early poem, the 'Description of U[pto]n G[rey]', written in 1728 when Fielding would have been just twenty-one, gives a hint of his youthful delight in painting 'low' scenes, declaring, 'I've thought (so strong with me Burlesque prevails,) / This Place design'd to ridicule *Versailles*.'

The light verse and amorous gallantries were, as Fielding explained, 'most of them written when I was very young, and are indeed Productions of the Heart rather than of the Head'.[3] They provide interesting evidence, however, that productions of the heart are no less in debt to traditional modes and turns of phrase than productions of the head: Fielding often echoes those Latin poets of love who first taught the hearts of English schoolboys

---

[1] *De officiis*, I. xxvi. 92; Cockman trans., p. 86. Cf. Fielding, *Preface*, p. 11 *et passim*.
[2] Eighteen of the poems (including the verse-essays) are in heroic couplets, fourteen in octosyllabics, four in anapestic tetrameter, and one (a song) has the form 868688 (ababcc).
[3] *Preface*, p. 3.

to flutter—Ovid, Catullus, Tibullus, Propertius[1]—and the
themes and phrases of Prior, and occasionally Carew, Waller,
and Cowley, identify some of his English masters in love poetry.
Prior's graceful Anacreontics seem particularly to have chimed in
Fielding's head (or heart), as we may see in the little epigram
'When Jove with Fair Alcmena Lay'; the poem to Celia subtitled
'Cupid Call'd to Account'; and 'To the Same. On Her Wishing
to Have a Lilliputian, to Play with'; and the poem 'To Euthalia'.
The satires and epigrams display an equal debt to Horace and
Juvenal and Martial, as well as to the obvious English models,
Dryden, Young, Gay, and Pope. The influence of Pope is, in-
deed, so all-pervasive that annotation in this volume has had to be
selective: he is everywhere in Fielding's poetry.

The five serious verse-essays can, in truth, be reasonably
described as Fielding's attempt to articulate some of his central
concerns in the poetic voice of Alexander Pope. Though thematic
echoes of other Latin and English reflective poets—Virgil and
Lucretius, Dryden, Young, and Thomson—also enter in, the
formal model is inescapably Pope. Fielding's personal estimate of
the wasp of Twickenham may have been ambivalent;[2] but when
he undertook to write serious poetry, he turned to the obvious
exemplar for his age.

That Fielding's skill as a poet never remotely approached
Pope's genius needs no argument; but his verse-essays possess a
thematic significance that transcends the occasionally limping
couplets. (As he somewhat self-consciously urged: 'Accept the
Muse whom Truth inspires to sing, / Who soars, tho' weakly, on
an honest Wing.')[3] For Fielding was trying to formulate some of
his major convictions in this verse; and the ideas displayed here
remain central to his view of life, whether expounded in periodical
essays, dramatized in plays, or woven into the ethical structure of
his novels. The poems treat in order the themes of greatness,
good-nature, liberty, love and marriage, and the inconsistency of
human actions.

The poem OF TRUE GREATNESS insists, in its very title, upon
the distinction that Fielding made in the preface to the *Miscellanies*: not only was there a polar opposition of 'Goodness' and

---

[1] See 'The Beggar: A Song', several of the poems to 'Celia', and 'To Euthalia'.
[2] See S. J. Sackett, 'Fielding and Pope', *N&Q*, cciv (1959), 200–4.
[3] *Liberty*, ll. 11–12.

'Greatness', but there was a further necessary discrimination
between false greatness and the true. The general attack upon false
greatness was a theme traditional enough, especially in the immediately preceding era of Louis XIV and Charles XII; and a
multitude of moralists had anticipated Fielding's anatomy of the
'Great Man', a phrase, however, that in the England of the 1730s
almost inevitably glanced at Sir Robert Walpole.[1] Fielding's most
notable unmasking of the spurious 'Great Man' is, of course, in
Jonathan Wild; what his poem seeks to do is to expose as false
the claims to 'greatness' of a more varied array of representative
figures: the court favourite, the ascetic hermit, the savage
conqueror, the pedant, the self-serving merchant, the bad writer,
and so on—all those sinners against *communitas* who are wrongly
honoured by a public which fails to see that pretenders to greatness, by usurping the praise due to genuine virtue, strike at the
very heart of civil society. Every community, of course, finds in
its central and typical figures exemplars both of superior virtue
and of brilliant degeneracy; and the moralist's aim must be to
revitalize, by dramatic example and exhortation, the urgent truth
that *mere* 'greatness' is more likely to bring mischief than
salvation to the admiring world. This is among the reasons that
Fielding found the classical biographers (such as Plutarch,
Cornelius Nepos, and Suetonius, the trio celebrated in the
opening pages of *Jonathan Wild*)[2] and the classical historians of
such immediate and vital relevance to his own age; and this is
perhaps why he came ultimately to declare that history was more
truthful and of greater intrinsic value than fiction.[3]

The companion poem, OF GOOD-NATURE, contemplates the
character most obviously opposed to greatness, namely natural
goodness, 'Virtue's Self'.[4] Fielding was by no means the first to
exalt Good-Nature to the rank of an indispensable ethical quality:
this emphasis is familiar to us in the 'Benevolist' school of
moralists from the late seventeenth century—one of whom had

[1] See W. R. Irwin, *The Making of Jonathan Wild* (New York, 1941), pp. 44–55 *et
passim*; David Worcester, *The Art of Satire* (Cambridge, Mass., 1940), pp. 82–8.
[2] See *Jonathan Wild*, I. i, cited below, p. xxxiii n. 3.
[3] See the preface to *The Journal of a Voyage to Lisbon*. On the exemplary function of
history, see among other statements that would have drawn Fielding's assent, Polybius,
Hist. I. xxxv. 7; Tacitus, *Annals*, III. lxv.
[4] *Of Good-Nature*, l. 7. Fielding's most detailed analysis of this central concept in his
ethical vocabulary is to be found in the *Champion*, 27 March 1740.

cried enthusiastically: 'They that maintain the Principle of good Nature, are the Representatives of God in the World.'[1] Fielding himself insisted that this virtue had been central to the classical moralists as well.[2] His poem declares that it is 'A Flow'r so fine, / It only grows in Soils almost divine';[3] but, like greatness, it is often mistaken by the undiscriminating, and meaner passions are honoured as good-nature. Hence Fielding seeks to provide a poetic definition in terms of 'the glorious Lust of doing Good'.[4] Most of the poem is, in fact, a paean to pecuniary charity, though it broadens its range with a diatribe against not only the un-charitable, but the envious and the censorious—antitheses of good-nature. The emphasis upon this benevolence of soul was crucial to Fielding, for although he never seriously denied the 'rational' component of ethics, temperamentally and by con-viction he felt that as the passions were the motive force to action, the cultivation of the 'good' passions was among the imperative tasks of an effective ethics. The presentation of ideals and exem-plars of natural benevolence, even in flawed young fellows like Tom Jones,[5] served as genial inspiration and encouragement to men of ordinary constitution, who might be put off by the grandeur of the Stoic sage or the purity of the Christian saint.[6] Fielding was after a workaday morality.

The third verse-essay, LIBERTY, addressed to Fielding's friend and patron, George Lyttelton, was clearly intended as a contri-bution to the 'patriot' opposition to Walpole in the 1730s, when 'liberty' was something of a shibboleth (or cant-phrase) to

---

[1] Benjamin Whichcote, Sermon VI, in *Select Sermons of Dr. Whichcot* (1698), p. 218. See the classic study of R. S. Crane, 'Suggestions toward a Genealogy of the "Man of Feeling"', *ELH*, i (1934), 205–30; supplemented, for Fielding, by James A. Work, 'Henry Fielding, Christian Censor', in *The Age of Johnson* (New Haven, 1949), pp. 139–48; Martin C. Battestin, *The Moral Basis of Fielding's Art* (Middletown, Conn., 1959); and Miller, *Essays on Fielding's Miscellanies*, pp. 66–88.

[2] See, for example, the discussion in the *Champion*, cited above, p. xxix n. 4.

[3] Fielding tended to alternate, according to mood and context, between an 'exclusive' conception of good-nature that saw it as the possession of a very few, and a more expansive feeling that benevolence was actually found in many human breasts (e.g. *Tom Jones*, vi. i).

[4] Cf. the definition of Charity in the *Covent-Garden Journal*, 29, as a delight in doing good.

[5] Cf. *Tom Jones*, ii. vii: 'The finest Composition of human Nature, as well as the finest China, may have a Flaw in it; and this, I am afraid, is, in either Case, is equally incurable; though, nevertheless, the Pattern may remain of the highest Value.'

[6] Cf. *Tom Jones*, x. i.

signalize enmity to the administration.[1] Fielding begins by surveying the 'historic' rise of society, in the manner of Lucretius,[2] to suggest the vicissitudes of the concept of liberty in human history; and then concludes his poem with a long apostrophe to Liberty, that traces her traditional 'progress' from Greece and Republican Rome, through the Gothic peoples of the north, to her natural home in Britain.[3] Implicit in the argument is Fielding's normal ideal of the 'mixed' government expounded by Locke ('Hence Right to Pow'r and Laws by Compact grew'); but the major image that emerges is of powerful and benevolent kingship: 'The People Pow'r, to keep their Freedom, gave, / And he who had it was the only Slave.'[4] The whole conception of 'liberty' in the poem is of a piece with Fielding's basic commitment to a hierarchical society in which the various classes functioned, after that favourite Renaissance metaphor, like the body and its members.[5]

The poem To a FRIEND ON THE CHOICE OF A WIFE is really untypical of Fielding, in its pose of Juvenalian misogyny.[6] It follows the formal pattern of Juvenal's *Sixth Satire*, which lay behind such contemporary models as Pope's *Epistle to a Lady* and Satires V and VI ('On Women') of Edward Young's *The Universal Passion*. Like Juvenal, Fielding here counsels a 'friend'

[1] An anonymous attack upon Walpole in 1741 blustered, 'Give us none of your Cant about *Allegiance, Oaths, Compacts,* and *Terms of Submission*: These Things will not go down now-a-days; LIBERTY, Sir, LIBERTY, I say, in its widest Extent, is what we want, and will have, cost what it will' (*A Seasonable Admonition to a Great Man*, pp. 21–2).

[2] *De rerum natura*, v. 925–1168.

[3] See Alan D. McKillop, *The Background of Thomson's Liberty* (Houston, Texas, 1951); Zera S. Fink, *The Classical Republicans* (Evanston, Ill., 1945); and Samuel Kliger, *The Goths in England* (Cambridge, Mass., 1952).

[4] As the episode of the gypsy king in *Tom Jones* (XII. xi–xii) suggests, Fielding liked to play with the utopian notion of a benevolent despot, but there, as in the poem *Liberty*, he expressed his conviction that absolute power almost inevitably corrupts. See Martin C. Battestin, 'Tom Jones and "His *Egyptian* Majesty": Fielding's Parable of Government', *PMLA*, lxxxii (1967), 68–77.

[5] See the *Champion*, 2 February 1740, and the Introduction to *An Enquiry into the Causes of the Late Increase of Robbers* (1751). On Fielding's social conservatism, see Malvin R. Zirker, Jr., *Fielding's Social Pamphlets* (Berkeley, 1966). One might express it in terms of an emphasis upon the Duties ('offices') of man, as opposed to a historically later emphasis upon the Rights of man.

[6] In apologizing for his 'Modernization' of Juvenal's *Sixth Satire*, the famous diatribe against women, Fielding hoped that it would 'give no Offence to that Half of our Species, for whom I have the greatest Respect and Tenderness. . . . For my Part, I am much more inclined to Panegyric on that amiable Sex' (*Preface*, p. 3).

who is contemplating marriage to consider the mistakes that are
often made in the matrimonial lottery: 'Whence come the Woes
which we in Marriage find, / But from a Choice too negligent,
too Blind?' And he proceeds to exhibit 'characters' of the
women one should hesitate to marry: reigning beauties, wits,
fools, heiresses, titled ladies, coquettes, and prudes. The conclusion, however, more typically frames an outline of the ideal
woman: 'If Fortune gives thee such a Wife to meet, / Earth
cannot make thy Blessing more complete.' For, if Fielding had
included on the title-page of *Amelia* a quotation from Simonides
to the effect that 'a man can be possessed of nothing better than a
virtuous woman, nor more terrible than a bad one', the portrait
of Amelia herself offers convincing evidence that he found more
pleasure in idealizing women than in arraigning them.

    The last of the verse-essays, the short poem To JOHN HAYES,
ESQ;, pursues the theme that Pope had explored in the *Epistle to
Cobham* and in the second epistle of the *Essay on Man*: namely,
the contradictions displayed in man's individual character and
the strange inconsistency of human nature in general. There is
perhaps no more traditional topic in ethical literature than this,
but for the eighteenth century it was particularly linked with
Montaigne and the revival of the Pyrrhonist tradition;[1] and most
of Fielding's points had been anticipated by the elegant sceptic
La Rochefoucauld. (Characteristically, however, Fielding himself cites a classical inspiration for his theme: 'Canst with thy
Horace see the human Elves / Not differ more from others than
themselves.') This natural inconsistency in man is further compounded, Fielding says, by the fact that men perversely struggle
to appear other than they really are, that they seek by 'art' to
dissimulate their true 'nature', and thus show forth in completely
variant lights, depending on the part that they are acting at the
moment. In the poem to Hayes, Fielding merely exclaimed at
the mighty maze of human inconsistency without looking for the
plan; but it was his acquiescence in a practical scepticism toward

---

[1] See Louis I. Bredvold, *The Intellectual Milieu of John Dryden* (Ann Arbor, Mich.,
1934); and cf. Pope's remarks to Spence: 'How wrong the greatest men have been in
judging the cause of human actions. . . . Montaigne hence concludes pyrrhonically that
nothing can be known of the workings of men's minds' (Joseph Spence, *Observations,
Anecdotes, and Characters of Books and Men,* ed. James M. Osborn [Oxford, 1966], i. 142).
See also the notes of F. W. Bateson on Pope's *Epistle to Cobham* and of Maynard Mack
on the *Essay on Man*, Epistle II, in the Twickenham Edition.

generalizations about fixed character[1] (perhaps joined with a fear of falling into Hobbism through emphasis upon the radical evil in men)[2] that forwarded Fielding's grateful acceptance of a theory arguing the mixed nature of the individual man.[3]

If we turn to the formal prose essays of this volume, we find further evidence of Fielding's overriding concern for the 'offices' of community and the moral life of the *bonus civis*. The Essay on Conversation is almost an epitome of the social values that for Fielding and the Augustans were an inseparable part of their estimate of human nature and of particular individuals: for, given the classical premiss that man is a social animal, it follows apodictically that an individual's genuine nature can emerge only in his relationships with other people. The essay is, typically enough, cast in the form of a miniature courtesy-book;[4] and, like others in the tradition, it moves easily between the idea of 'conversation' as social intercourse in its largest sense and the idea of social talk—which for the Augustans was no trifling art but, as Fielding declared, 'the noblest Privilege of human Nature, and productive of all rational Happiness'.[5] The topic had,

---

[1] This sceptical tradition serves in some degree as a qualification of the equally classical principle of *decorum* (see above, p. xxiv and n. 5). As to fixed conceptions of human nature, Fielding observed: 'Those who predicate of Man in general, that he is an Animal of this or that Disposition, seem to me not sufficiently to have studied Human Nature; for that immense Variety of Characters so apparent in Men even of the same Climate, Religion, and Education . . . could hardly exist, unless the Distinction had some original Foundation in Nature itself' (*Essay on the Knowledge of the Characters of Men*, below, p. 153). Thus a disclaimer of generalizations about human nature leads into an assertion that *individuals* may indeed have 'a very early and strong Inclination to Good or Evil'.

[2] Speaking of *Jonathan Wild*, Fielding declared in the preface to the *Miscellanies*, 'I solemnly protest, I do by no means intend in the Character of my Hero to represent Human Nature in general. Such Insinuations must be attended with very dreadful Conclusions . . .' (below, p. 9).

[3] Cf. the opening of *Jonathan Wild* (I. i): 'We may moreover learn from *Plutarch, Nepos, Suetonius*, and other Biographers this useful Lesson, not too hastily nor in the Gross to bestow either our Praise or Censure: Since we shall often find such a Mixture of Good and Evil in the same Character, that it may require a very accurate Judgment and elaborate Inquiry to determine which Side the Ballance turns: for tho' we sometimes meet with an *Aristides* or a *Brutus*, a *Lysander* or a *Nero*, yet far the greater Number are of the mixt Kind; neither totally good nor bad; their greatest Virtues being obscured and allayed by their Vices, and those again softened and coloured over by their Virtues.'

[4] See the informative survey of John E. Mason, *Gentlefolk in the Making* (Philadelphia, 1935); and Gertrude E. Noyes, *Bibliography of Courtesy and Conduct Books in Seventeenth-Century England* (New Haven, 1937).

[5] See below, p. 121. Few of the major Augustans failed to offer comment on the topic; see Herbert Davis, 'The Conversation of the Augustans', in *The Seventeenth Century:*

in fact, occupied a notable place in English social literature, from the sixteenth-century translations of Castiglione and Stefano Guazzo: sermons, moral tracts, satirical works, even volumes of philosophy, treated conversation as a theme worthy of the most serious concern.[1] A multitude of handbooks set forth the same rules and cautions against slander, blasphemy, indecency, and raillery—indeed, illustrated with brief Theophrastan 'characters' the same errors and gaucheries—that Fielding dramatizes in his own little treatise: such works, for instance, as *The Art of Complaisance, or the Means to Oblige in Conversation* (by 'S. C.', 1673), *The Whole Art of Converse* (by 'D. A. Gent', 1683), *The Art of Pleasing in Conversation* (John Ozell's translation of Pierre d'Ortigue, 1736), and *The Conversation of Gentlemen Considered* (1738). More generalized studies, such as Bellegarde's famous *Reflexions upon Ridicule* (trans., 2 vols., 1706–7), treated the topic of conversation as inseparable from good-breeding itself; and Fielding's strategy does not differ.

If the redefinition of the concept of the 'gentleman' that was crystallizing in the eighteenth century[2] can be seen as part of an intricate contest between the aristocracy and the mercantile classes for control of the term 'honour',[3] then Fielding may be said to occupy a middle ground in the struggle. As the *Essay on Conversation* makes clear, he accepted the rising view that 'true Good-Breeding consists in contributing, with our utmost Power,

Studies . . . by Richard Foster Jones and Others Writing in His Honor (Stanford, 1951), pp. 181–97.

[1] Anthony Blackwall declared that 'the best *Classics* lay down very valuable Rules for the Management of *Conversation*, for graceful and proper *Address* to those Persons with whom we converse' (*An Introduction to the Classics*, 4th edn., 1728, p. 76). The table of contents in George Stanhope's influential translation of *Epictetus His Morals with Simplicius His Comment* (1694) organized one set of precepts under the heading 'Rules for Conversation'.

[2] See George C. Brauer, Jr., *The Education of a Gentleman: Theories of Gentlemanly Education in England, 1660–1775* (New York, 1959); and W. Lee Ustick, 'Changing Ideals of Aristocratic Character and Conduct in Seventeenth-Century England', *MP*, xxx (1932), 147–66.

[3] As Mandeville said, 'the Principle of Honour in the beginning of the last Century was melted over again, and brought to a new Standard' (*Fable of the Bees*, 6th edn., 1732, p. 242). In Fielding's *Dialogue between Alexander and Diogenes*, the 'heroic' concept of honour is presented by Alexander, who accuses Diogenes of 'undermining the Foundation of all that Honour, which is the Encouragement to, and Reward of, every thing truly great and noble'; to which Diogenes replies that 'true' honour is of a different nature: 'It results from the secret Satisfaction of our own Minds, and is decreed us by Wise Men and the Gods; it is the Shadow of Wisdom and Virtue, and is inseparable from them' (below, p. 229).

to the Satisfaction and Happiness of all about us';[1] and he includes in his essay a savage attack upon social Pride and contempt of others. But he also honoured the traditional assumptions
of a hierarchical society[2] and the polite 'ceremony' (as opposed
to mere 'civility') that could only be learned in the best company.[3]
For, despite his mockery of the Lord Formals and their absurd
rituals, Fielding never underestimated the profound virtue to a
civilized community, of grace and decency in the conduct of
those social relationships that were peculiar to man.[4]

The ESSAY ON THE KNOWLEDGE OF THE CHARACTERS OF MEN
is really Fielding's *Scourge of Villanie* rather than his *Essay on Man*.
Though not strictly a satire, it belongs to the ancient homiletic
and literary tradition of attacks upon and warnings against
Hypocrisy, 'those great Arts, which the Vulgar call Treachery,
Dissembling, Promising, Lying, Falshood, &c. but which are by
GREAT MEN summed up in the collective Name of Policy, or
Politicks, or rather *Pollitricks. . .*'.[5] Fielding distinguishes two
kinds of Hypocrisy, that which seeks to gain the good opinion of
others in order to exploit them and that which by censoriousness
of others struggles to achieve a reputation as a 'saint'. The two
overlap, of course (as we see in a Tartuffe); but Fielding's distinction is between those who seek through flattery, professions
of esteem, promises, and the like, to persuade their victims to
sacrifice their own interests for the hypocrite's gain—a utili-
tarian hypocrisy, in other words—and, on the other hand, a kind
of pure and radical evil, whose envy and hatred of the good springs

[1] See below, p. 4. Cf. the *Covent-Garden Journal*, 55–6.

[2] For instance, in dealing with behaviour in 'public Assembly', he divides his topic into
behaviour to superiors, to equals, and to inferiors—as, indeed, Swift had, in his unpublished
essay, 'On Good-Manners and Good Breeding': 'One principal point of this art is to suit
our behaviour to the three several degrees of men; our superiors, our equals, and those
below us' (*Prose Works*, ed. Herbert Davis, iv. 213).

[3] Fielding's normal view; cf. *Tom Jones*, IX. i. As Bellegarde said, 'Nothing forms the
Mind like the Use of the World; this gives it that Tincture of Politeness which is only
obtain'd by the frequent Sight of polite Persons, and copying from their Plan' (*Reflexions
upon Ridicule*, 5th edn., i. 281).

[4] See Fielding's poignant comment upon the brutish malevolence of the watermen on
the Thames, in the *Journal of a Voyage to Lisbon*, under date of 26 June 1754.

[5] *Jonathan Wild*, II. v. The tradition is too broad, and perhaps too familiar, for survey;
the hypocrite has been a persistent type in literature, as in life, from the time of Homer:
'For hateful in my eyes, even as the gates of Hades, is the man that hideth one thing in his
mind and sayeth another' (*Iliad*, ix. 312–13; trans. A. T. Murray, Loeb Library); and
scripture offers copious warning that 'the hypocrite's hope shall perish' (Job. 8: 13).

from an inherent depravity of mind. Fielding's conviction that
the hypocrite flourished because the average citizen did not
trouble to make adequate moral distinctions—or even properly
judge his own interests and happiness—was made more bitter
by his belief that good men, in particular, were the hypocrite's
natural victims. Like Parson Adams, as they had never any
intention to deceive, so they never suspected such a design in
others.[1] However, in the faith that 'Simplicity, when set on its
Guard, is often a Match for Cunning',[2] Fielding sought to provide some cues to the disguises worn by 'the crafty and designing
Part of Mankind', even to a rather confused flirtation with the
art of physiognomy, shortly abandoned for a more convincing
analysis of the 'characters' of hypocrisy.

Perhaps the strategy of exhortation led him to begin his essay
with some premisses about human nature that are darker than the
popular conception of Fielding has normally taken into account.
But the numerous sombre reflections upon the malignity of man
that can be found in his various works suggest that this was no
transient mood,[3] and that Fielding's comic view of the human
predicament represented a hard-won victory over a more despairing persuasion that 'scarce a Day passes without inclining a
truly good-natured Man rather to Tears than Merriment'.[4] So
also, there are two major (and contradictory) emphases in
Fielding's view of man's educability: the first emphasis posited
an 'unacquired, original Distinction' between one soul and
another that suggests an almost deterministic view of original
good or evil.[5] The other emphasis, which is implicit in most of
Fielding's work, lay upon man's free will, his power to change
himself or win a conquest over his passions.[6] Nevertheless, he

---

[1] *Joseph Andrews*, I. iii.   [2] *Tom Jones*, VII. vi.
[3] See, for example, besides such bitter early plays as *The Modern Husband* (1732): the
Champion, 6 March 1740; *Joseph Andrews*, III. iii; *Amelia*, III. i; the *Covent-Garden
Journal*, 16 and 55; *A Clear State of the Case of Elizabeth Canning* (1753), p. 14; and the
Journal of a Voyage to Lisbon (1755), under date of 26 June 1754. On Fielding's general
view of human nature, see Morris Golden, *Fielding's Moral Psychology* (Amherst, Mass.,
1966) and the broad survey by Wolfgang Iser, *Die Weltanschauung Henry Fieldings*
(Tübingen, 1952).
[4] See below, p. 159.   [5] See below, p. 154.
[6] See, for example, the *Champion*, 2 February 1740 and 27 March 1740; *Jonathan Wild*,
revised edn., IV. xv (1754, p. 263); *Amelia*, VIII. iii; the *Covent-Garden Journal*, 16 and
29. This conviction lay behind Parson Adams's faith in (private) education, as the more
pessimistic view lay behind Joseph's demurrer (*Joseph Andrews*, III. v).

more than once declared that those who were inherently evil or who had been corrupted by a vicious education could not change;[1] and, giving up on these social monsters, he addressed his exhortations rather to 'the innocent and undesigning', either to inculcate some degree of suspicion and caution in their dealing with mankind[2] or to place in a true light the thoughtless follies and crimes of which even good men were sometimes capable.[3] Both the *Essay on Conversation* and the *Essay on the Knowledge of the Characters of Men* are contributions to this dual endeavour in moral education.

If there is a dark and a sceptical strain in Fielding that cannot be denied, his first anchor nevertheless remains the exalted tradition of the classical and Christian moralists, with its doubly 'optimistic' assertion of the ultimate rationality of the universe and the ultimate significance of man's often floundering pilgrimage. Few of his works more clearly attest his loyalty to that tradition than the soberly considered essay, OF THE REMEDY OF AFFLICTION FOR THE LOSS OF OUR FRIENDS, a cry from the heart, written after the death of his own daughter Charlotte.[4] Quite typically, though the essay is very individual Fielding and rings with an unquestionable sincerity, every appeal that it makes, every argument that it employs, is ancient and traditional.

The commonplaces, the *topoi*, of classic consolatory literature are revitalized in Fielding's intense forwarding of the arguments that the man of sound intelligence anticipates future sorrows and is better able therefore to accept them; that human life is at best but a brief span and death is common to all; that a public display of grief is not a duty expected of the mourner and that though tears are natural they are unavailing, and excessive grief is folly;

[1] 'I think we may with Justice suspect, at least so far as to deny him our Confidence, that a Man whom we once knew to be a Villain, remains a Villain still' (see below, p. 176). Cf. the *Champion*, 6 March 1740; *Jonathan Wild*, III. iv; *Tom Jones*, XIV. viii and VIII. i; *Amelia*, XII. ix. So Jonathan Swift had said: 'The Preaching of Divines helps to preserve well-inclined Men in the Course of Virtue; but seldom or never reclaims the Vicious' ('Thoughts on Various Subjects', *Prose Works*, ed. Herbert Davis, iv. 246).

[2] Cf. the *Champion*, 11 December 1739.

[3] See the arguments in the *Champion*, 6 March 1740 and 13 March 1740; and Fielding's conclusion, in the Dedication to *Tom Jones*, that 'it is much easier to make good Men wise, than to make bad Men good'.

[4] See below, p. 14 and n. Fielding introduced formal consolations into each of his novels: see *Jonathan Wild*, III. ii; *Joseph Andrews*, III. xi; *Tom Jones*, V. vii; *Amelia*, VII. ii. They serve quite different ends in the different contexts; but in every case they provide an authentic part of the texture of contemporary life.

that our loved ones are merely a loan that must be surrendered
on call; that death, indeed, may have rescued them from greater
ills; and that if 'Life be no general Good, Death is no general
Evil'.[1] These were precisely the arguments that the famed *conso-
lationes* of Cicero and Seneca and Plutarch had displayed[2] and
that had passed from them into the tradition of Christian consolation.[3] The Christian tradition had, however, stressed an
additional appeal: the certain hope of immortality and the bliss
of the other world, which should rob death of all its terrors.[4]
This is the assurance with which Fielding concludes, 'a Hope, the
sweetest, most endearing, and ravishing, which can enter into a
Mind capable of, and inflamed with, Friendship'. If the bulk of
the essay bears witness to the classic sources of Fielding's practical
morality, the conclusion just as certainly manifests his profound
emotional commitment to the promise affirmed by his religion.[5]

The lighter prose-pieces of the *Miscellanies* are all satires,
though each exploits a different form: mock-encomium, parody,
Lucianic dialogue, dramatic sketch. The ESSAY ON NOTHING
rings a set of ingenious changes upon the word 'nothing', to prove
—with a great show of formal logic and rhetorical fireworks—
that the moderns write on Nothing, theologians argue over
Nothing, ambition leads to Nothing, and that the dignity of an
empty nobility is Nothing: for 'NOTHING contains so much
Dignity as NOTHING'.[6] The amusement and the bite of this kind

[1] See below, p. 223.

[2] Cicero, *Tusculan Disputations*, i and iii; *Epistulae ad familiares*, IV. v and v. xvi;
Seneca, *De consolatione ad Marciam, Ad Polybium*, and *Epistulae morales ad Lucilium*, lxiii,
xcviii, xcix; Plutarch, *Consolatio ad Apollonium*.

[3] See Charles Favez, *La Consolation latine chrétienne* (Paris, 1937); Sister Mary E. Fern,
The Latin Consolatio as a Literary Type (St. Louis, 1941); and Benjamin Boyce, 'The Stoic
Consolatio and Shakespeare', *PMLA*, lxiv (1949), 771–80. As the *Spectator* observed (no.
163): 'Enquiries after Happiness, and Rules for attaining it, are not so necessary and useful
to Mankind as the Arts of Consolation, and supporting one self under Affliction.'

[4] Cf. the contrast between the operations of 'Religion and Philosophy' in *Tom Jones*,
III. i. In the *Remedy of Affliction*, Fielding eschewed most of the arguments, other than the
appeal to immortality, that were peculiar to the Christian *consolatio*, e.g., that no accident
happens to us without divine permission, that therefore it is the duty of the Christian to
submit patiently to affliction, that the anger of heaven toward our sins may be thereby
appeased, and that it is folly to complain against heaven's law; but these are precisely the
commonplaces that are urged in Parson Adams's brief sermon to Joseph in affliction
(*Joseph Andrews*, III. xi).

[5] Even here, however, Fielding balances a quotation from a good English divine with
a paraphrase of Cicero; see below, p. 225 and n.

[6] See below, p. 186.

of word-play had been exploited by a number of predecessors, from the distinguished Renaissance scholar Joannes Passerati, who wrote a Latin poem called *Nihil* in the sixteenth century, to perhaps the most famous of such productions, the Earl of Rochester's *Upon Nothing* (1679).[1] But Fielding's essay is also in the richer and more ancient tradition of the paradoxical encomium, a genre almost as old as formal rhetoric itself.[2] Aristophanes had included mock-encomiums in his plays (as Ben Jonson was later to do), and Lucian's solemn praise of the fly, *Laus muscae*, was a favourite with the learned wits of the Renaissance, whose ingenious variations upon the form reached a climax in the *Moriae encomium* of Erasmus (1509). Rabelais included a panegyric upon the codpiece and a celebration of debt in *Gargantua and Pantagruel*, and Swift sported with the technique throughout *A Tale of a Tub*. Fielding himself displays a learned familiarity with the traditional topics proper to this genre of mock-rhetoric, such as the antiquity, the dignity, and the utility of the object praised;[3] and like his eminent predecessors in the jest, he turned its traditional inversions to the service of valid and pungent satire upon the unsubstantial goods that men pursued for—nothing.

The parody, SOME PAPERS PROPER TO BE READ BEFORE THE R—L SOCIETY, is a delightfully authentic reproduction of the form and style of the Royal Society's *Philosophical Transactions*, and, in fact, follows an actual issue of that journal, in which the learned Swiss naturalist, Abraham Trembley, had described in excruciating detail his dissection of that interesting 'insect', the freshwater polypus—an experiment which resulted in each part becoming a new and whole polyp.[4] For the 'polypus' Fielding substituted the 'chrysipus' or English guinea, and solemnly

---

[1] As Swift said, at the conclusion of the *Tale of a Tub*: 'I am now trying an Experiment very frequent among Modern Authors; which is, to *write upon Nothing* . . .' (ed. A. C. Guthkelch and D. N. Smith, 2nd edn. [Oxford, 1958], p. 208).

[2] See Henry Knight Miller, 'The Paradoxical Encomium, with Special Reference to Its Vogue in England, 1600–1800', *MP*, liii (1956), 145–78; and, for a larger frame, Rosalie L. Colie, *Paradoxica Epidemica* (Princeton, 1966).

[3] Cf. Fielding's discourse upon the antiquity, the dignity, and the efficacy of the *argumentum baculinum*, or knock-down argument, in the *Champion*, 5 January 1740.

[4] *Philosophical Transactions*, no. 467 (13–21 January 1743). On Trembley, see John R. Baker, *Abraham Trembley of Geneva: Scientist and Philosopher 1710–1784* (1952); and for the fascinating philosophical reverberations of his discovery, Aram Vartanian, 'Trembley's Polyp, La Mettrie, and Eighteenth-Century French Materialism', *Journal of the History of Ideas*, xi (1950), 259–86.

followed out the order of topics proper to a biological report: a description of the 'chrysipus', complete with diagram, its size and species, general habitat, an attempt at classification, account of its motion and its methods of generation, a long section on experiments, and a conclusion on its longevity and local habitat, to which Fielding added an uncustomary account of the creature's 'virtues'. Although the Royal Society inspired consistently hostile passions in Fielding and most of his humanistic con-temporaries,[1] that distinguished body bears only the secondary (or formal) brunt of the satire here; for by replacing Trembley with a protagonist of his own, the learned 'Petrus Gualterus', Fielding turns the report into a cutting attack upon the usurer and miser, Peter Walter, who also yielded the pattern for Peter Pounce in *Joseph Andrews*.[2] Though it is comical to follow Petrus Gualterus's exposition of the art of producing many guineas from a single original, it is hard not to absorb also something of Fielding's total contempt for the figure he is mocking. If there was one sin that drove him to even greater fury than hypocrisy, it was avarice; for not only did this appear to him a deliberately chosen meanness (as opposed to a sin of inadvertence or extrava-gance), but it was clearly pernicious to society at large. The miser was one of those 'monsters' that baffled Fielding, something outside the human frame; and like his brother satirists of all ages, he used the moral weapons of ridicule and scorn against the monstrous as a way of reaffirming the norm.

The DIALOGUE BETWEEN ALEXANDER THE GREAT AND DIOGENES THE CYNIC offers a dramatic contrast between two types of False Greatness, the Conqueror and the Ascetic, overweening am-bition and churlish unsocial censuring. Cast in the form of a Lucianic dialogue,[3] Fielding's sketch seizes upon the supposedly

---

[1] See, among many other studies, Dorothy Stimson, *Scientists and Amateurs: A History of the Royal Society* (New York, 1948); W. P. Jones, *The Rhetoric of Science* (Berkeley, 1966); and C. S. Duncan, 'The Scientist as a Comic Type', *MP*, xiv (1916), 281–91. Fielding has satirical allusions to the Royal Society in many of his plays and in the journals, e.g. the *Champion*, 29 April 1740, and *Covent-Garden Journal*, 70. See also the *Journey from This World to the Next*, I. vii; his Letter XL contributed to Sarah Fielding's *Familiar Letters between the Principal Characters in David Simple* (1747); and *Tom Jones*, III. v and XVI. iii.

[2] See below, p. 193 and n.

[3] No adequate comment can here be offered on Lucian's pervasive influence in Fielding's work; for a tentative critical estimate, see Miller, *Essays on Fielding's Miscellanies*, pp. 365–86. Lucian had presented a dialogue between the shades of Alexander and Diogenes in his

historical meeting of Alexander and Diogenes as a dramatic
opportunity for allowing each to expose the claims of the other.
Thus Alexander, the very type of worldly greatness, is treated
with scorn by Diogenes: 'How vainly dost thou endeavour to
raise thyself on the Monuments of thy Disgrace!' But when the
tub-philosopher claims that his own invectives against vice drive
men into the 'Road of Virtue', Alexander provides the crushing
rejoinder (to an age schooled in *communitas*): 'For which Purpose
thou hast forsworn Society, and art retired to preach to Trees
and Stones'! Fielding could draw upon conventionally negative
views of Alexander and Diogenes for his dialogue;[1] but he seems
to have been the first to see the riper dramatic and symbolic
possibilities inherent in their confrontation.[2] As the dialogue proceeds, and the extremes of the active and the contemplative lives
cancel each other out, the implicit ideal emerges—the ideal that
lies behind the whole volume—of the good man who seeks
neither unjust power over others nor a hypocritical reputation for
virtue, a reputation actually based upon the negation of man's
most profound social instincts. Alexander and Diogenes sum up,
in their individual persons, the two vices that provide a major
focus for the moral energy of the *Miscellanies*.

Though Fielding described An Interlude between Jupiter,
Juno, Apollo, and Mercury as a playlet actually intended for
the stage,[3] it is, in effect, a Lucianic 'Dialogue of the Gods' in four
'scenes'.[4] The action, Jupiter's preparation for a descent to earth,

Dialogues of the Dead, xiii, and Diogenes appears in a number of his other works. Though
Fielding's 'imaginary conversation' is not a dialogue of the dead, Lucian is clearly its
ultimate inspiration. Fénelon had also offered a dialogue between Alexander and Diogenes,
taken almost directly from Lucian, in his *Dialogues des morts* (Paris, 1712).

[1] For typical views of Alexander as one of 'the principal *Directors* and *Disturbers* of the
Affairs of Mankind' (Thomas Gordon, *The Humourist*, 1720–5, ii. 23), see below, p. 229 n.
Diogenes was often treated sympathetically; but for negative views, see below, p. 231 n. 2.

[2] Earlier treatments featured the mockery of Alexander's greatness by Diogenes; but none,
so far as I know, thought to reverse the positions. Fielding frequently censured Alexander:
for example, in *The Temple Beau*, ii. vii; the *Champion*, 27 November 1739; the *Journey
from This World to the Next*, i. iv; *Jonathan Wild*, i. iii; the *True Patriot*, 8; and the
Covent-Garden Journal, 19; but outside the *Miscellanies* he had little to say about
Diogenes.

[3] The title-page in the *Miscellanies* says that it was intended as the introduction to a
comedy, *Jupiter's Descent on Earth*; but nothing is known of such a work.

[4] Lucian's *Dialogues of the Gods* were perhaps less influential in the eighteenth century
than his *Dialogues of the Dead*; but when Addison looked for an example of burlesque that
represented 'great Persons acting and speaking, like the basest among the People,' his
first thought was '*Lucian*'s Gods' (*Spectator*, 249).

which had been treated in comic terms by many others besides Fielding,[1] merely serves as the occasion for some random satire upon henpecked husbands and termagant wives,[2] poor poets, effusive dedications, and titled rogues. The mild humour turns upon Jupiter's deceived notion that the virtuous men described in dedications actually exist upon earth; though as Mercury rather sourly observes, 'Men are such Hypocrites, that the greatest Part deceive even themselves, and are much worse than they think themselves to be.'

A final item, having little to do with any of the other miscellaneous pieces,[3] the straightforward translation of THE FIRST OLYNTHIAC OF DEMOSTHENES, offers evidence only that Fielding had searched the very bottom drawers of his desk to make up a volume. The translation was possibly intended as a contribution to the anti-Walpole campaign of the war-party Opposition in the late 1730s, when it became the fashion to argue that Walpole's inertia in the face of insults from Philip V of Spain threatened the nation's safety, as that of the Athenian demagogues had doomed an Athens confronted by Philip of Macedon.[4] There is no evidence that Fielding's faithful but not very exciting translation was ever published before its inclusion in the *Miscellanies*.

3. DATE OF COMPOSITION

The earliest public reference to the *Miscellanies*, the 'Proposals' that appeared in the *Daily Post* of 5 June 1742 (see below, section

---

[1] Besides Charles Cotton's travesty of the Lucianic dialogues in *Burlesque upon Burlesque* (1675), there were light treatments of Jupiter's 'ranging' in John Crowne's masque *Calisto* (1675); Dryden's *Amphitryon* (1690); the anonymous translation from Louis Fuzelier, *Momus Turn'd Fabulist* (1729); the anonymous *Jupiter and Io* (1735); and *The Descent of the Heathen Gods; With the Loves of Jupiter and Alcmena*, performed at Bartholomew Fair in 1740!

[2] Perhaps with an eye upon George II and Queen Caroline; see William Peterson, 'Satire in Fielding's *An Interlude between Jupiter, Juno, Apollo, and Mercury*', *MLN*, lxv (1950), 200–2.

[3] Fielding declared in the preface to the *Miscellanies* that he was presenting 'various Matters; treating of Subjects which bear not the least Relation to each other' (see below, p. 3), which is in some measure true, though the collection has a moral unity, as suggested above, that provides it with more coherence than Fielding gives himself credit for.

[4] See the loose translations of Demosthenes in *Common Sense*, 26 November and 24 December 1737 and 4 February 1738, as well as the lofty reply in the administration paper, the *Daily Gazetteer*: 'Of Applying the Orations of Demosthenes' (22 February 1738). Mark Akenside wrote 'A British Philippic: Occasion'd by the Insults of the Spaniards, and the present Preparations for War,' that was published in the *Gentleman's Magazine*, August 1738, pp. 427–8.

4), suggests that Fielding had been receiving subscriptions for some time by that date, and that he had originally planned to have the volumes ready by the end of 1741 or the opening months of 1742.[1] The political overtones of much of his material would further suggest that the project was originally conceived when Fielding was still in the forefront of the anti-Walpole Opposition, that is, before he definitely broke with the *Champion,* no later than June of 1741.[2] One can only theorize about the stages in which *Jonathan Wild* was composed, a matter that will be discussed in the appropriate volume of this edition; but the most generally accepted hypothesis is that, as a satire of Sir Robert Walpole, it was substantially complete by the time Fielding began to project the *Miscellanies* and that it was considerably revised in the months after Walpole's fall from power (February 1742).[3] Most of the poems were already in his desk; the rest of the work (probably including the *Journey from This World to the Next,* which may have existed in embryo) he apparently assumed that he would be able to dash off in time, even though *Joseph Andrews* was already in the making and he was presumably pursuing his career in the law and riding the Western Circuit. Fielding was, after all, a professional writer; and his experience in the theatre and with the *Champion* must have given him full confidence in his ability to write under pressure and to meet deadlines. This is all speculative, to be sure; but one thing is certain: unforeseen events kept Fielding apologizing for his delays over a period of almost two years. And that his original plans never did achieve fruition is suggested by his filling out the volumes almost up to the date of publication with such things as a poem written in the autumn of 1742 and a satire written in February 1743.[4]

---

[1] The 'spirit-author' of *A Journey from This World to the Next* begins his story, 'On the first of *December* 1741, I departed this Life, at my Lodgings in *Cheapside*.' W. L. Cross (i. 395), reasonably enough, took this as the date at which Fielding probably began composition of the *Journey;* but it is equally reasonable to suppose that Fielding expected his narrative to be *published* at about that date. His 'Apology for the Delay in publishing these Volumes', in the *Preface* (pp. 13 ff.), refers vaguely to 'a Year or two backwards . . . whilst I have been engaged in these Works . . .'.

[2] See above, p. xii n. 3.

[3] The argument is summarized by Dudden, *Henry Fielding,* i. 480–3.

[4] Respectively, 'To Miss H—and at Bath' and *Some Papers Proper to be Read before the R—l Society.* The plays of Volume Two may also have been a late addition (see above, p. xi n. 1).

Evidence of date for the various items in the first volume of the *Miscellanies* is offered individually in the text; but it may be of service to present a brief chronological summary here. The earliest compositions are to be found among the poems: indeed, unless the parody of the *Aeneid* and the 'Simile' from Silius Italicus are seen as schoolboy work, the first of Fielding's extant writings that we possess in any form would be the burlesque of the *Sixth Satire* of Juvenal, 'originally sketched out before I was Twenty', i.e. before April 1727.[1] Two light-hearted amorous poems, 'To Euthalia' and 'A Description of U[pto]n G[rey]', are identified in their titles as having been written in 1728, before Fielding met Charlotte Cradock; and the little triplet 'To the Master of the Salisbury Assembly' probably belongs with these, since his lady-love is here called 'Jenny', whereas he almost invariably addressed Charlotte as 'Celia'. So, too, with the lines 'Written Extempore on a Half-Penny', addressed to 'Gloriana', and perhaps 'The Beggar', which gives no name to his inamorata. The first poem to mention Charlotte, beginning 'The Queen of Beauty, t'other Day . . .', links her with her sister Catherine, and probably belongs to the year 1729; by 1730 Charlotte has been singled out and her sister is heard of no more.[2] The group of epigrams and similes and romantic effusions specifically addressed to 'Celia' (about ten of the poems) presumably belongs to the period before November 1734, when Charlotte and Henry Fielding were married. One, the 'Advice to the Nymphs of New S[aru]m', is designated as written in 1730; and the diatribe against London, 'I hate the Town . . .', can be dated around 1730–1.

Several other poems offer reasonably clear evidence of date. One of the epistles to Sir Robert Walpole is described as 'Written in the Year 1730', and the other, 'Anno 1731'.[3] The 'Epigram on One Who Invited Many Gentlemen to a Small Dinner' must have been written after February 1733, the date of the poem by

[1] See below, *Preface*, p. 3; and cf. Cross, i. 50–2. Topical references of later date show that Fielding reworked his early lines: there are allusions to *Pamela* (November 1740), to the translation with Young of Aristophanes' *Plutus* (May 1742), and to the English army in Flanders in 1742.

[2] Cross (i. 174) suggested that the epigram, 'That Kate Weds a Fool' (below, p. 76), might represent an allusion to Catherine; and he also hinted that Amelia's evil sister might be drawn from Charlotte's sister.

[3] That these dates are a hoax has been cogently argued by Hugh Amory, 'Henry Fielding's *Epistles to Walpole*: A Reexamination', *PQ*, xlvi (1967), 236–47; but the present editor must accept their authenticity.

Pope on which it is based. The long poem *Liberty* was certainly written after 1735–6, for it echoes James Thomson's *Liberty*, published in those years. The epigram on the printer John Watts at a play and 'A Sailor's Song' probably (but not necessarily) belong to the years of Fielding's theatrical career, i.e. before the summer of 1737. So also with the brief playlet, *An Interlude between Jupiter, Juno, Apollo, and Mercury.*

The translation of Demosthenes' *First Olynthiac* was presumably written, or refurbished, to exploit the war fervour of 1737–8. The *Essay on the Knowledge of the Characters of Men* has numerous parallels with papers in the *Champion* in 1739 and 1740; an allusion to Pope's *Letters*, first published in 1735, provides a *terminus a quo*. The *Dialogue between Alexander the Great and Diogenes the Cynic*, though it has no datable allusions, expands a topic treated in the poem *Of True Greatness*, which was published in January 1741, as 'writ several Years ago'.

The other long poems would also seem to have been written in the late 1730s. Lines from *Of Good-Nature* were published in the *Champion* in 1739, though the poem was certainly revised for the *Miscellanies*. The verses *To John Hayes* include a compliment to David Garrick that must postdate his London debut in October 1741. The poem *To A Friend on the Choice of a Wife* is of uncertain date.[1] Fielding's *Essay on Conversation* refers to a treatise by his friend James Harris that Fielding read in manuscript and that we know to have been finished in December 1741.[2] The occasion for the sober essay *Of the Remedy of Affliction for the Loss of Our Friends* was surely the death of Fielding's father in June 1741, followed by the death of his daughter Charlotte in March 1742. The latest poem in the collection is the little compliment 'To Miss H[usb]and at Bath', probably written in the autumn of 1742; and the *Essay on Nothing* has a reference to James Hammond's *Love Elegies* of November 1742. Finally, *Some Papers Proper to be Read before the R—l Society*, which was separately published in February 1743, is a parody of the issue of the *Philosophical Transactions* that appeared in late January of that year.

---

[1] If Wilbur Cross (i. 384) was right in thinking that the poem was occasioned by Lyttelton's marriage, it could be dated around June 1742; but this guess cannot be substantiated.

[2] See below, p. 122 n.

4. HISTORY OF PUBLICATION

If we suppose that Fielding began to organize the materials of the *Miscellanies* sometime in 1741 for publication late that year or early in the next,[1] the first extant public notice of his project offers sad evidence in its 'Note' that his plans had gone awry. On 5 June 1742 the *Daily Post* advertised the following:

This Day are publish'd,

Proposals *for* printing *by* Subscription,

MISCELLANIES in Three VOLUMES

Octavo.

By HENRY FIELDING, *Esq;*

The first Volume will contain all his Works in Verse, and some short Essays in Prose.

The second Volume will contain, a Journey from this World to the next.

The third Volume will contain, the History of that truly renowned Person Jonathan Wyld, Esq; in which not only his Character, but that of divers other great Personages of his Time, will be set in a just and true Light.

The Price to Subscribers is One Guinea; and Two Guineas for the Royal Paper. One Half of which is to be paid at Subscribing, the other on the Delivery of the Book in Sheets. The Subscribers Names will be printed.

Note, The Publication of these Volumes hath been hitherto retarded by the Author's Indisposition last Winter, and a Train of melancholy Accidents scarce to be parallell'd [*sic*]; but he takes this Opportunity to assure his Subscribers, that he will most certainly deliver them within the Time mentioned in his last Receipts, viz. by the 25th of December next.

Subscriptions are taken in by Mr. A. Millar, Bookseller, opposite St. Clement's Church in the Strand.

As the Books will very shortly go to the Press, Mr. Fielding begs the Favour of those who intend to subscribe to do it immediately.[2]

In November the announcement of 5 June was repeated in the *Daily Post*, with a new final paragraph:

Whereas the Number of Copies to be printed is to be determin'd by the Number of Subscribers, Mr. Fielding will be oblig'd to all those who have subscrib'd to those Miscellanies, or who intend him that Favour, if they will please send their Names and first Payment (if not already made) to Mr. Millar, Bookseller, opposite to Katharine-Street in the Strand, before the 5th of December next.[3]

---

[1] See above, p. xliii.   [2] *Daily Post*, 7098 (5 June 1742).
[3] *Daily Post*, 7240 (18 November 1742).

Whatever the response to this appeal, Fielding did not have his materials ready for the printers in December. The next notice did not appear, in fact, until 12 February 1743, when the *Daily Post* announced that the volumes would be delivered to subscribers on the 28th of that month and that the subscription would be closed on the 22nd.[1] Again, however, the volumes were not delivered on the promised date. Toward the end of March they were advertised as ready for delivery on 7 April.[2] And this time Fielding was able to keep his promise. The *Miscellanies* were entered in the Stationers' Register on 6 April; and on 7 April 1743, the *Daily Post* announced: '*This Day will be deliver'd to the Subscribers*, MISCELLANIES in three Volumes, 8vo. *By* HENRY FIELDING, *Esq;* . . . . Printed for the Author, and to be had of A. Millar, opposite to Katherine-Street in the Strand.'[3]

Andrew Millar, the famous bookseller who was said by Dr. Johnson to have 'raised the price of literature' and who handled all of Fielding's novels, acted as publisher of the *Miscellanies*. Most of the proceeds, after deduction of printing costs, advertising, and the like (probably amounting to about £150), went to Fielding—although it is not certain what financial arrangements he made with Millar.[4] Since there were subscriptions by 427 subscribers to 342 copies on 'coarse' (demy 8vo) paper and 214 on 'fine' (royal 8vo) paper, the gross, at one guinea for the demy and two for the royal, could not have been less than 770 guineas— a pleasant sum, and one that satisfied Fielding's most 'urgent Motive' in publishing the *Miscellanies*.[5]

---

[1] *Daily Post*, 7314 (12 February 1743). The notice was repeated on 14 February in the *Daily Post* and also in the *Daily Advertiser*.

[2] Notices in the *St. James's Evening Post*, 22–4 March 1743 and thereafter, cited in John Edwin Wells, 'Fielding's "Miscellanies" ', *MLR*, xiii (1918), 481.

[3] *Daily Post*, 7358 (7 April 1743).

[4] The normal arrangement was for the subscription money to go to the author (after costs); the publisher's profit came from the sale of additional copies. See William M. Sale, Jr., *Samuel Richardson: Master Printer* (Ithaca, N.Y., 1950), pp. 106 ff. Millar farmed out the printing of the three volumes to three different houses, a not unusual practice in the period. The first volume was printed by William Strahan, whose ledger (British Museum Add. MS. 48800, p. 38 verso) records the charge to Millar: 'April 2 [1743]. For printing the first Volume of Fielding's Miscellanies 26½ Sheets Pica 8vo No. 1000 Coarse and 250 fine @ £1:2:6 p Sheet . . . [£]29/16/–.' Volume Three was printed by William Bowyer the younger, as his paper-stock ledger indicates (Bodleian Library MS. Don. b. 4, fol. 112 recto); and Volume Two was most likely the work of Henry Woodfall the elder, who had printed Fielding's 'Proposals' of 5 June 1742 (see Miller, *Essays on Fielding's Miscellanies*, pp. 12–13).

[5] Fielding's phrase, in the *Preface*, p. 7.

There is little evidence concerning the reception of the *Miscellanies* as a whole, which is not very surprising; that the entire project was probably viewed in something of a political light is perhaps suggested by the fact that the subscription list contains the names of many political acquaintances but very few literary men. We know, for instance, that Alexander Pope ordered copies for himself and Ralph Allen; but neither put his name down for public acknowledgement. Nor did Aaron Hill, who got his copy through the printer, Samuel Richardson; Richardson was not a subscriber.[1] Most of the names that do not reflect interlinked circles of political interest are those of professional friends and acquaintances. Fielding indeed declared that he had derived 'more than half the Names which appear to this Subscription' through the efforts of his fellows in the Inns of Court;[2] and many of his theatrical friends were subscribers: Charles Fleetwood, the manager of Drury Lane Theatre, who took twenty sets, David Garrick, Peg Woffington, Kitty Clive, and others. As an interesting final note: leaders of the 'patriot' Opposition to Walpole, with the significant exception of Carteret, were quite as strongly represented in the subscription list as one would expect; but so also were many friends and associates of Sir Robert Walpole, headed by the Great Man himself with a subscription to ten sets on royal paper.

Later in the month of April 1743,[3] after delivery of the subscription edition, Millar published for his own profit the so-called 'Second Edition' of the *Miscellanies* (unsold sheets of the original, bound up with a new title-page), and was still advertising it, in Fielding's *Jacobite's Journal*, as late as October and November of 1748. A Dublin reprint, of no textual authority, was offered in two volumes in 1743.

As one would anticipate, *Jonathan Wild* drew more attention than the other volumes of the *Miscellanies*; but a few allusions to the first volume can be gleaned. Arthur Murphy's notes to Smart's *Hilliad* (1753) offered this comment: 'Among our countrymen, I do not know any body that has handled this subject [Inanity] so well as the accurate Mr. Fielding, in his essay

[1] For Pope and Allen, see *Correspondence of Alexander Pope*, ed. George Sherburn (Oxford, 1956), iv. 452; for Hill, see Alan D. McKillop, *Samuel Richardson* (Chapel Hill, N.C., 1936), p. 77. [2] See below, *Preface*, p. 13.
[3] Publication was noted in the *General Evening Post* of 23–6 April, in the *Daily Advertiser* of 27 April, and in the *Daily Post* of 2 May 1743.

upon Nothing, which the reader may find in the first volume of his miscellanies. . . .'[1] And in later years Goldsmith observed that Fielding had said, 'he never knew a person with a steady glavering smile, but he found him a rogue', which is loosely quoted from the *Essay on the Knowledge of the Characters of Men*.[2] The author of *The History of Jack Connor* (1752) used some lines from the poem *Of Good-Nature* as an epigraph to his fourth chapter. The first epistle to Walpole was reprinted in a different text in Robert Dodsley's *Collection of Poems in Six Volumes* (1758). And the *Essay on Conversation* was apparently in the mind of William Creech when he declared that Fielding was one of the 'best writers on the subject of politeness'.[3]

But for the most part, the poems and essays and satires of the *Miscellanies* elicited comparatively little attention. When Arthur Murphy assembled the first collected edition of Fielding's *Works* in 1762, he even omitted the *Essay on Nothing* that he had praised in 1753, as well as all of the poetry (except for some citations in his Introduction); and it was not until the edition of J. P. Browne (1871–2) that the whole of the *Miscellanies*, including the poems, was reprinted in an edition of the *Works*. As in the Leslie Stephen and W. E. Henley editions, however, the various items were scattered through separate volumes; and until the present edition, the poems and prose of the first volume of the *Miscellanies* have never been reprinted together, as they were originally published.

HENRY KNIGHT MILLER

[1] *The Hilliad* (Dublin, 1753), p. 39.
[2] *An History of the Earth, and Animated Nature* (1774), ii. 94.
[3] *Edinburgh Fugitive Pieces, with Letters . . . by the Late William Creech* (1815), p. 150.

TEXTUAL INTRODUCTION

T H I S edition offers a critical, unmodernized text of Fielding's *Miscellanies*. The text is critical in that it has been established by the application of analytical criticism to the evidence of the various early documentary forms in which the material appeared. It is unmodernized in that every effort has been made to present the text in as close a form to Fielding's own inscription (and, when they appear, revisions) as the surviving documents permit, subject to normal editorial regulation.

General remarks about the editorial procedures are intended to apply to all three volumes of the *Miscellanies*. However, since each volume has its individual textual problems, which will need explication, the present introduction in these matters concerns itself only with the texts in Volume One. The peculiar problems of Volumes Two and Three will be treated in the respective introductions where the discussion will have an immediate application.

I. THE COPY-TEXT AND ITS TREATMENT

The details of publication leave no doubt as to the authoritative nature of the manuscripts that Fielding sent to Millar, the publisher of the volumes. The previously unpublished items, therefore, would have been set in the first edition almost certainly from Fielding's holograph papers, and for this material the first edition remains the only text with an over-all authority. The first volume of the *Miscellanies* was not reprinted in Fielding's lifetime save for the unauthoritative two-volume Dublin edition in 1743 with which Fielding had no connection. The Murphy collected edition of Fielding's *Works* in 1762 referred to no fresh authority. Signs of Fielding's individual characteristics are obscured by the variable habits of the compositors, even within the different printing-houses that set the three separate volumes, so that a wide variety of doublets occurs, such as *satire–satyr, music–musick, falshood–falsehood, tho'–though, would–wou'd, confess'd–confessed, shew–show,* and the like. Nevertheless, what authority there is in these 'accidentals' of the texts, as in the 'substantives', is contained only in the 1743 edition for the previously unpublished works.

Fragments of two poems, the first epistle to Walpole (p. 56) and the lines 'Written Extempore, on a Half-penny' (p. 59), had earlier been published in *The Gentleman's Magazine* and the *Champion* respectively. The connection of the copy for these fragments with the manuscripts from which the *Miscellanies* were set is obscure. Nevertheless, since it is certain that the magazine publication is in no sense an ancestor of these texts in the *Miscellanies*, no attempt at conflation has been made, and the magazine versions will be found separately reprinted in Appendices B and C

On the other hand, *Of True Greatness* had been published previously, complete, in January 1741, and *Some Papers Proper to be Read before the R——l Society* in February 1743. The *Miscellanies* omits the original preface to *Of True Greatness* (printed in Appendix A of the present edition, however) but is otherwise a word-for-word reprint save that *H——cote* is substituted in line 149 for *G——schal*. For the rest there are the usual corrections or 'improvements' of the accidentals. The reproduction in the *Miscellanies* of the untypical spelling *unreguarded* from 1741 at line 24 would indicate that the copy for the *Miscellanies* was the 1741 printed text. No such unique evidence is present in *Some Papers*, but the general conformity of the accidentals (the most notable change by the printers of the *Miscellanies* being the use of double-quotes in place of the original single-quotes) suggests with some certainty that, in turn, the *Miscellanies* used the earlier 1743 printed version as its copy.

In a situation of this sort textual critics recognize a double authority.[1] For an unmodernized edition the most authentic form of what are known as the 'accidentals' of a text—that is, the spelling, punctuation, capitalization, word-division, and such typographical matters as the use of italicized words—can be transmitted only in the document that lies nearest to the lost holograph, that is, in the first edition, the one printing that was set direct from manuscript. An editor will understand that the first edition by no means represents a diplomatic reprint of the lost manuscript and that in various respects the accidentals will

[1] Sir Walter Greg, 'The Rationale of Copy-Text', *Studies in Bibliography*, iii (1950), 19–36, is the main authority. See also F. Bowers, 'Textual Criticism', in *The Aims and Methods of Scholarship in Modern Languages and Literatures* (Modern Language Association of America, 1963), pp. 23–42, and citations.

be a mixture of the author's and the compositors'. But whatever the relative impurity, the first edition stands nearest to the author's own characteristics and represents the only authority in these matters that has been preserved for the texture in which his words were originally clothed.

On the other hand, when Fielding sent the marked-up pages of the printed versions to the press as copy for the *Miscellanies* there is no positive evidence that, in any major respect, he altered the accidentals of the copy. Moreover, the evidence at this date does not favour an author tinkering with the accidentals of printed copy so long as his meaning had not been altered as a result of house styling, and all seemed reasonably in order. Thus we may take it that the variations in the *Miscellanies* accidentals represent substantially the normal compositorial differences characteristic of reprints of the time. In this respect, in the *Miscellanies* the authority of the substantives and of the accidentals splits when the text had already appeared in an earlier printing. Given the general suggestion, and sometimes the specific evidence, that Fielding did occasionally revise the wording, almost all of these substantive variants must be accepted as authorial, whereas almost all of the changes in the texture of the accidentals must be labelled as compositorial and hence unauthoritative. Under these circumstances, Sir Walter Greg's classic theory of copy-text must hold. That is, a critical editor chooses as his copy-text —the basic authority for his old-spelling edition—that document which can be isolated as the supreme authority for the accidentals. In this respect, then, he comes as close as documentary evidence permits to the desirable reproduction of authorial characteristics in spelling, pointing, and the like. In this authoritative texture of the first edition, then, he inserts those verbal changes in later editions that in his estimate represent authorial correction or revision, and not compositorial variation and corruption. By this procedure an editor of the *Miscellanies* substantially reproduces the marked copy that was given to the press for the *Miscellanies* (in case of prior publication), a copy that was in the main followed by the printer in respect to the wording but was casually varied in the accidentals. This is a critical process almost exclusively, with only occasional bibliographical guidance, in which the editor shoulders his proper responsibility to separate the author's intended alterations from the verbal corruption that inevitably accompanies the transmission of a text through a series of reprints.

In these volumes Dr. Miller has made a few alterations to remove patent error, but he has not endeavoured to achieve an unnatural consistency in spelling, capitalization, or punctuation, especially one not to be expected from the miscellaneous collection of manuscripts, and occasional annotated printed copy, that formed the printer's copy. Wanting the manuscripts, no editor could determine whether the compositor(s) or Fielding himself was responsible for the casual variation.

With few exceptions, all accidental as well as all substantive alterations have been recorded in the textual apparatus so that a critic may reconstruct the copy-text in detail as well as the substantive variation from it in the present edition. However, in a few purely formal matters the following editorial changes have been made silently. (1) Typographical errors such as turned letters or wrong fount are not recorded. (2) The small capitals and the exact size of the heading capital at the beginning of poems and essays have been ignored. (3) Running quotation marks in the left margin have been omitted and quotations have been indicated according to the modern custom. (4) Simple arabic numbers have been spelled out. (5) When the apostrophe and roman 's' follow an italicized name, the roman is retained only when it indicates the contraction for 'is' and is normalized to italic when the possessive case is required. (6) The fount of punctuation is normalized without regard for the variable practice of the original. Pointing within an italic passage is italicized; but pointing following an italicized word that is succeeded by roman text is silently placed in roman. (7) The diacritical marks that sometimes were applied to Latin texts of the eighteenth century have been silently removed in Fielding's Latin quotations (and in the text of Juvenal's *Sixth Satire*), as Dr. Miller takes it that they do not possess even antiquarian interest. The diacriticals in Greek words or phrases have, in several cases, been silently emended. (8) The speech-prefixes in the *Interlude* have been silently expanded ('Jup.' to 'Jupiter', and so on) for the convenience of the modern reader.

The more important noted emendation of accidentals (as of substantives) has been conservative. In Fielding's time, apostrophes were frequently introduced in plural nouns (and even sometimes

0

liv *Textual Introduction*

in verbs), and these have not been trifled with. Contrariwise, the apostrophe was not customarily employed for the plural possessive, and it has not been supplied in this text. A number of items in Volume One were prefaced by individual title-pages. Dr. Miller has not reprinted these with two exceptions: the title-page of *Some Papers Proper to be Read before the R——l Society* is an organic part of the text and has been retained; the title-page of *An Interlude between Jupiter, Juno, Apollo, and Mercury* contains additional material not included in the head-title, and this has been retained in the title of the present edition.

2. THE EARLY EDITIONS

The first editions of the three volumes of *Miscellanies* have been described in detail by Donald D. Eddy,[1] and his technical descriptions and account of the method of printing need not be repeated here. The printer of Volume One was William Strahan. Two issues of this text were made, the first—in two states—to the subscribers, and the second issue to the public. In the first issue copies were advertised as to be printed on royal paper (royal 8vo) and on ordinary paper (demy 8vo). These two papers were machined in order for each forme, the fine-paper sheets first, without removing the type from the press. Except for the size and quality of the paper, therefore, they are identical save for a few accidentally dropped press-figures. Each copy of this issue contained a prefatory 'List of Subscrebers' [*sic*] in Volume One, except for a few sports or remainders.[2] The title-page has no mention of the edition number. The second issue is also of the same impression for the text-sheets and, being on the same coarse paper as the demy 8vo first or subscription issue, these were undoubtedly printed merely as an over-run without any original distinction. However, its title-page advertises it as the 'Second Edition' and the subscription list is wanting, this accompanied by some rearrangement of the imposition of the

---

[1] 'The Printing of Fielding's *Miscellanies* (1743)', *Studies in Bibliography*, xv (1962) 247–56.

[2] Various odd combinations may appear. For example, the University of Pennsylvania's copy of the coarse-paper first issue does not include the list of subscribers, and John Edwin Wells ('Fielding's "Miscellanies"', *Modern Language Review*, xiii [1918], 481–2) remarked that he possessed a copy of the 'Second Edition' (i.e. the second issue) that included the subscription list. Yale University has a copy of the royal paper (as indicated by its watermarks) that at some time has been cut down to the size of the demy.

preliminary sheets and the final single leaf of the text. Except for the omission of the List of Subscribers and the altered typography of the title-page in order to insert the notation 'Second Edition' in place of 'Printed for the Author', the two issues are textually identical.

3. THE APPARATUS

All the textual apparatus is placed in appendices. For the principles and procedures followed in this edition, see the Textual Introduction to the Wesleyan Edition of *Joseph Andrews*, pp. xliv–xlv.

4. COLLATION

The copy-text of the present edition of Volume One of the *Miscellanies* is (with the exceptions noted below) the Princeton University coarse-paper state of the first issue (Ex 3738. 1743). This has been collated against the coarse-paper copies of the first issue in the Houghton Library of Harvard College (*EC7. F460. 743ma), the University of Pennsylvania (EC7. F4605. B743m), and the Peabody Library in Baltimore, Maryland (828. F460. 743); as well as the royal-paper copies of the Houghton Library (*EC7. F460. 743m) and the Beinecke Library of Yale University (Fielding Coll. C743Ac); and also the second-issue copies at Harvard (*EC7. F460. 743mb) and at Yale (Fielding Coll. C743b). No press-variants were discovered in the course of this collation.

The copy-text for the poem 'Of True Greatness' is the first edition of that poem (1741) in the Houghton Library at Harvard College (*fEC7. F 460. 741o), which has been collated against the Yale copy (Fielding Coll. 741n), without indication of press-variation; this edition is, of course, the copy-text also for the poem's 'Preface', which is reprinted in Appendix A. The copy-text for the prose parody 'Some Papers Proper to be Read before the R—l Society' is the first edition (1743) in the library of Princeton University (EX 3738. 386), collated against the Yale copy (Fielding Coll. 743s) without the discovery of any press-variants.

FREDSON BOWERS

MISCELLANIES,

BY

Henry Fielding Efq;

In THREE VOLUMES.

L O N D O N:
Printed for the AUTHOR:
And fold by A. MILLAR, oppofite to
Catharine-Street, in the *Strand.*
MDCCXLIII.

B

PREFACE

THE Volumes[1] I now present the Public, consist, as their Title indicates, of various Matter; treating of Subjects which bear not the least Relation to each other; and perhaps, what *Martial* says of his Epigrams, may be applicable to these several Productions.

Sunt bona, sunt quædam mediocria, sunt mala PLURA.[2]

At least, if the *Bona* be denied me, I shall, I apprehend, be allowed the other Two.

The Poetical Pieces which compose the First Part of the First Volume, were most of them written when I was very young, and are indeed Productions of the Heart rather than of the Head. If the Good-natured Reader thinks them tolerable, it will answer my warmest Hopes. This Branch of Writing is what I very little pretend to, and will appear to have been very little my Pursuit, since I think (one or two Poems excepted) I have here presented my Reader with all I could remember, or procure Copies of.[3]

My Modernization of Part of the sixth Satire of *Juvenal*, will, I hope, give no Offence to that Half of our Species, for whom I have the greatest Respect and Tenderness. It was originally sketched out before I was Twenty, and was all the Revenge taken by an injured Lover.[4] For my Part, I am much more inclined to Panegyric on that amiable Sex, which I have always thought treated with a very unjust Severity by ours, who censure them for Faults (if they are truly such) into which we allure and betray them, and of which we ourselves, with an unblamed Licence, enjoy the most delicious Fruits.

As to the *Essay on Conversation*, however it may be executed, my Design in it will be at least allowed good; being to ridicule out of Society, one of the most pernicious Evils which attends it, *viz.* pampering the gross Appetites of Selfishness and Ill-nature, with the Shame and Disquietude of others; whereas I have

---

[1] Three volumes in the original edition of 1743.

[2] *Epigrammata*, I. xvi ('There are good things, there are some middling, there are more things bad . . .').

[3] Fielding ignores his prologues and epilogues and the songs in his plays; the 'Poems excepted' would include *The Masquerade* (1728) and the *Vernoniad* (1741).

[4] See W. L. Cross, *History of Henry Fielding*, i. 50–2, for the theory that Fielding's revenge' was directed against Sarah Andrew, the young heiress of Lyme Regis.

endeavoured in it to shew, that true Good-Breeding consists in contributing, with our utmost Power, to the Satisfaction and Happiness of all about us.

In my *Essay on the Knowledge of the Characters of Men*, I have endeavoured to expose a second great Evil, namely, Hypocrisy; the Bane of all Virtue, Morality, and Goodness; and to arm, as well as I can, the honest, undesigning, open-hearted Man, who is generally the Prey of this Monster, against it. I believe a little Reflection will convince us, that most Mischiefs (especially those which fall on the worthiest Part of Mankind) owe their Original to this detestable Vice.

I shall pass over the remaining Part of this Volume, to the *Journey from this World to the next*, which fills the greatest Share of the second.

It would be paying a very mean Compliment to the human Understanding, to suppose I am under any Necessity of vindicating myself from designing, in an Allegory of this Kind, to oppose any present System, or to erect a new one of my own: but perhaps the Fault may lie rather in the Heart than in the Head; and I may be misrepresented, without being misunderstood. If there are any such Men, I am sorry for it; the Good-natured Reader will not, I believe, want any Assistance from me to disappoint their Malice.

Others may (and that with greater Colour) arraign my Ignorance; as I have, in the Relation which I have put into the Mouth of *Julian*, whom they call the Apostate, done many Violences to History, and mixed Truth and Falshood with much Freedom. To these I answer. I profess Fiction only; and tho' I have chosen some Facts out of History, to embellish my Work, and fix a Chronology to it, I have not, however, confined myself to nice Exactness; having often ante-dated, and sometimes post-dated the Matter I have found in the Historian, particularly in the *Spanish* History, where I take both these Liberties in one Story.[1]

The Residue of this Volume is filled with two Dramatic Pieces, both the Productions of my Youth, tho' the latter was not acted 'till this Season.[2] It was the third Dramatic Performance I

[1] Cf. *A Journey from This World to the Next*, I. xvii, based on Juan de Mariana, *The General History of Spain*, trans. John Stevens (1699).

[2] *Eurydice, or the Devil Henpeck'd*, a one-act musical farce, produced at Drury Lane 19 February 1737; and *The Wedding Day*, acted at Drury Lane 17 February 1743, and published separately in February 1743, before the *Miscellanies* appeared.

ever attempted;[1] the Parts of *Millamour* and *Charlotte* being originally intended for Mr. *Wilks* and Mrs. *Oldfield*;[2] but the latter died before it was finished; and a slight Pique which happened between me and the former, prevented him from ever seeing it. The Play was read to Mr. *Rich*[3] upwards of twelve Years since, in the Presence of a very eminent Physician of this Age,[4] who will bear me Testimony, that I did not recommend my Performance with the usual Warmth of an Author. Indeed I never thought, 'till this Season, that there existed on any one Stage, since the Death of that great Actor and Actress abovementioned, any two Persons capable of supplying their Loss in those Parts: for Characters of this Kind do, of all others, require most Support from the Actor, and lend the least Assistance to him.

From the Time of its being read to Mr. *Rich*, it lay by me neglected and unthought of, 'till this Winter,[5] when it visited the Stage in the following Manner.

Mr. *Garrick*,[6] whose Abilities as an Actor will, I hope, rouse up better Writers for the Stage than myself, asked me one Evening, if I had any Play by me; telling me, he was desirous of appearing in a new Part. I answered him, I had one almost finished: but I conceived it so little the Manager's Interest to produce any thing new on his Stage this Season, that I should not think of offering it him, as I apprehended he would find some Excuse to refuse me, and adhere to the Theatrical Politics, of never introducing new Plays on the Stage, but when driven to it by absolute Necessity.

[1] Presumably after *Love in Several Masques*, produced in 1728, and *Don Quixote in England*, sketched out at Leyden 1728–9, though not produced until 1734. If Mrs. Oldfield's death (October 1730) occurred before the play was finished, however, one would have to place ahead of it Fielding's completed plays acted in the season of 1730: *The Temple Beau, The Author's Farce, Tom Thumb*, and *Rape upon Rape* (*The Coffee-House Politician*), as well as the first draft of *The Modern Husband*, which he submitted to Lady Mary Wortley Montagu's inspection in September 1730.

[2] Robert Wilks (1665?–1732) and Anne Oldfield (1683–1730) both acted in Fielding's first play, *Love in Several Masques*, at Drury Lane.

[3] John Rich (1692–1761), the great pantomime actor, was manager of the 'New House' in Lincoln's Inn Fields from 1714, and of the new Covent Garden Theatre after December 1732. Fielding's vague chronology would indicate that *The Wedding Day* was designed for Lincoln's Inn Fields in the season of 1731. That it was originally intended for the Drury Lane company, however, is clear from the reference to Wilks and Mrs. Oldfield.

[4] Not identified. Possibly Dr. Benjamin Hoadly (1706–57).

[5] i.e. the winter of 1742–3.

[6] David Garrick (1717–79). His career at Drury Lane had just begun (in 1742) after his great success at Goodman's Fields in 1741.

Mr. *Garrick's* Reply to this was so warm and friendly, that, as I was full as desirous of putting Words into his Mouth, as he could appear to be of speaking them, I mentioned the Play the very next Morning to Mr. *Fleetwood*,[1] who embraced my Proposal so heartily, that an Appointment was immediately made to read it to the Actors who were principally to be concerned in it.

When I came to revise this Play, which had likewise lain by me some Years, tho' formed on a much better Plan, and at an Age when I was much more equal to the Task, than the former; I found I had allowed myself too little Time for the perfecting it; but I was resolved to execute my Promise, and accordingly, at the appointed Day I produced five Acts, which were entitled, THE GOOD-NATURED MAN.[2]

Besides, that this Play appeared to me, on the Reading, to be less completely finished than I thought its Plan deserved; there was another Reason which dissuaded me from bringing it on the Stage, as it then stood, and this was, that the very Actor on whose Account I had principally been inclined to have it represented, had a very inconsiderable Part in it.

Notwithstanding my private Opinion, of which I then gave no Intimation, *The Good-natured Man* was received, and ordered to be writ into Parts, Mr. *Garrick* professing himself very ready to perform his; but as I remained dissatisfied, for the Reasons abovementioned, I now recollected my other Play, in which I remembered there was a Character I had originally intended for Mr. *Wilks*.

Upon Perusal, I found this Character was preserved with some little Spirit, and (what I thought would be a great Recommendation to the Audience) would keep their so justly favourite Actor almost eternally before their Eyes. I apprehended (in which I was not deceived) that he would make so surprising a Figure in this Character, and exhibit Talents so long unknown to the Theatre, that, as hath happen'd in other Plays, the Audience

---

[1] Charles Fleetwood (d. 1747), manager of the Drury Lane Theatre, 1734–45. He had staged three of Fielding's earlier plays, *An Old Man Taught Wisdom* and *The Universal Gallant* in 1735, and the unhappy *Eurydice* of 1737, before accepting *Miss Lucy in Town* and *The Wedding Day* in 1743. He was the largest single subscriber to Fielding's *Miscellanies*, taking twenty copies, presumably for distribution to theatrical friends.

[2] On the later history of this play, see Cross, iii. 99–109. Lost for some years, it came to light again in 1776 and, probably retouched by Garrick and Sheridan, was given nine performances under the title of *The Fathers*.

might be blinded to the Faults of the Piece, for many I saw it had, and some very difficult to cure.

I accordingly sat down with a Resolution to work Night and Day, during the short Time allowed me, which was about a Week, in altering and correcting this Production of my more juvenile Years; when unfortunately, the extreme Danger of Life into which a Person, very dear to me,[1] was reduced, rendered me incapable of executing my Task.

To this Accident alone, I have the Vanity to apprehend, the Play owes most of the glaring Faults with which it appeared. However, I resolved rather to let it take its Chance, imperfect as it was, with the Assistance of Mr. *Garrick*, than to sacrifice a more favourite, and in the Opinion of others, a much more valuable Performance, and which could have had very little Assistance from him.

I then acquainted Mr. *Garrick* with my Design, and read it to him, and Mr. *Macklin*;[2] Mr. *Fleetwood* agreed to the Exchange, and thus the WEDDING DAY was destined to the Stage.

Perhaps it may be asked me, Why then did I suffer a Piece, which I myself knew was imperfect, to appear? I answer honestly and freely, that Reputation was not my Inducement; and that I hoped, faulty as it was, it might answer a much more solid, and in my unhappy Situation, a much more urgent Motive. If it will give my Enemies any Pleasure to know that they totally frustrated my Views, I will be kinder to them, and give them a Satisfaction which they denied me: for tho' it was acted six Nights, I received not 50 *l.* from the House for it.[3]

This was indeed chiefly owing to a general Rumour spread of its Indecency;[4] which originally arose, I believe, from some

---

[1] Fielding's wife, Charlotte. See below, p. 13.

[2] Charles Macklin (1697?–1797), who wrote and spoke the prologue for *The Wedding Day*, and acted Mr. Stedfast in it.

[3] *The Wedding Day* opened at Drury Lane on 17 February 1743, and was thereafter performed on 19, 21, 22, 24, and 26 February. Scouten cites comments from the Winston MS. on Fielding's two benefit nights: 21 February: 'Benefit the author of this bad new play, which would have sunk the 1st night but for Garrick's acting'; and 26 February: 'Author's second Benefit. He did not get above £30 each Benefit' (*The London Stage 1660–1800: Part 3: 1729–1747*, ed. Arthur H. Scouten, ii. 1035–7).

[4] The Countess of Hertford wrote to her son Lord Beauchamp that 'Mr. Fielding has wrote a comedy which has been refused by the Licenser, not as a reflecting one, but on account of its immorality' (25 January 1743), and added a few weeks later (19 February): 'Mr. Fielding by suffering his bawd to be carted, though she is his favorite character in the new play, has obtained a license to have it acted, and it was performed on Thursday for the first time, but so much disliked that it is believed that it will be impossible to prevail

Objections of the Licenser,[1] who had been very unjustly censured
for being too remiss in his Restraints on that Head; but as every
Passage which he objected to was struck out, and I sincerely
think very properly so, I leave to every impartial Judge to decide,
whether the Play, as it was acted, was not rather freer from such
Imputation than almost any other Comedy on the Stage. However, this Opinion prevailed so fatally without Doors, during its
Representation, that on the sixth Night, there were not above
five Ladies present in the Boxes.

But I shall say no more of this Comedy here, as I intend to
introduce it the ensuing Season,[2] and with such Alterations as
will, I hope, remove every Objection to it, and may make the
Manager some Amends for what he lost by very honourably
continuing its Representation, when he might have got much
more by acting other Plays.

I come now to the Third and last Volume, which contains the
History of *Jonathan Wild*. And here it will not, I apprehend, be
necessary to acquaint my Reader, that my Design is not to enter
the Lists with that excellent Historian, who from authentic
Papers and Records, &c. hath already given so satisfactory an
Account of the Life and Actions of this Great Man. I have not
indeed the least Intention to depreciate the Veracity and Im-
partiality of that History; nor do I pretend to any of those Lights,
not having, to my Knowledge, ever seen a single Paper relating
to my Hero, save some short Memoirs, which about the Time of
his Death were published in certain Chronicles called News-
Papers, the Authority of which hath been sometimes questioned,[3]
and in the Ordinary of *Newgate* his Account,[4] which generally

with a second audience to hear it through' (Helen Sard Hughes, *The Gentle Hertford*, New
York, 1940, pp. 238, 242).

[1] The Licenser of the Stage, who held office under the Lord Chamberlain (the Duke of
Grafton), was then William Chetwynd, who had assumed his post in 1738 (cf. *Gent. Mag.*
viii. 222). Scouten says that 'the Larpent MS. shows many question marks and deletions of
suggestive, passionate, and physiological references' (ii. 1035).

[2] Brave words; but *The Wedding Day* was not acted again.

[3] Daniel Defoe published two accounts of Wild in 1725: viz. *The Life of Jonathan Wild*
and *The True and Genuine Account of the Life and Actions of the Late Jonathan Wild . . .
taken from His Own Mouth, and Collected from Papers of His Own Writing*. There were
various other such 'histories', including Alexander Smith's *Memoirs of the Life and Times
of the Famous Jonathan Wild* (1726).

[4] Thomas Purney, *The Ordinary of Newgate His Account of the Behaviour, Last Dying
Speeches and Confessions of the Four Malefactors Who Were Executed at Tyburn . . . the 24th
of May, 1725* (1725).

contains a more particular Relation of what the Heroes are to suffer in the next World, than of what they did in this. To confess the Truth, my Narrative is rather of such Actions which he might have performed, or would, or should have performed, than what he really did; and may, in Reality, as well suit any other such great Man, as the Person himself whose Name it bears.

A second Caution I would give my Reader is, that as it is not a very faithful Portrait of *Jonathan Wild* himself, so neither is it intended to represent the Features of any other Person. Roguery, and not a Rogue, is my Subject; and as I have been so far from endeavouring to particularize any Individual, that I have with my utmost Art avoided it; so will any such Application be unfair in my Reader, especially if he knows much of the Great World, since he must then be acquainted, I believe, with more than one on whom he can fix the Resemblance.[1]

In the third Place, I solemnly protest, I do by no means intend in the Character of my Hero to represent Human Nature in general. Such Insinuations must be attended with very dreadful Conclusions; nor do I see any other Tendency they can naturally have, but to encourage and soothe Men in their Villainies, and to make every well-disposed Man disclaim his own Species, and curse the Hour of his Birth into such a Society.[2] For my Part, I understand those Writers who describe Human Nature in this depraved Character, as speaking only of such Persons as *Wild* and his Gang; and I think it may be justly inferred, that they do not find in their own Bosoms any Deviation from the general Rule.[3] Indeed it would be an insufferable Vanity in them to conceive themselves as the only Exception to it.

[1] Cf. *Joseph Andrews*, III. i. Walpole had fallen from power in February 1742, over a year before the publication of the *Miscellanies*. Fielding now takes the opportunity to hint that some members of the triumphant Opposition could equally well serve as models for his portrait. Cf. the revisions in *Joseph Andrews* (e.g. II. x) for the second edition of June 1742.

[2] Cf. Allworthy's speech in *Tom Jones*, II. v; and the sentiments expressed in the *Champion*, 11 December 1739.

[3] Fielding usually has Hobbes and Mandeville (and perhaps La Rochefoucauld) in mind in such references as this and in the *Champion*, 11 December 1739 and 22 January 1740. See below, *Of Good Nature*, 3–4. That their sentiments were merely a projection of their own evil natures remained a favourite conclusion of his: cf. the *True Patriot*, 17 (18–25 February 1746); *Tom Jones*, VI. i and VIII. xv; and *Amelia*, VIII. viii. See the *Spectator*, 537 and 588; and for older analogues, Plato, *Republic*, III. xvi (409 a–c); and Montaigne on Francesco Guicciardini's habit of assigning evil motives for every action (*Essays*, II. x).

But without considering *Newgate* as no other than Human Nature with its Mask off, which some very shameless Writers have done, a Thought which no Price should purchase me to entertain, I think we may be excused for suspecting, that the splendid Palaces of the Great are often no other than *Newgate* with the Mask on. Nor do I know any thing which can raise an honest Man's Indignation higher than that the same Morals should be in one Place attended with all imaginable Misery and Infamy, and in the other, with the highest Luxury and Honour. Let any impartial Man in his Senses be asked, for which of these two Places a Composition of Cruelty, Lust, Avarice, Rapine, Insolence, Hypocrisy, Fraud and Treachery, was best fitted, surely his Answer must be certain and immediate; and yet I am afraid all these Ingredients glossed over with Wealth and a Title, have been treated with the highest Respect and Veneration in the one, while one or two of them have been condemned to the Gallows in the other.

If there are then any Men of such Morals who dare to call themselves Great, and are so reputed, or called at least, by the deceived Multitude, surely a little private Censure by the few is a very moderate Tax for them to pay, provided no more was to be demanded: But I fear this is not the Case. However the Glare of Riches, and Awe of Title, may dazzle and terrify the Vulgar; nay, however Hypocrisy may deceive the more Discerning, there is still a Judge in every Man's Breast,[1] which none can cheat nor corrupt, tho' perhaps it is the only uncorrupt Thing about him. And yet, inflexible and honest as this Judge is, (however polluted the Bench be on which he sits) no Man can, in my Opinion, enjoy any Applause which is not thus adjudged to be his Due.

Nothing seems to me more preposterous than that, while the Way to true Honour lies so open and plain, Men should seek false by such perverse and rugged Paths: that while it is so easy and safe, and truly honourable, to be good, Men should wade through Difficulty and Danger, and real Infamy, to be *Great*, or, to use a synonimous Word, *Villains*.[2]

[1] A familiar classical theme: cf. Seneca, *Epist. mor.* xcvii. 16, *De brevitate vitae*, x. 3; Polybius, *Hist.* xviii. 43; Juvenal, *Sat.* xiii. 2–3. See *Tom Jones*, IV. vi.

[2] Cf. Shaftesbury, *Misc. Reflections*, III. ii: 'How shall we explain this preposterous *Relish*, this odd Preference of *Subtlety* and *Indirectness*, to true *Wisdom*, open *Honesty*, and *Uprightness* ?' (*Characteristicks*, 6th edn., 1737, iii. 172). The theme is repeated throughout *Jonathan Wild*.

Nor hath Goodness less Advantage in the Article of Pleasure, than of Honour over this kind of Greatness. The same righteous Judge always annexes a bitter Anxiety to the Purchases of Guilt, whilst it adds a double Sweetness to the Enjoyments of Innocence and Virtue: for Fear, which all the Wise agree is the most wretched of human Evils, is, in some Degree, always attending on the former, and never can in any manner molest the Happiness of the latter.

This is the Doctrine which I have endeavoured to inculcate in this History, confining myself at the same Time within the Rules of Probability. (For except in one Chapter, which is visibly meant as a Burlesque on the extravagant Accounts of Travellers,[1] I believe I have not exceeded it.) And though perhaps it sometimes happens, contrary to the Instances I have given, that the Villain succeeds in his Pursuit, and acquires some transitory imperfect Honour or Pleasure to himself for his Iniquity; yet I believe he oftner shares the Fate of my Hero, and suffers the Punishment, without obtaining the Reward.

As I believe it is not easy to teach a more useful Lesson than this, if I have been able to add the pleasant to it, I might flatter myself with having carried every Point.[2]

But perhaps some Apology may be required of me, for having used the Word *Greatness*, to which the World have affixed such honourable Ideas, in so disgraceful and contemptuous a Light. Now if the Fact be, that the Greatness which is commonly worshipped is really of that Kind which I have here represented, the Fault seems rather to lie in those who have ascribed it to those Honours, to which it hath not in Reality the least Claim.

The Truth, I apprehend, is, we often confound the Ideas of Goodness and Greatness together, or rather include the former in our Idea of the latter. If this be so, it is surely a great Error, and no less than a Mistake of the Capacity for the Will. In Reality, no Qualities can be more distinct: for as it cannot be doubted but that Benevolence, Honour, Honesty, and Charity, make a good Man; and that Parts, Courage, are the efficient Qualities of a Great Man, so must it be confess'd, that the Ingredients which compose the former of these Characters, bear no Analogy to, nor Dependence on those which constitute the latter. A Man

---

[1] Book IV, chap. ix (omitted in the second and most subsequent editions of *Jonathan Wild*).   [2] An echo, of course, of Horace, *Ars Poetica*, 343-4.

may therefore be Great without being Good, or Good without being Great.

However, tho' the one bear no necessary Dependence on the other, neither is there any absolute Repugnancy among them which may totally prevent their Union so that they may, tho' not of Necessity, assemble in the same Mind, as they actually did, and all in the highest Degree, in those of *Socrates* and *Brutus*; and perhaps in some among us. I at least know one to whom Nature could have added no one great or good Quality more than she hath bestowed on him.[1]

Here then appear three distinct Characters; the Great, the Good, and the Great and Good.

The last of these is the *true Sublime* in Human Nature. That Elevation by which the Soul of Man, raising and extending itself above the Order of this Creation, and brighten'd with a certain Ray of Divinity, looks down on the Condition of Mortals. This is indeed a glorious Object, on which we can never gaze with too much Praise and Admiration. A perfect Work! the *Iliad* of Nature! ravishing and astonishing, and which at once fills us with Love, Wonder, and Delight.[2]

The Second falls greatly short of this Perfection, and yet hath its Merit. Our Wonder ceases; our Delight is lessened; but our Love remains; of which Passion, Goodness hath always appeared to me the only true and proper Object. On this Head I think proper to observe, that I do not conceive my Good Man to be absolutely a Fool or a Coward; but that he often partakes too little of Parts or Courage, to have any Pretensions to Greatness.

Now as to that Greatness which is totally devoid of Goodness, it seems to me in Nature to resemble the *False Sublime*[3] in Poetry; whose Bombast is, by the ignorant and ill-judging Vulgar, often mistaken for solid Wit and Eloquence, whilst it is in Effect the very Reverse. Thus Pride, Ostentation, Insolence, Cruelty, and every Kind of Villany, are often construed into True Greatness of Mind, in which we always include an Idea of Goodness.

---

[1] Probably Chesterfield (though Fielding may have intended to gratify several friends with this general compliment).

[2] See Cicero, *De Officiis*, II. x. 37, among other portraits of the classical *sapiens*. Cf. below, *Of True Greatness*, 251 ff.

[3] The 'False Sublime' is a favourite phrase of Shaftesbury's. Cf. also Edward Young, *Love of Fame*, vii. 178: 'Be wise, and quit the false *sublime* of life' (2nd edn., 1728, p. 172).

This Bombast Greatness then is the Character I intend to expose; and the more this prevails in and deceives the World, taking to itself not only Riches and Power, but often Honour, or at least the Shadow of it, the more necessary is it to strip the Monster of these false Colours, and shew it in its native Deformity: for by suffering Vice to possess the Reward of Virtue, we do a double Injury to Society, by encouraging the former, and taking away the chief Incentive to the latter. Nay, tho' it is, I believe, impossible to give Vice a true Relish of Honour and Glory, or tho' we give it Riches and Power, to give it the Enjoyment of them, yet it contaminates the Food it can't taste, and sullies the Robe which neither fits nor becomes it, 'till Virtue disdains them both.

Thus have I given some short Account of these Works. I come now to return Thanks to those Friends who have with uncommon Pains forwarded this Subscription: for tho' the Number of my Subscribers be more proportioned to my Merit, than their Desire or Expectation, yet I believe I owe not a tenth Part to my own Interest. My Obligations on this Head are so many, that for Fear of offending any by Preference, I will name none. Nor is it indeed necessary, since I am convinced they served me with no Desire of a public Acknowledgment; nor can I make any to some of them, equal with the Gratitude of my Sentiments.

I cannot, however, forbear mentioning my Sense of the Friendship shewn me by a Profession of which I am a late and unworthy Member, and from whose Assistance I derive more than half the Names which appear to this Subscription.[1]

It remains that I make some Apology for the Delay in publishing these Volumes, the real Reason of which was, the dangerous Illness of one from whom I draw all the solid Comfort of my Life, during the greatest Part of this Winter.[2] This, as it is most sacredly true, so will it, I doubt not, sufficiently excuse the Delay to all who know me.

Indeed when I look a Year or two backwards, and survey the Accidents which have befallen me, and the Distresses I have waded through whilst I have been engaged in these Works, I could almost challenge some Philosophy to myself, for having

---

[1] Fielding had been called to the bar 20 June 1740. The subscription list of the *Miscellanies* is dotted with names from all the Inns of Court.

[2] His wife, Charlotte, who died a year and a half later in November 1744.

been able to finish them as I have; and however imperfectly that may be, I am convinced the Reader, was he acquainted with the whole, would want very little Good-Nature to extinguish his Disdain at any Faults he meets with.

But this hath dropt from me unawares: for I intend not to entertain my Reader with my private History: nor am I fond enough of Tragedy, to make myself the Hero of one.

However, as I have been very unjustly censured, as well on account of what I have not writ, as for what I have; I take this Opportunity to declare in the most solemn Manner, I have long since (as long as from *June* 1741) desisted from writing one Syllable in the *Champion*,[1] or any other public Paper; and that I never was, nor will be the Author of anonymous Scandal on the private History or Family of any Person whatever.

Indeed there is no Man who speaks or thinks with more Detestation of the modern Custom of Libelling. I look on the Practice of stabbing a Man's Character in the Dark, to be as base and as barbarous as that of stabbing him with a Poignard in the same Manner; nor have I ever been once in my Life guilty of it.

It is not here, I suppose, necessary to distinguish between Ridicule and Scurrility; between a Jest on a public Character, and the Murther of a private one.

My Reader will pardon my having dwelt a little on this Particular, since it is so especially necessary in this Age, when almost all the Wit we have is applied this Way; and when I have already been a Martyr to such unjust Suspicion. Of which I will relate one Instance. While I was last Winter[2] laid up in the Gout, with a favourite Child dying in one Bed, and my Wife in a Condition very little better, on another, attended with other Circumstances, which served as very proper Decorations to such a Scene, I received a Letter from a Friend,[3] desiring me to vindicate myself from two very opposite Reflections, which two opposite Parties thought fit to cast on me, *viz.* the one of writing in the *Champion*, (tho' I had not then writ in it for upwards of half a Year) the other, of writing in the *Gazetteer*, in which I never had the Honour of inserting a single Word.

---

[1] See G. M. Godden, *Henry Fielding* (1910), pp. 115–16, 138–9.

[2] The reference here is to the winter of 1741–2. On the child, Charlotte, who died in March 1742, see the General Introduction, pp. xv–xvi.   [3] Not identified.

To defend myself therefore as well as I can from all past, and to enter a Caveat against all future Censure of this Kind; I once more solemnly declare, that since the End of *June* 1741, I have not, besides *Joseph Andrews*, published one Word, except *The Opposition, a Vision. A Defence of the Dutchess of Marlborough's Book. Miss Lucy in Town*, (in which I had a very small Share.)[1] And I do farther protest, that I will never hereafter publish any Book or Pamphlet whatever, to which I will not put my Name.[2] A Promise, which as I shall sacredly keep, so will it, I hope, be so far believed, that I may henceforth receive no more Praise or Censure, to which I have not the least Title.

And now, my good-natured Reader, recommending my Works to your Candour, I bid you heartily farewell; and take this with you, that you may never be interrupted in the reading these Miscellanies, with that Degree of Heart-ach[3] which hath often discomposed me in the writing them.

[1] Fielding forgets his translation, with William Young, of Aristophanes' *Plutus* (May 1742); and perhaps *The Wedding Day* and *Some Papers Proper to be Read before the Royal Society* (both published in February 1743), though the preface may have been written before the latter date. He may have had 'a very small Share' in writing *Miss Lucy*, but Fielding nevertheless owned the copyright, which he sold to Andrew Millar in 1742 (Cross, i. 316). David Garrick has been suggested as Fielding's anonymous collaborator; see Charles B. Woods, 'The "Miss Lucy" Plays of Fielding and Garrick', *PQ*, xli (1962), 294–310.

[2] Fielding withdrew this promise in the Preface to the second edition of his sister Sarah's *Adventures of David Simple* (1744). Among Fielding's other protests against the attribution to him of anonymous scurrility, cf. the *Covent-Garden Journal* 72.

[3] The spelling was normal; cf. Prior, 'The Ladle', 151: 'His Head achs for a Coronet' (*Literary Works*, ed. Wright-Spears, i. 206).

CONTENTS[1]

PREFACE   3

I. POETRY   19

   1. Of True Greatness   19

   2. Of Good-Nature   30

   3. Liberty   36

   4. To a Friend on the Choice of a Wife   42

   5. To John Hayes, Esq;   51

   6. A Description of U—n G—   53

   7. To the Right Honourable Sir Robert Walpole   56

   8. To the Same   59

   9. Written Extempore, on a Half-penny   59

  10. The Beggar. A Song   61

  11. An Epigram   62

  12. The Question   62

  13. J—n W—ts at a Play   63

  14. To Celia   63

  15. On a Lady, Coquetting with a Very Silly Fellow   65

  16. On the Same   65

  17. Epitaph on Butler's Monument   66

  18. Another. On a Wicked Fellow   66

  19. Epigram on One Who Invited Many Gentlemen to a Small Dinner   67

  20. A Sailor's Song   67

  21. Advice to the Nymphs of New S—m   68

  22. To Celia. Occasioned by Her Apprehending Her House Would Be
      Broke Open   70

  23. To the Same. On Her Wishing to Have a Lilliputian   72

  24. Similes. To the Same   74

[1] The original edition had no list of Contents; the present list has been supplied by the editor.

25. The Price. To the Same   75

26. Her Christian Name. To the Same. A Rebus   75

27. To the Same; Having Blamed Mr. Gay   75

28. An Epigram   76

29. Another   76

30. To the Master of the Salisbury Assembly   76

31. The Cat and Fiddle   77

32. Untitled [The Queen of Beauty]   77

33. A Parody, from the First Aeneid   80

34. A Simile, from Silius Italicus   81

35. To Euthalia   82

36. Juvenalis Satyra Sexta   84

37. Part of Juvenal's Sixth Satire, Modernized in Burlesque Verse   85

38. To Miss H——and at Bath   118

II. AN ESSAY ON CONVERSATION   119

III. AN ESSAY ON THE KNOWLEDGE OF THE CHARACTERS OF MEN   153

IV. AN ESSAY ON NOTHING   179

V. SOME PAPERS PROPER TO BE READ BEFORE THE R——L SOCIETY   191

VI. THE FIRST OLYNTHIAC OF DEMOSTHENES   205

VII. OF THE REMEDY OF AFFLICTION FOR THE LOSS OF OUR FRIENDS   212

VIII. A DIALOGUE BETWEEN ALEXANDER THE GREAT AND DIOGENES THE CYNIC   226

IX. AN INTERLUDE BETWEEN JUPITER, JUNO, APOLLO, AND MERCURY   236

OF TRUE GREATNESS[1]

An EPISTLE to
GEORGE DODINGTON, Esq;[2]

'Tis strange, while all to Greatness Homage pay,
So few should know the Goddess they obey.
That Men should think a thousand Things the same,
And give contending Images one Name.
Not *Greece*, in all her Temples wide Abodes,[3]   5
Held a more wild Democracy of Gods[4]
Than various Deities we serve, while all
Profess before one common Shrine to fall.
Whether ourselves of Greatness are possest,
Or worship it within another's Breast.   10
While a mean Crowd of Sycophants attend,
And fawn and flatter, creep and cringe and bend;[5]
The Fav'rite blesses his superior State,
Rises o'er all, and hails Himself the Great.
Vain Man! can such as these to Greatness raise?   15
Can Honour come from Dirt? from Baseness, Praise?
Then *India's* Gem on *Scotland's* Coast shall shine,
And the *Peruvian* Ore enrich the *Cornish* Mine.[6]

---

[1] *Of True Greatness* had been previously published in January 1741, with a preface not reprinted in the *Miscellanies* (see Appendix A), which stated that the poem 'was writ several Years ago, and comes forth now with a very few Additions or Alterations . . .' (p. 3). For the literary strategy of the poem, cf. Pope's poetic search after the abode of Happiness in the *Essay on Man*, Epistle IV.

[2] George Bubb (1691–1762), who took the name of Dodington when he came into the estates of his uncle, George Dodington, in 1720. Satirized by Pope, as 'Bubo' (see Twickenham edn., III. ii. 134, and n. 20), he was nevertheless a friend and patron to such writers as Young, Thomson, and Fielding. Among the many compliments paid to him by Fielding was the somewhat unmeasured assertion in *Amelia* (XI. ii), that he was 'one of the greatest Men this Country ever produced'.

[3] The apparent off-rhyme, 'abodes . . . Gods', like many others in Fielding's poems (e.g. approved–loved, good–food, form–worm), has the sanction of Dryden and Pope.

[4] Cf. Swift, 'To Mr. Congreve': 'O'er Nile, with all its wilderness of gods' (*Poems*, ed. Sir Harold Williams, i. 46). See Pausanias, *Descriptio Graeciae*, Book VI.

[5] Cf. Pope, 'Bounce to Fop', 9–10: 'Fop! You can dance, and make a Leg, / Can fetch and carry, cringe and beg . . .' (Twickenham edn., vi. 366).

[6] Cf. Pope, *Imitations of Horace*, Sat. I. vi. 71: 'For Indian spices, for Peruvian gold' (Twickenham edn., iv. 241). On the tin mines of Cornwall, see Defoe's *Tour* (3 vols. 1724–6), Letter III.

Behold, in blooming *May*, the May-pole stand,
Dress'd out in Garlands by the Peasant's Hand;[1]   20
Around it dance the Youth, in mirthful Mood;
And all admire the gaudy, drest up Wood.
See, the next Day, of all its Pride bereft,
How soon the unreguarded Post is left.
So thou, the Wonder of a longer Day,   25
Rais'd high on Pow'r, and drest in Titles, gay,
Stript of these Summer Garlands, soon wouldst see,
The mercenary Slaves ador'd not thee;
Wouldst see them thronging thy Successor's Gate,
Shadows of Power, and Properties of State.[2]   30
As the Sun Insects, Pow'r Court-Friends begets,
Which wanton in its Beams and vanish as it sets.[3]
    Thy highest Pomp the Hermit dares despise,
Greatness (crys this) is to be good and wise.
To Titles, Treasures, Luxury and Show,   35
The gilded Follies of Mankind, a Foe.
He flies Society, to Wilds resorts,
And rails at busy Cities, splendid Courts.[4]
Great to himself, he in his Cell, appears,
As Kings on Thrones, or Conquerors on Cars.[5]   40

---

[1] Cf. Robert Herrick, 'The Country Life', 53: 'Thy Maypoles, too, with garlands graced'.

[2] The victor in Prior's *Solomon* reflects that if he were defeated by a foe,

> Yon' Crowd. . . .
> Would for That Foe with equal Ardor wait
> At the high Palace, or the crowded Gate;
> With restless Rage would pull my Statues down;
> And cast the Brass a-new to His Renown.

(*Solomon*, iii. 323, 327–30; *Literary Works*, ed. Wright-Spears, i. 370.) Cf. Cleanthes in Dryden's *Cleomenes*: 'Well said again, Father! Comply, comply: / Follow the Sun, True Shadow' (Act II; *Works*, 1701, ii. 455).

[3] Cf. Pope, 'The Words of the King of Brobdingnag', 1–2: 'In Miniature see *Nature's* Power appear; / Which wings the Sun-born Insects of the Air . . .' (Twickenham edn., vi. 280); Richard Crashaw, 'An Hymne of the Nativity': '. . . those gay flyes / Guilded i' the beames of earthly Kings' (*Steps to the Temple*, 2nd edn., 1648, p. 46); Milton, *Samson Agonistes*, 676. On the ephemera or May-fly, see Pliny, *Naturalis Historia*, XI. xliii. 120. For Fielding's phrasing, cf. Otway, *Don Carlos*, iv: 'Bask'd in his Shine, and wanton'd in his Shade' (*Works*, 1768, i. 159), and his own play, *The Modern Husband*, I. viii.

[4] See Aristotle, *Nic. Eth.* IX. ix. 3: 'And it would be strange to represent the supremely happy man as a recluse . . . for man is a social being, and designed by nature to live with others' (trans. H. Rackham, Loeb Library).

[5] Here, of course, triumphal chariots.

O Thou, that dar'st thus proudly scorn thy Kind,
Search, with impartial Scrutiny, thy Mind;
Disdaining outward Flatterers to win,
Dost thou not feed a Flatterer within?
While other Passions Temperance may guide,   45
Feast not with too delicious Meals thy Pride.
On Vice triumphant while thy Censures fall,
Be sure, no Envy mixes with thy Gaul.[1]
Ask thy self oft, to Pow'r and Grandeur born,
Had Pow'r and Grandeur then incurr'd thy Scorn: 50
If no Ill-nature in thy Breast prevails,
Enjoying all the Crimes at which it rails.[2]
A peevish sour Perverseness of the Will,
Oft we miscall Antipathy to Ill.
    Scorn and Disdain the little *Cynick*[3] hurl'd   55
At the exulting Victor of the World.
Greater than this what Soul can be descry'd?
His who contemns the *Cynick's* snarling Pride.
Well might the haughty Son of *Philip* see
Ambition's second Lot devolve on thee;[4]   60
Whose Breast Pride fires with scarce inferior Joy,
And bids thee hate and shun Men, him destroy.
    But hadst thou, *Alexander*, wish'd to prove
Thy self the real Progeny of *Jove*,
Virtue another Path had bid thee find,   65
Taught thee to save, and not to slay Mankind.[5]
    Shall the lean Wolf, by Hunger fierce and bold,
Bear off no Honours from the bloody Fold?[6]

[1] Variant spelling of 'gall'. See *OED*.

[2] Cf. Marcus Aurelius, *Meditations*, xii. 27: 'For the conceit that is conceited of its freedom from conceit is the most insufferable of all' (trans. C. R. Haines, Loeb Library). See Burton, *Anat. Melancholy*, i. 2. 3. 14.

[3] Diogenes. See below, *A Dialogue between Alexander the Great and Diogenes the Cynic*.

[4] Cf. Dryden, *Religio Laici*, 110: 'And all his Righteousness devolv'd on thee' (*Works*, 1701, III. i. 71).

[5] The phrasing is reminiscent of Samson's reproof to Dalila (Milton, *Samson Agonistes*, 873–5):

> But had thy love, still odiously pretended,
> Been, as it ought, sincere, it would have taught thee
> Far other reasonings, brought forth other deeds.

(*Samson Agonistes*, p. 18; *Poetical Works*, 1695.)

[6] Cf. Gay, *Fables*, Part I, xvii. 1–2: 'A Wolf, with hunger fierce and bold, / Ravag'd the plains and thinn'd the fold' (*Fables. By Mr. Gay*, 3rd edn., 1729, p. 65).

Shall the dead Flock his Greatness not display;
But Shepherds hunt him as a Beast of Prey?   70
While Man, not drove by Hunger from his Den,
To Honour climbs o'er Heaps of murder'd Men.
Shall ravag'd Fields, and burning Towns proclaim
The Hero's Glory, not the Robber's Shame?[1]
Shall Thousands fall, and Millions be undone   75
To glut the hungry Cruelty of one?
    Behold, the Plain with human Gore grow red,
The swelling River heave along the Dead.
See, through the Breach the hostile Deluge flow,
Along it bears the unresisting Foe: 80
Hear, in each Street the wretched Virgin's Cries,
Her Lover sees her ravish'd as he dies.
The Infant wonders at its Mother's Tears,
And smiling feels its Fate before its Fears.
Age, while in vain for the first Blow it calls,   85
Views all its Branches lopp'd before it falls.[2]
Beauty betrays the Mistress it should guard,
And, faithless, proves the Ravisher's Reward:
Death, their sole Friend, relieves them from their Ills,
The kindest Victor he, who soonest kills.[3]   90
    Could such Exploits as these thy Pride create?
Could these, O *Philip's* Son, proclaim thee Great?
Such Honours *Mahomet* expiring crav'd,

---

[1] Cf. Dryden, trans. Juvenal, *Sat.* i. 110–11: 'Wou'dst thou to Honours and Preferments climb, / Be bold in Mischief, dare some mighty Crime' (1693, p. 7). So Defoe on Louis XIV:

> If Flaming Towns, if ravish'd Vertue lies,
> As steps to mount a Monarch to the Skies;
> *Lewis* to reign above the Gods may claim,
> And *Jove* resigns his Thunder and his Name.

(*Jure Divino*, 1706, Book I, p. 21.)

[2] The imagery derives from the battle scenes in Dryden's version of the *Aeneid* and Pope's *Iliad* (esp. Book XXI); but see also Cowley's *Davideis*, Book II:

> At last in rushes the prevailing foe,
> Does all the mischief of prcud *conquest* show.
> The wondring babes from mothers breasts are rent,
> And suffer ills they neither *fear'd* nor *meant*.
> No silver rev'rence guards the stooping age,
> No rule or method ties their boundless rage.

(*The Works*, 1668, p. 60.)

[3] See Milton, *Samson Agonistes*, 1262–3; *Paradise Lost*, xi. 491–3.

Such were the Trophies on his Tomb engrav'd.[1]
If Greatness by these Means may be possest,   95
Ill we deny it to the greater Beast.
Single and arm'd by Nature only, He,
That Mischief does, which Thousands do for thee.
  Not on such Wings, to Fame did *Churchill* soar,
For *Europe* while defensive Arms he bore.[2]   100
Whose Conquests, cheap at all the Blood they cost,
Sav'd Millions by each noble Life they lost.
  Oh, Name august! in Capitals of Gold,
In Fame's eternal Chronicle enroll'd!
Where *Cæsar*, viewing thee, asham'd withdraws,   105
And owns thee Greater in a greater Cause.
Thee, from the lowest Depth of Time, on high
Blazing, shall late Posterity[3] descry;
And own the Purchase[4] of thy glorious Pains,
While Liberty, or while her Name remains.   110
  But quit, great Sir, with me this higher Scene,
And view false Greatness with more aukward Mien.
For now, from Camps to Colleges retreat;
No Cell, no Closet here without the Great.
See, how Pride swells the haughty Pedant's Looks;   115
How pleas'd he smiles o'er Heaps of conquer'd Books.
Tully to him, and *Seneca*, are known,
And all their noblest Sentiments his own.
These, on each apt Occasion, he can quote; ⎫
Thus the false Count affects the Man of Note, ⎬   120
Aukward and shapeless in a borrow'd Coat. ⎭

---

[1] The reference is not, of course, to the Prophet, but to the great fifteenth-century conqueror, Mahomet II, of whom it is said that his epitaph read, 'I intended to conquer Rhodes, and proud Italy' (see Bayle's *Dictionary*, 2nd edn., 1734–8, iv. 54 n.). Fielding may have known a different version of the epitaph: cf. the *Champion*, 3 May 1740.

[2] John Churchill, first Duke of Marlborough (1650–1722), ranked high among Fielding's personal heroes. See, among other praises, *A Journey from This World to the Next*, I. iv, the *Vernoniad*, and *A Full Vindication of the Dutchess Dowager of Marlborough*. For the comparison with Alexander, cf. George Lyttelton's *Blenheim*: '. . . for with different views they fought; / This to *subdue*, and that to *free* mankind' (*Works*, 1774, p. 595).

[3] A Latinism: cf. 'postera recens' (Horace, *Carm.* III. xxx). See Addison, *Poem to His Majesty*: 'Our late Posterity, with secret dread, / Shall view thy Battels, and with Pleasure read' (*Works*, 1721, i. 10); Thomson, *Autumn*, 912–13.

[4] 'That which is obtained, gained, or acquired . . . *esp.* that which is taken in the chase . . . or in war' (*OED*). Cf. Addison, *The Campaign*: 'But now a purchase to the sword she lies'.

Thro' Books some travel, as thro' Nations some,
Proud of their Voyage, yet bring nothing home.
Criticks thro' Books, as Beaus thro' Countries stray,
Certain to bring their Blemishes away.　　　　　　　　125
　　Great is the Man, who with unwearied Toil
Spies a Weed springing in the richest Soil.
If *Dryden's* Page with one bad Line be blest,
'Tis Great to shew it, as to write the rest.[1]
　　Others, with friendly Eye run Authors o'er,　　　130
Not to find Faults, but Beauties to restore;
Nor scruple (such their Bounty) to afford
Folios of Dulness to preserve a Word:[2]
Close, as to some tall Tree the Insect cleaves,
Myriads still nourish'd by its smallest Leaves.　　　135
So cling these Scriblers round a *Virgil's* Name,
And on his least of Beauties soar to Fame.
　　Awake, ye useless Drones, and scorn to thrive
On the Sweets gather'd by the lab'ring Hive.[3]
Behold, the Merchant give to Thousands Food,　　　140
His Loss his own, his Gain the Public Good.
Her various Bounties Nature still confines,
Here gilds her Sands, there silvers o'er her Mines:
The Merchant's Bounty Nature's hath outdone,
He gives to all, what she confines to one.[4]　　　145
And is he then not Great? Sir *B.* denies

[1] See *Tatler,* 158 on Pedants: 'These Persons set a greater Value on themselves for having found out the Meaning of a Passage in *Greek,* than upon the Author for having written it . . .'; and Sir Thomas Browne, *Religio Medici*: 'I have seen a Grammarian Towr and Plume himself over a single line in *Horace,* and show more pride in the construction of one Ode, than the Author in the composure of the whole Book' (8th edn., 1685, p. 39).

[2] Cf. the *Champion,* 15 March 1740, on 'overdoing'.

[3] See Dryden's translation of the *Georgics,* iv. 241–2: 'All, with united Force, combine to drive / The lazy Drones from the laborious Hive' (*Works of Virgil,* 1697, p. 129: a couplet that Dryden, following his master, economically made use of again in his *Aeneid,* i. 606–7).

[4] Encomiums on trade were, of course, the order of the day among Whig wits; e.g., Lyttelton, *Letters from a Persian in England* (1735), Letter XLI; Gay, *Fables,* Part II, viii. 16–18:

> On trade alone thy glory stands.
> That benefit is unconfin'd,
> Diffusing good among mankind.

(*Works,* 1772, iii. 184) or the *Spectator,* 69, on merchants: 'a Body of Men thriving in their own private Fortunes, and at the same time promoting the Publick Stock'. Cf. Fielding's *Vernoniad,* 99–104 and note.

True Greatness to the Creature whom he buys;
Blush the Wretch wounded, conscious of his Guile.
B—*nard* and H—*cote* at such Satyr smile.[1]
But if a Merchant lives, who meanly deigns   150
To sacrifice his Country to his Gains.
Tho' from his House, untrusted and unfed,
The Poet bears off neither Wine nor Bread;
As down *Cheapside* he meditates the Song,[2]
He ranks that Merchant with the meanest Throng.   155
Nor Him the Poet's Pride contemns alone,
But all to whom the Muses are unknown.
These, cries the Bard, true Honours can bestow,
And separate true Worth from outward Show;[3]
Scepters and Crowns by them grow glorious Things,   160
(For tho' they make not, they distinguish Kings.)
Short-liv'd the Gifts which Kings to them bequeath;
Bards only give the never-fading Wreath.[4]
Did all our Annals no *Argyle* afford,[5]
The Muse constrain'd could sing a common Lord.   165
But should the Muse with-hold her friendly Strain,
The Hero's Glory blossoms fair in vain;
Like the young Spring's, or Summer's riper Flow'r,
The Admiration of the present Hour.

[1] 'Sir B.' is doubtless intended to suggest 'Sir Bob' or 'Sir Brass', both popular appellations for Walpole. Sir John Barnard (1685–1764), knighted 1732, Lord Mayor 1737, was perhaps the most respected merchant of the day; Sir Gilbert Heathcote (1651 ?–1733) was one of the richest. It is possible that Fielding had his nephew, George Heathcote, in mind here. In the 1741 version the second name was 'G—schal', i.e. Sir Robert Godschall (c. 1692–1742), who died while holding the office of Lord Mayor, 26 June 1742. Cf. *A Journey from This World to the Next*, I. vii.

[2] Cf. Pope, *Dunciad*, iii. 15–16: 'A slip-shod Sibyl led his steps along, / In lofty madness meditating song' (Twickenham edn., v. 320–1); Gay, *Mr. Pope's Welcome from Greece*, 74. See Virgil, *Eclogues*, i. 2: 'Silvestrem . . . musam meditaris'.

[3] Cf. Gay, *Fables*, Part I, xxxii. 30: 'How false we judge by outward show' (*Fables by Mr. Gay*, 3rd edn., 1729, p. 124); and *Fables*, Part II, vii. 83–4.

[4] The familiar theme of Theocritus (*Idylls*, xvi) and of Horace's *Odes* (IV. viii and IX. viii); in Pope's words: 'They had no Poet and are dead!' (Twickenham edn., iv. 159). Cf. Nathaniel Lee: 'For Death would to their Acts an End afford, / Did not Immortal Verse out-do the Sword' ('To the Prince and Princess of Orange, upon their Marriage', in *The Third Part of Miscellany Poems*, 5th edn., 1727, p. 75); George Granville, Lord Lansdowne, 'To the Immortal Memory of Mr. Edmund Waller', in *Genuine Works*, 1736, i. 10–12; or Shaftesbury, *Soliloquy*, II. i: 'their Fame is in the hands of *Penmen* . . .' (*Characteristicks*, 6th edn., 1737, i. 223).

[5] John Campbell, second Duke of Argyle (1680 ?–1743). See below, ll. 257–8, and Introduction, p. xiii.

She gleans from Death's sure Scythe the noble Name,   170
And lays up in the Granaries of Fame.
Thus the great tatter'd Bard, as thro' the Streets
He cautious treads, least any Bailiff meets:
Whose wretched Plight the Jest of all is made;
Yet most, if hapless, it betray his Trade.   175
Fools in their Laugh at Poets are sincere,
And wiser Men admire them thro' a Sneer:
For Poetry with Treason shares this Fate,
Men like the Poem and the Poet hate.[1]
And yet with Want and with Contempt opprest,   180
Shunn'd, hated, mock'd, at once Men's Scorn and Jest,
Perhaps, from wholesome Air itself confin'd,
Who hopes to drive out Greatness from his Mind?
    Some Greatness in myself, perhaps I view;
Not that I write, but that I write to you.   185
    To you! who in this *Gothick* Leaden Age,
When Wit is banish'd from the Press and Stage,[2]
When Fools to greater Folly make Pretence,
And those who have it, seem asham'd of Sense;
When Nonsense is a Term for the Sublime,   190
And not to be an Ideot is a Crime;[3]
When low Buffoons in Ridicule succeed,
And Men are largely for such Writings fee'd,
As *W—'s*[4] self can purchase none to read;
Yourself th' unfashionable Lyre have strung,   195
Have own'd the Muses and their Darling *Young*.[5]
    All court their Favour when by all approv'd;
Ev'n Virtue, if in Fashion, would be lov'd.

---

[1] A variation on Dryden's lines on the Test Act: 'T'abhor the makers, and their laws approve, / Is to hate Traytors, and the treason love' (*Hind and the Panther*, iii. 2001–2; *Works*, 1701, III. i. 118). Cf. Farquhar, *The Recruiting Officer*, III. ii; and ultimately Plutarch, *Romulus*, xvii. 3.

[2] Hence presumably after the passage of the Licensing Act in June 1737, though the complaint may simply be general. Cf. *The Temple Beau* (1730), II. xii: 'Posterity may call this the Leaden Age.'

[3] Cf. Dryden, *Eleonora*, 363–4: 'And dares to sing thy Praises, in a Clime / Where Vice Triumphs, and Virtue is a Crime' (*Works*, 1701, III. i. 184); and Pope, *Epilogue to the Satires*, Dialogue i. 159–60.

[4] Walpole.

[5] Edward Young (with the like complaint of a declining age) dedicated Satire III of his *Love of Fame* (1725–8) to Dodington.

You for their Sakes with Fashion dare engage,
Mæcenas you in no *Augustan* Age.   200
Some Merit then is to the Muses due;
But oh! their Smiles the Portion of how few!
Tho' Friends may flatter much, and more ourselves,
Few, *Dodington*, write worthy of your Shelves.
Not to a Song which *Cælia's* Smiles make fine,   205
Nor Play which *Booth* had made esteem'd divine;[1]
To no rude Satyr from Ill-nature sprung,
Nor Panegyrick for a Pension sung;
Not to soft Lines that gently glide along,
And vie in Sound and Sense with *Handel's* Song;[2]   210
To none of these will *Dodington* bequeath,
The Poet's noble Name and laureate Wreath.
   Leave, Scriblers, leave, the tuneful Road to Fame,
Nor by assuming damn a Poet's Name.
Yet how unjustly we the Muses slight,   215
Unfir'd by them because a Thousand write!
Who would a Soldier or a Judge upbraid,
That — wore Ermine, — a Cockade.[3]
   To Greatness each Pretender to pursue,
Would tire, Great Sir, the jaded Muse and you.   220
   The lowest Beau that skips about a Court,
The Lady's Play-thing, and the Footman's Sport;
Whose Head adorn'd with Bag or Tail of Pig,
Serves very well to bear about his Wig;[4]
Himself the Sign-Post of his Taylor's Trade,   225
That shews abroad, how well his Cloaths are made;
This little, empty, silly, trifling Toy,
Can from Ambition feel a Kind of Joy;
Can swell, and even aim at looking wise,

---

[1] Barton Booth (1681–1733), who took the role of Cato in Addison's tragedy in 1713. See below, p. 64.
[2] George Frederick Handel (1685–1759). The decade of his great oratorios had just begun, with the *Messiah* in 1742; and the compliment here is dubious. But Fielding had praised him in the *Champion* (10 June 1740) and usually referred to him warmly (cf. *Tom Jones*, IV. ii. v; *Amelia*, IV. ix).
[3] This Verse may be filled up with any two Names out of our Chronicles, as the Reader shall think fit. [Fielding's note.]
[4] These Verses attempt (if possible) to imitate the Meanness of the Creature they describe. [Fielding's note.]

And walking Merit from *its* Chair despise.[1]   230
  Who wonders then, if such a Thing as this
At Greatness aims, that none the Aim can miss!
Nor Trade so low, Profession useless, thrives,
Which to its Followers not Greatness gives.
What Quality so mean, what Vice can shame   235
The base Possessors from the mighty Claim?
To make our Merits little Weight prevail,
We put not Virtue in the other Scale;
Against our Neighbour's Scale our own we press,
And each Man's Great who finds another Less.   240
In large Dominions some exert their State,
But all Men find a Corner to be Great.
The lowest Lawyer, Parson, Courtier, Squire,
Is somewhere Great, finds some that will admire.[2]
  Where shall we say then that true Greatness dwells?   245
In Palaces of Kings, or Hermits Cells?
Doth she confirm the Minister's Mock-State,
Or bloody on the Victor's Garland wait?
Warbles, harmonious, she the Poet's Song,
Or, graver, Laws pronounces to the Throng?   250
  To no Profession, Party, Place confin'd,
True Greatness lives but in the noble Mind;[3]
Him constant through each various Scene attends,
Fierce to his Foes, and faithful to his Friends.[4]
In him, in any Sphere of Life she shines,   255
Whether she blaze a *Hoadley* 'mid Divines,[5]
Or, an *Argyle*, in Fields and Senates dare,

---

[1] Perhaps a reminiscence of Juvenal, i. 158–9: 'Qui dedit ergo tribus patruis aconita, / vehatur / pensilibus plumis atque illinc dispiciat nos?' Cf. Gay, *Trivia*, i. 117–18: 'In saucy state the griping broker sits, / And laughs at honesty, and trudging wits' (*Poems on Several Occasions*, 1737, i. 138).

[2] So Young, *Love of Fame*, ii. 17: 'For every soul finds reasons to be proud' (2nd edn., 1728, p. 24). Cf. *Spectator*, 49 and 219: 'There is a kind of Grandeur and Respect, which the meanest and most insignificant part of Mankind endeavour to procure in the little Circle of their Friends and Acquaintance.'

[3] An echo of Gay on True Happiness: ''Tis to no rank of life confin'd, / But dwells in ev'ry honest mind' (*Fables*, Part II, vii. 143–4; *Works*, 1772, iii. 183).

[4] Cf. Waller, 'On the Duke of Monmouth's Expedition': 'Firm to his Friends, and fatal to his Foes' (*Poems &c.*, 9th edn., 1712, p. 232).

[5] Benjamin Hoadly (1676–1761), Bishop of Winchester, 1734–61. Cf. *Joseph Andrews*, I. xvii; *Tom Jones*, II. vii.

Supreme in all the Arts of Peace and War.[1]
Greatness with Learning deck'd in *Carteret* see,[2]
With Justice, and with Clemency in *Lee*;[3]   260
In *Chesterfield* to ripe Perfection come,[4]
See it in *Littleton* beyond its Bloom.[5]
   Lives there a Man, by Nature form'd to please,[6]
To think with Dignity, express with Ease;
Upright in Principle, in Council strong,   265
Prone not to change, nor obstinate too long:
Whose Soul is with such various Talents bless'd,
What he now does seems to become him best;[7]
Whether the Cabinet demands his Pow'rs,
Or gay Addresses sooth his vacant Hours,   270
Or when from graver Tasks his Mind unbends,
To charm with Wit the Muses or his Friends.
His Friends! who in his Favour claim no Place,
From Titles, Pimping, Flattery or Lace.
To whose blest Lot superior Portions fall,   275
To most of Fortune, and of Taste to all,
Aw'd not by Fear, by Prejudice not sway'd,
By Fashion led not, nor by Whim betray'd,
By Candour only biass'd, who shall dare
To view and judge and speak Men as they are.   280
In him, (if such there be) is Greatness shewn,
Nor can he be to *Dodington* unknown.

[1] See above, line 164. Cf. Pope, *Epilogue to the Satires*, Dialogue ii. 86–7: 'Argyle, the State's whole Thunder born to wield, / And shake alike the Senate and the Field' (Twicken-ham edn., iv. 318); Young, *Love of Fame*, vii. 129: '[*Fame*] bids *Argyle* in fields, and senates shine' (2nd edn., 1728, p. 169). See also Thomson, *Autumn*, 929–43. The conceit is classical: cf. Martial's 'clarum militiae . . . togaque decus' (I. lv. 2) and Juvenal's 'utilis et bellorum et pacis rebus agendis' (*Sat.* xiv. 72).

[2] John, Lord Carteret (1690–1763), later Earl Granville (1744), one of the leaders of the Opposition in the 1730s. See above, Introduction, p. xiv.

[3] Sir William Lee (1688–1754), Chief Justice of the King's Bench (1737) and later Lord Chief Justice of England.

[4] Philip Dormer Stanhope, fourth Earl of Chesterfield (1694–1773).

[5] On Lyttelton, see below, *Liberty*.

[6] In rhythm, if not in sentiment, a clear echo of Pope's lines to Atticus (*Epistle to Dr. Arbuthnot*, 193–214), perhaps with a hint of Martial's epigram, 'Si quis erit raros inter numerandus amicos' (I. xxxix) and Horace's praise of Lollius (*Carm.* IV. ix). See Tacitus, *Agricola*, ix; and *Hist.* IV. v (the famous portrait of Helvidius Priscus).

[7] Cf. Milton, *Paradise Lost*, viii. 549–50: '. . . that what she wills to do or say, / Seems wisest, virtuousest, discreetest, best' (P. 216: *Poetical Works*, 1695). See Tibullus, IV. ii. 10–14.

OF GOOD-NATURE

To his GRACE the
DUKE of *RICHMOND*.[1]

What is Good-nature?[2] Gen'rous *Richmond*, tell;
He can declare it best, who best can feel.
Is it a foolish Weakness in the Breast,
As some who know, or have it not, contest?[3]
Or is it rather not the mighty whole   5
Full Composition of a virtuous Soul?
Is it not Virtue's Self? A Flow'r so fine,
It only grows in Soils almost divine.[4]
Some Virtues flourish, like some Plants, less nice,
And in one Nature blossom out with Vice.   10
Knaves may be valiant, Villains may be Friends;
And Love in Minds deprav'd effect its Ends.

[1] Charles Lennox, second Duke of Richmond (1701–50), was a member of George II's Privy Council and a strong supporter of Walpole; but Fielding apparently looked to him for patronage. *The Miser* had been dedicated to him in 1733, and Fielding alludes to him in the *Enquiry into the Causes of the Late Increase of Robbers*, 1751. Richmond's name does not appear in the subscription list to the *Miscellanies*, though that of his duchess does. Part of Fielding's poem had been sketched out as early as November 1739 (see p. 35 n. 1), but the allusion to Montfort (p. 35 n. 6) must post-date May 1741.

[2] On good nature see, among many other passages, the *Champion*, 16 February and 27 March 1740: the *True Patriot*, 8 (24 December 1745); the *Jacobite's Journal*, 31–2 (2 and 9 July 1748); *Tom Jones*, IV. vi; and the *Covent-Garden Journal*, 44.

[3] Fielding may have had in mind partly the Stoic belief ('misericordia . . . vitium animi est') that pity was a weakness of the mind (cf. Seneca, *De clementia*, II. iv. 4 and II. v. 1) and partly the arguments of such writers as Machiavelli, Hobbes, Rochester, La Rochefoucauld, and Mandeville. Cf. Shaftesbury's attack on the philosophers of self-interest: 'Thus Kindness of every sort, Indulgence, Tenderness, Compassion, and in short, all natural Affection shou'd be industriously suppress'd, and, as mere Folly, and Weakness of Nature, be resisted and overcome . . .' (*Inquiry concerning Virtue and Merit*, 1711, II. i. 1; *Characteristicks*, 6th edn., 1737, ii. 80). But the association with weakness was proverbial. Cf. Robert South: 'When this Word passes between Equals, commonly by a *good-natur'd* Man is meant, either some easy, soft-headed Piece of Simplicity, who suffers himself to be led by the Nose, and wip'd of his Conveniences by a Company of sharping, worthless Sycophants, who will be sure to despise, laugh, and droll at him, as a weak, empty Fellow, for all his ill-plac'd Cost and Kindness' ('Third Instance of the Fatal Influence of Words and Names Falsely Applied', *Sermons*, 6th edn., 1727, vi. 106). See also *Tatler*, 76; *Spectator*, 169; Lyttelton, *Persian Letters* (1735), Letter XXXIII; John Armstrong, *The Art of Preserving Health* (1744), Book IV. A classical analogue is Plato, *Republic*, III. xvi (409 a–b).

[4] Cf. Pope on Happiness: 'Plant of celestial seed! if dropt below, / Say in what mortal soil thou deign'st to grow?' (*Essay on Man*, iv. 7–8; Twickenham edn., III. i. 128). See Fielding's preface to *The Tragedy of Tragedies*.

Good-nature, like the delicatest Seeds,
Or dies itself, or else extirpates Weeds.[1]
Yet in itself howe'er unmix'd and pure,   15
No Virtue from Mistakes is less secure.
Good-nature often we those Actions name,
Which flow from Friendship, or a softer Flame.[2]
Pride may the Friend to noblest Efforts thrust,
Or Salvages grow gentle out of Lust.[3]   20
The meanest Passion may this best appear,
And Men may seem good-natur'd, from their Fear.
What by this Name, then, shall be understood?
What? but the glorious Lust of doing Good?[4]
The Heart that finds it Happiness to please,   25
Can feel another's Pain, and taste his Ease.
The Cheek that with another's Joy can glow,
Turn pale, and sicken with another's Woe;[5]
Free from Contempt and Envy, he who deems
Justly of Life's two opposite Extremes.   30
Who to make all and each Man truly blest,
Doth all he can, and wishes all the rest?[6]
   Tho' few have Pow'r their Wishes to fulfil,
Yet all Men may do Good, at least in Will.
Tho' few, with you or *Marlborough*[7] can save   35

---

[1] A version of the Stoic paradox that vice and virtue cannot consist together; cf. Dryden's *Persius, Sat.* v. 175–6: 'Virtue and Vice are never in one Soul: / A Man is wholly Wise, or wholly is a Fool' (1693, p. 67). See Diogenes Laertius, vii. 125–7.

[2] See La Rochefoucauld, *Maxims*, xvi (trans. 1706, p. 8); Pope, *Epistle to Cobham*, 61–70 (Twickenham edn., III. ii. 19); and Fielding on 'Good Humour' below, pp. 158 ff.

[3] Fielding may have carried an imperfect recollection of the 'Salvage man' and Serena in the early cantos of Spenser's *Faerie Queene*, Book VI; and see Burton, *Anat. Melancholy*, iii. 2. 3. 1 (ed. Shilleto, iii. 197–8).

[4] Cf. Bubb Dodington's *Epistle to . . . Sir Robert Walpole*: 'Indulge thy boundless Thirst of doing Good' (3rd edn., 1726, p. 10).

[5] Cf. Pope, 'The Universal Prayer,' 37. 'Teach me to feel another's Woe' (Twickenham edn., vi. 148); Thomson, *Spring* (1746 version), 875–6: '. . . Ye sordid sons of earth, / Hard, and unfeeling of another's woe' (*Poetical Works*, ed. Robertson, p. 36). See Cicero, *De finibus*, I. xx. 67–8 ('Nam et laetamur amicorum laetitia aeque nostra et pariter dolemus angoribus'), and Juvenal, *Sat.* xv. 131 ff.

[6] In *Guardian*, 166, Steele says: 'I never saw an Indigent Person in my Life, without reaching out to him some of this imaginary Relief. I cannot but Sympathise with every one I meet that is in Affliction; and if my Abilities were equal to my Wishes, there should be neither Pain nor Poverty in the World' (5th edn., 1729, ii. 315).

[7] i.e. Sarah, 'the Old Duchess', Hervey's 'Beldam of Bedlam', whose patronage Fielding earnestly sought in his *Full Vindication of the Dutchess Dowager of Marlborough*, 1742.

From Poverty, from Prisons, and the Grave;
Yet to each Individual Heav'n affords
The Pow'r to bless in Wishes, and in Words.
   Happy the Man[1] with Passions blest like you,
Who to be ill, his Nature must subdue.[2]   40
Whom Fortune fav'ring, was no longer blind,
Whose Riches are the Treasures of Mankind.[3]
O! nobler in thy Virtues than thy Blood,
Above thy highest Titles place THE GOOD.
   High on Life's Summit rais'd, you little know   45
The Ills which blacken all the Vales below;[4]
Where Industry toils for Support in vain,
And Virtue to Distress still joins Disdain.
Swelt'ring[5] with Wealth, where Men unmov'd can hear
The Orphans sigh, and see the Widow's Tear:[6]   50
Where griping Av'rice slights the Debtor's Pray'r,
And Wretches wanting Bread deprives of Air.[7]
   Must it not wond'rous seem to Hearts like thine,
That God, to other Animals benign,

---

[1] The familiar 'Beatus ille . . .' (Horace, *Epodes*, ii).

[2] The moral rigorists reversed this argument to declare that, since Good-nature was a natural affection, 'it is the Creator's Goodness, and not the Creature's. . . . A high Degree of it may make Men almost passive in Acts of Kindness; as it gives their Minds so strong a Bias towards such acts, that the very Forbearance of them is a kind of Violence and Self-denial' (John Balguy, preface to *The Law of Truth*, 2nd edn., in *A Collection of Tracts Moral and Theological*, 1734).

[3] Cf. Edward Young, *Love of Fame*, vi. 319 ff., on those 'great souls' who do not hoard their treasure,

> Nor think their wealth *their own*, till well bestow'd.
> Grand *reservoirs* of publick happiness,
> Thro' *secret* streams diffusively they bless . . .

(2nd edn., 1728, p. 140.)

[4] Prior's Solomon thus compares the happiness of angels with that of men: 'Why, whilst We struggle in this Vale beneath, / With Want and Sorrow, with Disease and Death . . . ' (*Solomon*, i. 621–2; *Lit. Works*, ed. Wright-Spears, i. 328). On the social implications of this separation, cf. Booth in *Amelia*, x. ix.

[5] 'To be bathed in liquid; hence, to welter, wallow' (*OED*).

[6] The conventional coupling, from the scriptural 'widows and fatherless': Addison, *A Poem to His Majesty*: 'The Cries of Orphans, and the Widow's Tears' (*Works*, 1721, i. 12); Gay, *Trivia*, ii. 451–2: 'Proud coaches pass regardless of the moan / Of infant orphans, and the widow's groan' (*Poems on Several Occasions*, 1737, i. 168).

[7] Cf. the *True Patriot*, 3 December 1745; and, among many other attacks on the practice of imprisoning for debt, *Covent-Garden Journal*, 39, which cites Locke, Cumberland, Grotius, Pufendorf, and Barbeyrac (as well as Scripture) against it.

Shou'd unprovided[1] Man alone create,   55
And send him hither but to curse his Fate!
Is this the Being for whose Use the Earth
Sprung out of nought, and Animals had Birth?[2]
This he, whose bold Imagination dares
Converse with Heav'n, and soar beyond the Stars?[3]   60
Poor Reptile! wretched in an Angel's Form,
And wanting that which Nature gives the Worm.[4]
Far other Views our kind Creator knew,
When Man the Image of himself he drew.
So full the Stream of Nature's Bounty flows,[5]   65
Man feels no Ill, but what to Man he owes.[6]

[1] Lat. *imparatus*; cf. Shakespeare, *King Lear*, I. i. 54: 'With his prepared sword he charges home / My unprovided body' (*Works*, 1733, v. 135).

[2] Cf. Pope, *Essay on Man*, i. 185–6: 'Each beast, each insect, happy in its own; / Is Heav'n unkind to Man, and Man alone?' (See the whole passage, 173–88, Twickenham edn., III. i. 37–8, and citations there; cf. also i. 123–6, Twickenham edn., III. i. 30–1.) Cf. Milton, *Samson Agonistes*, 667–73; the Earl of Roscommon, 'On Mr. Dryden's *Religio Laici*' (*The First Part of Miscellany Poems*, 5th edn., p. 56); and Rochester's *Satyr against Mankind*, 60 ff.

[3] Cf. Pope, *Essay on Man*, i. 173–4: 'What would this Man? Now upward will he soar, / And little less than Angel, would be more' (Twickenham edn., III. i. 36); Dryden, *Religio Laici*, 62: 'Thus Man by his own strength to Heaven wou'd soar' (*Works*, 1701, III. i. 70); Boileau, *Satire VIII*. 165–8; Lucretius, *De rerum nat.* i. 72–4; Horace, *Carm.* I. iii. 38 and I. xxviii; Seneca, *De otio*, v. 6.

[4] Cf. Prior, *Solomon*, i. 635–6: '. . . the poor Reptile with a reas'ning Soul, / That miserable Master of the Whole' (*Lit. Works*, ed. Wright-Spears, i. 328); Pope, 'To Mr. John Moore', 5–6: 'Man is a very Worm by Birth, / Vile Reptile, weak, and vain!' (Twickenham edn., vi. 161); Shaftesbury, *Miscellaneous Reflections*, iii. chap. i: '. . . that *Planet*, in which, with other Animals of various sorts, We (poor Reptiles!) were also bred and nourish'd' (*Characteristicks*, 6th edn., 1737, iii. 144).

[5] See Seneca's summary of the Golden Age commonplaces, *Epist. mor.* xc. 36–40; and Cicero on the Stoic view 'quae in terris gignantur, ad usum hominum omnia creari' (*De officiis*, I. vii. 22). So Dryden, 'Of the Pythagorean Philosophy' (from Ovid, *Metam.* xv), 111–12: 'While Earth not only can your Needs supply, / But lavish of her Store, provides for Luxury' (*Works*, 1701, III. ii. 507); Milton, *Paradise Lost*, iv. 242–3; Robert South: 'The great Business of Providence is to be continually issuing out fresh Supplies of the Divine Bounty to the Creature . . .' ('Covetousness an Absurdity in Reason and a Contradiction to Religion,' *Sermons*, 6th edn., 1727, iv. 441); and see the letter of 'Misargurus' in Fielding's *Covent-Garden Journal*, 35 (2 May 1752). Pope expands Horace's 'dives opia natura suae' (*Serm.* I. ii. 74) to 'Hath not indulgent Nature spread a Feast, / And giv'n enough for Man, enough for Beast?' ('Sober Advice from Horace', 96–7; Twickenham edn., iv. 83).

[6] See Pliny, *Nat. Hist.* VII. i. 5: 'homini plurima ex homine sunt mala', in the context of his famous argument that Nature is rather a stepmother than a mother to man. Cf. Cicero, *De officiis*, II. v. 16; Rochester, *Satyr against Mankind*, 130: 'But Savage *Man* alone, does *Man* betray' (*Poems on Several Occasions*, 1680, p. 10); Shaftesbury, *The Moralists*, I. ii (*Characteristicks*, 6th edn., 1737, ii. 192); Mandeville, *Fable of the Bees*, Part II (1729), p. 274.

The Earth abundant furnishes a Store,
To sate the Rich, and satisfy the Poor.
These wou'd not want, if those did never hoard;
Enough for *Irus* falls from *Dives'* Board.[1]   70
   And dost thou, common Son of Nature, dare
From thy own Brother to with-hold his Share?
To Vanity, pale Idol, offer up
The shining Dish, and empty golden Cup!
Or else in Caverns hide thy precious Ore, ⎫   75
And to the Bowels of the Earth restore   ⎬
What for our Use she yielded up before?[2] ⎭
Behold, and take Example, how the Steed
Attempts not, selfish, to engross the Mead.[3]
See how the lowing Herd, and bleating Flock,   80
Promiscuous[4] graze the Valley, or the Rock;
Each tastes his Share of Nature's gen'ral Good,
Nor strives from others to with-hold their Food.
But say, O Man! wou'd it not strange appear
To see some Beast (perhaps the meanest there)   85
To his Repast the sweetest Pastures chuse,
And ev'n the sourest to the rest refuse.
Wouldst thou not view, with scornful wond'ring Eye,
The poor, contented, starving Herd stand by?
All to one Beast a servile Homage pay,   90
And, boasting, think it Honour to obey.
   Who wonders that Good-nature in so few,
Can Anger, Lust, or Avarice subdue?
When the cheap Gift of Fame our Tongues deny,
And risque our own, to poison with a Lie.   95
   Dwells there a base Malignity in Men,
That 'scapes the Tiger's Cave, or Lion's Den?

---

[1] Irus, the beggar in the *Odyssey*, proverbial for the poor man, as Dives for the wealthy man. For the argument cf. Fénelon, *Les avantures de Télémaque* (Paris, 1699), xii; 1743 edn., p. 212.

[2] For the conceit, see Pope, *Epistle to Bathurst*, 7–14 (Twickenham edn., III. ii. 81–2), and Waller, 'Of a War with Spain', 69–74 (*Poems, &c.*, 9th edn., 1712, p. 134). Cf. also Virgil, *Georgics*, ii. 507; Horace, *Carm.* III. iii. 49; Milton, *Paradise Lost*, i. 687–8.

[3] The theme of 'Sumite in exemplum pecudes ratione carentes' (cf. Ovid, *Amores*, I. x).

[4] Lat. *promiscuus*, mixed, in common; so Milton, *Paradise Lost*, i. 380: 'the promiscuous croud'. Cf. Thomson's description of the State of Nature (*Spring*, 262–3): '. . . . o'er the swelling mead / The herds and flocks commixing played secure' (ed. Robertson, pp. 12–13); and Dryden's Virgil, *Pastorals*, viii. 40; *Georgics*, i. 125–8.

Does our Fear dread, or does our Envy hate
To see another happy, good, or great?
Or does the Gift of Fame, like Money, seem?   100
Think we, we lose, whene'er we give Esteem?[1]
  Oh! great Humanity, whose Beams benign,
Like the Sun's Rays, on just and unjust shine;[2]
Who turning the Perspective[3] friendly still,
Dost magnify all Good, and lessen Ill;   105
Whose Eye, while small Perfections it commends,
Not to what's better, but what's worse attends:
Who, when at Court it spies some well-shap'd Fair,
Searches not through the Rooms for *Shaftsb'ry's* Air;[4]
Nor when *Clarinda's* Lillies are confest,   110
Looks for the Snow that whitens *Richmond's* Breast.[5]
Another's Sense and Goodness when I name,
Why wouldst thou lessen them with *Mountford's* Fame?[6]
Content, what Nature lavishes admire,
Nor what is wanting in each Piece require.[7]   115
Where much is Right, some Blemishes afford,
Nor look for *Ch—d* in ev'ry Lord.[8]

[1] An earlier version of these lines appeared in the *Champion*, 27 November 1739, as 'from a Poem not yet communicated to the Public':

> Nor in the Tyger's Cave, nor Lion's Den,
> Dwells our Malignity. For selfish Men,
> The Gift of Fame like that of Money deem;
> And think they lose, whene'er they give Esteem.

(Coll. edn., 1741, i. 35; italics reversed.)

[2] Cf. Matt. 5: 45.

[3] A telescope or spy-glass; cf. Steele, *The Tender Husband*, I. i: 'I have seen such a one with a Pocket Glass to see his own Face, and an affected Perspective to know others' (*Dramatick Works*, 1723, p. 99); Dryden, 'To My honor'd Friend Sir Robert Howard', 77–8.

[4] Susannah Noel Cooper, Countess of Shaftesbury (d. 1758).

[5] Sarah Lennox, second Duchess of Richmond (d. 1751). See below, p. 79.

[6] Henry Bromley (1705–55), elevated to the peerage as first Baron Montfort 9 May 1741 O.S.

[7] For this usage, cf. Addison, *The Campaign*: 'Eager for glory, and require the fight' (*Works*, 1721, i. 69).

[8] Chesterfield.

LIBERTY

TO

GEORGE LYTTLETON, *Esq*;[1]

To *Lyttleton* the Muse this Off'ring pays;
Who sings of Liberty, must sing his Praise.
This Man, ye grateful *Britons*, all revere;
Here raise your Altars, bring your Incense here.[2]
To him the Praise, the Blessings which ye owe,   5
More than their Sires your grateful Sons shall know.[3]
O! for thy Country's Good and Glory born!
Whom Nature vy'd with Fortune to adorn!
Brave, tho' no Soldier; without Titles, great;
Fear'd, without Pow'r; and envy'd, without State.[4]   10
Accept the Muse whom Truth inspires to sing,
Who soars, tho' weakly, on an honest Wing.[5]
   See Liberty, bright Goddess, come along,
Rais'd at thy Name, she animates the Song.[6]
Thy Name, which *Lacedemon* had approv'd,   15
Rome had ador'd, and *Brutus*' Self had lov'd.[7]

---

[1] George Lyttelton (1709–73), later first Baron Lyttelton (1757). He was, after Ralph Allen, perhaps Fielding's most generous patron; and Fielding repaid the debt in full, with the dedication of *Tom Jones*. The present poem must have been written after 1735–6, the date of Thomson's *Liberty*, which it echoes.

[2] Cf. Prior, *Carmen Seculare*, 506: 'New Incense They shall bring, new Altars raise' (*Lit. Works*, ed. Wright-Spears, i. 179); see Horace, *Carm.* I. xix.

[3] See Dryden, *Annus Mirabilis*, 203–4.

[4] An echo of Pope, *Imit. of Horace*, Epist. I. i. 181, 183 (of Bolingbroke): 'Great without Title, without Fortune bless'd . . . / Lov'd without youth, and follow'd without power' (Twickenham edn., iv. 293; cf. also Epist. II. i. 204, ibid., p. 211).

[5] Cf. Pope, *Essay on Criticism*, 197: 'That on weak Wings, from far, pursues your Flights' (Twickenham edn., i. 263).

[6] Cf. Pope, *Imit. of Horace*, Odes, IV. i. 27–8: 'There, every Grace and Muse shall throng, / Exalt the Dance, or animate the Song' (Twickenham edn., iv. 153).

[7] The traditional association of Sparta and Republican Rome with the theme of Liberty. The republic of Venice was often added as a third (cf. John Locke, *Two Treatises of Government*, 1690, II. viii. 102–3). Alan D. McKillop, *The Background of Thomson's Liberty* (1951), provides an admirable context for Fielding's poem as well. Both Thomson and Fielding drew upon the standard classical authorities, Polybius, Plutarch, Lucan, and Tacitus; and both apparently made use of the Abbé Vertot's *Histoire des Révolutions de la république romaine* (Paris, 1720). It seems likely that Fielding also knew Charles Rollin's *Histoire ancienne* (10 vols., 1734–6), though no copy is listed in his library.

Come, then, bright Maid, my glowing Breast inspire;
Breathe in my Lines, and kindle all thy Fire.[1]
Behold, she cries, the Groves, the Woods, the Plains,
Where Nature dictates, see how Freedom reigns;   20
The Herd, promiscuous, o'er the Mountain strays;
Nor begs this Beast the other's Leave to graze.
Each freely dares his Appetite to treat,
Nor fears the Steed to neigh, the Flock to bleat.[2]
Did God, who Freedom to these Creatures gave,   25
Form his own Image, Man, to be a Slave?[3]
But Men, it seems, to Laws of Compact yield;
While Nature only governs in the Field.[4]
Curse on all Laws which Liberty subdue,
And make the Many wretched for the Few.[5]   30
However deaf to Shame, to Reason blind,
Men dare assert all Falshoods of Mankind;
The Publick never were, when free, such Elves
To covet Laws pernicious to themselves.
Presumptuous Pow'r assumes the publick Voice,   35
And what it makes our Fate, pretends our Choice.[6]

[1] Cf. Dryden's *Aeneid*, vii. 52–3; and Ovid, *Metam.* i. 2–3: 'coeptis . . . adspirate meis'.

[2] See above, *Of Good Nature*, 80–3. Fielding's somewhat unlikely view of the animal estate runs counter to Locke's, who contrasted the rule of beasts, 'where the strongest carries it', with that of man, where the natural state is that of 'perfect Freedom' (*Two Treatises*, II. i. 1 and II. ii. 4).

[3] See St. Augustine, *De civitate dei*, xix. 15; Milton, *Paradise Lost*, xii. 63–71.

[4] On the history of contract theory, see J. W. Gough, *The Social Contract* (2nd edn., 1957). Lyttleton's *Letters from a Persian in England* (1735), Letters X–XXI, sought, through a continuation of Montesquieu's history of the 'Troglodites' (*Lettres Persanes*, Letters XI–XIV), 'to shew . . . by what steps, and through what changes, the original good of society is overturned, and mankind become wickeder and more miserable in a state of government, than they were when left in a state of nature' (*Works*, 1774, p. 122). Needless to say, Lyttelton, like Fielding, had Walpole's 'state of government' in mind.

[5] Cf. Pope, *Eloisa to Abelard*, 74: 'Curse on all laws but those which love has made!' (Twickenham edn., ii. 305); and, for the theme of the rise and corruption of society, *Essay on Man*, iii. 199 ff.: 'Who first taught souls enslav'd, and realms undone, / Th' enormous faith of many made for one' (iii. 241–2; Twickenham edn., III. i. 116–17). This kind of complaint could be turned, with embarrassing ease, to support of the 'libertine' position: see the speech that Otway gives to Don John of Austria in *Don Carlos* (1676), II. i, beginning, 'Why should dull Law rule Nature, who first made / That Law by which herself is now betray'd?' (*Works*, 1768, i. 117). The first act of Dryden's *Conquest of Granada*, Part I (1672) offers debate on this topic.

[6] See Locke, *Two Treatises*, II. viii. 114, on obligations to Father or to Prince: ''Tis plain Mankind never owned nor considered any such natural subjection that they were born in, to one or to the other, that tied them, without their own Consents, to a subjection to them and their Heirs' (1698 edn., p. 254).

To whom did Pow'r original belong? ⎫
Was it not first extorted by the Strong? ⎬
And thus began, where it will end, in Wrong. ⎭
These scorn'd to Pow'r another Claim than Might,   40
And in Ability establish'd Right.[1]
    At length a second nobler Sort arose,
Friends to the Weak, and to Oppression Foes;
With warm Humanity their Bosoms glow'd,
They felt to Nature their great Strength they ow'd.[2]   45
And as some Elder born of noble Rate,[3]
To whom devolves his Father's rich Estate,
Becomes a kind Protector to the rest,
Nor sees, unmov'd, the younger Branch distrest.
So these, with Strength whom Nature deign'd to grace,   50
Became the Guardians of their weaker Race;
Forc'd Tyrant Pow'r to bend its stubborn Knee,
Broke the hard Chain, and set the People free.[4]
O'er abject Slaves they scorn'd inglorious Sway,[5]
But taught the grateful freed Man to obey;   55
And thus by giving Liberty, enjoy'd
What the first hop'd from Liberty destroy'd.
    To such the Weak for their Protection flew,
Hence Right to Pow'r and Laws by Compact grew.[6]
With Zeal embracing their Deliv'rer's Cause,   60
They bear his Arms, and listen to his Laws.

1 Fielding's account of the rise of society seems to owe its largest debt to Lucretius, *De rerum natura*, v. 925–1168. On the 'power original', see v. 958–61. Fielding omits the earlier 'pre-governmental' stage of patriarchal powers, found in Pufendorf, Harrington, Algernon Sidney, and Locke, and poetized in Defoe's *Jure Divino* (1706).

2 See Lucretius, v. 1105–7, 1143 ff.; cf. Thomson, *Liberty*, ii. 38–40: 'Heroes then arose, / Who, scorning coward self, for others lived, / Toiled for their ease, and for their safety bled' (*Poetical Works*, ed. Robertson, p. 325). The distinction is essentially that of Aristotle, between tyrants, who serve only their own advantage, and kings, who are guardians of society (*Politics*, v. x. 9). Cf. also Machiavelli, *Discourses*, I. ii.

3 Mode of living. Cf. Shakespeare, *Merchant of Venice*, I. i. 127–8: 'Nor do I now make moan to be abridg'd / From such a noble rate . . .' (*Works*, 1733, ii. 7).

4 Cf. Prior, 'Presented to the King . . . 1696', 7–8: 'But Tyrants dread Ye, lest your just Decree / Transfer the Pow'r, and set the People free' (*Lit. Works*, ed. Wright-Spears, i. 154).

5 Cf. Gay, 'Epistle to William Pulteney', 246: 'And scorns to rule a wretched race of slaves' (*Poems on Several Occasions*, 1737, ii. 31).

6 In contrast to lines 27–30 above, the compact, here derived from humane guardians, is seen as a good—though it ends in corruption by evil. See Lucretius, v. 1143–60; Locke, *Two Treatises*, II. viii.

Liberty 39

Thus Pow'r superior, Strength superior wears,
In Honour chief, as first in Toils and Cares.
The People Pow'r, to keep their Freedom, gave,
And he who had it was the only Slave.[1]   65
But Fortune wills to wisest human Schemes,
The Fate that Torrents bring to purest Streams,
Which from clear Fountains soon polluted run,
Thus ends in Evil what from Good begun.
For now the Savage Host, o'erthrown and slain,   70
New Titles, by new Methods, Kings obtain.
To Priests and Lawyers soon their Arts apply'd,
The People these, and those the Gods bely'd.[2]
The Gods, unheard, to Pow'r Successors name,
And silent Crowds their Rights divine proclaim.[3]   75
Hence all the Evils which Mankind have known,
The Priest's dark Mystery, the Tyrant's Throne;
Hence Lords, and Ministers, and such sad Things;
And hence the strange Divinity of Kings.[4]
Hail Liberty! Boon worthy of the Skies,   80
Like fabled *Venus* fair, like *Pallas* wise.
Through thee the Citizen braves War's Alarms,
Tho' neither bred to fight, nor pay'd for Arms;
Thro' thee, the Lawrel crown'd the Victor's Brow,
Who serv'd before his Country at the Plough: 85
Thro' thee (what most must to thy Praise appear)
Proud Senates scorn'd not to seek Virtue there.[5]

[1] Thus Addison's Cato: 'Am I distinguish'd from you but by toils, / Superior toils, and heavier weight of cares!' (*Cato*, III. v; *Works*, 1721, i. 345). Cf. Boabdelin's lines concluding the first act of *The Conquest of Granada*, Part I: ''Tis just, some Joys on weary Kings should wait; / 'Tis all we gain by being Slaves to State' (*Works*, 1701, i. 391); also the gypsy king in *Tom Jones*, XII. xii. Fénelon's Telemachus concludes that 'l'état d'un roi est bien malheureux: il est l'esclave de tous ceux auxquels il paroît commander' (*Les avantures de Télémaque*, Paris, 1699, xxiv; 1743 edn., p. 411).
[2] On the priesthood, see Lucretius, v. 1161–1240. The rubric to Pope's *Essay on Man*, iii. 235 ff., reads: 'Origine of TRUE RELIGION and GOVERNMENT from the Principle of LOVE: and of SUPERSTITION and TYRANNY, from that of FEAR' (Twickenham edn., III. i. 116 n).
[3] Fielding's catachresis varies Dryden's lines: 'The Crowd with silent Admiration stand / And heard him, as they heard their God's Command' ('Of the Pythagorean Philosophy', 86–7; *Works*, 1701, III. ii. 506). He may have had in mind Cicero's 'cum tacent, clamant' (*In Catilinam*, I. viii. 21).
[4] Cf. Locke, *Two Treatises*, II. viii. 112: 'Though they never dream'd of Monarchy being *Jure Divino*, which we never heard of among Mankind, till it was revealed to us by the Divinity of this last Age' (1698 edn., p. 252).   [*For footnote 5 see overlehf*

O thou, than Health or Riches dearer far,
Thou gentle Breath of Peace, and Soul of War;
Thou that hast taught the Desart Sweets to yield, 90
And shame the fair *Campania's* fertile Field;[1]
Hast shewn the Peasant Glory, and call'd forth
Wealth from the barren Sand, and Heroes from the North;
The southern Skies, without thee, to no End
In the cool Breeze, or genial[2] Show'rs descend: 95
Possess'd of thee, the *Vandal*, and the *Hun*,
Enjoy their Frost, nor mourn the distant Sun.[3]
As Poets *Samos*, and the *Cyprian* Grove,
Once gave to *Juno*, and the Queen of Love;[4]
Be thine *Britannia*: ever friendly smile, 100
And fix thy Seat eternal in this Isle.
Thy sacred Name no *Romans* now adore,
And *Greece* attends thy glorious Call no more.
To thy *Britannia*, then, thy Fire transfer,
Give all thy Virtue, all thy Force to her; 105
Revolve, attentive, all her Annals o'er,
See how her Sons have lov'd thee heretofore.
While the base Sword oppress'd *Iberia* draws,
And slavish *Gauls* dare fight against thy Cause,
See *Britain's* Youth rush forth, at thy Command, 110
And fix thy Standard in the hostile Land.[5]
With noble Scorn they view the crowded Field,
And force unequal Multitudes to yield.

[5] On Lucius Quinctius Cincinnatus, see Livy, iii. 26 et seq., and Cicero, *De senectute*, xvi. 56. Cf. Thomson, *Liberty*, iii. 143–7.

[1] See Thomson, *Summer* (1746 version), 953–5: '. . . Liberty retired, / Her Cato following through Numidian wilds— / Disdainful of Campania's gentle plains' (*Poetical Works*, ed. Robertson, p. 87).

[2] Generative: cf. Pope, *Essay on Man*, iii. 118: 'the genial seeds'.

[3] Addison's *Letter from Italy* (1703) contrasts the 'blooming mountains' and 'sunny Shores' of Italy with the oppression and tyranny found there, and concludes: 'We envy not the warmer clime. . . . / 'Tis Liberty that crowns *Britannia's* Isle, / And makes her barren rocks and her bleak mountains smile' (*Works*, 1721, i. 53). On the popular theme of the *translatio libertatis* from Republican Rome to the northern barbarians, see Samuel Kliger, *The Goths in England* (1952). Cf. Thomson, *Liberty*, Parts III–V.

[4] On Juno and Samos see Pausanias, *Descript. Graec.* VII. iv. 4; for Venus and Cyprus, Hesiod, *Theogony*, 188–200.

[5] The allusion is probably not to the War of Jenkins's Ear and of the Austrian Succession, beginning in 1739 (cf. below, p. 97), but to the War of the Spanish Succession, 1701–13, celebrated below (Blenheim).

So Wolves large Flocks, so Lions Herds survey,
Not Foes more num'rous, but a richer Prey.   115
O! teach us to withstand, as they withstood,
Nor lose the Purchase of our Father's Blood.[1]
Ne'er blush that Sun that saw in *Blenheim's* Plain
Streams of our Blood, and Mountains of our Slain;[2]
Or that of old beheld all *France* to yield   120
In *Agincourt* or *Cressy's* glorious Field;
Where Freedom *Churchill, Henry, Edward* gave,
Ne'er blush that Sun to see a *British* Slave.[3]
   As Industry might from the Bee be taught,
So might Oppression from the Hive be brought: 125
Behold the little Race laborious stray,
And from each Flow'r the hard-wrought Sweets convey,
That in warm Ease in Winter they may dwell,
And each enjoy the Riches of its Cell.
Behold th' excising Pow'r of Man despoil   130
These little Wretches of their Care and Toil.[4]
Death's the Reward of all their Labour lost,
Careful in vain, and provident to their Cost.
   But thou, great Liberty, keep *Britain* free,
Nor let Men use us as we use the Bee.   135
Let not base Drones upon our Honey thrive,
And suffocate the Maker in his Hive.[5]

[1] Cf. Addison, *Cato*, III. v; and *A Poem to His Majesty*:
     Oh, did our *British* Peers thus court Renown,
     And grace the Coats their great Fore-fathers won! . . .
     What might not *England* hope, if such abroad
     Purchas'd their country's honour with their Blood.
(*Works*, 1721, i. 15.)
[2] So Addison, *The Campaign*: 'Rivers of blood I see, and hills of slain' (*Works*, 1721, i. 65); later lines gives us 'streams of blood' (i. 77) and 'Mountains of slain' (i. 78).
[3] On Agincourt (Henry V) and Crécy (Edward III), see Pope, *Windsor Forest*, 305; *Imit. of Horace*, Epist. II. i. 7; Thomson, *Summer*, 1484; *Liberty*, iv. 840, 865; Samuel Johnson, *London*, 99–122; and Lord Lansdowne's 'Ode: On the Present Corruption of Mankind', st. viii: 'Not such the Men who fill'd with Heaps of Slain / Fam'd Agincourt and Cressy's bloody Plain' (*Genuine Works*, 1736, i. 142).
[4] Presumably a remembrance of the 'tyrannical' Excise Bill that Walpole sought unsuccessfully to achieve in 1733. The suggestion that government has the duty to protect private property is a central focus in Cicero, *De officiis*, II. xxi. 73 *et passim*, and Locke, *Two Treatises*, II. v, vii *et passim*.
[5] See above, *Of True Greatness*, 138–9. Cf. Thomson, *Liberty*, iv. 852–3: 'To be luxurious drones, that only rob / The busy hive . . .' (*Poetical Works*, ed. Robertson, p. 381). See also Fielding's *Amelia*, IV. viii. Ultimately, perhaps, Plato, *Republic*, VIII. vii (552 c–d).

TO A FRIEND

ON THE

CHOICE of a WIFE

'Tis hard (Experience long so taught the wise)
Not to provoke the Person we advise.
Counsel, tho' ask'd, may very oft offend,
When it insults th' Opinion of my Friend.
Men frequent wish another's Judgment known,   5
Not to destroy, but to confirm their own.
With feign'd Suspence for our Advice they sue,
On what they've done, or are resolv'd to do.[1]
The favour'd Scheme should we by Chance oppose,
Henceforth they see us in the Light of Foes.   10
For could Mankind th' Advice they ask receive,
Most to themselves might wholesome Counsel give.
Men in the beaten Track of Life's Highway,   ⎫
Ofter through Passion than through Error stray,   ⎬
Want less Advice than Firmness to obey.[2]   ⎭   15
   Nor can Advice an equal Hazard prove
To what is given in the Cause of Love;
None ask it here 'till melting in the Flame.   ⎫
If we oppose the now victorious Dame,   ⎬
You think her Enemy and yours the same.[3]   ⎭   20
   But yet, tho' hard, tho' dangerous the Task,
Fidus must grant, if his *Alexis* ask.
Take then the friendly Councils of the Muse;
Happy, if what you've chosen she should chuse.
   The Question's worthy some diviner Voice,   25
How to direct a Wife's important Choice.[4]

---

[1] Cf. *Tatler*, 25: 'For some People will ask Council of you, when they have already acted what they tell you is still under Deliberation'; *Spectator*, 475 and 512; La Rochefoucauld, *Maxims*, cxvi (trans. 1706, pp. 48–9).

[2] Contrary to the Socratic view that 'Error est causa pecandi'.

[3] Cf. Ovid, *Remedia amoris*, 123–4; James Miller, *The Universal Passion* (1737), I. i: 'I am glad your Opinion, *Lucentius*, agrees with my own, for, like a true Lover, I have been asking Advice when 'twas too late to take it . . .' (p. 2).

[4] The genre of advice on contemplated marriage, which would include the *Sixth Satire* of Juvenal, the last three books of Rabelais, Ben Jonson's *Epicoene*, and numerous *Spectator*

In other Aims if we should miss the White,[1]
Reason corrects, and turns us to the Right:
But here, a Doom irrevocable's past,
And the first fatal Error proves the last.   30
Rash were it then, and desperate, to run
With Haste to do what cannot be undone.[2]
Whence come the Woes which we in Marriage find,
But from a Choice too negligent, too blind?
    Marriage, by Heav'n ordain'd is understood,   35
And bounteous Heav'n ordain'd but what is good.
To our Destruction we its Bounties turn,
In Flames, by Heav'n to warm us meant, we burn.
What draws Youth heedless to the fatal Gin?[3]
Features well form'd, or a well polish'd Skin.   40
What can in riper Minds a Wish create?
Wealth, or Alliance with the Rich and Great:
Who to himself, now in his Courtship, says,
I chuse a Partner of my future Days;
Her Face, or Pocket seen, her Mind they trust;   45
They wed to lay the Fiends of Avarice or Lust.[4]
    But thou, whose honest Thoughts the Choice intend
Of a Companion, and a softer Friend;
A tender Heart, which while thy Soul it shares,
Augments thy Joys, and lessens all thy Cares.   50
One, who by thee while tenderly carest,
Shall steal that God-like Transport to thy Breast,
The Joy to find you make another blest.
Thee in thy Choice let other Maxims move,
They wed for baser Passions; thou for Love.   55

papers, shades easily into the genre of anti-feminist literature; and of this, Burton (quoting Christopher Fonseca) has very truly said: 'non possunt invectivae omnes, et satirae in faeminas scriptae, uno volumine comprehendi' (*Anat. Melancholy*, iii. 2. 5. 3; ed. Shilleto, iii. 249). For the structure of a set of female characters, see also Pope's *Epistle to a Lady*.

  [1] In archery, a circular band of white on the target; cf. Cotton's translation of Montaigne, I. ix: 'there are a thousand ways to miss the White, there is only one to hit it' (3rd edn., 1700, i. 50).

  [2] The theme of Ovid's *Remedia amoris*, 79 ff.

  [3] 'A contrivance for catching game, etc.; a snare, net, trap, or the like' (*OED*).

  [4] Cf. *Spectator*, 268: 'But how few are there who seek after these Things [Virtue, Wisdom, &c.], and do not rather make Riches their chief if not their only Aim? How rare is it for a Man, when he engages himself in the Thoughts of Marriage, to place his Hopes of having in such a Woman a constant, agreeable Companion? One who will divide his Cares and double his Joys?'

Of Beauty's subtle Poison well beware;
Our Hearts are taken e'er they dread the Snare:[1]
Our Eyes, soon dazzled by that Glare, grow blind,
And see no Imperfections in the Mind.[2]
Of this appriz'd, the Sex, with nicest Art,   60
Insidiously adorn the outward Part.[3]
But Beauty, to a Mind deprav'd and ill,
Is a thin Gilding to a nauseous Pill;
A cheating Promise of a short-liv'd Joy,
Time must this Idol, Chance may soon destroy.   65
See *Leda*, once the Circle's proudest Boast,
Of the whole Town the universal Toast;
By Children, Age, and Sickness, now decay'd,
What Marks remain of the triumphant Maid?
Beauties which Nature and which Art produce,   70
Are form'd to please the Eye, no other Use.[4]
The Husband, sated by Possession grown,
Or indolent to flatter what's his own;
With eager Rivals keeps unequal Pace:
But oh! no Rival flatters like her Glass.[5]   75
There still she's sure a thousand Charms to see,
A thousand Times she more admires than he:
Then soon his Dulness learns she to despise,
And thinks she's thrown away too rich a Prize.
To please her, try his little Arts in vain;   80
His very Hopes to please her move Disdain.

---

[1] Cf. Ovid, *Remedia amoris*, 105–6, 148; *Tom Jones*, IV. v.

[2] Cf., in a like context, Prior, *Solomon*: 'How shall our Thought avoid the various Snare ?' (ii. 547) and 'Nor find, how Beauty's Rays elude our Sight: / Struck with her Eye whilst We applaud her Mind' (ii. 563–4; *Lit. Works*, ed. Wright-Spears, i. 348); Cowley, 'Against Fruition': '*Beauty* at first moves wonder, and delight; / 'Tis *Natures juggling trick* to cheat the sight . . .' (*The Mistress*, p. 33, in *Works*, 1668).

[3] Cf. Ovid, *Remedia amoris*, 343–4; Lucretius, iv. 1185–91; Dryden, *Aureng-Zebe*, iv: 'Nature took care to dress you up for Sin: / Adorn'd without; unfinish'd left, within' (*Works*, 1701, ii. 39).

[4] Cf. *Tatler*, 2: 'Beauty is a Thing which palls with Possession; and the Charms of this Lady soon wanted the Support of good Humour and Complaisancy of Manners.' And Gulliver on the Lilliputians: 'For, their Maxim is, that among People of Quality, a Wife should be always a reasonable and agreeable Companion, because she cannot always be young' (*Gulliver's Travels*, I. vi; *Prose Works of Swift*, ed. Herbert Davis, xi. 46).

[5] So La Rochefoucauld, *Maxims*, ii: 'Self-Love is of all Flatterers the greatest' (trans. 1706, p. 2).

The Man of Sense, the Husband, and the Friend,
Cannot with Fools and Coxcombs condescend
To such vile Terms of tributary Praise,
As Tyrants scarce on conquer'd Countries raise. 85
Beauties think Heav'n they in themselves bestow,
All we return is Gratitude too low.
A gen'ral[1] Beauty wisely then you shun;
But from a Wit, as a Contagion, run.
Beauties with Praise if difficult to fill; 90
To praise a Wit enough, is harder still.
Here with a thousand Rivals you'll contest;
He most succeeds, who most approves the Jest.
Ill-nature too with Wit's too often join'd;
Too firm Associates in the human Mind. 95
Oft may the former for the latter go,
And for a Wit we may mistake a Shrew.[2]
How seldom burns this Fire, like *Sappho's*, bright?
How seldom gives an innocent Delight?
Flavia's a Wit at Modesty's Expence; 100
Iris to Laughter sacrifices Sense.
Hard Labour undergo poor *Delia*'s Brains, ⎫
While ev'ry Joke some Mystery contains; ⎬
No Problem is discuss'd with greater Pains.⎭
Not *Lais* more resolv'd, through thick and thin, 105
Will plunge to meet her ever-darling Sin,
Than *Myrrha*, through Ingratitude and Shame,
To raise the Laugh, or get a witty Fame.
No Friendship is secure from *Myrrha's* Blows;
For Wits, like Gamesters, hurt both Friends and Foes.[3] 110

---

[1] 'Prefixed to personal designations of function or employment: Not restricted to one department; concerned with, or skilled in, all the branches of one's business or pursuit: said, e.g. of a scholar, an artist' (*OED*). Cf. *Joseph Andrews*, I. v: ' "O then", said the Lady, "you are a general Lover." '

[2] Cf. above, *Of True Greatness*, 53–4, 207.

[3] Cf. Burton on prodigals in gaming, who consume 'not themselves only, but even all their friends, as a man desperately swimming drowns him that comes to help him' (*Anat. Melancholy*, i. 2. 3. 13; ed. Shilleto, i. 336). See Prior and Charles Montagu, *The Hind and the Panther Transvers'd* (1687), 650–1: '*Bayes*. 'Tis no matter for that, these general reflections are daring, and savour most of a *noble Genius*, that spares neither *Friend* nor *Foe*' (*Lit. Works*, ed. Wright-Spears, i. 54); cf. Drawcansir in *The Rehearsal* (1672); Young, *Love of Fame*, ii. 111–12: 'He spares nor friend, nor foe; but calls to mind, / Like Doom's-day*, all the faults of all mankind' (2nd edn., 1728, p. 29).

Besides, where'er these shining Flowers appear,⎫
Too nice the Soil more useful Plants to bear; ⎬
Her House, her Person, are below her Care. ⎭
In a domestick Sphere she scorns to move,
And scarce accepts the vulgar Joys of Love.   115
But while your Heart to Wit's Attacks is cool,
Let it not give Admission to a Fool.
He who can Folly in a Wife commend,
Proposes her a Servant, not a Friend.
Thou too, whose Mind is generous and brave,   120
Wouldst not become her Master, but her Slave;
For Fools are obstinate, Advice refuse,
And yield to none but Arts you'd scorn to use.
When Passion grows, by long Possession, dull,
The sleepy Flame her Folly soon must lull;   125
Tho' now, perhaps, those childish Airs you prize.
Lovers and Husbands see with diff'rent Eyes.
A rising Passion will new Charms create;
A falling seeks new Causes for its Hate.
Wisely the Bee, while teeming Summer blooms,   130
Thinks of the Dearth which with cold Winter glooms,[1]
So thou should'st, in thy Love's serener Time,
When Passion reigns, and *Flora*'s in her Prime,[2]
Think of that Winter which must sure ensue,
When she shall have no Charms, no Fondness you.   135
How then shall Friendship to fond Love succeed?
What Charms shall serve her then in Beauty's Stead?
What then shall bid the Passion change, not cool?
No Charm's in the Possession of a Fool.
Next for the all-attracting Power of Gold,   140
That as a Thing indifferent you hold,
I know thy am'rous Heart, whose honest Pride
Is still to be on the obliging Side,
Would wish the Fair One, who your Soul allures,
Enjoy'd a Fortune rather less than yours.   145
Those whom the dazzling Glare of Fortune strikes,
Whom Gold allures to what the Soul dislikes;

---

[1] Cf. Dryden's Virgil, *Georgics*, iv. 230–1, on the bees: 'Mindful of coming Cold, they
share the Pain: / And hoard, for Winter's use, the Summer's gain' (*Works of Virgil*, 1697,
p. 129).   [2] Cf. Spenser, *Faerie Queene*, I. iv. xvii. 3.

If counterfeit Affection they support,
Strict Pennance do, and golden Fetters court.[1]
But if ungrateful for the Boon they grow,   150
And pay the bounteous Female back with Woe,
These are the worst of Robbers in their Wills,
Whom Laws prevent from doing lesser Ills.
   Many who Profit in a Match intend,
Find themselves clearly Losers in the End.   155
Fulvius, who basely from *Melissa* broke,
With richer *Chloe* to sustain the Yoke,
Sees, in her vast Expence, his Crimes repaid,
And oft laments the poor forsaken Maid.
And say, What Soul, that's not to Slav'ry born,   160
Can bear the Taunts, th' Upbraidings, and the Scorn,
Which Women with their Fortunes oft bestow?
Worse Torments far than Poverty can know.
   Happy *Alexis*, sprung from such a Race,
Whose Blood would no Nobility disgrace.[2]   165
But O prefer some tender of a Flock,
Who scarce can graft one Parson on her Stock,
To a fair Branch of *Churchil's* Noble Line,
If Thou must often hear it match'd with thine.
Hence, should I say, by her big Taunts compell'd, ⎫   170
With *Tallard* taken, *Villars* forc'd to yield, ⎬
And all the Glories of great *Blenheim's* Field.[3] ⎭
While thus secure from what too frequent charms,
Small Force against the rest your Bosom arms.
Ill-nature, Pride, or a malicious Spleen,   175
To be abhorr'd, need only to be seen;
But to discover 'em may ask some Art:
Women to Lovers seldom Faults impart.
She's more than Woman, who can still conceal
Faults from a Lover, who will watch her well.   180

---

[1] Cf. Juvenal, *Sat.* vi. 136–41.

[2] Cross (i. 384), perhaps influenced by this description of 'Alexis', which would fit Lyttelton adequately, saw the whole poem as 'evidently complimenting Lyttelton on his marriage in the summer of 1742'; but the verses are addressed to someone planning to marry rather than just married, and there is no convincing evidence for the suggestion.

[3] French marshals defeated by Marlborough: Tallard, taken prisoner at Blenheim, 1704; Villars, defeated at Malplaquet, 1709. For the syntax, cf. below, 'Juvenal's Sixth Satire Modernized', 262–3.

The Dams of Art may Nature's Stream oppose,
It swells at last, and in a Torrent flows.[1]
But Men, too partial, think, when they behold
A Mistress rude, vain, obstinate, or bold,
That she to others who a Dæmon proves,   185
May be an Angel to the Man she loves.
Mistaken Hope, that can expect to find
Pride ever humble, or Ill-nature kind.
No, rest assur'd, the Ill which now you see
Her act to others, she will act to thee.[2]   190
Shun then the Serpent, when the Sting appears,[3]
Nor think a hurtful Nature ever spares.
Two Sorts of Women never should be woo'd,
The wild Coquette, and the censorious Prude:
From Love both chiefly seek to feed their Pride,   195
Those to affect it strive, and these to hide.
Each gay Coquette would be admir'd alone
By all, each Prude be thought to value none.
Flaretta so weak Vanities enthrall,
She'd leave her eager Bridegroom for a Ball.   200
Chloe, the darling Trifle of the Town,
Had ne'er been won but by her Wedding Gown;
While in her fond *Myrtillo's* Arms caress'd,
She doats on that, and wishes to be dress'd.
Like some poor Bird, just pent within the Cage,   205
Whose rambling Heart in vain you would engage,
Cold to your Fondness, it laments its Chain,
And wanton longs to range the Fields again.
But Prudes, whose Thoughts superior Themes employ,
Scorn the dull Transports of a carnal Joy: 210

[1] Cf. Horace, *Epist.* I. x. 24: 'Naturam expellas furca, tamen usque recurret.' See Defoe, *Jure Divino*:

> Art may by mighty Dams keep out the Tide . . .
> But when *the injur'd Stream's* retain'd *too long*,
> And *Nature calls it* to resent the Wrong;
> It breaks th' Illegal Opposition down,
> And *Claims by Force* the Channel for its own.

(1706; Book IV, p. 12.)

[2] Cf. Shakespeare, *Othello*, I. iii. 293–4.

[3] The conventional image; cf. Otway, *Venice Preserv'd*, Act IV: '. . . there's a lurking Serpent / Ready to leap, and sting thee to thy Heart' (*Works*, 1768, iii. 302); Milton *Samson Agonistes*, 997–8.

With screw'd-up Face, confess they suffer Raptures,
And marry only to obey the Scriptures.
But if her Constitution take the Part
Of honest Nature 'gainst the Wiles of Art;
If she gives loose to Love, she loves indeed;   215
Then endless Fears and Jealousies succeed.
If Fondness e'er abate, you're weary grown,
And doat on some lewd Creature of the Town.
If any Beauty to a Visit come;
Why can't these gadding[1] Wretches stay at Home?   220
They think each Compliment conveys a Flame,
You cannot both be civil to the same.
Of all the Plagues with which a Husband's curst,
A jealous Prude's, my Friend sure knows, the worst.
   Some sterner Foes to Marriage bold aver,   225
That in this Choice a Man must surely err:
Nor can I to this Lottery advise,
A thousand Blanks appearing to a Prize.[2]
Women by Nature form'd too prone to Ill,
By Education are made proner still,   230
To cheat, deceive, conceal each genuine Thought,
By Mothers, and by Mistresses are taught.[3]
The Face and Shape are first the Mother's Care;
The Dancing-Master next improves the Air.
To these Perfections add a Voice most sweet;   235
The skill'd Musician makes the Nymph compleat.

[1] Cf. Dryden, Prologue to *The Princess of Cleves*, 28: 'No sooner out of sight, but they are gadding' (*Works*, III. i. 216); and cf. Steele's prosing of Milton's 'that strange Desire of wand'ring' (*Paradise Lost*, ix. 1135–6): 'when that strange Desire of Gadding possessed you' (*Tatler*, 217).

[2] Cf. Burton, *Anat. Melancholy*, iii. 2. 5. 3: ''tis twenty to one thou wilt not marry to thy contentment: but as in a lottery forty blanks were drawn commonly for one prize, out of a multitude you shall hardly choose a good one' (ed. Shilleto, iii. 254); Cowley, 'Against Hope', st. 3: 'Hope, Fortunes cheating *Lottery*!/Where for one *prize* an hundred *blanks* there be' (*The Mistress*, p. 42; in *Works*, 1668); Eustace Budgell, *Memoirs of . . . the Late Earl of Orrery* (1732), citing Robert Boyle on Love and Marriage: 'a Lottery, *in which there are many* Blanks *to one* Prize' (p. 138).

[3] See the *Champion*, 4 September 1740; *Tom Jones*, XIV. i; Otway, *The Atheist*, iii:
       Their Sex is one gross Cheat; their only Study
       How to deceive, betray, and ruin Man:
       They have it by Tradition from their Mothers,
       Which they improve each Day, and grow more exquisite.
(*The Works*, 1768, ii. 323.) Cf. Juvenal, *Sat.* vi. 231–41.

Thus with a Person well equipp'd, her Mind ⎫
Left, as when first created, rude and blind, ⎬
She's sent to make her Conquests on Mankind. ⎭
But first inform'd the studied Glance to aim,   240
Where Riches shew the profitable Game:
How with unequal Smiles the Jest to take,
When Princes, Lords, or Squires, or Captains speak;
These Lovers careful shun, and those create;
And Merit only see in an Estate.   245
But tho' too many of this Sort we find,
Some there are surely of a nobler Kind.
Nor can your Judgment want a Rule to chuse,
If by these Maxims guided you refuse.
His Wishes then give *Fidus* to declare,   250
And paint the chief Perfections of the Fair.
May she then prove, who shall thy Lot befall,
Beauteous to thee, agreeable to all.
Nor Wit, nor Learning proudly may she boast;
No low-bred Girl, nor gay fantastic Toast: 255
Her tender Soul, Good-nature must adorn,
And Vice and Meanness be alone her Scorn.
Fond of thy Person, may her Bosom glow
With Passions thou hast taught her first to know.
A warm Partaker of the genial Bed,   260
Thither by Fondness, not by Lewdness led.[1]
Superior Judgment may she own thy Lot;
Humbly advise, but contradict thee not.
Thine to all other Company prefer;
May all thy Troubles find Relief from her.   265
If Fortune gives thee such a Wife to meet,
Earth cannot make thy Blessing more complete.

[1] Cf. Martial, x. xlvii. 10: 'non tristis torus et tamen pudicus'.

TO *JOHN HAYES*, Esq;[1]

That *Varius* huffs, and fights it out to Day,
Who ran last Week so cowardly away,[2]
In *Codrus*[3] may surprize the little Skill,
Who nothing knows of Humankind, but Ill:
Confining all his Knowledge, and his Art,   5
To this, that each Man is corrupt at Heart.
But thou who Nature thro' each Maze canst trace,
Who in her Closet forcest her Embrace;
Canst with thy *Horace* see the human Elves[4]
Not differ more from others than themselves:[5]   10
Canst see one Man at several Times appear,
Now gay, now grave, now candid, now severe;[6]
Now save his Friends, now leave 'em in the Lurch;
Now rant in Brothels, and now cant in Church.[7]

---

[1] Probably John Hayes of Wolverhampton, Staffordshire, admitted to the Middle Temple 13 February 1723, called to the bar 8 May 1730 (*Register of Admissions to the . . . Middle Temple*, ed. H. A. C. Sturgess, 1949, i. 292). Admitted to Corpus Christi, Cambridge, in 1723, matriculated in the Lent term (*Alum. Cantabrig.*, ed. John and J. A. Venn, Part I, ii. 339). The poem may possibly date after July 1742 (see p. 53 n. 3), but this is uncertain; the compliment to Garrick would fall after his debut at Goodman's Fields in October 1741.

[2] See Montaigne, *Essays*, II. i ('Of the Inconstancy of Our Actions'): 'The Man you saw yesterday so adventurous and brave, you must not think it strange to see him as great a Poltro[o]n the next . . .' (trans. Cotton, 3rd edn., 1700, ii. 8). Parson Adams makes a like point about Paris and Hector (*Joseph Andrews*, II. ix) and Fielding later uses the argument to excuse the flight of Adams (III. vi).

[3] Fielding may have Juvenal's poor poet, Codrus, in mind (*Sat.* iii. 203 ff.); cf. the *Champion*, 15 March 1740; and Pope, 'To the Author of a Poem, intitled, *Successio*' (Twickenham edn., vi. 15). Pope himself had been called 'Codrus' in an anonymous attack (by Elizabeth Thomas ?), *Codrus: or The Dunciad Dissected* (1728); and it is not impossible that he is Fielding's target.

[4] Cf. Prior, 'The Ladle', 9–10: 'And frankly leave us Human Elves, / To cut and shuffle for our selves' (*Lit. Works*, ed. Wright-Spears, i. 202).

[5] Horace, *Serm.* i. 3; cf. also *Epist.* I. i. 97–9. Seneca further moralizes Horace's portrait, with imagery from play-acting (*Epist. mor.* cxx). Cf. Montaigne, II. i: '. . . and there is as much difference betwixt us and our selves, as betwixt us and others' (trans. Cotton, 3rd edn., 1700, ii. 12); La Rochefoucauld, *Maxims*, cxxxv: 'A Man is some times as different from himself, as he is from others' (trans. 1706, p. 55); Pope, *Epistle to Cobham*, 19–20.

[6] For the anaphora of 'Now . . . Now . . .', cf. Pope, *Epistle to a Lady*, 63–5, and *Epistle to Augustus* (Hor. *Ep.* II. i), 155–60.

[7] Cf. Butler, *Hudibras*, I. iii. 763–4: 'And though th'art of a diff'rent Church, / I will not leave thee in the Lurch' (1761 edn., p. 99).

Yet farther with the Muse pursue the Theme,   15
And see how various Men at once will seem;[1]
How Passions blended on each other fix,
How Vice with Virtues, Faults with Graces mix;
How Passions opposite, as sour to sweet,
Shall in one Bosom at one Moment meet.   20
With various Luck for Victory contend,
And now shall carry, and now lose their End.
The rotten Beau, while smelt along the Room,
Divides your Nose 'twixt Stenches and Perfume:
So Vice and Virtue lay such equal Claim,   25
Your Judgment knows not when to praise or blame.
Had Nature Actions to one Source confin'd,
Ev'n blund'ring *Codrus* might have known Mankind.
But as the diff'ring Colours blended lie
When *Titian* variegates his clouded Sky;   30
Where White and Black, the Yellow and the Green,
Unite, and undistinguish'd form the Scene.[2]
So the Great Artist diff'ring Passions joins,
And Love with Hatred, Fear with Rage combines.[3]

Nor Nature this Confusion makes alone,   35
She gives us often Half, and Half's our own.

Men what they are not struggle to appear,
And Nature strives to shew them as they are;[4]
While Art, repugnant thus to Nature, fights,
The various Man appears in different Lights.   40

---

[1] Thus Montaigne, I. i: 'Man (in good earnest) is a Marvellous vain, fickle, and unstable Subject, and on whom it is very hard to form any certain or proportionate Judgment' (3rd edn., 1700, i. 6); La Rochefoucauld, *Maxims*, ccclxxviii (trans. 1706, p. 192).

[2] On the blending and union of colours in the Venetian school, see Dryden's translation of Dufresnoy, *De Arte Graphica* (2nd edn., 1716, pp. 47–55, 188–9); Thomson, *Liberty*, iv. 237 ff. Mrs. Clerimont, in Steele's *Tender Husband* (1705), III. i, says: 'The Ladies abroad us'd to call me *Madamoiselle Titian*, I was so famous for my Colouring' (*Dramatic Works*, 1723, p. 127). For the imagery of blending, cf. Pope, *Essay on Criticism*, 488–91, and the *Epistle to Mr. Jervas*; Prior, *Alma*, ii. 25–30. And for this use of 'undistinguished', cf. Pope's *Iliad*, xvi. 262.

[3] Cf. Pope, *Essay on Man*, ii. 111–12, 119–22 (Twickenham edn., III. i. 68–70).

[4] Cf. Congreve, 'To Sir R. Temple: Of Pleasing': 'Thus, Man, perverse, against plain Nature strives, / And to be artfully absurd, contrives' (*Works*, 5th edn., 1730, iii. 333); Montaigne, II. i: 'Vertue cannot be followed, but for her self, and if one sometimes borrow her Mask for some other occasion, she presently pulls it away again' (3rd edn., 1700, II. 11); Bacon, *Essays*, xxxviii: '*Nature* is often Hidden, sometimes Overcome, seldom Extinguished' (1701 edn., p. 105); La Rochefoucauld, *Maxims*, xii (trans. 1706, p. 6); *Spectator*, 352. Cf. above, *To a Friend*, 181–2.

The Sage or Heroe on the Stage may show
Behind the Scenes the Blockhead or the Beau.
For tho' with *Quin's*, or *Garrick's* matchless Art,
He acts; my Friend, he only acts a Part:
For *Quin* himself, in a few Moments more,   45
Is *Quin* again, who *Cato* was before.¹
Thus while the Courtier acts the Patriot's Part,²
This guides his Face and Tongue, and that his Heart.
Abroad the Patriot shines with artful Mien,
The naked Courtier glares behind the Scene.   50
What Wonder then to Morrow if he grow
A Courtier good, who is a Patriot now.³

A DESCRIPTION OF
U—n G—, (alias *New Hog's Norton*) in *Com. Hants.*⁴

Written to a young Lady in the Year 1728

To *Rosalinda*, now from Town retir'd,⁵
Where noblest Hearts her brilliant Eyes have fir'd;

---

¹ On the stage metaphor, cf. *Tom Jones*, VII. i. James Quin (1693–1766) followed Booth in the role of Cato, and was London's leading actor until the arrival of Garrick in 1741. See below, p. 136, and the *Jacobite's Journal*, 6 February 1748; *Covent-Garden Journal*, 26.

² Cf. Thomson, *Autumn*, 21–2: '. . . and fondly tries / To mix the patriot's with the poet's flame' (ed. Robertson, p. 134).

³ If a particular 'Patriot', the obvious candidate is William Pulteney, who, after leading the opposition to Walpole through the 1730s, accepted (in July 1742) a peerage as Earl of Bath, after Walpole's fall. See *Jonathan Wild*, II. xii; and cf. Pope, '1740. A Poem', 9–10 (Twickenham edn., iv. 332). Charles Hanbury Williams tirelessly sprayed squibs at Pulteney, among them:

> Each hour a different face he wears,
> Now in a fury, now in tears,
>   Now laughing, now in sorrow;
> Now he'll command, and now obey,
> Bellows for liberty to-day,
>   And roars for pow'r to morrow.

(*Works*, 1822, i. 138.)

⁴ Upton Grey is a village in northeast Hampshire, on the northern edge of the Hampshire Downs. A document of 1725 describes it as Fielding's usual abode at that date (see J. Paul de Castro, 'Fielding and Lyme Regis', *TLS*, 4 June 1931, p. 447). 'Hog's Norton' is said to be derived from a village in Oxfordshire, Hock Norton, once proverbial for

[*For footnote 4 cont. and 5 see overleaf*

54   *Miscellanies*

Whom Nightingales in fav'rite Bow'rs delight,
Where sweetest Flow'rs perfume the fragrant Night;
Where Music's Charms enchant the fleeting Hours,   5
And Wit transports with all *Thalia's* Pow'rs;
Alexis sends: Whom his hard Fates remove
From the dear Scenes of Poetry and Love,
To barren Climates, less frequented Plains,
Unpolish'd Nymphs, and more unpolish'd Swains.   10
In such a Place how can *Alexis* sing?
An Air ne'er beaten by the Muse's Wing!
In such a Place what Subject can appear?
What not unworthy *Rosalinda's* Ear?
Yet if a Charm in Novelty there be,   15
Sure it will plead to *Rosalind* for me;
Whom Courts or Cities nought unknown can shew,
Still *U— G—* presents a Prospect new.
    As the dawb'd Scene, that on the Stage is shewn,
Where this Side Canvas is, and that a Town;[1]   20
Or as that Lace which *Paxton* Half Lace calls,[2]
That decks some Beau Apprentice out for Balls;
Such our Half House erects its mimick Head,
This Side an House presents, and that a Shed.
Nor doth the inward Furniture excel,   25
Nor yields it to the Beauty of the Shell:[3]
Here *Roman* Triumphs plac'd with aukward Art,
A Cart its Horses draws, an Elephant the Cart.
On the House-Side a Garden may be seen,

boorishness. Cf. Swift, *Polite Conversation*: 'I believe he was bred at *Hogsnorton,* where the Pigs play upon the Organs' (*Prose Works,* ed. Davis, iv. 190); Goldsmith, *Life of Richard Nash* (1762), p. 38: 'As *Hogs-Norton* 'squires in boots'; Fielding, *Author's Farce,* III. i.

5 Fielding combines the 'dulcius urbe quid est?' theme of Tibullus (IV. viii) and Martial's lugubrious complaint on the tiny 'rus sub urbe' given him by Lupus (XI. xviii), in a burlesque Ovidian epistle. He may have known the *Hoglandiae Descriptio* (1710) of John Richards. But he seems, in his opening stanza, to have played with the first sixteen lines of Addison's *Letter from Italy,* beginning, 'While you, my Lord, the rural shades admire, / And from *Britannia's* publick posts retire . . .' (*Works,* 1721, i. 43).

1 Cf. the image in the *Champion,* 10 May 1740.

2 A laceman associated with the theatres. Cf. the £100 paid to 'Mr. Paxton Laceman' in the Lincoln's-Inn Fields accounts for 1724–5 (*The London Stage 1660–1800: Part 2: 1700–1729,* ed. Emmett L. Avery, II. lxvi; cf. also II. lxviii).

3 Here, a dome-shaped roof. Cf. the description of an orangery roof in *Tatler,* 179: 'The Shell, you see, is both agreeable and convenient. . . .' In Fielding's poem, the roof has, of course, been decorated with the painting of a Roman triumphal procession.

Which Docks and Nettles keep for ever green.[1]   30
Weeds on the Ground, instead of Flow'rs, we see,
And Snails alone adorn the barren Tree.
Happy for us, had *Eve's* this Garden been;
She'd found no Fruit, and therefore known no Sin.[2]
Nor meaner Ornament the Shed-Side decks,   35
With Hay-Stacks, Faggot Piles, and Bottle-Ricks;[3]
The Horses Stalls, the Coach a Barn contains;
For purling Streams, we've Puddles fill'd with Rains.
What can our Orchard without Trees surpass?
What, but our dusty Meadow without Grass?[4]   40
I've thought (so strong with me Burlesque prevails,)
This Place design'd to ridicule *Versailles*;[5]
Or meant, like that, Art's utmost Pow'r to shew,
That tells how high it reaches, this how low.
Our Conversation does our Palace fit,   45
We've ev'ry Thing but Humour, except Wit.
  O then, when tir'd with laughing at his Strains,
Give one dear Sigh to poor *Alexis'* Pains;
Whose Heart this Scene wou'd certainly subdue,
But for the Thoughts of happier Days, and You;   50
With whom one happy Hour makes large Amends
For ev'ry Care his other Hours attends.

[1] Cf. Dryden's Virgil, *Aeneid*, i. 233–4: 'Betwixt two rows of Rocks, a Sylvan Scene / Appears above, and Groves for ever green' (*Works of Virgil*, 1697, p. 208).

[2] Cf. Dryden, *Eleanora*, 172–3, on a second Eve: 'Had she been first, still Paradise had bin, / And Death had found no entrance by her sin' (*Works*, 1701, III. i. 181).

[3] 'Bottle-Ricks' is a compound not recorded by the *OED*; presumably it refers to bundles (bottles) of hay made up into stacks.

[4] Addison's version of Virgil's *Fourth Georgic* provides a sample of the pastoral setting burlesqued by Fielding:

> Let purling streams, and fountains edg'd with moss,
> And shallow rills run trickling through the grass;
> Let branching Olives o'er the fountain grow,
> Or Palms shoot up, and shade the streams below . . .

(*Works*, 1721, i. 18.)

[5] Cf. Prior, *Down Hall*, 160–1: 'I wish you cou'd tell what a Duce your head ails; / I show'd you DOWN-HALL; did you look for VERSAILLES?' (*Lit. Works*, ed. Wright-Spears, i. 557).

TO THE

RIGHT HONOURABLE

Sir *ROBERT WALPOLE*,

(Now Earl of *ORFORD*)[1]

Written in the YEAR 1730.[2]

Sir,
    While at the Helm of State you ride,
Our Nation's Envy, and its Pride;
While foreign Courts with Wonder gaze,
And curse those Councils which they praise;[3]
Would you not wonder, Sir, to view   5
Your Bard a greater Man than you?
Which that he is, you cannot doubt,
When you have read the Sequel out.
    You know, great Sir, that antient Fellows,
Philosophers, and such Folks, tell us,   10
No great Analogy between
Greatness and Happiness is seen.[4]
If then, as it might follow strait,
Wretched to be, is to be great.
Forbid it, Gods, that you should try   15
What 'tis to be so great as I.[5]

---

[1] Sir Robert Walpole was created Earl of Orford by letters patent dated 6 February 1742. Though Fielding indulged in some light jests upon Walpole in *Tom Thumb* (1730) and the *Grub-Street Opera* (1731), and other early plays, he repeated the overtures for patronage in this and the following poem more seriously in the dedication to *The Modern Husband* (1732).

[2] A shorter version of this poem was published in the *Gentleman's Magazine*, December 1738, p. 653 (See Appendix B); and a variant of that version appeared many years later in the 1758 edition of Dodsley's *Collection* (v. 117–18).

[3] See Horace, *Epist.* II. i. 1–4.

[4] e.g., Seneca, *Epist. mor.* xliv. 7 and xciv. 73. Cf. Bacon, *Essays*, xi: 'Certainly Great Persons had need to borrow other mens Opinions, to think themselves happy' (ed. 1701, p. 26); Otway, *Alcibiades*, IV. i, and *Don Carlos*, I. i (*Works*, 1768, i. 49 and 112); Prior, *Solomon*, ii. 804–5 (*Lit. Works*, ed. Wright-Spears, i. 355); *Spectator*, 312; Pope, *Essay on Man*, IV. 217 ff.

[5] For the 'heroick' style, cf. Cowley: 'Forbid it *God*, that where *thy* right is try'd, / The strength of *man* should find just cause for *pride*!' (*Davideis*, iii, p. 94; in *The Works* 1668).

The Family that dines the latest,
Is in our Street esteem'd the greatest;[1]
But latest Hours must surely fall
Before him who ne'er dines at all.[2]   20
Your Taste in Architect, you know,
Hath been admir'd by Friend and Foe;[3]
But can your earthly Domes compare
To all my Castles—in the Air?
We're often taught it doth behove us   25
To think those greater who're above us.
Another Instance of my Glory,
Who live above you twice two Story,
And from my Garret can look down[4]
On the whole Street of *Arlington*.[5]   30
Greatness by Poets still is painted
With many Followers acquainted;
This too doth in my Favour speak,
Your Levée is but twice a Week;
From mine I can exclude but one Day,   35
My Door is quiet on a *Sunday*.[6]

---

[1] Steele (as Bickerstaff) said in 1710: 'In my own Memory the Dinner has crept by Degrees from Twelve a Clock to Three, and where it will fix no Body knows'; and the supper, he says, has had 'to make his Retreat into the Hours of Midnight' (*Tatler*, 263).

[2] Cf. Pope's Horace, *Epist*. I. vi. 37: 'Plead much, read more, dine late, or not at all' (Twickenham edn., iv. 239); Prior, 'To Fleetwood Shephard', 40: 'Writes best, who never thinks at all' (*Lit. Works*, ed. Wright-Spears, i. 86).

[3] Walpole's handsome estate of Houghton in Norfolk normally brought eulogies from friends (cf. J. H. Plumb, *Sir Robert Walpole*, ii. 82) and diatribes from foes. Cf. Fielding's later comment upon Houghton as the Palace of Mammon in *The Vernoniad* (1741).

[4] See John E. Wells, 'Fielding's First Poem to Walpole and His Garret in 1730', *MLN*, xxix (1914), 29–30. Wells took the garret allusion seriously and decided that it must be located in Piccadilly; but Fielding was more likely parodying the *cenaculum* of Martial (I. cviii) or Juvenal (*Sat*. vii. 28), and playing out the proper role of Distressed Poet.

[5] Where the present Lord *Orford* then lived. [Fielding's note.] Walpole lived in Arlington Street from 1716 until the autumn of 1732. He returned to the street in midsummer of 1742, though to a different house. (See the *Yale Edition of the Correspondence of Horace Walpole*, xvii. 478; xiii–xiv. 1 and n. 1, 56 n. 1).

[6] i.e., when debtors were free from arrest, by the act of 29 Charles II, c. 7 (cf. *Amelia*, IV. vi). For the conceit of a levee of duns, cf. Swift, 'The Run upon the Bankers':

> Because 'tis Lordly not to pay,
> Quakers and Aldermen, in State,
> Like Peers, have Levees ev'ry Day
> Of Duns, attending at their Gate.

(*Poems*, ed. Sir Harold Williams, i. 239.)

Nor in the Manner of Attendance
Doth your great Bard claim less Ascendance.
Familiar you to Admiration,
May be approach'd by all the Nation: 40
While I, like the Mogul in *Indo*,
Am never seen but at my Window.[1]
If with my Greatness you're offended,
The Fault is easily amended.
For I'll come down, with wond'rous Ease,   45
Into whatever Place you please.
    I'm not ambitious; little Matters
Will serve us great, but humble Creatures.
Suppose a Secretary o' this Isle,
Just to be doing with a While;   50
Admiral, Gen'ral, Judge or Bishop;
Or I can foreign Treaties dish up.
If the good Genius of the Nation
Should call me to Negotiation;
Tuscan and *French* are in my Head;   55
Latin I write, and *Greek* I—read.
    If you should ask, what pleases best?
To get the most, and do the least,
What fittest for?—you know, I'm sure,
I'm fittest for a—*Sinecure*.[2]   60

---

[1] Cf. Pope, *Elegy to the Memory of an Unfortunate Lady*, 21-2: 'Like Eastern Kings a lazy state they keep, / And close confin'd to their own palace sleep' (Twickenham edn., II. 341-2) and *Epistle to Arbuthnot*, 220. See François Bernier, *History of the Late Revolution of the Empire of the Great Mogol*: 'In the midst of the Wall, which separateth this Hall [the great hall at Delhi] from the *Seraglio*, there is an opening, or a kinde of great window high and large, and so high that a man cannot reach to it from below with his hand: There it is where the King appears seated upon his Throne . . .' (trans. H. Oldenburg, 1671-2, iii. 39).

[2] It is just possible that Fielding was here glancing at Joseph Mitchell, who climaxed a notable series of begging epistles in the 1720s with 'The Sine-Cure: A Poetical Petition to the Right Honourable Robert Walpole, Esq; For the Government of Duck-Island in St. James's Park', in the course of which poem he also mentioned the possibility of a Secretary's place (repr. in his *Poems on Several Occasions*, 1729, vol. ii). Mitchell became known as 'Sir Robert Walpole's Poet'.

To the same. *Anno* 1731.

Great Sir, as on each Levée Day
I still attend you[1]—still you say
I'm busy now, To-morrow come;
To-morrow, Sir, you're not at Home.
So says your Porter, and dare I   5
Give such a Man as him the Lie?[2]
   In Imitation, Sir, of you,
I keep a mighty Levée too;
Where my Attendants, to their Sorrow,
Are bid to come again To-morrow.   10
To-morrow they return, no doubt,
And then like you, Sir, I'm gone out.
So says my Maid—but they, less civil,
Give Maid and Master to the Devil;
And then with Menaces depart,   15
Which could you hear would pierce your Heart.
   Good Sir, or make my Levée fly me,
Or lend your Porter to deny me.

Written *Extempore*, on a Half-penny, which a young Lady gave a Beggar, and the Author redeem'd for Half a Crown.[3]

Dear little, pretty, fav'rite Ore,[4]
That once encreas'd *Gloriana's* Store;
That lay within her Bosom blest,
Gods might have envy'd thee thy Nest.[5]

[1] The anonymous *Historical View of the . . . Political Writers in Great Britain* (1740) presents an anecdote of Fielding at a Walpole levee (p. 50).

[2] Cf. Martial's like complaint to one of his patrons: 'Illud adhuc gravius quod te post mille labores, / Paule, negat lasso ianitor esse domi' (v. xxii).

[3] A shorter version of this poem, in sixteen lines, had appeared in the *Champion*, 27 May 1740. See Appendix C. If one supposes that only the 'Celia' poems were addressed to Charlotte Cradock, this effusion would presumably be earlier than that relationship *c.* 1730; but the matter is uncertain.

[4] Cf. Prior's imitation of Hadrian's 'animula, vagula, blandula': 'Poor little, pretty, flutt'ring Thing . . .' (*Lit. Works*, ed. Wright-Spears, i. 196).

[5] Cf. Sophia's pet bird which seemed 'almost sensible of its own Happiness', as it nestled in her bosom (*Tom Jones*, IV. iii); Waller, 'To a Fair Lady, playing with a Snake':

I've read, imperial *Jove* of old,   5
For Love transform'd himself to Gold:[1]
And why, for a more lovely Lass,
May he not now have lurk'd in Brass?
Oh! rather than from her he'd part,
He'd shut that charitable Heart,   10
That Heart whose Goodness nothing less
Than his vast Pow'r, cou'd dispossess.

From *Gloriana's* gentle Touch
Thy mighty Value now is such,
That thou to me art worth alone   15
More than his Medals are to *Sloan*.[2]

Not for the Silver and the Gold
Which *Corinth* lost shouldst thou be sold:[3]
Not for the envy'd mighty Mass
Which Misers wish, or *M—h* has:[4]   20
Not for what *India* sends to *Spain*,
Nor all the Riches of the Main.

While I possess thy little Store,
Let no Man call, or think me poor:
Thee, while alive, my Breast shall have,[5]   25
My Hand shall grasp thee in the Grave;
Nor shalt thou be to *Peter* giv'n,
Tho' he should keep me out of Heav'n.[6]

'Contented in a Nest of Snow / He lies, as he his Bliss did know' (*Poems, &c.*, 9th edn., 1712, p. 118); Carew, 'On a Damask-Rose Sticking upon a Ladies Breast' (*Poems, Songs, and Sonnets*, 4th edn., 1670, pp. 161–2). See the like conceit in the Lilliputian poem below, p. 73.

[1] Cf. Cowley: 'What should those *Poets* mean of old / That made their *God* to woo in *Gold*?' ('The Given Love', st. vi, in *The Mistress*, p. 7; *The Works*, 1668). On Danae, see Apollodorus, *Bibliotheca*, II. iv. 1.

[2] Cf. Ovid on the lucky gift-ring that will be handled by his mistress: 'Felix, a domina tractaberis, anule, nostra' (*Amores*, II. xv. 7). Sir Hans Sloane (1660–1753), the famous collector; cf. Pope: 'And Books for Mead, and Butterflies for Sloane' (*Epistle to Burlington*, 10; Twickenham edn., III. ii. 132).

[3] On the sack of Corinth by Mummius, see Strabo, *Geographica*, VIII. vi. 20.

[4] Marlborough. Presumably the old Duchess. See above, p. 31.

[5] Cf. Joseph Andrews, clutching Fanny's gold-piece to his bosom (I. xiv); *Spectator*, 30; and Burton, *Anat. Melancholy*, iii. 2. 3. 1: 'If he get any remnant of hers, a busk-point, a feather of her fan, a shoe-tie, a lace, a ring, a bracelet of hair . . . he wears it for a favour . . . next his heart' (ed. Shilleto, iii. 192 et seq.).

[6] In allusion to the Custom of *Peter-Pence*, used by the *Roman Catholicks*. [Fielding's note.]

THE BEGGAR

A SONG

I.

While cruel to your wishing Slave,
You still refuse the Boon I crave,
Confess, what Joy that precious Pearl
Conveys to thee, my lovely Girl?

II.

Dost thou not act the Miser's Part,   5
Who with an aking, lab'ring Heart,
Counts the dull joyless shining Store,
Which he refuses to the Poor?

III.

Confess then, my too lovely Maid,
Nor blush to see thy Thoughts betray'd;   10
What, parted with, gives Heav'n to me;
Kept, is but Pain and Grief to thee.

IV.

Be charitable then, and dare
Bestow the Treasure you can spare;
And trust the Joys which you afford   15
Will to yourself be sure restor'd.[1]

[1] Cf. Carew, 'To A. L. Perswasions to Love':

> But 'twere a madness not to grant
> That which affords (if you consent)
> To you the giver, more content
> Than me the begger; Oh then be
> Kind to your self, if not to me . . .

(*Poems, Songs, and Sonnets*, 4th edn., 1670, p. 3.) The conceit is ultimately, perhaps, from Ovid, *Amores*, I. x. 33–6. Cf. the first sestiad of Marlowe's *Hero and Leander*, 234–6; Shakespeare, Sonnet IV and *Venus and Adonis*, 767–78.

AN EPIGRAM

When *Jove* with fair *Alcmena* lay,
He kept the Sun a-bed all Day;[1]
That he might taste her wond'rous Charms,
Two Nights together in her Arms.
Were I of *Celia's* Charms possest,   5
Melting on that delicious Breast,
And could, like *JOVE*, thy Beams restrain,
Sun, thou should'st never rise again;
Unsated with the luscious Bliss,
I'd taste one dear eternal Kiss.   10

THE QUESTION

In *Celia's* Arms while bless'd I lay,
My Soul in Bliss dissolv'd away;[2]
Tell me, the Charmer cry'd, how well
You love your *Celia*; *Strephon*, tell.
Kissing her glowing burning Cheek,   5
I'll tell, I cry'd—but could not speak.
At length my Voice return'd, and she
Again began to question me.
I pull'd her to my Breast again,
And try'd to answer, but in vain: 10

[1] The mythographers do not agree on the precise length of Jove's heroic night; but see Apollodorus, *Bibliotheca*, II. iv. 8. Cf. Prior, 'The Wedding Night', 1–2: 'When *Jove* lay blest in his *Alcmaena*'s Charms, / Three Nights in one he prest her in his Arms . . .' (*Lit. Works*, ed. Wright-Spears, i. 213); Doggrel's verses in Gay's *The Wife of Bath*, Act IV; the anonymous poem, 'The Enjoyment,' in *Fourth Part of Miscellany Poems*, 5th edn., 1727, pp. 57–9.

[2] Cf. the song on Strephon and Chloe in *Joseph Andrews*, II. xii; Dryden's song from *Marriage à la Mode*: 'Whil'st Alexis lay prest / In her Arms he lov'd best' etc. (*Works*, 1701, i. 500); Pope, *Sapho to Phaon*, 61–2: 'Till all dissolving in the Trance we lay, / And in tumultuous Raptures dy'd away' (Twickenham edn., i. 396); Otway, *Don Carlos*, II. i; and the poem attributed to Sir Charles Sedley, 'On Fruition':

> None, but a Muse in Love, can tell
> The sweet tumultuous joys I feel,
> When on *Caelia*'s Breast I lye,
> When I tremble, faint, and dye . . .

(*The Poetical Works*, 1707, p. 139.)

Short falt'ring Accents from me broke,
And my Voice fail'd before I spoke.
The Charmer pitying my Distress,
Gave me the tenderest Caress,
And sighing cry'd, You need not tell;   15
Oh! *Strephon*, Oh! I feel how well.

J—N W—TS at a PLAY.[1]

While Hisses, Groans, and Cat-calls thro' the Pit,
Deplore the hapless Poet's want of Wit:
J—n W—ts, from Silence bursting in a Rage,
Cry'd, *Men are mad who write in such an Age.*
Not so, reply'd his Friend, a sneering Blade,   5
The Poet's only dull, the Printer's mad.

TO CELIA

I Hate the Town, and all its Ways;[2]
Ridotto's, Opera's, and Plays;
The Ball, the Ring,[3] the Mall, the Court;
Wherever the Beau-Monde resort;
Where Beauties lie in Ambush for Folks,   5
Earl *Straffords*, and the Duke of *Norfolks*;[4]
All Coffee-Houses, and their Praters;
All Courts of Justice, and Debaters;
All Taverns, and the Sots within 'em;

[1] John Watts (d. 1763), one of the best-known printers of the day, printed many of Fielding's plays; there are allusions to him in *Pasquin* and *Eurydice Hiss'd*.

[2] Cf. Alcyon's catalogue of 'I hates' in Spenser's *Daphnaida*, sect. v, concluding, 'So all the world, and all in it I hate' (428); though in a different metre and different context, it belongs to the same tradition of *vituperatio*. See also the opening of Pope's *Second Satire of Dr. John Donne*: 'Yes; thank my stars! as early as I knew / This Town, I had the sense to hate it too' (Twickenham edn., iv. 133). An ultimate source would be Juvenal's *Third Satire*, also imitated by Samuel Johnson in 1738. Fielding's poem can be roughly dated, by allusions, as written between January 1730 (p. 64 n. 1) and January 1731 (p. 64 n. 6).

[3] The Ring, fashionable riding circle in Hyde Park, was partly destroyed when the Serpentine was formed, *c.* 1730–3.

[4] Presumably chosen because the families of both had been under suspicion as Jacobites. Cf. also his early poem, *The Masquerade*, 110.

All Bubbles, and the Rogues that skin 'em.   10
I hate all Critics; may they burn all,
From *Bentley* to the *Grub-street Journal*.[1]
All Bards, as *Dennis* hates a Pun:[2]
Those who have Wit, and who have none.
All Nobles, of whatever Station;   15
And all the Parsons in the Nation.
All Quacks and Doctors read in Physick,
Who kill or cure a Man that is sick.
All Authors that were ever heard on,
From *Bavius* up to *Tommy Gordon*;[3]   20
Tradesmen with Cringes ever stealing,
And Merchants, whatsoe'er they deal in.
I hate the Blades professing Slaughter,
More than the Devil Holy Water.[4]
I hate all Scholars, Beaus, and Squires;   25
Pimps, Puppies, Parasites, and Liars.[5]
All Courtiers, with their Looks so smooth;
And Players, from *Boheme* to *Booth*.[6]
I hate the World, cram'd all together,
From Beggars, up the Lord knows whither.   30
    Ask you then, *Celia*, if there be
The Thing I love? My Charmer, Thee.
Thee more than Light, than Life adore,

[1] Richard Bentley (1662–1742), the great classical scholar, burlesqued by Fielding in the *Tragedy of Tragedies* and *The Vernoniad*. The *Grub-Street Journal*, with which Fielding carried on a running battle in the 1730s (see James T. Hillhouse, *The Grub-Street Journal*, pp. 173–85 *et passim*), ran from January 1730 to December 1737.

[2] John Dennis (1657–1734) is supposed to have remarked that 'He that would Pun, would pick a Pocket' (see Pope, *Variorum Dunciad*, i. 61 and n.; Twickenham edn., v. 67). Cf. *The Tragedy of Tragedies*, III. ii, note *d*.

[3] Bavius, the poetaster scorned by Virgil in the *Third Eclogue*; see also Pope's note to the *Variorum Dunciad*, iii. 16 (Twickenham edn., v. 151). Thomas Gordon (d. 1750), a journalist, pamphleteer, and translator (Tacitus and Sallust), who served Walpole from about 1727 on; cf. the *Dunciad* (1743), iv. 492 ff. (Twickenham edn., v. 390–3).

[4] Cf. Arbuthnot, *The History of John Bull* (1712), Part III, chap. ix: 'No question, as the Devil loves Holy-water!' (ed. H. Teerink, p. 199). The phrase was already spoken of in 1576 as an 'olde Proverbe' (*Oxford Dictionary of English Proverbs*, ed. W. G. Smith, 2nd edn., p. 141).

[5] Cf. Butler, *Hudibras*, I. ii. 1016: 'Pimps, Buffoons, Fidlers, Parasites' (1761 edn., p. 70).

[6] Anthony Boheme (d. January 1731), actor at Lincoln's Inn Fields; Barton Booth (1681–1733), the first actor of Cato, had, as one of the managers of Drury Lane, been concerned in the rejection of Fielding's *Don Quixote in England*, which may help to explain his inclusion here.

Thou dearest, sweetest Creature, more
Than wildest Raptures can express;   53
Than I can tell,—or thou canst guess.
Then tho' I bear a gentle Mind,
Let not my Hatred of Mankind
Wonder within my *Celia* move,
Since she possesses all my Love.   40

ON A LADY

Coquetting with a very silly Fellow

Corinna's Judgment do not less admire,
That she for *Oulus*[1] shews a gen'rous Fire;
Lucretia toying thus had been a Fool,
But wiser *Helen* might have us'd the Tool.[2]
Since *Oulus* for one Use alone is fit,   5
With Charity judge of *Corinna's* Wit.

On the Same

While Men shun *Oulus* as a Fool;
Dames prize him as a Beau;
What Judgment form we by this Rule?
Why this it seems to shew.
Those apprehend the Beau's a Fool,   5
These think the Fool's a Beau.[3]

---

[1] Of the various meanings attached to *Oulus*, Fielding probably intended 'pernicious'; cf. H. Junius, *Lexicon graeco-latinum* (1548): 'οὖλος. perniciosus'.

[2] Cf. Mrs. Fitzpatrick on the ladies who choose silly fellows for favourites (*Tom Jones*, XI. iv), and Fielding's *Masquerade*, 268–9: 'Some half a Year he's made that Tool, / The wise yclepe a Woman's Fool.' Cassandra, mistress of the foolish king Ptolemy in Dryden's *Cleomenes*, says: 'Fools we must have, or else we cannot sway; / For none but Fools will Woman-kind Obey . . .' (Act IV; *Works*, 1701, ii. 467).

[3] Cf. John Heywood's 'A Fool Taken for Wise':

> Wisdom and folly in thee, (as men scan),
> Is as it were a thing by itself sool:
> Among fools thou art taken a wise man;
> And, among wise men, thou art known a fool.

(*Proverbs, Epigrams, and Miscellanies of John Heywood*, ed. John S. Farmer, p. 148.) See also Prior's well-known epigram (*Lit. Works*, ed. Wright-Spears, i. 454), and Pope's 'Epigram from the French' (Twickenham edn., vi. 347).

EPITAPH

on *BUTLER's* MONUMENT.[1]

What tho' alive neglected and undone,
O let thy Spirit triumph in this Stone.
No greater Honour could Men pay thy Parts,
For when they give a Stone, they give their Hearts.

ANOTHER.

On a wicked Fellow, who was a great
BLUNDERER

Interr'd by Blunder in this sacred Place,
Lies *William's* wicked Heart, and smiling Face.
Full Forty Years on Earth he blunder'd on,
And now the L——d knows whither he is gone.
But if to Heav'n he stole, let no Man wonder,   5
For if to Hell he'd gone, he'd made no Blunder.[2]

---

[1] Eighteenth-century writers carefully nurtured the legend that Samuel Butler, who died in 1680, had expired in poverty and neglect. See Dryden, *Hind and the Panther*, iii. 1541–4; John Oldham, 'A Satyr [concerning Poetry]', in *Poems and Translations* (1683), pp. 173–4; *Athenian Sport* (1707), p. 149; Joseph Mitchell, *Poems on Several Occasions* (1729), i. 294; *The Honey-Suckle* (1734), p. 105; Samuel Wesley, *Poems on Several Occasions* (1736), p. 62; and other allusions by Fielding in *Eurydice Hiss'd*; the *Champion*, 27 November 1739; and *Tom Jones*, IV. viii. The monument to Butler in Westminster Abbey had been set up in 1721 by John Barber, the well-known London printer.

[2] Cf. Swift, 'A Quibbling Elegy on . . . Judge Boat': '*A* Boat *a Judge! yes, where's the Blunder?* | *A* wooden *Judge is no such Wonder*' (*Poems*, ed. Sir Harold Williams, i. 286). If Fielding was here emulating Pope's jest of writing epitaphs upon living persons, one might suggest Walpole's henchman, Sir William Yonge (d. 1755), as the recipient of this mock.

(67)

EPIGRAM
On one who invited many Gentlemen to a small Dinner.

Peter (says *Pope*) won't poison with his Meat;[1]
'Tis true, for *Peter* gives you nought to eat.[2]

A SAILOR'S SONG
Design'd for the S T A G E[3]

Come, let's aboard, my jolly Blades,
   That love a merry Life;
To lazy Souls leave home-bred Trades,
   To Husbands home-bred Strife;
Through *Europe* we will gayly roam,   5
And leave our Wives and Cares at Home.[4]
         With a Fa la, &c.

If any Tradesman broke should be,
   Or Gentleman distress'd,
Let him away with us to Sea,   10
   His Fate will be redress'd:
The glorious Thunder of great Guns,
Drowns all the horrid Noise of Duns.
         With a Fa la, &c.

[1] See Pope's Horace, *Sat.* II. i. 89–90: 'So drink with *Waters*, or with *Chartres* eat, / They'll never poison you, they'll only cheat' (Twickenham edn., iv. 13). On Peter Walter, see below, *Some Papers Proper to be Read before the Royal Society*. The epigram must post-date Pope's satire (February 1733).

[2] Cf. Swift (?) on Carthy and the news-boy: 'My Works, he said, cou'd ne'er afford him Meat, / And Teeth are useless, where there's nought to eat' (*Poems*, ed. Sir Harold Williams, ii. 670).

[3] Possibly intended for *The Sailor's Opera*, an anonymous ballad-opera performed with Fielding's *Historical Register* at the Little Theatre in the Haymarket, 3 May 1737, and several times thereafter (see *The London Stage 1660–1800: Part 3: 1729–1747*, ed. A. H. Scouten, ii. 666–70). For the general movement of this chanty, cf. the famous song by Charles Sackville, Earl of Dorset, 'To All You Ladies Now at Land'.

[4] Cf. Cowley's 'Ode' (*Verses on Several Occasions*, p. 8, in *The Works*, 1668): 'What dull men are those who tarry at home, / When abroad they might wantonly rome. . . .'

And while our Ships we proudly steer   15
  Through all the conquer'd Seas,
We'll shew the World that *Britons* bear
  Their Empire where they please:
Where'er our Sails are once unfurl'd,
Our King rules that Part of the World.¹   20
                              With a Fa la, &c.

The *Spaniard* with a solemn Grace
  Still marches slowly on,
We'd quickly make him mend his Pace,
  Desirous to be gone: 25
Or if we bend our Course to *France*,
We'll teach Monsieur more brisk to dance.
                              With a Fa la, &c.

At length, the World subdu'd, again
  Our Course we'll homeward bend;   30
In Women, and in brisk Champaign,
  Our Gains we'll freely spend:
How proud our Mistresses will be
To hug the Men that fought as we.
                              With a Fa la, &c.   35

ADVICE

TO THE

NYMPHS of *New S—m.*²

Written in the Year 1730.

Cease, vainest Nymphs, with *Celia* to contend,
And let your Envy and your Folly end.

¹ See Pope, *Windsor Forest*, 385 ff. (Twickenham edn., i. 189–93); Prior, 'Presented to the King . . . 1696', 55–8 (*Lit. Works*, ed. Wright-Spears, i. 156); *Solomon*, i. 442–4 (ibid., i. 323):

> And [Britannia] rules an Empire by no Ocean bound;
> Knows her Ships anchor'd, and her Sails unfurl'd
> In other INDIES, and a second World.

² New Sarum: Salisbury, where Fielding lived for a time in the 1720s with his maternal grandmother, Lady Gould (d. 1733), and thereafter frequently spent his summers. It was, after Shaftesbury, the nearest town of size to his legal residence (in 1730) of East Stour, Dorset.

With her Almighty Charms when yours compare,
When your blind Lovers think you half so fair,
Each *Sarum* Ditch, like *Helicon* shall flow,   5
And *Harnam Hill*, like high *Parnassus*, glow;[1]
The humble Dazie trod beneath our Feet,
Shall be like Lillies fair, like Violets sweet;
Winter's black Nights outshine the Summer's Noon,
And Farthing Candles shall eclipse the Moon: 10
T—b—ld shall blaze with Wit, sweet *Pope* be dull,[2]
And *German* Princes vie with the *Mogul*.[3]
Cease then, advis'd, O cease th' unequal War,
'Tis too much Praise to be o'ercome by her.
With the sweet Nine so the *Pierians* strove;   15
So poor *Arachne* with *Minerva* wove:
'Till of their Pride just Punishment they share;
Those fly and chatter, and this hangs in Air.[4]
Unhappy Nymphs! O may the Powers above,
Those Powers that form'd this second Queen of Love,   20
Lay all their wrathful Thunderbolts aside,
And rather pity than avenge your Pride;
Forbid it Heaven, you should bemoan too late
The sad *Pierian's* or *Arachne's* Fate;
That hid in Leaves, and perch'd upon a Bough,   25
You should o'erlook those Walks you walk in now;
The gen'rous Maid's Compassion, others Joke,

[1] Harnham Hill is south-west of Salisbury. The species of hyperbole employed here is called *adynaton* (see Ernest Dutoit, *Le Thème de l'adynaton dans la poésie antique*, 1936). It is a common feature of the 'Give place, you ladies' theme, as well as of 'protestations' (cf. Propertius, I. xv. 29 ff.; Herrick, 'His Protestation to Perilla'; Carew, 'The Protestation'). Cf. Garth, *The Dispensary*, Canto II: 'Or Highgate-Hill with lofty *Pindus* vie: . . . / And Hare-Court Pump with *Aganippe*'s Streams' (6th edn., 1706, p. 27); and see Fielding's *Covent-Garden Tragedy*, II. i, ii.

[2] The compliment to Pope at the expense of his first Dunce recalls Virgil's comparison of Orpheus and Tityrus (*Eighth Eclogue*, 52–6). Lewis Theobald (1688–1744) was a better scholar than either Pope or Fielding gave him credit for; though Fielding subscribed to Theobald's edition of Shakespeare in 1734, he mocked its pedantry in the *Journey from This World to the Next* (I. viii). In the notes to his and Young's translation of Aristophanes' *Plutus* (1742) Fielding was very severe on 'Mr. Theobald, who being a Critic of great Nicety himself, and great Diligence in correcting Mistakes in others, cannot be offended at the same Treatment' (p. xiii).

[3] Fielding's normal bias (at least until the Pelham administration) was anti-Hanoverian. See above, p. xiv.

[4] On the daughters of Pierus, see Ovid, *Metam.* v. 294 ff.; on Arachne, vi. 1–145.

Should chatter Scandal which you once have spoke;
Or else in Cobwebs hanging from the Wall,
Should be condemn'd to overlook the Ball:[1]   30
To see, as now, victorious *Celia* reign,
Admir'd, ador'd by each politer Swain.
O shun a Fate like this, be timely wise,[2]
And if your Glass be false, if blind your Eyes,
Believe and own what all Mankind aver,   35
And pay with them the Tribute due to her.

TO CELIA

Occasioned by her apprehending her House would be broke
open, and having an old Fellow to guard it, who sat up all
Night, with a Gun without any Ammunition.

CUPID call'd to Account.[3]

Last Night, as my unwilling Mind
To Rest, dear *Celia*, I resign'd;
For how should I Repose enjoy,
While any Fears your Breast annoy?
Forbid it, Heav'n, that I should be   5
From any of your Troubles free.[4]
Oh! would kind Fate attend my Pray'r,
Greedy, I'd give you not a Share.
Last Night then, in a wretched taking,
My Spirits toss'd 'twixt Sleep and waking,[5]   10

---

[1] Cf. Pope, *Rape of the Lock*, i. 54, and *Epistle to a Lady*, 241–2. See *Spectator*, 90, on the 'Platonick Notion' that the ruling passion survives after death.

[2] Cf. Prior, 'Satyr on the Poets', 29: 'Repent fond Mortal, and be timely wise' (*Lit. Works*, ed. Wright-Spears, i. 29); Gay, 'Story of Arachne', 41.

[3] This Anacreontic is very much in the vein of Prior (e.g. 'Love Disarm'd'; and see notes below). On the ultimate sources of the *amor* conceits, see M. B. Ogle, 'The Classical Origin and Tradition of Literary Conceits', *AJPhilol.* xxxiv (1913), 125–52, and Floyd A. Spencer, 'The Literary Lineage of Cupid in Greek Literature', *Classical Weekly*, xxv (1932), 121–7, 129–34, 139–44.

[4] Cf. Cowley, 'Love Undiscovered', st. 2: 'Forbid it Heaven my *Life* should be / Weigh'd with her least *Conveniency*' (*The Mistress*, p. 33; in *The Works*, 1668).

[5] Cf. Dryden, Epilogue to *Tyrannic Love*, 13–14: 'And 'faith you'll be in a sweet kind of taking, / When I surprise you between sleep and waking' (*Works*, 1701, i. 339); Prior 'Paulo Purganti and His Wife', 123–6.

I dreamt (ah! what so frequent Themes
As you and *Venus* of my Dreams!)
That she, bright Glory of the Sky,
Heard from below her Darling's Cry:
Saw her Cheeks pale, her Bosom heave,   15
And heard a distant Sound of Thieve.
Not so you look when at the Ball,
Envy'd you shine, outshining all.
Not so at Church, when Priest perplext,
Beholds you, and forgets the Text.   20
   The Goddess frighten'd, to her Throne
Summon'd the little God her Son,
And him in Passion thus bespoke;
'Where, with that cunning Urchin's Look,
Where from thy Colours hast thou stray'd?   25
Unguarded left my darling Maid?
Left my lov'd Citadel of Beauty,
With none but *Sancho* upon Duty!
Did I for this a num'rous Band
Of Loves send under thy Command![1]   30
Bid thee still have her in thy Sight,
And guard her Beauties Day and Night!
Were not th' *Hesperian* Gardens taken?
The hundred Eyes of *Argus* shaken?[2]
What Dangers will not Men despise,   35
T' obtain this much superior Prize?
And didst thou trust what *Jove* hath charm'd,
To a poor Centinel unarm'd?
A Gun indeed the Wretch had got,
But neither Powder, Ball, nor Shot.   40
Come tell me, Urchin, tell no Lies;
Where was you hid, in *Vince's* Eyes?
Did you fair *Bennet's* Breast importune?
(I know you dearly love a Fortune.)'[3]
Poor *Cupid* now began to whine;   45

---

[1] Cf. Belinda's sylphs in *The Rape of the Lock*.
[2] On the Garden of the Hesperides, see Apollodorus, *Bibliotheca*, II. v. 11; on Argus Panoptes, Ovid, *Metam.* i. 622 ff.
[3] The setting is presumably Salisbury, but these Wiltshire beauties remain unidentified. Bennett is a familiar Wiltshire name and several Bennetts have been mayors of Salisbury.

'Mamma, it was no Fault of mine.
I in a Dimple lay *perdue*,
That little Guard-Room chose by you.[1]
A hundred Loves (all arm'd) did grace
The Beauties of her Neck and Face;   50
Thence, by a Sigh I dispossest,
Was blown to *Harry Fielding's* Breast;[2]
Where I was forc'd all Night to stay,
Because I could not find my Way.
But did Mamma know there what Work   55
I've made, how acted like a Turk;
What Pains, what Torment he endures,
Which no Physician ever cures,[3]
She would forgive.' The Goddess smil'd,
And gently chuck'd her wicked Child,   60
Bid him go back, and take more Care,
And give her Service to the Fair.

To the SAME

On her wishing to have a LILLIPUTIAN, to play with

Is there a Man who would not be,
My *Celia*, what is priz'd by thee?[4]
A Monkey Beau, to please thy Sight,
Would wish to be a Monkey quite.

---

[1] Prior's Cupid also calls Venus 'Mamma' and he is called an 'urchin' (e.g. 'Cupid Mistaken', 'The Dove'). Cf. 'Her Right Name', 13–14: 'He [Cupid] in the Dimple of her Chin, / In private State by Friends is seen' (*Lit. Works*, ed. Wright-Spears, i. 444).

[2] The familiar 'et possessa ferus pectora versat Amor' (Ovid, *Amores*, I. ii. 8). And cf. Carew, 'A Prayer to the Wind':

> Goe thou gentle whispering Wind,
> Bear this sigh; and if thou find
> Where my cruel fair doth rest
> Cast it in her snowie brest . . .

(*Poems, Songs, and Sonnets*, 4th edn., 1670, p. 13.)

[3] 'Quod amor non est medicabilis herbis!' (Ovid, *Heroides*, v. 149). See below, p. 118.

[4] Cf. Burton, *Anat. Melancholy*, iii. 2. 3. 1, on the Lover: 'He wisheth himself a saddle for her to sit on, a posy for her to smell to . . . *Ovid* would be a Flee, a Gnat, a Ring, *Catullus* a Sparrow . . ., *Anacreon*, a glass, a gown, a chain, any thing' (ed. Shilleto, iii. 194).

Or (couldst thou be delighted so)   5
Each Man of Sense would be a Beau.
Courtiers would quit their faithless Skill,
To be thy faithful Dog *Quadrille*.
P—*lt*—*y*, who does for Freedom rage,
Would sing confin'd within thy Cage;   10
And *W*—*lp*–*le*, for a tender Pat,
Would leave his Place to be thy Cat.[1]
May I, to please my lovely Dame,
Be five Foot shorter than I am;
And, to be greater in her Eyes,   15
Be sunk to *Lilliputian* Size.
While on thy Hand I skipt the Dance,
How I'd despise the King of *France*!
That Hand! which can bestow a Store
Richer than the *Peruvian* Ore,   20
Richer than *India*, or the Sea,
(That Hand will give yourself away)
Upon your Lap to lay me down,
Or hide in Plaitings of your Gown.[2]
Or on your Shoulder sitting high,   25
What Monarch so enthron'd as I?
Now on the rosy Bud I'd rest,
Which borrows Sweetness from thy Breast.[3]
Then when my *Celia* walks abroad,
I'd be her Pocket's little Load: 30
Or sit astride, to frighten People,
Upon her Hat's new-fashion'd Steeple.[4]

---

[1] William Pulteney (1684–1764), later Earl of Bath; see above, p. 53. Sir Robert Walpole, his great opposite in the 1730s.   [2] Cf. Catullus, ii. 2: 'quem in sinu tenere'.
[3] Cf. Carew, 'On a Damask-Rose sticking upon a Ladies breast':

> O then what Monarch would not think't a grace,
> To leave his Regal Throne to have thy place.
> My self to gain thy blessed seat do vow
> Would be transform'd into a Rose as thou.

(*Poems, Songs, and Sonnets*, 4th edn., 1670, p. 162.)
[4] Cf. *Guardian*, 154: 'a Gigantick Woman with a high crowned Hat, that stood up like a Steeple over the Heads of the whole Assembly' (5th edn., 1729, ii. 266). In the early 1730s 'The High-Crowned Hat, after having been confined to cots and villages for so long a time, is become the favourite mode of quality, and is the politest distinction of a fashionable undress' (quoted from the *Weekly Register*, 10 July 1731, in James P. Malcolm, *Anecdotes of the Manners and Customs of London during the Eighteenth Century*, p. 436).

These for the Day; and for the Night,
I'd be a careful, watchful Spright.[1]
Upon her Pillow sitting still,   35
I'd guard her from th' Approach of Ill.
Thus (for afraid she could not be
Of such a little Thing as me)
While I survey her Bosom rise,
Her lovely Lips, her sleeping Eyes,   40
While I survey, what to declare
Nor Fancy can, nor Words must dare,
Here would begin my former Pain,
And wish to be myself again.[2]

SIMILES

To the SAME

As wildest Libertines would rate,
Compar'd with Pleasure, an Estate;
Or as his Life a Heroe'd prize,
When Honour claim'd the Sacrifice;
Their Souls as strongest Miser's Hold,   5
When in the Ballance weigh'd with Gold;[3]
Such, was thy Happiness at Stake,
My Fortune, Life, and Soul, I'd make.

[1] Cf. Pope, *Rape of the Lock*, i. 106: 'A watchful Sprite, and *Ariel* is my Name '(Twicken-ham edn., ii. 153).

[2] Cf. Ovid, *Amores*, II. xv. 25–6; Prior, 'A Lover's Anger', 15–16: 'That Seat of Delight I with Wonder survey'd; / And forgot ev'ry Word I design'd to have said' (*Lit. Works*, ed. Wright-Spears, i. 441).

[3] The apostrophe in a plural noun ('Miser's') is common practice in the time. See above, p. 63 ('Ridotto's, Opera's . . .'). For the simile, cf. Otway's *Orphan*, i:

> Though she be dearer to my Soul, than Rest
> To weary Pilgrims, or to Misers Gold,
> To great Men Pow'r, or wealthy Cities Pride . . .

(*Works*, 1768, iii. 19.) See Luckless's song to Harriot in *The Author's Farce*, I. iii.

THE PRICE

To the SAME

Can there on Earth, my *Celia*, be,
A Price I would not pay for thee?
Yes, one dear precious Tear of thine
Should not be shed to make thee mine.

Her CHRISTIAN NAME

To the SAME. A Rebus

A very good Fish, very good Way of Selling
A very bad Thing, with a little bad Spelling,[1]
Make the Name by the Parson and Godfather giv'n,
When a Christian was made of an Angel from Heav'n.

To the SAME;

Having blamed Mr. GAY for his Severity on her Sex.[2]

Let it not CELIA's gentle Heart perplex,
That GAY severe hath satyriz'd her Sex:
Had they, like her, a Tenderness but known,
Back on himself each pointed Dart had flown.
But blame thou last, in whose accomplish'd Mind   5
The strongest Satire on thy Sex we find.[3]

---

[1] To explain a puzzle is perhaps gratuitous. However, this play on Charlotte Cradock's first name involves a fish (the Char, a trout-like fish), a way of selling (by Lot), and a very bad thing (presumably Tea).

[2] Cf. Gay, 'Epistle to William Pulteney', 67–8: 'Think not, ye Fair, that I the Sex accuse: / How shall I spare you, prompted by the Muse?' (*Poems on Several Occasions*, 1737, ii. 23). Fielding's poem, like all the 'Celia' poems, is presumably to be dated before November 1734, when he married Charlotte.

[3] Cf. Dryden, *Eleonora*, 365–6: 'Where ev'n to draw the Picture of thy Mind, / Is Satyr on the most of Humane Kind' (*Works*, 1701, III. i. 184). See the poem by a certain 'Mr. Izard' ('The Excuse: To Caelia, who blam'd him for writing a Satire on some Ladies') in the *Gentleman's Magazine*, October 1738, p. 538.

AN EPIGRAM

That *Kate* weds a Fool what Wonder can be,
Her Husband has married a Fool great as she.[1]

ANOTHER

Miss *Molly* lays down as a positive Rule,
That no one should marry for Love, but a Fool:
Exceptions to Rules even *Lilly* allows;[2]
Moll has sure an *Example* at Home in her Spouse.

To the MASTER of the
SALISBURY ASSEMBLY;

Occasioned by a Dispute, whether the Company should have
fresh Candles.[3]

Take your Candles away, let your Musick be mute,
My Dancing, however, you shall not dispute;
Jenny's Eyes shall find Light, and I'll find a Flute.

---

[1] Cross (i. 174) saw in 'Kate' an allusion to Fielding's sister-in-law, Catherine Cradock. One could equally well suppose the lady of the epigram to be the same as the 'black Kate' of Lady Mary Wortley Montagu's satiric 'Epithalamium' (*Letters and Works*, ed. Lord Wharncliffe, 3rd edn., rev. by W. Moy Thomas, ii. 492–3).

[2] William Lily's sixteenth-century Latin grammar, still standard in Fielding's time, and his schoolbook at Eton. Cf. below, p. 184 n. 1.

[3] If we suppose that 'Jenny' was an earlier flame than 'Celia' (Charlotte Cradock), this poem would date before *c*. 1730.

THE CAT and FIDDLE[1]

TO THE

Favourite CAT of a Fiddling MISER

Thrice happy Cat, if in thy A— House,[2]
Thou luckily shouldst find a half-starv'd Mouse.
The Mice, that only for his Musick stay,
Are Proofs that *Orpheus* did not better play.[3]
Thou too, if Danger could alarm thy Fears,   5
Hast to this *Orpheus* strangely ty'd thy Ears:
For oh! the fatal Time will come, when he,
Prudent, will make his Fiddle-strings of thee.

[Untitled]

The Queen of Beauty, t'other Day,
(As the *Elysian* Journals say)
To ease herself of all her Cares,
And better carry on Affairs;
By Privy-Council mov'd above,   5
And *Cupid* Minister of Love,
To keep the Earth in due Obedience,
Resolv'd to substitute Vice Regents;
To Canton out[4] her Subject Lands,
And give the fairest the Commands.   10
She spoke, and to the Earth's far Borders
Young *Cupid* issued out his Orders,

---

[1] Cf. Pope, 'Epigram. On the Toasts of the Kit-Cat Club', 3–4: 'Some say from *Pastry Cook* it came, and some from *Cat* and *Fiddle*' (Twickenham edn., vi. 177 and n.). The *Spectator*, 28, complaining about London signs, excused this one: 'As for the Cat and Fiddle, there is a Conceit in it. . . .' The famous nursery rime seems to be of earlier date, though its first appearance in print was *c.* 1765 (*Oxford Dictionary of Nursery Rhymes*, ed. Iona and Peter Opie, pp. 203–5).

[2] Not identified.

[3] An epigram by Lucillius in the Greek Anthology presents a mouse retorting to a miser: 'thou hast no cause to fear; / I only *lodge* with thee, I *eat* elsewhere' (trans. John Jortin; cited by Henry P. Dodd, *The Epigrammatists*, p. 49).

[4] To subdivide into cantons or districts. Cf. *OED*, citing Defoe, *The True-Born Englishman*, i. 152: 'He Canton'd out the Country to his Men.'

That every Nymph in its Dimensions
Should bring or send up her Pretensions.[1]
Like Lightning swift the Order flies,   15
Or swifter Glance from *Celia's* Eyes:
Like Wit from sparkling *W—tley's* Tongue,[2]
Or Harmony from *Pope*, or *Young*.[3]
Why should I sing what Letters came;
Who boasts her Face, or who her Frame?   20
From black and brown, and red, and fair,
With Eyes and Teeth, and Lips and Hair.
One fifty hidden Charms discovers;
A second boasts as many Lovers:
This Beauty all Mankind adore;   25
And this all Women envy more.
This witnesses, by *Billetsdoux*,
A thousand Praises, and all true;
While that by Jewels makes Pretences
To triumph over Kings and Princes;   30
Bribing the Goddess by that Pelf,
By which she once was brib'd herself.
So Borough Towns, Election brought on,
E'er yet Corruption Bill was thought on.[4]
Sir Knight, to gain the Voters Favour,   35
Boasts of his former good Behaviour;
Of Speeches in the Senate made;
Love for its Country, and its Trade.
And, for a Proof of Zeal unshaken,
Distributes Bribes he once had taken.   40
What matters who the Prizes gain,
In *India*, *Italy*, or *Spain*;

[1] Fielding's poem is a literary *Kallisteia*, or competition of beauties; cf. the anonymous
Callistia; or the Prize of Beauty. A Poem, 1738.

[2] Lady Mary Wortley Montagu (1689–1762), second cousin to Fielding, and sponsor
of his early dramatic career. She went abroad in 1739, and did not return till the year of
her death (which may account for the fact that her name does not appear in the List of
Subscribers to the *Miscellanies*). Cf. Lansdowne, 'The Progress of Beauty': 'With what
Delight my Muse to Sandwich flies! / Whose Wit is piercing as her sparkling Eyes . . .'
(*Genuine Works*, 1736, i. 61).

[3] Edward Young (1683–1765). Fielding admired Young as a satirist and craftsman, and
frequently linked his name with Pope's (see below, p. 136).

[4] Presumably the act of 1729 (2 Geo. II, c. 24), a bill for the more effectual preventing
of bribery and corruption at Parliamentary elections.

Or who requires[1] the brown Commanders
Of *Holland*, *Germany*, and *Flanders*.
Thou *Britain*, on my Labours smile,   45
The Queen of Beauty's favour'd Isle;[2]
Whom she long since hath priz'd above
The *Paphian*, or the *Cyprian* Grove.[3]
And here, who ask the Muse to tell,
That the Court Lot to *R–chmond* fell?[4]   50
Or who so ignorant as wants
To know that *S—per*'s chose for *Hants*.[5]
Sarum, thy Candidates be nam'd,
Sarum, for Beauties ever fam'd,
Whose Nymphs excel all Beauty's Flowers,   55
As thy high Steeple doth all Towers.[6]
The Court was plac'd in Manner fitting;
Venus upon the Bench was sitting;
Cupid was Secretary made.
The Cryer an *O Tes* display'd;   60
Like Mortal Cryer's loud Alarum,
Bring in Petitions from *New Sarum*.[7]
When lo,[8] in bright celestial State,

[1] 'To seek after, search for. Also, to inquire after; to call upon, summon' (*OED*). See above, 'Of Good Nature', 115.

[2] Cf. Fielding, *The Lovers Assistant*; and Venus in Prior's 'Henry and Emma', 764: 'As on the *British* Earth, my Fav'rite Isle . . .' (*Lit. Works*, ed. Wright-Spears, i. 300).

[3] The conflated myth of Aphrodite offers two abodes: Paphos, in Cyprus, and Cythera (cf. Hesiod, *Theogony*, 188–200; the *Second Homeric Hymn to Aphrodite*, 1–2). Hence Fielding's epithets are redundant; he may have confused the island of Paphos with the Cyprian city of that name. Cf. Charles Hanbury Williams's rendering of Horace, *Carm.* I. xxx (to Venus): 'Quit Paphos, and the Cyprian isle' (*Works*, 1822, i. 235); and Spenser, *Faerie Queene*, IV. x. v.

[4] See above, p. 35, for another compliment to the Duchess of Richmond—'Cruel R[ichmon]d, the first *toast*' (Young, *Love of Fame*, vi. 224; 2nd edn., 1728, p. 134).

[5] Possibly Patience Soper, the (apparent) eldest daughter and heiress of John Soper of Preston Candover. Their manor of Nutley was, like Upton Grey (see above, p. 53), in the Bermondspit Hundred (*Victoria County History of Hampshire*, iii. 370–3).

[6] Cf. Gay, 'A Journey to Exeter', 68, 72: 'See *Sarum*'s steeple o'er yon hill ascend; . . ./ The proud Cathedral, and the lofty spire' (*Poems on Several Occasions*, 1737, ii. 15–16).

[7] The image seems to be that of a Grand Jury, at assizes or quarter sessions, hearing petitions (cf. Blackstone, *Commentaries*, 12th edn., 1793, i. 143), rather than a Parliamentary hearing. For the form of *oyez*, cf. Chambers's *Cyclopaedia*, 5th edn., 1741–3: 'O Yes, a corruption of the French, *Oyez*, hear ye. . . .'

[8] The middle Part of this Poem (which was writ when the Author was very young) was filled with the Names of several young Ladies, who might perhaps be uneasy at seeing themselves in Print, that Part therefore is left out; the rather, as some Freedoms, tho'

Jove came and thunder'd at the Gate.
'And can you, Daughter, doubt to whom   65
(He cry'd) belongs the happy Doom,
While *C—cks* yet make bless'd the Earth,[1]
C—cks, whom long before their Birth,
I, by your own Petition mov'd,
Decreed to be by all belov'd.   70
C—cks, to whose celestial Dower
I gave all Beauties in my Power;
To form whose lovely Minds and Faces,
I stript half Heaven of its Graces.[2]
Oh let them bear an equal Sway,   75
So shall Mankind well-pleas'd obey.'
The God thus spoke, the Goddess bow'd;
Her rising Blushes strait avow'd
Her hapless Memory and Shame,
And *Cupid* glad writ down their Name.   80

A PARODY,

FROM THE

FIRST ÆNEID

Dixit; et avertens Rosea Cervice refulsit,
Ambrosiæque Comæ divinum Vertice Odorem
Spiravere: Pedes vestis defluxit ad imos,
Et vera Incessu patuit Dea.—[3]

gentle ones, were taken with little Foibles in the amiable Sex, whom to affront in Print, is,
we conceive, mean in any Man, and scandalous in a Gentleman. [Fielding's note.]

[1] The fact that Fielding treats Charlotte and Catherine Cradock with equal fervour
here, combined with the allusion to the 'Corruption Bill', would seem to date the poem
sometime in 1729 or 1730. His marriage to Charlotte took place 28 November 1734.

[2] A variation on the Zeuxis legend (see Cicero, *De inventione*, II. i. 1–3). Cf. also Catullus,
lxxxvi. 5–6: 'Lesbia formosast, quae cum pulcherrima totast, / tum omnibus una omnis
surripuit Veneres.'

[3] Virgil, *Aeneid*, i. 402–5. Cf. Fielding's comment in the note to *The Vernoniad*, 109.
Dryden's version of these lines is:

> Thus having said, she turn'd, and made appear
> Her Neck refulgent, and dishevel'd Hair;
> Which flowing from her Shoulders, reach'd the Ground,
> And widely spread Ambrosial Scents around:
> In length of Train descends her sweeping Gown,
> And by her graceful Walk, the Queen of Love is known.

She said; and turning shew'd her wrinkled Neck,
In Scales and Colour like a Roach's Back.[1]
Forth from her greasy Locks such Odours flow,
As those who've smelt *Dutch* Coffee-Houses, know.[2]
To her Mid-Leg her Petticoat was rear'd,   5
And the true Slattern in her Dress appear'd.

A SIMILE,

FROM

SILIUS ITALICUS.

Aut ubi Cecropius formidine Nubis aquosæ
Sparsa super Flores examina tollit *Hymettos*;
Ad dulceis Ceras et odori Corticis Antra,
Mellis Apes gravidæ properant, densoque volatu
Raucum connexæ glomerant ad Limina murmur.[3]   5

Or when th' *Hymettian* Shepherd, struck with Fear
Of wat'ry Clouds thick gather'd in the Air,
Collects to waxen Cells the scatter'd Bees
Home from the sweetest Flowers, and verdant Trees;
Loaded with Honey to the Hive they fly,
And humming Murmurs buzz along the Sky.[4]

(*Æneis*, i. 556–61; *Works of Virgil*, 1697, p. 218.) With this may be compared Charles Cotton's travesty, beginning, 'With that she turn'd to go away, / And did her freckl'd Neck display' (*Scarronides or Virgil Travestie*, i, in *Genuine Poetical Works*, 5th edn., 1765, p. 36).

[1] The opening couplet appears verbatim at the end of an unfinished poem by Lady Mary Wortley Montagu (*Letters and Works*, ed. Lord Wharncliffe, 3rd edn., rev. by W. Moy Thomas, ii. 470). Who borrowed from whom is uncertain.

[2] Cf. *A Journey from This World to the Next*, I. ii, on The Hague. Travellers agreed that the neatness of the Dutch was only equalled by the badness of their air: cf. Sir William Temple, *Observations upon the United Provinces* (in *Works*, 1757, i. 170); Arbuthnot, *History of John Bull* (1712), chap. xv; James Grainger, *Letters*, ed. J. P. Malcolm (1805), p. 43: 'Leyden the neatest of all their towns, and has the worst air.' Or, to cite an unfriendly view, Samuel Butler's 'Description of Holland' saw it as inhabited by men 'That always ply the Pump, and never think / They can be safe, but at the Rate they stink' (*The Genuine Remains*, 1759, i. 270).   [3] *Punica*, ii. 217–21.

[4] Fielding is clearly seeking an effect like Shakespeare's 'And husht with buzzing night-flies to thy slumber' (*2 Hen. IV*, III. i. 11; *Works*, 1733–4, iii. 484).

TO *EUTHALIA*

Written in the Year 1728

Burning with Love, tormented with Despair,
Unable to forget or ease his Care;
In vain each practis'd Art *Alexis* tries;
In vain to Books, to Wine or Women flies;
Each brings *Euthalia's* Image to his Eyes.   5
In *Lock's* or *Newton's* Page her Learning glows;
Dryden the Sweetness of her Numbers shews;
In all their various Excellence I find
The various Beauties of her perfect Mind.[1]
How vain in Wine a short Relief I boast!   10
Each sparkling Glass recalls my charming Toast.
To Women then successless I repair,
Engage the Young, the Witty, and the Fair.
When *Sappho's* Wit each envious Breast alarms,[2]
And *Rosalinda* looks ten thousand Charms;[3]   15
In vain to them my restless Thoughts would run;
Like fairest Stars, they show the absent Sun.

[1] Cf. Tibullus, I. v. 37–40; Propertius, II. iii. 7; Cowley, 'The Thief', st. iii–iv (*The Mistress*, pp. 24–5; in *Works*, 1668); Prior, 'To Mr. Charles Montagu, on His Marriage', 7–12:

> In Company I strove for Ease in vain
> Whilst Mirth in others but encreas't my Pain.
> Med'cines from Books as vain I often took,
> They that Writ best but told me how You spoke
> In vain I saw; each Object thrô my Eye
> Touch'd my Soul quick with Something still of Thee.

(*Lit. Works*, ed. Wright-Spears, i. 61; Fielding might have seen this then unpublished poem in manuscript.)

[2] The use of 'Sappho' as an antonomasia for Lady Mary Wortley Montagu was familiar enough that by 1733 Pope expected no difficulty in the recognition of his 'furious Sappho' (*Imit. of Horace*, Sat. II. i. 84; Twickenham edn., iv. 13).

[3] Prior's Alexis tells his Clorinda: 'Your Eyes ten thousand Dangers dart: / Ten thousand Torments vex My Heart' ('The Despairing Shepherd', 28–9; *Lit. Works*, ed. Wright-Spears, i. 197). Cf. also 'To a Child of Quality', 7–8: '[lest her Eyes] Shou'd dart their kindling Fires, and look / The Pow'r they have to be obey'd' (ibid., p. 190).

JUVENALIS

SATYRA SEXTA.[1]

Credo pudicitiam Saturno rege[2] moratam

In terris, visamque diu; cum frigida parvas

Præberet spelunca domos, ignemque, Laremque,

Et pecus, et dominos communi clauderet umbra:

Silvestrem montana torum cum sterneret uxor   5

Frondibus et culmo, vicinarumque[3] ferarum

Pellibus, haud similis tibi, Cynthia, nec tibi, cujus

Turbavit nitidos extinctus passer ocellos;[4]

Sed potanda ferens infantibus ubera magnis,[5]

Et sæpe horridior glandem ructante marito.   10

Quippe aliter tunc orbe novo, cœloque recenti

[1] Fielding's Latin text follows, with a few individual departures and flourishes, that of the Delphin edition of Juvenal and Persius, edited by Ludovicus Prateus (the 5th edn., 1722, was in Fielding's library). His Latin notes are largely drawn from this edition and from that of Eilhardus Lubinus (Hanover, 1603; several later editions); there is nothing individual about them and they have not here been translated. Diacritical marks in Latin text and notes have been silently removed.

[2] Aureo scilicet sæculo; quod viguisse Saturno, Coeli et Vestæ filio, in Latio regnante a Poetis fingitur. Regem hunc eleganter satis Poeta profert, cum de moribus in Latio muatis agitur. [Fielding's note.]

[3] Contubernalium. Vel forsan non longe petitarum sicut nunc; et exprobrare vult sui Temporis Romanis, qui ex longinquo, mollitiei vel odoris causa, Ferarum pelles maximo cum pretio comparabant. [Fielding.]

[4] Cynthia Propertii, Lesbia Catulli amica. Quarum quidem hanc ineptam, illam delicatulam fuisse innuit noster. [Fielding.]

[5] Grangæum quendam hic refutat Lubinus. Qui per magnos, adultæ vel saltem provectioris Ætatis pueros, intelligit. Ego tamen cum Grangæo sentio. Nam delicatulis et nobilissimis Matronis consuetudinem pueros a Matris Mammis arcendi objicere vult Poetu, ob quam Romanas mulieres, Juvenalis Temporibus, sicut et nostræ, infames et Reprehensione dignas fuisse ne minimum quidem dubito. [Fielding's note.] Isaacus Grangæus and Eilhardus Lubinus.

PART OF

Juvenal's Sixth SATIRE,

MODERNIZED IN

BURLESQUE VERSE[1]

Dame *Chastity,* without Dispute,
Dwelt on the Earth with good King *Brute*;[2]
When a cold Hut of modern *Greenland*
Had been a Palace for a Queen *Anne*;
When hard and frugal Temp'rance reign'd,   5
And Men no other House contain'd
Than the wild Thicket, or the Den;
When Houshold Goods, and Beasts, and Men,
Together lay beneath one Bough,
Which Man and Wife would scarce do now;   10
The Rustick Wife her Husband's Bed
With Leaves and Straw, and Beast-Skin made.
Not like Miss *Cynthia,* nor that other,
Who more bewail'd her Bird than Mother;[3]
But fed her Children from her Bubbies,   15
'Till they were grown up to great Loobies:[4]
Herself an Ornament less decent
Than Spouse, who smelt of Acorn recent.
For, in the Infancy of Nature,

---

[1] This poem is probably Fielding's earliest (extant) work; he says in the Preface to the *Miscellanies* (see above, p. 3) that it 'was originally sketched out before I was Twenty, and was all the Revenge taken by an injured Lover'. The present version, however, was clearly brought up to date with recent allusions. Cross (i. 50–2) argued that the occasion of the poem was Fielding's abortive affair with Sarah Andrew, the youthful heiress of Lyme Regis, in the autumn of 1725.

[2] The *Roman* Poet mentions *Saturn,* who was the first King of *Italy*; we have therefore rendered *Brute* the oldest to be found in our Chronicles, and whose History is as fabulous as that of his *Italian* Brother. [Fielding's note.]

[3] This is the first satyrical Stroke, in which the Poet inveighs against an over Affectation of Delicacy and Tenderness in Women. [Fielding's note.] For 'Cynthia', see Propertius; the 'Lesbia' of Catullus is generally identified as Clodia, sister of Publius Clodius Pulcher, Cicero's great enemy: see his attack upon her in the *Pro Caelio.*

[4] Here the Poet slyly objects to the Custom of denying the Mother's Breast to the Infant; there are among us truly conscientious Persons, who agree with his Opinion. [Fielding's note.] Among such persons was Samuel Richardson; see *Pamela,* Part II, Letter XLV et seq.

Vivebant homines; qui rupto robore nati,[1]

Compositique luto nullos habuere parentes.

Multa pudicitiæ veteris vestigia forsan,

Aut aliqua extiterant, et sub Jove,[2] sed Jove nondum   15

Barbato, nondum Græcis jurare paratis[3]

Per caput alterius; cum furem nemo timeret

Caulibus, aut pomis, sed aperto viveret horto.

Paulatim deinde ad superos Astræa recessit

Hac comite; atque duæ pariter fugere sorores.   20

Antiquum et vetus est, alienum, Posthume, lectum

Concutere, atque sacri Genium contemnere fulcri.

Omne aliud crimen mox ferrea protulit ætas:

Viderunt primos argentea secula mœchos.

Conventum tamen, et pactum, et sponsalia nostra   25

Tempestate paras; jamque a tonsore magistro[4]

Pecteris, et digito pignus fortasse dedisti.

Certe sanus eras: uxorem, Posthume, ducis?

Dic, qua Tisiphone? quibus exagitare colubris?

---

[1] Sic Virgilius [*Aeneid*, viii. 315].
Gensque virum truncis, et rupto Robore nati.
Hanc Fabulam ex eo natam fuisse volunt, quod habitantes in arborum cavitibus exinde egredi solebant. Ridicula sane Conjectura, et quæ Criticulorum Homunculorum Hallucinantem Geniunculum satis exprimit. Hæc Fabula et aliæ quæ de Hominis origine extiterunt, ab uno et eodem Fonte effluxisse videntur, ab Ignorantia scilicet humana cum vanitate conjuncta. Homines enim cum sui Generis originem prorsus ignorarent, et hanc ignorantiam sibi probro verterent, causas varias genitivas, ad suam cujusque Regionem accommodatas invenerunt et tradiderunt; Alii ab arboribus, alii a Luto, alii a Lapidibus originem suam ducentes. [Fielding.]

[2] Argenteo Sæculo, Jove Saturni filio regnante. Miram hujus Loci Elegantiam nemine prætereundam censeo. Quanta enim acerbitate in vitia Humana insurgit Poeta noster, qui non nisi vestigia Pudicitiæ argenteo sæculo attribuit, neque hæc asserit, sed *forsan* extitisse sæculo hoc *ineunte* dicit; mox Jove pubescente ad superos avolasse. [Fielding.]

[3] Apud Romanos Punica Fides, et apud Græcos, ut liquet ex Demosthene in I Olynth. *Macedonica* Fides, Proverbio Locum tribuerunt: Asiaticos etiam ob Perjuriam infectatur Noster Sat. sequente vers. 14. Sed hic originem Perjurii Græcis attribuere videtur. [Fielding.]

[4] Adprime docto. Hic et ad vers. 78, 79. Ritus nuptiales exhibet Poeta. [Fielding.]

Man was a diff'rent sort of Creature;   20
When Dirt-engender'd Offspring broke
From the ripe Womb of Mother Oak.¹
Ev'n in the Reign of *Jove*, perhaps,
The Goddess may have shewn her Chaps;
But it was sure in its Beginning,   25
E'er *Jupiter* had Beard to grin in.
Not yet the *Greeks* made Truth their Sport,
And bore false Evidence in Court;
Their Truth was yet become no Adage;²
Men fear'd no Thieves of Pears and Cabbage.   30
By small Degrees *Astrea* flies
With her two Sisters to the Skies.³
O 'tis a very ancient Custom,
To taint the genial Bed, my Posthum!
Fearless lest Husband should discover it,   35
Or else the Genius that rules over it.
The Iron Age gave other Crimes,
Adult'ry grew in Silver Times.
But you, in this Age, boldly dare
The Marriage Settlements prepare;   40
Perhaps have bought the Wedding Garment,
And Ring too, thinking there's no Harm in't.
Sure you was in your Senses, Honey.
You marry. Say, what *Tisiphone*⁴

---

¹ We have here varied a little from the Original, and put the two Causes of Generation together. [Fielding's note.]

² They were so infamous for Perjury, that to have Regard to an Oath was a great Character among them, and sufficient to denote a Gentleman. See our Notes on the *Plutus* of *Aristophanes*. [Fielding's note.] The point in the Fielding–Young *Plutus* is not quite the same: '*A Gentleman*.] The *Greek* is *a Man who hath regard to his Oath*. . . . The *Athenians* in common with the other *Greeks*, had so religious a Regard to an Oath, that Perjury was the most base and infamous Imputation with which any Character could be aspersed' (*Plutus*, 1742, pp. 7–8 n.). In the *Covent-Garden Journal*, 12, Juvenal (*Sat*. x. 174–5) is cited on Greek mendacity.

³ Truth and Modesty. [Fielding's note.] Fielding mistranslates, perhaps purposely. Juvenal draws upon the myth that Astraea, emblem of Justice, was the last immortal to leave the earth at the close of the Golden Age (cf. Ovid, *Metam*. i. 149–50), and that her sister Chastity accompanied her. Fielding may have recalled Dryden's rendering of Ovid's earlier lines (*Metam*. i. 129): 'Truth, Modesty, and Shame, the World forsook' (*Examen Poeticum*, 1693, p. 12).

⁴ One of the Furies. We have presumed to violate the Quantity of this Word. [Fielding's note.] i.e., Tisiphōne for Tisiphŏne.

Ferre potes dominam salvis tot restibus ullam?

Cum pateant altæ, caligantesque fenestræ?

Cum tibi vicinum se præbeat Æmilius pons?

Aut si de multis nullus placet exitus; illud

Nonne putas melius, quod tecum pusio dormit?

Pusio qui noctu non litigat: exigit a te   35

Nulla jacens illic munuscula, nec queritur quod

Et lateri parcas, nec, quantum jussit, anheles.

Sed placet Ursidio lex Julia:[1] tollere dulcem

Cogitat hæredem, cariturus turture magno,

Mullorumque jubis,[2] et captatore macello.   40

Quid fieri non posse putes, si jungitur ulla

Ursidio? si mœchorum notissimus[3] olim

Stulta maritali jam porrigit ora capistro,

Quem toties texit periturum cista Latini?

---

[1] De Adulterijs; qua lata est Pœna Adulterii, ideoque ad Matrimonium viri ab ea Lege impelluntur. [Fielding.]

[2] i.e. Mullatis jubis. Sic Phædrus [Lib. iv. Fab. xiii]: Aviditas canis pro avido cane, et etiam apud Græcus Βίη Πρίαμοιο pro Βίαιος Πρίαμος. [Fielding.]

[3] Al[iter] Turpissimus, perperam: nam si ita legas diminuitur hujus Loci vis; quo quis enim majorem Adulterarum habuit Notitiam, eo magis Maritali Capistro porrecturus, ora Exemplum præbet ridiculum. [Fielding.]

Possesses you with all her Snakes,   45
Those Curls which in her Pole she shakes?
What, wilt thou wear the Marriage Chain,
While one whole Halter doth remain;
When open Windows Death present ye,
And *Thames* hath Water in great Plenty?   50
But Verdicts of Ten Thousand Pound
Most sweetly to *Ursidius* sound.
'We'll all (he cries) be Cuckolds, *Nem. Con.*
While the rich Action lies of *Crim. Con.*'¹
And who would lose the precious Joy   55
Of a fine thumping darling Boy?
Who, while you dance him, calls you Daddy,
(So he's instructed by my Lady.)
What tho' no Ven'son, Fowl, or Fish,
Presented, henceforth grace the Dish: 60
Such he hath had, but dates no Merit hence;
He knows they came for his Inheritance.²
What would you say, if this *Ursidius*,
A Man well known among the Widows,
First of all Rakes, his Mind should alter,   65
And stretch his simple Neck to th' Halter?³
Often within *Latinus*' Closet,⁴
(The Neighbours, nay, the whole Town knows it,)
He hath escap'd the Cuckold's Search;

¹ *Nemine contradicente* (no one contradicting) and 'Criminal Conversation' or adultery. This addition to the original is probably intended to identify Ursidius with Theophilus Cibber, who, having for some time played the role of contented cuckold, brought charges in 1738 against William Sloper for criminal conversation with Cibber's wife, Susannah Maria. Dismissed with £10 damages, he again brought suit in 1739 and was successful in gaining £500 damages for the loss of Mrs. Cibber's theatrical income while she was with Mr. Sloper. See *An Account of the Life of That Celebrated Actress Mrs. Susannah Maria Cibber* (1887), and cf. Fielding's remark on 'T. Pistol' in the *Champion*, 17 May 1740.

² This Custom of making Presents to rich Men who had no Children in order to become their Heirs, is little known to us. Mr. *Ben. Johnson*, indeed, hath founded a Play on it, but he lays the scene in *Venice*. [Fielding's note.] *Volpone*, of course.

³ We have endeavoured to preserve the Beauty of this Line in the Original. The Metaphor is taken from the Posture of a Horse holding forth his Neck to the Harness. [Fielding's note.]

⁴ We have here a little departed from the *Latin*. This *Latinus* was a Player, and used to act the Part of the Gallant; in which, to avoid the Discovery of the Husband, he used to be hid in a Chest, or Cloaths-Basket, as *Falstaff* is concealed in the *Merry Wives of Windsor*. The Poet therefore here alludes to that Custom. [Fielding's note.] The Delphin edition cites the authority of Adrianus Turnebus for this story.

Quid, quod et antiquis uxor de moribus illi 45

Quæritur? O medici mediam pertundite venam:

Delicias hominis![1] Tarpeium limen adora

Pronus, et auratam Junoni cæde juvencam,

Si tibi contigerit capitis matrona pudici.

Paucæ adeo Cereris vittas[2] contingere dignæ; 50

Quarum non timeat pater oscula. necte coronam

Postibus, et densos per limina tende corymbos.

Unus Iberinæ vir sufficit? ocyus illud

Extorquebis, ut hæc oculo contenta sit uno.

Magna tamen fama est cujusdam rure paterno 55

Viventis: vivat Gabijs, ut vixit in agro;

Vivat Fidenis, et agello cedo paterno.

Quis tamen affirmat nil actum in montibus, aut in

Speluncis? adeo senuerunt Jupiter et Mars?

---

[1] Delicatum Hominem. Sic monstrum hominis, pro monstrosus Homo. [Fielding.]
[2] Mysteria Eleusynia his respicit. Quæ quidem a Warburtono illo doctissimo in Libro suo de Mosaica Legatione accuratissime nunc demum explicantur. [Fielding.]

Yet now he seeks a Wife most starch;   70
With good old-fashion'd Morals fraught.
Physicians give him a large Draught,
And Surgeons ope his middle Vein.[1]
O delicate Taste! go, prithee strain
Thy Lungs to Heav'n, in Thanksgivings;   75
Build Churches, and endow with Livings.
If a chaste Wife thy Lot befall,
'Tis the Great Prize drawn in *Guildhall.*[2]
  Few worthy are to touch those Mysteries,
Of which we lately know the Histories,   80
To *Ceres* sacred,[3] who requires
Strict Purity from loose Desires.
Whereas at no Crime now they boggle,
Ev'n at their Grandfathers they ogle.
  But come, your Equipage make ready,   85
And dress your House out for my Lady.
Will one Man *Iberine* supply?
Sooner content her with one Eye.
  But hold; there runs a common Story
Of a chaste Country Virgin's Glory.   90
At *Bath* and *Tunbridge* let her be;
If there she's chaste, I will agree.
And will the Country yield no Slanders?
Is all our Army gone to *Flanders?*[4]

[1] Cf. Dryden's version, 65: 'Run for the Surgeon; breathe the middle Vein' (1693, p. 91). Of the major veins of the arm, the *vena mediana* seems most often to have been employed in bleeding (see Robert James, *A Medicinal Dictionary*, 1743–5, s.v. 'Phlebotomia').

[2] In the state lottery; cf. Swift to Stella, 15 September 1710: 'To-day Mr. Addison, colonel Freind and I went to see the million lottery drawn at Guildhall' (*Journal to Stella*, Letter III, ed. Harold Williams, i. 18–19). Cf. the third scene in the revised version of Fielding's ballad-opera, *The Lottery*.

[3] Which the Reader may see explain'd in a most masterly Stile, and with the profoundest Knowledge of Antiquity, by Mr. *Warburton*, in the first Vol. of his *Divine Legation of Moses vindicated.* [Fielding's note.] William Warburton (1698–1779). The exposition of the Eleusinian Mysteries occurs in Book II, sec. 4, of Warburton's *Divine Legation*, of which Part I (Books I–III) was published in 1738. See *A Journey from This World to the Next*, I. viii. Both compliments presumably arise from the close relationship that Warburton had established with Ralph Allen, Fielding's new patron; and that both were late additions is suggested by the fact that in commenting on the Eleusinian Mysteries in a note to Aristophanes' *Plutus*, IV. ii (1742, p. 82 n.) in May of 1742, Fielding (and Young) had cited Potter's *Antiquities*, with no mention of Warburton.

[4] As the Patron of these Gentlemen is mentioned in the Original, we thought his Votaries might be pleased with being inserted in the Imitation. [Fielding's note.] English troops in

Porticibusne tibi monstratur fœmina voto   60

Digna tuo? cuneis an habent spectacula totis

Quod securus ames, quodque inde excerpere possis?

Chironomon Ledam molli saltante Bathyllo,

Tuccia vesicæ non imperat; Appula gannit

(Sicut in amplexu) subitum, et miserabile longum:[1]   65

Attendit Thymele; Thymele tunc rustica discit.

Ast aliæ, quoties aulæa recondita cessant,

Et vacuo clausoque sonant fora sola theatro,

Atque a plebeijs longe Megalesia; tristes

Personam, thyrsumque tenent, et subligar Acci.   70

Urbicus exodio risum movet Attellanæ

Gestibus Autonoes; hunc diligit Ælia pauper.

Solvitur his magno comœdi fibula; sunt quæ

---

[1] Hæc et sequentia ut minus a castis intelligenda, sic ab Interpretibus minime intellecta videntur. Omnes quos unquam vidi, Codd. ita se habent.

> *—Appula gannit*
> *Sicut in Amplexu; subitum, et miserabile longum*
> *Attendit Thymele.*

Quid sibi vult hæc Lectio, me omnino latere fateor; Sin vero nobiscum legas, tribus illis verbis parenthesi inclusis, invenies planam quidem (licet castiore Musa indignam) Sententiam. [Fielding's note.] The codical reading cited is that of the Delphin edition; the emendation seems to be Fielding's own.

Can the full *Mall*[1] afford a Spouse,   95
Or Boxes, worthy of your Vows?
While some soft Dance *Bathyllus* dances,
Can *Tuccy* regulate her Glances?
Appula chuckles, and poor *Thomyly*
Gapes, like a Matron at a Homily.   100
But others, when the House is shut up,
Nor Play-Bills, *by Desire*,[2] are put up;
When Players cease, and Lawyer rises
To harangue Jury at Assizes;[3]
When Drolls at *Barthol'mew* begin,   105
A Feast Day after that of *Trin'*.[4]
Others, I say, themselves turn Players,
With *Clive* and *Woffington's* gay Airs;
Paint their fair Faces out like Witches,
And cram their Thighs in *Fle—w—d's* Breeches.[5]   110
Italian Measures while *Fausan*[6]
Mov'd, what a Laugh thro' Gall'ry ran?
Poor *Ælia* languishes in vain;
Fausan is bought with greater Gain.

considerable numbers began embarking for Flanders in April 1742, in response to the threat offered by France and Prussia in the War of the Austrian Succession. Horace Walpole's letters to Mann of 1742 and 1743 are full of references to the Flanders troops.

[1] The *Portico's* in the Original; where both Sexes used to assemble. [Fielding's note.]

[2] A constant Puff at the Head of our Play-Bills; Designed to allure Persons to the House, who go thither more for the sake of the Company than of the Play; but which has proved so often fallacious (Plays having been acted *at the particular Desire of several Ladies of Quality, when there hath not been a single Lady of Quality in the House*) that at present it hath very little Signification. [Fielding's note.]

[3] Viz. in the Vacation. In the Original, *As the* Megalesian *Festival is so long distant from the* Plebeian. The latter being celebrated in the Calends of *December*, the former in the Nones of *April*. [Fielding's note.] The 'Vacation' was any time of the year outside of the four terms during which superior courts were open; here, the Long Vacation from June to November, after Trinity Term (May–June).

[4] Bartholomew Fair began on St. Bartholomew's Day, 24 August. Trinity Sunday is the first Sunday after Pentecost, in May or June.

[5] Kitty Clive (1711–85), Fielding's favourite actress, who took leads in many of his plays, and to whom he dedicated *The Intriguing Chambermaid* in 1734; Margaret (Peg) Woffington (1714?–60), whose London career began with the season of 1740, and who acted in Fielding's *The Wedding Day* (1743); Charles Fleetwood (d. 1747), manager of the Drury Lane Theatre from 1734 to 1745. The popularity of actresses dressed 'in Man's-Cloaths' continued unabated in the eighteenth century.

[6] Signor and Signora Fausan were comic dancers who appeared at Drury Lane and the opera in the season of 1742. Horace Walpole refers to them several times (*Yale Edition of the Corr.* xviii. 339, 358).

Chrysogonum cantare vetent; Hispulla tragœdo

Gaudet: an expectas, ut Quintilianus ametur?   75

Accipis uxorem, de qua citharœdus Echion

Aut Glaphyrus fiat pater, Ambrosiusve choraules.

Longa per angustos figamus pulpita vicos:

Ornentur postes, et grandi janua lauro,

Ut testudineo tibi, Lentule, conopeo   80

Nobilis Euryalum mirmillonem exprimat infans.

   Nupta senatori comitata est Hippia Ludium[1]

Ad Pharon et Nilum, famosaque mœnia Lagi;

Prodigia, et mores urbis damnante Canopo.[2]

Immemor illa domus, et conjugis, atque sororis,   85

Nil patriæ indulsit; plorantesque improba gnatos,

Utque magis stupeas, ludos, Paridemque reliquit.

---

[1] Salmas. Ludum mavult, et hoc pro Ludio, ut Regna pro Regibus, positum censet: sed synæresis hæc frequenter occurrit apud Poetas. Sic τὸ Omnia apud Virgilium Dissyllabum est. [Fielding's note.] Claudius Salmasius (1588–1653 ?), the great Renaissance scholar, Milton's adversary.

[2] Urbs erat Ægyptiaca ad ostium Nili, sed hic pro tota Ægypto usurpatur. Hujus Populi mores tam apud Græcos quam Romanos maxime infames fuere, adeo ut αἰγυπτιαστὶ perinde valeat ac turpiter. His duobus versibus nihil acerbius esse potest. [Fielding.]

Others make *B—rd* their wiser Choice,   115
And wish to spoil his charming Voice.[1]
Hispulla sighs for Buskin's Wit,
Cou'd she love *Lyt—n* or *P—t?*[2]
Chuse you a Wife, whom the blind Harper,[3]
Or any Fidler else, or Sharper,   120
Fine Rivals! might with Ease enjoy,
And make thee Father of a Boy?
Come then, prepare the Nuptial Feast,
Adorn the Board, invite the Guest;
That Madam may, in Time, be big,   125
And bring an Heir resembling *Fig*.[4]
Hippia[5] to Parl'ment Man was wed,
But left him for a Fencer's Bed:
With him she went to some Plantation,
Which damn'd the Morals of our Nation;   130
Forgetful of her House and Sister,
And Spouse and Country too, which miss'd her:
Her brawling Brats ne'er touch'd her Mind;
Nay more, young *C—r*'s left behind.[6]

[1] John Beard (*c.* 1716–91), famous tenor, who played in Fielding's *Miss Lucy in Town* (1742). Horace Walpole, who did not care for him, called him 'a man with one note in his voice' (*Yale Edition of the Corr.* xviii. 180; and cf. xvii. 435).
[2] Lyttelton (see above, p. 36) or Pitt. William Pitt (1708–78), later first Earl of Chatham, had been at Eton with Fielding and was a member of the 'patriot' opposition to Walpole. Fielding celebrated his oratory in *Tom Jones*, XIV. i.
[3] If a specific person, perhaps John Parry (d. 1782), called 'the Blind Harper', who was harper to Sir Watkin Williams Wynne. But the phrase was apparently in general use: cf. Charles Cotton's *Scarronides*, Book I: 'Quoth he, Blind Harpers, have among ye; / 'Tis ten to one but I bedung ye' (*Genuine Poetical Works*, 5th edn., 1765, p. 12); and Puttenham, *Arte of English Poesie*, II. ix (1589), p. 69; Shakespeare, *Love's Labour's Lost*, V. ii. 405; Jonson, *Volpone*, I. i. 500.
[4] A celebrated Prize-fighter. [Fielding's note.] James Figg (d. 1734) had a famous academy of swordsmanship and pugilism in Marylebone Fields (cf. the *Champion*, 29 January 1740).
[5] She was Wife to *Fabricius Vejento*, a noble rich *Roman*, who was infamous for his Luxury and Pride. This last Quality was so eminent in him, that he scorned to salute any almost of his Fellow Citizens; for which he is lashed by our Poet, Sat. III. v[erse] 185. He is likewise introduced in the fourth Satyr [IV. 113]. His wife *Hippia* ran away to *Egypt* with the Gladiator *Sergius*. [Fielding's note.]
[6] In the Original *Paris*, a Player, of whom *Domitian* was so fond, that our Author was banished for his abusing him. He afterwards was put to Death for an Amour with the Empress. [Fielding's note.] 'Young Cibber' is, of course, Theophilus again.

Sed quanquam in magnis opibus, plumaque paterna,

Et segmentatis dormisset parvula cunis,

Contempsit pelagus; famam contempserat olim,   90

Cujus apud molles minima est jactura cathedras.

Tyrrhenos igitur fluctus, lateque sonantem

Pertulit Ionium constanti pectore, quamvis

Mutandum toties esset mare. Justa pericli

Si ratio est, et honesta, timent; pavidoque gelantur   95

Pectore, nec tremulis possunt insistere plantis:

Fortem animum præstant rebus, quas turpiter audent.

Si jubeat conjux, durum est conscendere navim;

Tunc sentina gravis; tunc summus vertitur aer.

Quæ mœchum sequitur, stomacho valet: illa maritum   100

Convomit: hæc inter nautas et prandet, et errat

Per puppim, et duros gaudet tractare rudentes.

Qua tamen exarsit forma? qua capta juventa

Hippia? Quid vidit, propter quod ludia dici

Sustinuit? nam Sergiolus[1] jam radere guttur   105

Cœperat, et secto requiem sperare lacerto.[2]

Præterea multa in facie deformia; sicut

---

[1] Diminutivo blandulo quam facete utitur Poeta! [Fielding.]

[2] Missionem impetrabant Gladiatores, Brachio, vel aliquo alio Membro mutilato. Vide ut Sergii Laudes enumeret noster; eum nempe Formæ Decorem, propter quem Hippia, Famæ suæ oblita, Ludia dici sustinuit. Senex erat, mutilatus, et forma turpissima. Hæc omnia munere suo Gladiatorio compensavit. [Fielding.]

Nor was this Nymph bred up to Pattins,[1] 135
But swaddled soft in Silks and Sattins;
Yet she despis'd the Sea's loud Roar;
Her Fame she had despis'd before:
For that's a Jewel, in Reality,
Of little Value 'mongst the Quality.[2] 140
Nor *Bay of Biscay* rais'd her Fears,
Nor all the *Spanish* Privateers.[3]
But should a just Occasion call
To Danger, how the Charmers squall!
Cold are their Breasts as addled Eggs, 145
Nor can they stand upon their Legs,
More than an Infant that is ricketty;
But they are stronger in Iniquity.
Should Spouse decoy them to a Ship,
Good Heavens! how they'd have the Hip![4] 150
"Tis hard to clamber up the Sides;
O filthy Hold! and when she rides,
It turns one's Head quite topsy-turvy,
And makes one sicker than the Scurvy.'
Her Husband is the nauseous Physick, 155
With her Gallant, she's never Sea-sick.
To dine with Sailors then she's able,
And even bears a Hand to Cable.
But say, what Youth or Beauty warm'd thee
What, *Hippia*, in thy Lover charm'd thee? 160
For little *Sergy*, like a Goat,
Was bearded down from Eyes to Throat:
Already had he done his best;
Fit for an Hospital, and Rest.[5]
His Face wore many a Deformity, 165

[1] Wooden shoes or clogs.
[2] We have inserted this rather to stick as close to the Original as possible, than from any Conceit that it is justly applicable to our own People of Fashion. [Fielding's note.]
[3] Allusions suitable to the period before 1739 and the War of Jenkins's Ear. Cf. the host in *Joseph Andrews* (II. xvii) on 'those cursed *Guarda-Costas* . . .'.
[4] i.e. 'hyp' (hypochondria; the 'spleen'). Cf. *Tatler*, 230: '*Will Hazzard* has got the *Hipps* . . .'; George Cheyne, *The English Malady* (1733): 'the constant Complaints, common to *Hypish* People' (p. 335).
[5] The Gladiators, when they were maimed, received their Dismission; as a Token of which, a Wand was presented to them. *Sergius* had not, however, yet obtained this Favour; our Poet hints only, that he was intitled to it. [Fielding's note.]

Attritus galea, medijsque in naribus ingens
Gibbus; et acre malum semper stillantis ocelli.
Sed gladiator erat; facit hoc illos Hyacinthos: 110
Hoc pueris, patriæque, hoc prætulit illa sorori,
Atque viro: ferrum est, quod amant: hic Sergius idem
Accepta rude, cœpisset Veiento videri.
Quid privata domus, quid fecerit Hippia, curas?
Respice rivales Divorum: Claudius audi   115
Quæ tulerit: dormire virum cum senserat uxor,
(Ausa Palatino tegetem præferre cubili,
Sumere nocturnos meretrix Augusta cucullos,)
Linquebat, comite ancilla non amplius una;
Et nigrum flavo crinem abscondente galero,   120
Intravit calidum veteri centone lupanar,
Et cellam vacuam, atque suam: tunc nuda papillis

Upon his Nose a great Enormity.
His Eyes distill'd a constant Stream;
In Matter not unlike to Cream.
But he was still of the Bear-Garden,¹
Hence her Affection fond he shar'd in: 170
This did, beyond her Children, move; ⎞
Dearer than Spouse or Country prove; ⎬
In short, 'tis Iron which they love. ⎠
Dismiss this *Sergius* from the Stage;
Her Husband could not less engage.   175
　But say you, if each private Family
Doth not produce a perfect *Pamela*;²
Must ev'ry Female bear the Blame
Of one low private Strumpet's Shame?
　See then a dignify'd Example,   180
And take from higher Life a Sample;
How Horns have sprouted on Heads Royal,
And *Harry's* Wife hath been disloyal.³
When she perceiv'd her Husband snoring,
Th' Imperial Strumpet went a Whoring: 185
Daring with private Rakes to solace,
She preferr'd *Ch–rl–s-Street*⁴ to the Palace:
Went with a single Maid of Honour,
And with a *Capuchin* upon her,
Which hid her black and lovely Hairs;   190
At *H—d's*⁵ softly stole up Stairs:
There at Receipt of Custom sitting,

¹ On the famous Bear-Garden in Hockley-in-the-Hole, near Clerkenwell Green, see
Tatler, 28; *Spectator*, 141 and 436; Pope, *Dunciad*, i. 222, 326; and, of course, Fielding's
Champion, passim.
² Richardson's *Pamela* was published 6 November 1740. Fielding here, as in *Joseph
Andrews*, IV. xii, mocks the low pronunciation of Paměla, rather than Paměla (as in
Sidney's *Arcadia*).
³ This may be, perhaps, a little applicable to one of *Henry* VIII's Wives. [Fielding's
note.] Presumably Catherine Howard.
⁴ Charles Street, Covent Garden.
⁵ A useful Woman in the Parish of *Covent-Garden*. [Fielding's note.] Fielding called
the bawd in *The Wedding Day* 'Mrs. Useful'. Mother Haywood, who died in December
1743, was memorialized by the *London Magazine* of that month (p. 621): 'The noted
Mrs. *Haywood*, who for many Years kept the Bagnio in *Charles-street*, *Covent Garden*,
a Lady well known to the polite Part of the World, said to have died worth 10,000*l*'. The
original setting of *Miss Lucy in Town* had been the bagnio of 'Mrs. Haycock'; and cf.
Joseph Andrews, III. iii.

Constitit auratis, titulum mentita Lyciscæ,

Ostenditque tuum, generose Britannice, ventrem.

Excepit blanda intrantes, atque æra poposcit.[1]   125

Mox, lenone suas jam dimittente puellas,

Tristis abit; sed, quod potuit, tamen ultima cellam

Clausit, adhuc ardens rigidæ tentigine vulvæ;

Et lassata viris, nondum satiata recessit:

Obscurisque genis turpis, fumoque lucernæ   130

Fœda, lupanaris tulit ad pulvinar odorem.

Hippomanes, carmenque loquar, coctumque venenum,

Privignoque datum? faciunt graviora coactæ

Imperio sexus, minimumque libidine peccant.

    Optima sed quare Cesennia teste marito?   135

Bis quingenta dedit; tanti vocat ille pudicam:

Nec Veneris pharetris macer est; aut lampade fervet:

Inde faces ardent; veniunt a dote sagittæ.

Libertas emitur: coram licet innuat, atque

Rescribat; vidua est, locuples quæ nupsit avaro.   140

    Cur desiderio Bibulæ Sertorius ardet?

Si verum excutias, facies, non uxor amatur.

[Tres rugae subeant et se cutis arida laxet,][2]

Fiant obscuri dentes, oculique minores;

Collige sarcinulas, dicet libertus,[3] et exi;   145

---

1 Following line 125, most modern editions of Juvenal include a line 126 ('Et resupina jacens multorum absorbuit ictus') in their line-numbering, even when they do not include the passage. The present text follows the numbering of the Delphin edition, which does not include this line.

2 Fielding's Latin text inadvertently dropped line 143, which is here restored from the Delphin edition.

3 Sensus hujus loci non subolet Interpretibus. Divitem maritum e Libertino genere hic ostendi volunt: cum Poeta plane servum manumissum, vel primi ordinis servum intendit: quem nos anglice, *the Gentleman, the Steward,* &c. nominamus. [Fielding's note.]

She boldly call'd herself the *Kitten*;[1]
Smil'd, and pretended to be needy,
And ask'd Men to *come down the Ready*.[2]   195
But when for Fear of Justice' Warrants,
The Bawd dismiss'd her Whores on Errands,[3]
She staid the last—then went, they say,
Unsatisfy'd, tho' tir'd, away.
    Why should I mention all their Magick   200
Poison, and other Stories tragick?
Their Appetites are all such rash ones,
Lust is the least of all their Passions.
    Cesennia's Husband call, you cry,
He lauds her Virtues to the Sky.   205
She brought him twice ten thousand Pounds,
With all *that* Merit she abounds.
Venus ne'er shot at him an Arrow,
Her Fortune darted through his Marrow:
She bought her Freedom, and before him   210
May wink, forgetful of Decorum,
And Lovers Billet-doux may answer:
For he who marries Wives for Gain, Sir,
A Widow's Privilege must grant 'em,
And suffer Captains to gallant 'em.   215
    But *Bibula* doth *Sertorius* move:
I'm sure he married her for Love.
Love I agree was in the Case;
Not of the Woman, but her Face.
Let but one Wrinkle spoil her Forehead;   220
Or should she chance to have a sore Head;
Her Skin grow flabby, or Teeth blacken,
She quickly would be sent a packing.
'Be gone—(the Gentleman[4] would cry)
Are those d—n'd Nostrils never dry?   225

    [1] A young Lady of Pleasure. [Fielding's note.]
    [2] This is a Phrase by which loose Women demand Money of their Gallants. [Fielding's note.] Cf. *The Covent-Garden Tragedy*, II. i.
    [3] In *Rome*, the Keepers of evil Houses used to dismiss their Girls at Midnight; at which Time those who follow the same Trade in this City, first light up their Candles. [Fielding's note.]
    [4] That is, her Husband's Gentleman. The Commentators have wretchedly blunder'd here, in their Interpretation of the Latin. [Fielding's note.]

Jam gravis es nobis, et sæpe emungeris; exi

Ocyus, et propera; sicco venit altera naso.

Interea calet, et regnat, poscitque maritum

Pastores, et ovem Canusinam, ulmosque Falernas.

Quantulum in hoc? pueros omnes, ergastula tota,　　　　150

Quodque domi non est, et habet vicinus, ematur.

Mense quidem brumæ, cum jam mercator Iason

Clausus, et armatis obstat casa candida nautis,

Grandia tolluntur crystallina, maxima rursus

Myrrhina, deinde adamas notissimus, et Berenices　　　155

In digito factus pretiosior: hunc dedit olim

Barbarus incestæ; dedit hunc[1] Agrippa sorori;

Observant ubi festa mero pede sabbata reges,

Et vetus indulget senibus clementia porcis.

　　Nullane de tantis gregibus[2] tibi digna videtur?　　160

Sit formosa, decens, dives, fœcunda, vetustos

---

[1] Repetitionem hujus vocis *dedit* sunt qui conantur abjicere, licet elegantissimam; ideoque Interpretum Gustui minus gratam. [Fielding's note.]

[2] Ambiguitatem qua Greges refert tam ad mulieres quam ad porcos miratur Lubinus, et queritur quod ab aliis non animadvertatur. Sed nescio annon inurbanus potius quam argutus hic dicendus sit Poeta. [Fielding.]

Defend me, Heav'n, from a Strumpet,
Who's always playing on a Trumpet.'
But while her beauteous Youth remains,
With Power most absolute she reigns.
Now Rarities she wants; no matter   230
What Price they cost—they please the better.
Italian Vines, and *Spanish* Sheep.¹
But these are Trifles—you must keep
An Equipage of six stout Fellows;²
Of no Use to 'em, as they tell us,   235
Unless to walk before their Chairs,
When they go out to shew their Airs.
However liberal your Grants,
Still what her Neighbour hath she wants;
Even *Pit's* precious Diamond—that   240
Which *Lewis* Fifteen wear's in's Hat;³
Or what *Agrippa* gave his Sister,⁴
Incestuous Bribe! for which he kiss'd her.
(Sure with less Sin a *Jew* might dine,
If hungry, on a Herd of Swine.)   245
But of this Herd, I mean of Women,
Will not an Individual do Man?
No, none my Soul can e'er inflame,
But the rich, decent, lovely Dame:

¹ In the Original, *Falernian* Vines and *Canusian* Sheep: for *Falernia* produced the most
delicious Wine, and the Sheep which came from *Canusium*, a Town or Village of *Apulia*,
the finest Wool. I know not whether either of the Instances by which I have attempted to
modernize this Passage be at present in Fashion, but if they are not, it is probable the only
Reason is, that we forget *Italian* Vines, as they would require the Assistance of artificial
Heat; and *Spanish* Sheep, as they are to be fetched a great Way by Sea, would be extreamly
expensive, and consequently well worth our having. [Fielding's note.]
² The *Latin* hath it—*All the Fellows in the Work-House*: but this is an Instance that our
Luxury is not yet so extravagant as that of the *Romans* was in *Juvenal's* Days. [Fielding's
note.]
³ The famous Pitt diamond had been bought in India by Thomas Pitt (1653–1726),
grandfather of the elder William Pitt, and sold by him in 1717 to the Regent Duc d'Orléans
for Louis XV. See *Gent. Mag.* xcv (August 1825), pp. 105–7; Pope, *Epist. to Bathurst*, 339 ff.
(Twickenham edn., III. ii. 117 ff. and notes); Sir Charles Hanbury Williams, 'To Sir
Thomas Robinson' (*Works*, 1822, ii. 2); Horace Walpole to George Montagu, 6 May
1736 (*Yale Edition of the Corr.* ix. 2).
⁴ Berenice. [Fielding's note.] On Berenice, daughter of Agrippa I, king of Judah, who
married her uncle Herod, King of Chalcis, and after his death lived with her brother
Agrippa II, see Josephus, *De Bello Judaico*, II. xi. 6 and xv. 1–2; and *Antiq.* XVIII. v. 4
and XIX. v. 1; and Bayle's *Dictionary*, s.v. 'Berenice'.

Porticibus disponat avos, intactior omni

Crinibus effusis bellum dirimente Sabina:

(Rara avis in terris, nigroque simillima cygno.)

Quis feret uxorem, cui constant omnia? malo,　　　　165

Malo Venusinam, quam te, Cornelia,[1] mater

Gracchorum, si cum magnis virtutibus affers

Grande supercilium, et numeras in dote triumphos.

Tolle tuum, precor, Hannibalem, victumque Syphacem

In castris, et cum tota Carthagine migra.　　　　170

　　Parce, precor, Pæan; et tu, Dea, pone sagittas;

Nil pueri faciunt; ipsam configite matrem;

Amphion clamat: sed Pæan contrahit arcum.

Extulit ergo gregem natorum, ipsumque parentem,

Dum sibi nobilior Latonæ gente videtur,　　　　175

Atque eadem scrofa Niobe fœcundior alba.

Quæ tanti gravitas? quæ forma, ut se tibi semper

Imputet? hujus enim rari, summique voluptas

Nulla boni, quoties animo corrupta superbo

---

[1] Scipionis Africani Filia, Cornelio Graccho nupta, et Caii et Tiberii mater, hic maximæ Laudis, non vituperationis causa, memorata [Fielding's note.] Cornelia's husband was, of course, not Cornelius, but Tiberius Sempronius Gracchus; Fielding follows Lubinus here.

Her Womb with Fruitfulness attended;   250
Of a good ancient House descended:
A Virgin too, untouch'd, and chaste,
Whom Man ne'er took about the Waiste.
She's a rare Bird! find her who can,
And much resembling a black Swan.   255
   But who could bear a Wife's great Merit,
Who doth such Qualities inherit?
I would prefer some Country Girl
To the proud Daughter of an Earl;
If my Repose must still be hindred   260
With the great Actions of her Kindred.
Go to the Devil, should I say,
With the *West-Indies* ta'en—away.[1]
'Hold, *Pæan*, hold; thou Goddess, spare
My Children,—was *Amphion's* Pray'r—   265
They have done nought to forfeit Life;
O shoot your Arrows at my Wife.'
His Pray'r nor God nor Goddess heard,
Nor Child, nor ev'n the Mother spar'd.
For why, the Vixen proudly boasted,[2]   270
More than *Latona* she was toasted;
And had been oft'ner in the Straw,
Than the white Sow *Æneas* saw.[3]
   But say, tho' Nature should be lavish,
Can any Mien or Beauty ravish,   275
Whose Mind is nothing but Inanity,
Meer Bladder blown with Wind of Vanity?
Trust, if for such you give your Money,
You buy more Vinegar than Honey.

---

[1] Juvenal here mentions *Cornelia*, the Daughter of *Scipio Africanus*, Wife of *Cornelius Gracchus*, and Mother of the *Gracchi*, *Caius* and *Tiberius*. The Beauty of the Original here is inimitable. [Fielding's note.] See comment on Latin note opposite. If Fielding had a specific Earl's daughter in mind, perhaps the Lady Lucy Pitt, daughter of Thomas Pitt, first Earl of Londonderry (1688 ?–1729), governor of the Leeward Islands at his death.

[2] Our Poet here alludes to the Story of *Niobe* Wife of *Amphion* King of *Thebes*, who affronted *Latona*, in preferring her own Fruitfulness to that of the Goddess; for which Reason *Apollo* and *Diana* destroyed all her Children; the Number of which Authors report variously. [Fielding's note.] See Ovid, *Metam*. vi. 146–312; Aulus Gellius, xx. vi; Aelian, *Var. hist.* XII. xxxvi.

[3] Which produced thirty Pigs at a Litter. [Fielding's note.] See Virgil, *Aeneid*, iii. 389–93; viii. 81–5.

Plus aloes, quam mellis, habet. Quis deditus autem 180
Usque adeo est, ut non illam, quam laudibus effert,
Horreat? inque diem septenis oderit horis?
Quædam parva quidem; sed non toleranda maritis.
Nam quid rancidius, quam quod se non putat ulla
Formosam, nisi quæ de Thusca Græcula facta est? 185
De Sulmonensi mera Cecropis omnia Græce;
Cum sit turpe minus nostris nescire Latine.
Hoc sermone pavent; hoc iram, gaudia, curas,
Hoc cuncta effundunt animi secreta. Quid ultra?
Concumbunt Græce. dones tamen ista puellis: 190
Tune etiam, quam sextus et octogesimus annus
Pulsat, adhuc Græce? non est hic sermo pudicus
In vetula. quoties lascivum intervenit illud,
ΖΩΗ ΚΑΙ ΨΥΧΗ, modo sub lodice relictis
Uteris in turba. quod enim non excitat inguen 195
Vox blanda et nequam? digitos habet: ut tamen omnes
Subsidant pennæ: dicas hæc mollius Æmo
Quanquam, et Carpophoro; facies tua computat annos.
   Si tibi legitimis pactam, junctamque tabellis
Non es amaturus, ducendi nulla videtur 200
Causa; nec est quare cœnam et mustacea perdas,
Labente officio, crudis donanda, nec illud,
Quod prima pro nocte[1] datur; cum lance beata
Dacicus, et scripto radiat Germanicus auro.
Si tibi simplicitas uxoria, deditus uni 205
Est animus; submitte caput cervice parata
Ferre jugum: nullam invenies, quæ parcat amanti.

---

[1] Mos erat præmium aliquod novæ nuptæ donandi, quasi Virginitatis depositæ pretium: Hæc est autem hujus loci vis. *Si non amaturus es Nuptam quam ducis, ne nox prima quidem grata erit; Quam solam in Matrimonio jucundam esse expectare debes.* [Fielding.]

Who is there such a Slave in Nature,   280
That while he praises would not hate her?
Some smaller Crimes, which seem scarce nominable,
Are yet to Husbands most abominable:
For what so fulsome—if it were new t' ye,
That no one thinks herself a Beauty,   285
'Till *Frenchify'd*[1] from Head to Foot,
A meer *Parisian* Dame throughout.
She spells not *English*, who will blame her?
But *French* not understood would shame her.
  This Language 'tis in which they tremble,   290
Quarrel, are happy, and dissemble;
Tell Secrets to some other Miss;
What more?—'tis this in which they kiss.
  But if to Girls we grant this Leave;
You, Madam, whom fast by your Sleeve   295
Old Age hath got—must you still stammer
Soft Phrases out of *Bowyer's* Grammar?[2]
Mon ame, mon Mignon! how it comes
Most graceful from your toothless Gums!
Tho' softer spoke than by Lord *Fanny*,[3]   300
Can that old Face be lik'd by any?
  If Love be not your Cause of Wedding,
There is no other for your Bedding;
All the Expence of Wedding-Day
Would then, my Friend, be thrown away.   305
  If, on the contrary, you doat,
And are of the uxorious Note,
For heavy Yoke your Neck prepare;
None will the tender Husband spare:
Ev'n when they love they will discover   310
Joys in the Torments of a Lover:
The Hope to govern them by Kindness,

---

[1] The *Romans* were (if I may be allowed such a Word) *Greecify'd*, at this Time, in the same manner as we are *Frenchify'd*. [Fielding's note.]

[2] Presumably for 'Boyer's Grammar': Abel Boyer, *The Compleat French Master* (1694; many later editions).

[3] Pope had, in 1733, fixed this name indelibly upon John, Lord Hervey (1696–1743), with *The First Satire of the Second Book of Horace, Imitated*, 6 (Twickenham edn., iv. 4–5 and n.). On Hervey as 'Beau Didapper', see *Joseph Andrews*, IV. ix, in the Wesleyan edition.

Ardeat ipsa licet, tormentis gaudet amantis,

Et spoliis, igitur longe minus utilis illi

Uxor, quisquis erit bonus, optandusque maritus.　　　　210

Nil unquam invita donabis conjuge: vendes

Hac obstante nihil: nihil, hæc si nolit, emetur.

Hæc dabit affectus: ille excludetur amicus

Jam senior, cujus barbam tua janua vidit.

Testandi cum sit lenonibus, atque lanistis　　　　215

Libertas, et juris idem contingat arenæ,

Non unus tibi rivalis dictabitur hæres.

Pone crucem servo: meruit quo crimine servus

Supplicium? quis testis adest? quis detulit? audi:

Nulla unquam de morte hominis cunctatio longa est.　　　　220

O demens, ita servus homo est? nil fecerit, esto:

Hoc volo, sic jubeo, sit pro ratione voluntas.

Imperat ergo viro: sed mox hæc regna relinquit,

Permutatque domos, et flammea conterit: inde

Avolat, et spreti repetit vestigia lecti;　　　　225

Ornatas paulo ante fores, pendentia linquit

Vela domus, et adhuc virides in limine ramos.

Sic crescit numerus; sic fiunt octo mariti[1]

Quinque per autumnos: titulo res digna sepulchri.

Desperanda tibi salva concordia socru:　　　　230

Illa docet spoliis nudi gaudere mariti:

Illa docet, missis a corruptore tabellis,

---

[1] Quot nempe a Lege permissi sunt. Nam prohibitum erat mulieribus, pluribus quam octo maritis nubere, cum hunc numerum ergo minime liceret transire, necessitate coacta uxor ab octavo Marito redit iterum ad primum. [Fielding.]

Argues, my Friend, a total Blindness.
For Wives most useless ever prove
To those most worthy of their Love.   315
  Before you give, or sell, or buy,
She must be courted to comply:
She points new Friendships out—and strait
'Gainst old Acquaintance shuts your Gate.
  The Privilege which at their Birth   320
Our Laws bequeath the Scum o'th' Earth,
Of making Wills, to you's deny'd;
You for her Fav'rites must provide;
Those your sole Heirs creating, who
Have labour'd to make Heirs for you.   325
  Now, come Sir, take your Horse-whip down,
And lash your Footman there, *Tom Brown.*
What hath *Tom* done? or who accuses him?
Perhaps some Rascal, who abuses him.
Let us examine first—and then—   330
'Tis ne'er too late to punish Men.
Men! Do you call this abject Creature
A Man?—He's scarce of human Nature.[1]
What hath he done?—no matter what—
If nothing—lash him well for that: 335
My Will is a sufficient Reason
To constitute a Servant's Treason.
  Thus she commands; but strait she leaves
This Slave, and to another cleaves;
Thence to a third and fourth, and then   340
Returns, perhaps, to you again.
Thus in the Space of seven short Years
Possessing half a score of Dears.
  Be sure, no Quiet can arrive
To you while her Mamma's alive: 345
She'll teach her how to cheat her Spouse,
To pick his Pocket, strip his House:
Answers to Love-Letters indite,
And make her Daughter's Stile polite.

[1] The *Romans* derived from the *Greeks* an Opinion, that their Slaves were of a Species inferior to themselves. As such a Sentiment is inconsistent with the Temper of Christianity, this Passage loses much of its Force by being modernized. [Fielding's note.]

Nil rude, nil simplex rescribere: decipit illa

Custodes, aut ære domat: tunc corpore sano

Advocat Archigenem, onerosaque pallia jactat.   235

Abditus interea latet accersitus adulter,

Impatiensque moræ silet, et præputia ducit.

Scilicet expectas, ut tradat mater honestos,

Aut alios mores, quam quos habet? utile porro

Filiolam turpi vetulæ producere turpem.   240

    Nulla fere causa est, in qua non fœmina litem

Moverit. accusat Manilia, si rea non est.[1]

Componunt ipsæ per se, formantque libellos,

Principium atque locos Celso dictare paratæ.

    Endromidas Tyrias, et fœmineum ceroma   245

Quis nescit? vel quis non vidit vulnera pali?

Quem cavat assiduis sudibus, scutoque lacessit,

Atque omnes implet numeros; dignissima prorsus

Florali matrona tuba;[2] nisi si quid in illo

Pectore plus agitet, veræque paratur arenæ.   250

Quem præstare potest mulier galeata pudorem?

Quæ fugit a sexu, vires amat;[3] hæc tamen ipsa

---

[1] Accusator et reus eandem habent quam in Lege nostra Querens et defendens, significationem. [Fielding.]

[2] Tuba ad impudicos ludos vocante. Hos a Flora meretrice quadam in honorem Floræ Deæ institutos docet Ovid Fast: [v. 185 ff.] Acerbius quidem hoc in matronas a Poeta dictum. [Fielding.]

[3] Ita prorsus legendum existimo, finita interrogatione ad vocem pudorem? sensus tum erit. *Quamquam amat* vires *mulier quæ fugit a sexu, tamen omnino* vir *fieri nolit, quia, &c.*— Multo elegantior ita fiet sententia. Alii legunt *Quæ fugita sexu et vires amat.*—Sed minus recte. [Fielding.]

With Cunning she'll deceive your Spies,   350
Or bribe with Money to tell Lies.
   Then, tho' Health swells her Daughter's Pulse,
She sends for *Wasey, Hoadley, Hulse*.[1]
So she pretends,—but in their Room,
Lo, the Adulterer is come.   355
Do you expect, you simple Elf,
That she who hath them not herself,
Should teach Good Manners to your Lady,
And not debauch her for the Ready?[2]
   In Courts of Justice what Transactions?   360
Manilia's never without Actions:
No Forms of *Litigation* 'scape her,
In Special Pleading next to *Dr–per*.[3]
   Have you not heard of fighting Females,
Whom you would rather think to be Males?   365
Of Madam *Sutton*, Mrs. *Stokes*,[4]
Who give confounded Cuts and Strokes?
They fight the Weapons through complete,
Worthy to ride along the Street.[5]
   Can Female Modesty so rage,   370
To draw a Sword, and mount the Stage?
Will they their Sex entirely quit?
No, they have not so little Wit:
Better they know how small our Shares

---

[1] Fashionable physicians: William Wasey (1691–1757), later President of the Royal College of Physicians; Benjamin Hoadly (1706–57), son of the Bishop of Winchester, and later author of *The Suspicious Husband* (1747); Sir Edward Hulse (d. 1759), Physician in Ordinary to Queen Anne, George I, and George II; and Walpole's doctor in his last illness.

[2] Cf. line 196 and note.

[3] The subscription-list to the *Miscellanies* records a 'Thomas Draper, Esq; Serjeant at Law'; this is possibly an error for the Richard Draper of Gray's Inn (d. 1756) who is listed as one of 'His Majesty's Serjeants at Law' by J. Chamberlayne, *Magna Britanniae Notitia* (1743), Part II, p. 270. See also Edward Foss, *The Judges of England* (1848–64), viii. 89.

[4] Mrs. Elizabeth Stokes, 'the city championess', fought at Figg's amphitheatre in Marylebone Fields and at Hockley-in-the-Hole, apparently both at boxing and quarter-staff, in the 1720s (see William B. Boulton, *Amusements of Old London*, i. 30–1); Madam Sutton is presumably the wife of Ned Sutton, the Champion of Kent, who fought Figg at quarterstaff and, with 'a courageous female heroine', took on Bob Stokes and 'his much admired consort' in 1725 (*ibid.*, pp. 28, 31).

[5] Prize-Fighters, on the Day of Battle, ride through the Streets with a Trumpet before them. [Fielding's note.]

Vir nollet fieri: nam quantula nostra voluptas?

Quale decus rerum, si conjugis auctio fiat,

Balteus, et manicæ, et cristæ, crurisque sinistri   255

Dimidium tegmen! vel si diversa movebit

Prælia, tu felix, ocreas vendente puella.

Hæ sunt, quæ tenui sudant in cyclade, quarum

Delicias et panniculus bombycinus urit.

Aspice, quo fremitu monstratos perferat ictus,   260

Et quanto galeæ curvetur pondere; quanta

Poplitibus sedeat; quam denso fascia libro;

Et ride, scaphium positis cum sumitur armis.

Dicite vos neptes Lepidi, cæcive Metelli,

Gurgitis aut Fabii, quæ ludia sumpserit unquam   265

Hos habitus? quando ad palum gemat uxor Asylli?

   Semper habet lites, alternaque jurgia lectus,

In quo nupta jacet: minimum dormitur in illo.

Tunc gravis illa viro, tunc orba tigride pejor,

Cum simulat gemitus occulti conscia facti,   270

Aut odit pueros, aut ficta pellice plorat

Uberibus semper lachrymis, semperque paratis

In statione sua, atque expectantibus illam,

Quo jubeat manare modo: tu credis amorem;

Of Pleasure—how much less than theirs.   375
    But should your Wife by Auction sell,
(You know the modern Fashion well)
Should *Cock* aloft his Pulpit mount,¹
And all her Furniture recount,
Sure you would scarce abstain from Oaths,   380
To hear, among your Lady's Cloaths,
Of those superb *fine Horseman's Suits*,
And those magnificent *Jack-Boots*.
    And yet, as often as they please,
Nothing is tenderer than these.   385
A Coach!—O Gad! they cannot bear
Such Jolting!—*John*, go fetch a Chair.
Yet see, through *Hide-Park* how they ride!
How masculine! almost astride!
Their Hats fierce cock'd up with Cockades,   390
Resembling Dragoons more than Maids.²
    Knew our Great Grandmothers these Follies?
Daughters of *Hampden, Baynton, Hollis*?³
More Modesty they surely had,
Decently ambling on a Pad.   395
    Sleep never shews his drowsy Head
Within the Reach of Marriage-Bed:
The Wife thence frightens him with Scolding.
—Then chiefly the Attack she's bold in,
When, to conceal her own Amours,   400
She falls most artfully on yours:
Pretends a Jealousy of some Lady,
With Tears in Plenty always ready;
Which on their Post true Cent'nels stand,
The Word still waiting of Command,   405
How she shall order them to trickle.
—Thou thinkest Love her Soul doth tickle,

---

¹ Christopher Cock (d. 1748), famous auctioneer. Fielding uses the same image of Cock aloft in his pulpit in *Joseph Andrews*, III. vi; and he was the model for Christopher Hen in *The Historical Register*, Act II.
² Cf. *Spectator*, 104.
³ These, according to *Sidney*, are some of the best Families in *England*, and superior to many of our modern Nobility. [Fielding's note.] See Algernon Sidney, *Discourses Concerning Government* (1698), III. xxviii (p. 385).

Tu tibi tunc, curruca, places, fletumque labellis 275

Exorbes; quæ scripta, et quas lecture tabellas,

Si tibi zelotypæ retegantur scrinia mœchæ!

Sed jacet in servi complexibus, aut equitis: dic,

Dic aliquem, sodes hic, Quintiliane, colorem.

Hæremus: dic ipsa: olim convenerat, inquit, 280

Ut faceres tu quod velles; necnon ego possem

Indulgere mihi: clames licet, et mare cœlo

Confundas,¹ homo sum. Nihil est audacius illis

Deprensis: iram atque animos a crimine sumunt.

Unde hæc monstra tamen, vel quo de fonte requiris? 285

Præstabat castas humilis fortuna Latinas

Quondam, nec vitiis contingi parva sinebat

Tecta labor, somnique breves, et vellere Thusco

Vexatæ, duræque manus, ac proximus urbi

Hannibal, et stantes Collina in turre mariti. 290

Nunc patimur longæ pacis mala: sævior armis

Luxuria² incubuit, victumque ulciscitur orbem.

---

¹ Exclamando scilicet, ut apud Terentium [*Adelphi*, v. iii. 4], O Cœlum! O Terra! O Maria! [Fielding.]

² Eximiæ sunt hi versus Notæ, et vix satis laudandi. [Fielding]

Poor Hedge-Sparrow—with fifty Dears,
Lickest up her fallacious Tears.
Search her Scrutore, Man, and then tell us   410
Who hath most Reason to be jealous.
   But, in the very Fact she's taken;
Now let us hear, to save her Bacon,
What *Murray*, or what *Henley* can say;[1]
Neither Proof positive will gainsay: 415
It is against the Rules of Practice;
Nothing to her the naked Fact is.
'You know (she cries) e'er I consented
To be, what I have since repented,
It was agreed between us, you   420
Whatever best you lik'd should do;
Nor could I, after a long Trial,
Persist myself in Self-Denial.'
You at her Impudence may wonder,
Invoke the Lightning and the Thunder: 425
'You are a Man (she cries) 'tis true;
We have our human Frailties too.'
   Nought bold is like a Woman caught,
They gather Courage from the Fault.
   Whence come these Prodigies? what Fountain,   430
You ask, produces them? I'th' Mountain
The *British* Dames were chaste, no Crimes
The Cottage stain'd in elder Times;
When the laborious Wife slept little,
Spun Wool, and boil'd her Husband's Kettle: 435
When the *Armada* frighten'd *Kent*,
And good Queen *Bessy* pitch'd her Tent.
Now from Security we feel
More Ills than threaten'd us from Steel;
Severer Luxury abounds,   440

1 Eloquent barristers: William Murray (1705–93), later first Earl of Mansfield, was
made Solicitor-General, November 1742, and Lord Chief Justice, 1756–88; Robert
Henley (1708?–72), later first Earl of Northington, was a friend of Fielding and probably
rode the Western circuit with him. He ultimately became Lord Chancellor, 1761–6. See
below, p. 118 n.

Nullum crimen abest, facinusque libidinis, ex quo
Paupertas Romana perit: hinc fluxit ad istos
Et Sybaris colles, hinc et Rhodos, atque Miletos, 295
Atque coronatum, et petulans, madidumque Tarentum.
Prima peregrinos obscœna pecunia mores
Intulit, et turpi fregerunt secula luxu
Divitiæ molles.—

Avenging *France* of all her Wounds.[1]
When our old *British* Plainness left us,
Of ev'ry Virtue it bereft us:
And we've imported from all Climes,
All sorts of Wickedness and Crimes: 445
French Finery, *Italian* Meats,
With *German* Drunkenness, *Dutch* Cheats.
Money's the Source of all our Woes;
Money! whence Luxury o'erflows,
And in a Torrent, like the *Nile*,[2]   450
Bears off the Virtues of this Isle.[3]

---

[1] Cf. Butler, *Hudibras*, I. iii. 923–4: 'And as the French we conquer'd once, / Now give us Laws for Pantaloons . . .' (1761 edn., p. 103); and Dryden, prologue to *The Spanish Friar*:

> The *French* and we still change, but here's the Curse.
> They change for better, and we change for worse;
> They take up our old Trade of Conquering,
> And we are taking theirs, to Dance and Sing.

(*Works*, 1701, ii. 260.)

[2] Cf. Dryden, *The Medal*, 171–2: 'I call'd thee *Nile*; the parallel will stand: / Thy tydes of Wealth o'erflow the fatten'd Land' (*Works*, 1701, III. i. 26).

[3] We shall here close our Translation of this Satire; for as the Remainder is in many Places too obscene for chaste Ears; so, to the Honour of the *English* Ladies, the *Latin* is by no Means applicable to them, nor indeed capable of being modernized. [Fielding's note.] Cf. Dryden, in the Argument to his translation: '*Whatever his* Roman *Ladies, were, the* English *are free from all his Imputations*' (1693, p. 87).

TO Miss H—AND[1] at *Bath*.

Written *Extempore* in the Pump-Room, 1742.

Soon shall these bounteous Springs thy Wish bestow,
Soon in each Feature sprightly Health shall glow;
Thy Eyes regain their Fire, thy Limbs their Grace,
And Roses join the Lillies in thy Face.[2]
But say, sweet Maid, what Waters can remove   5
The Pangs of cold Despair, of hopeless Love?
The deadly Star which lights th' autumnal Skies[3]
Shines not so bright, so fatal as those Eyes.
The Pains which from their Influence[4] we endure,
Not *Brewster*,[5] Glory of his Art, can cure.[6]   10

[1] The lady has been plausibly identified as Miss Jane Husband, who later (December 1743) married Fielding's friend, Robert Henley, the future Earl of Northington and Lord Chancellor (see J. Paul de Castro, 'Fieldingiana', *N&Q*, 12th ser., i [1916], 483–4; Cross, i. 377–9). The allusion in line 7 to 'autumnal Skies' may (but need not) indicate that the poem was written in that season.

[2] Cf. Tibullus, IV. iv; and Thomson's imitation, 'To Amanda' (*Poetical Works*, ed. Robertson, pp. 469–70).

[3] Probably Arcturus, rather than Sirius, though both were considered malevolent at their heliacal rising (cf. Hippocrates, *Airs, Waters, Places*, xi. 11–15). The rising of Sirius was in late summer, that of Arcturus near the time of the autumnal equinox. On Arcturus, see Plautus, *Rudens*, 70–1; Horace, *Carm.* III. i. 27; Pope, *Windsor Forest*, 119; Garth, *The Dispensary*, iv: 'The bleak *Arcturus* still forbid the Seas' (6th edn., 1706, p. 68). Fielding refers to the ancient belief in the malign influence of Sirius in the notes to *The Vernoniad*.

[4] 'Influence', in its original sense, of course, an emanation from the stars, transferred to the lady's eyes, as in Milton, *L'Allegro*, 121–2: 'With store of Ladies, whose bright eyes / Rain influence . . .'; and Lord Lansdowne's lines, 'Their Praises for that gentle influence, / Which those auspicious lights, your Eyes, dispense' (*Genuine Works*, 1736, i. 5).

[5] Dr. Thomas Brewster (b. 1705), translator of Persius. He is praised in the *Essay on Conversation* (below, p. 150) and (presumably) mentioned in *Tom Jones*, XVIII. iv, as attendant on Mr. Square.

[6] On the topos of Love as the disease for which there is no cure, see Theocritus, XI. i; Tibullus, II. iii. 13–14; Propertius, II. i. 57–8; Ovid, *Heroides*, v. 149; xii. 166–7; Herrick, 'On Himself'; Carew, 'The Mistake'; Lansdowne, 'The Progress of Beauty' (*Genuine Works*, 1736, i. 62); and Pope, 'Summer', 11–12, addressed to Garth: 'Hear what from Love unpractis'd Hearts endure, / From Love, the sole Disease thou canst not cure!' (Twickenham edn., i. 72).

AN ESSAY ON
CONVERSATION[1]

Man is generally represented as an Animal formed for and delighting in Society:[2] In this State alone, it is said, his various Talents can be exerted, his numberless Necessities relieved, the Dangers he is exposed to can be avoided, and many of the Pleasures he eagerly affects, enjoyed. If these Assertions be, as I think they are, undoubtedly and obviously certain, those few who have denied Man to be a social Animal,[3] have left us these two Solutions of their Conduct: either that there are Men as bold in Denial as can be found in Assertion; and as *Cicero* says, there is no Absurdity which some Philosopher or other hath not asserted;[4] so we may say, there is no Truth so glaring, that some have not denied it. Or else; that these Rejecters of Society borrow all their Information from their own savage Dispositions,[5] and are indeed themselves the only Exceptions to the above general Rule.

But to leave such Persons to those who have thought them more worthy of an Answer; there are others who are so seemingly fond of this social State, that they are understood absolutely to confine it to their own Species; and, entirely excluding the tamer and gentler, the herding and flocking Parts of the Creation,

---

[1] The allusion to James Harris's dialogue, 'Concerning Happiness', which was completed in December 1741 (see p. 121 n. 1) and read by Fielding in manuscript, may offer a *terminus a quo* for the *Essay on Conversation*—though, as with most allusions, it could be a late addition. Another allusion, to Dr. Thomas Brewster (see p. 150 n. 4) as the 'late ingenious Translator' of Persius, is ambiguous: Brewster's translation appeared in 1741–2 and this may be what Fielding means by 'late'; there is no record of the date of Brewster's death, but he is the logical candidate for the 'Dr. Brewster' complimented in *Tom Jones*, XVIII. iv, so that he was presumably still alive in 1749.

[2] Aristotle, *Polit.* I. i. 9; Cicero, *De officiis*, I. iv. 12; I. xliv. 157; Marcus Aurelius, II. i, v. xvi, *et passim*; Locke, *Essay Concerning Human Understanding*, III. i. 1; Shaftesbury, *Sensus Communis*, III. ii.

[3] e.g., Hobbes, from his definition of the State of Nature, and Mandeville, for his argument that 'what renders [Man] a Sociable Animal, consists not in his desire of Company, Good-nature, Pity, Affability, and other Graces of a fair Outside . . .' (*Fable of the Bees*, 6th edn., 1732, Preface, p. iv). Epicurus was, of course, often seen as the ancient villain of the piece (cf. *Spectator*, 588).

[4] *De divinatione*, II. lviii. 119. Cf. Swift, *Gulliver's Travels*, III. vi.

[5] On this favourite topos in Fielding, see above, p. 9.

from all Benefits of it, to set up this as one grand general Distinction, between the Human and the Brute Species.[1]

Shall we conclude this *Denial* of all Society to the Nature of Brutes, which seems to be in Defiance of every Day's Observation, to be as bold, as the Denial of it to the Nature of Men? Or, may we not more justly derive the Error from an improper understanding of this Word *Society* in too confined and special a Sense? In a Word; Do those who utterly deny it to the Brutal Nature, mean any other by Society than Conversation?

Now if we comprehend them in this Sense, as I think we very reasonably may, the Distinction appears to me to be truly just; for though other Animals are not without all Use of Society, yet this noble Branch of it seems, of all the Inhabitants of this Globe, confined to Man only;[2] the narrow Power of communicating some few Ideas of Lust, or Fear, or Anger, which may be observable in Brutes, falling infinitely short of what is commonly meant by Conversation, as may be deduced from the Origination of the Word itself, the only accurate Guide to Knowledge. The primitive and literal Sense of this Word is, I apprehend, to *Turn round together*;[3] and in its more copious Usage we intend by it, that reciprocal Interchange of Ideas, by which Truth is examined, Things are, in a manner, *turned round*, and sifted, and all our Knowledge communicated to each other.

In this Respect Man stands, I conceive, distinguished from and superior to all other Earthly Creatures: it is this Privilege which, while he is inferior in Strength to some, in Swiftness to others; without Horns, or Claws, or Tusks to attack them, or even to defend himself against them, hath made him Master of them all. Indeed, in other Views, however vain Men may be of

---

[1] Cicero alludes to the Peripatetic doctrine that 'man is the only animal endowed . . . with a desire for intercourse and society with his fellows' (*De finibus*, IV. vii. 18; trans. H. Rackham, Loeb Library).

[2] Cf. Locke, *Essay*, III. vi. 21; Descartes, *Discours*, V; Cicero, *De officiis*, I. xvi. 50; Seneca, *De ira*, I. iii. 7. In what follows, Fielding may be glancing at Montaigne's witty argument (ultimately from Plutarch) that beasts have speech (II. xii; Cotton trans., 3rd edn., 1700, ii. 191–4, 200–1). See the *Champion*, 17 January 1740.

[3] Fielding's etymology is reasonably sound: the *OED* derives 'to converse' from (ultimately) 'L. *conversārī* lit. to turn oneself about . . .'. For the rest, cf. the *Guardian*, 24: 'The Faculty of interchanging our Thoughts with one another, or what we express by the Word *Conversation*, has always been represented by Moral Writers as one of the noblest Privileges of Reason, and which more particularly sets Mankind above the Brute Part of the Creation' (5th edn., 1729, i. 101).

their Abilities, they are greatly inferior to their animal Neighbours.[1] With what Envy must a Swine, or a much less voracious Animal, be survey'd by a Glutton; and how contemptible must the Talents of other Sensualists appear, when oppos'd, perhaps, to some of the lowest and meanest of Brutes: But in Conversation Man stands alone, at least in this Part of the Creation;[2] he leaves all others behind him at his first Start, and the greater Progress he makes, the greater Distance is between them.

Conversation is of three Sorts. Men are said to converse with God, with themselves, and with one another.[3] The two first of these have been so liberally and excellently spoken to by others, that I shall, at present, pass them by, and confine myself, in this Essay, to the third only: Since it seems to me amazing, that this grand Business of our Lives, the Foundation of every Thing, either useful or pleasant, should have been so slightly treated of;[4] that while there is scarce a Profession or Handicraft in Life, however mean and contemptible, which is not abundantly furnished with proper Rules to the attaining its Perfection, Men should be left almost totally in the Dark, and without the least Light to direct, or any Guide to conduct them in the proper exerting of those Talents, which are the noblest Privilege of human Nature, and productive of all rational Happiness; and the rather as this Power is by no means self-instructed, and in the Possession of the artless and ignorant, is of so mean Use, that it raises them very little above those Animals who are void of it.

As Conversation is a Branch of Society, it follows, that it can be proper to none who is not in his Nature social. Now Society is agreeable to no Creatures who are not inoffensive to each other; and we therefore observe in Animals who are entirely guided by Nature, that it is cultivated by such only, while those of more noxious Disposition addict themselves to Solitude, and,

---

[1] The familiar theriophilic argument; cf. George Boas, *The Happy Beast in French Thought of the Seventeenth Century* (1933).

[2] Presumably Fielding means as opposed to angels; but he may have the 'plurality of worlds' in mind.

[3] So *Spectator*, 381, on 'Chearfulness': 'If we consider Chearfulness in three Lights, with regard to our selves, to those we converse with, and to the great Author of our Being. . . .'

[4] The conventional gambit; cf. Samuel Parker the Younger: 'You wonder, and not without reason, so little has been publish'd upon so considerable a Subject as that of Conversation' ('Of Conversation', in *Sylva*, 1701, p. 70).

unless when prompted by Lust, or that necessary Instinct implanted in them by Nature, for the Nurture of their Young, shun as much as possible the Society of their own Species. If therefore there should be found some human Individuals of so savage a Habit, it would seem they were not adapted to Society, and consequently, not to Conversation: nor would any Inconvenience ensue the Admittance of such Exceptions, since it would by no means impeach the general Rule of Man's being a social Animal; especially when it appears (as is sufficiently and admirably proved by my Friend, the Author of *An Enquiry into Happiness*)[1] that these Men live in a constant Opposition to their own Nature, and are no less Monsters than the most wanton Abortions, or extravagant Births.[2]

Again; if Society requires that its Members should be inoffensive, so the more useful and beneficial they are to each other, the more suitable are they to the social Nature, and more perfectly adapted to its Institution: for all Creatures seek their own Happiness,[3] and Society is therefore natural to any, because it is naturally productive of this Happiness. To render therefore any Animal social is to render it inoffensive; an Instance of which is to be seen in those the Ferocity of whose Nature can be tamed by Man. And here the Reader may observe a double Distinction of Man from the more savage Animals by Society, and from the social by Conversation.

But if Men were meerly inoffensive to each other, it seems as if Society and Conversation would be meerly indifferent; and that in order to make it desirable by a sensible Being, it is necessary we should go farther, and propose some positive Good to ourselves from it; and this presupposes not only negatively, our not receiving any Hurt; but positively, our receiving some Good,

---

[1] The Treatise here mentioned is not yet public. [Fielding's note.] 'Concerning Happiness: A Dialogue', by James Harris (1709–80), the author of *Hermes*, was published in his *Three Treatises*, 1744. A note by his son, the Earl of Malmesbury, who edited Harris's *Works* in 1801, says that the treatise was '*Finished Dec.* 15, A.D. 1741' (i. 61).

[2] Berkeley, in *Guardian*, 126, declared that from an innate social principle 'arises that diffusive Sense of Humanity so unaccountable to the selfish Man who is untouch'd with it, and is, indeed, a sort of Monster or Anomalous Production' (5th edn., 1729, ii. 160). Cf. Bacon, *Essays*, xxvii ('Of Friendship'): 'For it is most true, that a natural and secret hatred, and aversation towards *Society* in any Man, hath somewhat of the Savage Beast . . .' (1701 edn., p. 69).

[3] Aristotle, *Nic. Eth.* I. vii. 8: 'Happiness . . . is the end at which all actions aim.' Cf. Cicero, *De finibus*, II. xxvii. 86; Locke, *Essay*, I. ii. 3.

some Pleasure or Advantage from each other in it, something
which we could not find in an unsocial and solitary State: otherwise we might cry out with the Right Honourable Poet;

Give us our Wildness and our Woods,
Our Huts and Caves again.[1]

The Art of pleasing or doing Good to one another is therefore
the Art of Conversation.[2] It is this Habit which gives it all its
Value. And as Man's being a social Animal (the Truth of which
is incontestably proved by that excellent Author of *An Enquiry*,
&c. I have above cited) presupposes a natural Desire or Tendency this Way, it will follow, that we can fail in attaining this
truly desirable End from Ignorance only in the Means; and how
general this Ignorance is, may be, with some Probability, inferred
from our want of even a Word to express this Art by: that which
comes the nearest to it, and by which, perhaps, we would sometimes intend it, being so horribly and barbarously corrupted, that
it contains at present scarce a simple Ingredient of what it seems
originally to have been designed to express.

The Word I mean is *Good Breeding*; a Word, I apprehend,
not at first confined to Externals, much less to any particular
Dress or Attitude of the Body: nor were the Qualifications
expressed by it to be furnished by a Milliner, a Taylor, or a
Perriwig-maker; no, nor even by a Dancing-Master himself.
According to the Idea I myself conceive from this Word, I should
not have scrupled to call *Socrates* a well-bred Man, though I
believe he was very little instructed by any of the Persons I have
above enumerated. In short, by *Good Breeding* (notwithstanding
the corrupt Use of the Word in a very different Sense) I mean
the Art of pleasing, or contributing as much as possible to the
Ease and Happiness of those with whom you converse.[3] I shall

[1] The Duke of *Buckingham*. [Fielding's note.] The lines occur in the chorus between
the first and second acts of his *Julius Caesar*:
Oh! rather than be Slaves to bold imperious Men,
Give us our Wildness, and our Woods, our Huts, and Caves again.
(*The Works of John Sheffield . . . Duke of Buckingham*, 3rd edn., 1740, i. 241.)
[2] One of the most famous of the courtesy-books on conversation was, in fact, *L'Art de
plaire dans la conversation* (1688), by Pierre d'Ortigue, sieur de Vaumorière (numerous
English translations). But almost all the Augustan writers on conversation insisted that the
Art of Pleasing was its central feature.
[3] Cf. Locke, *Some Thoughts Concerning Education* (1693): '*Good-Breeding* . . . has no
other use nor end, but to make People easie and satisfied in their conversation with us'
(p. 169).

contend therefore no longer on this Head: for whilst my Reader
clearly conceives the Sense in which I use this Word, it will not
be very material whether I am right or wrong in its original
Application.

Good Breeding then, or the *Art of pleasing in Conversation,* is
expressed two different Ways, *viz.* in our Actions and our Words,
and our Conduct in both may be reduced to that concise, comprehensive Rule in Scripture; *Do unto all Men as you would they
should do unto you.*[1] Indeed, concise as this Rule is, and plain as
it appears, what are all Treatises on Ethics, but Comments
upon it? And whoever is well read in the Book of Nature, and
hath made much Observation on the Actions of Men, will
perceive so few capable of judging, or rightly pursuing their
own Happiness, that he will be apt to conclude, that some
Attention is necessary (and more than is commonly used) to
enable Men to know truly, *what they would have done unto them,*
or at least, what it would be their Interest *to have done.*[2]

If therefore Men, through Weakness or Inattention, often err
in their Conceptions of what would produce their own Happiness,
no wonder they should miss in the Application of what will contribute to that of others; and thus we may, without too severe a
Censure on their Inclinations, account for that frequent Failure in
true Good Breeding, which daily Experience gives us Instances of.

Besides, the Commentators have well paraphrased on the
abovementioned divine Rule, that it is, to *do unto Men what you
would they,* IF THEY WERE IN YOUR SITUATION AND CIRCUM-
STANCES, AND YOU IN THEIRS, *should do unto you:*[3] And as this
Comment is necessary to be observed in Ethics, so is it particularly useful in this our Art, where the Degree of the Person is
always to be considered, as we shall explain more at large hereafter.

We see then a Possibility for a Man well disposed to this
Golden Rule, without some Precautions, to err in the Practice;
nay, even Good-Nature itself, the very Habit of Mind most

---

[1] Matt. 7: 12, Luke 6: 31. Cf. the *Covent-Garden Journal,* 55.

[2] Cf. Juvenal, *Sat.* x. 1–4: 'Look round the Habitable World: how few / Know their
own Good; or knowing it, pursue' (Dryden trans.).

[3] See, e.g., Henry Hammond, *A Paraphrase and Annotations upon All the Books of the
New Testament* (1653), p. 42; Daniel Whitby, *A Paraphrase and Commentary on the New
Testament* (4th edn., 1718), i. 79. Cf. Seneca, *Epist. mor.* xlvii. 11: 'sic cum inferiore vivas,
quemadmodum tecum superiorem velis vivere.'

essential to furnish us with true Good Breeding, the latter so nearly resembling the former, that it hath been called, and with the Appearance at least of Propriety, artificial *Good Nature*.[1] This excellent Quality itself sometimes shoots us beyond the Mark, and shews the Truth of those Lines in *Horace*:

Insani sapiens nomen ferat, æquus iniqui
Ultra quam satis est VIRTUTEM *si petat ipsam*.[2]

Instances of this will be naturally produced where we shew the Deviations from those Rules, which we shall now attempt to lay down.

As this Good Breeding is the Art of pleasing, it will be first necessary, with the utmost Caution, to avoid hurting or giving any Offence to those with whom we converse. And here we are surely to shun any kind of actual Disrespect, or Affront to their Persons, by Insolence, which is the severest Attack that can be made on the Pride of Man, and of which *Florus* seems to have no inadequate Opinion, when speaking of the second *Tarquin*, he says; *In omnes superbia (quæ Crudelitate gravior est* BONIS) *grassatus*; 'He trod on all with INSOLENCE, which sits heavier on Men of great Minds than Cruelty itself.'[3] If there is any Temper in Man, which more than all others disqualifies him for Society, it is this Insolence or Haughtiness, which, blinding a Man to his own Imperfections, and giving him a Hawk's Quick-sightedness to those of others, raises in him that Contempt for his Species, which inflates the Cheeks, erects the Head, and stiffens the Gaite of those strutting Animals, who sometimes stalk in Assemblies, for no other Reason, but to shew in their Gesture and Behaviour the Disregard they have for the Company. Though to a truly great and philosophical Mind, it is not easy to conceive a more ridiculous Exhibition than this Puppet; yet to others he is little less than a Nusance; for Contempt is a murtherous Weapon, and there is this Difference only between the greatest and weakest Men, when attacked by it; that, in order to wound the former, it must be just; whereas without the Shields

[1] Cf. *Spectator*, 169: 'There is no Society or Conversation to be kept up in the World without Good-nature. . . . For this Reason Mankind have been forced to invent a kind of artificial Humanity, which is what we express by the Word *Good-Breeding*.'

[2] *Epist*. I. vi. 15–16: 'Let the wise man bear the name of madman, the just of unjust, should he pursue Virtue herself beyond due bounds' (trans. H. R. Fairclough, Loeb Library). Cf. the *Champion*, 15 March 1740; *Covent-Garden Journal*, 55; and Shaftesbury, *Characteristicks* (6th edn., 1737), ii. 90–1.   [3] *Epitomae*, I. i. 7. 4.

of Wisdom and Philosophy, which God knows are in the Possession of very few, it wants no Justice to point it; but is certain
to penetrate, from whatever Corner it comes. It is this Disposition
which inspires the empty *Cacus* to deny his Acquaintance, and
overlook Men of Merit in Distress; and the little, silly, pretty
Phillida, or *Foolida*, to stare at the strange Creatures round her.
It is this Temper which constitutes the supercilious Eye, the
reserved Look, the distant Bowe, the scornful Leer, the affected
Astonishment, the loud Whisper, ending in a Laugh directed
full in the Teeth of another. Hence spring, in short, those
numberless Offences given too frequently, in public and private
Assemblies, by Persons of weak Understandings, indelicate
Habits, and so hungry and foul-feeding a Vanity, that it wants to
devour whatever comes in its Way. Now, if Good-Breeding be
what we have endeavoured to prove it, how foreign, and indeed
how opposite to it, must such a Behaviour be? And can any Man
call a Duke or a Dutchess who wears it, well-bred? or are they
not more justly entitled to those inhuman Names which they
themselves allot to the lowest Vulgar? But behold a more pleasing
Picture on the Reverse. See the Earl of *C*—[1] noble in his Birth,
splendid in his Fortune, and embellished with every Endow-
ment of Mind; how affable, how condescending![2] himself the
only one who seems ignorant that he is every Way the greatest
Person in the Room.

But it is not sufficient to be inoffensive, we must be profitable
Servants to each other: we are, in the second Place, to proceed
to the utmost Verge in paying the Respect due to others. We
had better go a little too far than stop short in this Particular.
My Lord *Shaftsbury* hath a pretty Observation, that the Beggar,
in addressing to a Coach with, my Lord, is sure not to offend,
even though there be no Lord there; but, on the contrary,
should plain Sir fly in the Face of a Nobleman, what must be
the Consequence?[3] And indeed, whoever considers the Bustle

[1] Chesterfield (see above, p. 29).
[2] Without its modern overtones; cf. Addison in *Tatler*, 152: 'the same noble Condescension, which never dwells but in truly great Minds . . .'; Shaftesbury, *Soliloquy*, III. iii: 'that
Modesty, Condescension, and just *Humanity* which is essential to the Success of all friendly
Counsel and *Admonition*' (*Characteristicks*, 6th edn., 1737, i. 364).
[3] *A Letter Concerning Enthusiasm*, iv (*Characteristicks*, 6th edn., 1737, i. 35-6). See
A Journey from This World to the Next, I. xix. Cf. Martial, VI. lxxxviii, on losing a gift of
money by failing to address a patron as 'dominus'.

and Contention about Precedence, the Pains and Labours undertaken, and sometimes the Prices given for the smallest Title or Mark of Pre-eminence, and the visible Satisfaction betray'd in its Enjoyment, may reasonably conclude this is a Matter of no small Consequence. The Truth is, we live in a World of common Men, and not of Philosophers; for one of these, when he appears (which is very seldom) among us, is distinguished, and very properly too, by the Name of an *odd Fellow*: for what is it less than extream Oddity to despise what the Generality of the World think the Labour of their whole Lives well employed in procuring: we are therefore to adapt our Behaviour to the Opinion of the Generality of Mankind, and not to that of a few odd Fellows.

It would be tedious and perhaps impossible, to specify every Instance, or to lay down exact Rules for our Conduct in every minute Particular. However, I shall mention some of the chief which most ordinarily occur, after premising, that the Business of the whole is no more than to convey to others an Idea of your Esteem of them, which is indeed the Substance of all the Compliments, Ceremonies, Presents, and whatever passes between well-bred People.[1] And here I shall lay down these Positions.

First, that all meer Ceremonies exist in *Form* only, and have in them no Substance at all: but being imposed by the Laws of Custom, become essential to Good Breeding, from those high-flown Compliments paid to the Eastern Monarchs, and which pass between *Chinese* Mandarines, to those coarser Ceremonials in use between *English* Farmers and *Dutch* Boors.[2]

Secondly, That these Ceremonies, poor as they are, are of more Consequence than they at first appear,[3] and, in Reality, constitute the only external Difference between Man and Man. Thus, His Grace, Right Honourable, My Lord, Right Reverend, Reverend, Honourable, Sir, Esquire, Mr. &c. have, in a Philosophical Sense, no Meaning, yet are, perhaps, politically essential, and must be preserved by Good Breeding; because,

---

[1] So Hamlet (II. ii. 389): 'the appurtenance of welcome is fashion and ceremony'.

[2] Cf. *Spectator*, 62: '*French* Huguenots, or *Dutch* Boors, brought over in Herds, but not Naturalized'.

[3] Cf. Fielding's comment upon the ceremonies surrounding the ancient oath of fealty, in the Preface to *An Enquiry into the Causes of the Late Increase of Robbers* (1751).

Thirdly, They raise an Expectation in the Person by Law and Custom entitled to them, and who will consequently be displeased with the Disappointment.

Now, in order to descend minutely into any Rules for Good Breeding, it will be necessary to lay some Scene, or to throw our Disciple into some particular Circumstance. We will begin then with a Visit in the Country; and as the principal Actor on this Occasion is the Person who receives it, we will, as briefly as possible, lay down some general Rules for his Conduct; marking, at the same Time, the principal Deviations we have observed on these Occasions.

When an expected Guest arrives to Dinner at your House, if your Equal, or indeed not greatly your Inferior, he should be sure to find your Family in some Order, and yourself dress'd and ready to receive him at your Gate with a smiling Countenance. This infuses an immediate Cheerfulness into your Guest, and perswades him of your Esteem and Desire of his Company. Not so is the Behaviour of *Polysperchon*, at whose Gate you are obliged to knock a considerable Time before you gain Admittance. At length, the Door being opened to you by a Maid, or some improper Servant, who wonders where the Devil all the Men are; and being asked if the Gentleman is at home, answers, She believes so; you are conducted into a Hall, or back Parlour, where you stay some Time, before the Gentleman, in *Dishabille* from his Study or his Garden, waits upon you, asks Pardon, and assures you he did not expect you so soon.

Your Guest being introduced into a Drawing-Room, is, after the first Ceremonies, to be asked, whether he will refresh himself after his Journey, before Dinner, (for which he is never to stay longer than the usual or fixed Hour.) But this Request is never to be repeated oftner than twice, in Imitation of *Chalepus*, who, as if hired by a Physician, crams Wine in a Morning down the Throats of his most temperate Friends, their Constitutions being not so dear to them as their present Quiet.

When Dinner is on the Table, and the Ladies have taken their Places, the Gentlemen are to be introduced into the Eating-Room, where they are to be seated with as much seeming Indifference as possible, unless there be any present whose Degrees claim an undoubted Precedence. As to the rest, the general Rules of Precedence are by Marriage, Age, and Profession. Lastly; in placing your Guests, Regard is rather to be had to Birth than Fortune: for though Purse-Pride is forward enough to exalt itself, it bears a Degradation with more secret Comfort and Ease than the former, as being more inwardly satisfied with itself, and less apprehensive of Neglect or Contempt.

The Order in helping your Guests is to be regulated by that of placing them: but here I must with great Submission recommend to the Lady at the upper End of the Table, to distribute her Favours as equally, and as impartially as she can. I have sometimes seen a large Dish of Fish extend no farther than to the fifth Person, and a Haunch of Venison lose all its Fat before half the Table had tasted it.

A single Request to eat of any particular Dish, how elegant soever, is the utmost I allow. I strictly prohibit all earnest Solicitations, all Complaints that you have no Appetite, which are sometimes little less than Burlesque, and always impertinent and troublesome.

And here, however low it may appear to some Readers, as I have known Omissions of this kind give Offence, and sometimes make the Offenders, who have been very well-meaning Persons, ridiculous, I cannot help mentioning the Ceremonial of drinking Healths at Table, which is always to begin with the Lady's, and next the Master's of the House.

When Dinner is ended, and the Ladies retired, though I do not hold the Master of the Feast obliged to fuddle himself through Complacence; and indeed it is his own Fault generally, if his Company be such as would desire it, yet he is to see that the Bottle circulate sufficiently to afford every Person present a moderate Quantity of Wine, if he chuses it; at the same Time permitting those who desire it, either to pass the Bottle, or fill their Glass as they please. Indeed, the beastly Custom of besotting, and ostentatious Contention for Pre-eminence in their Cups, seems at present pretty well abolished among the better sort of People. Yet *Methus* still remains, who measures the Honesty and Understanding of Mankind by the Capaciousness of their Swallow; who sings forth the Praises of a Bumper, and complains of the Light in your Glass; and at whose Table it is as difficult to preserve your Senses, as to preserve your Purse at a Gaming Table, or your Health at a B——y-House.[1] On the other Side,

---

[1] Bawdy-House.

K

Sophronus eyes you carefully whilst you are filling out his Liquor. The Bottle as surely stops when it comes to him, as your Chariot at *Temple-Bar*;[2] and it is almost as impossible to carry a Pint of Wine from his House, as to gain the Love of a reigning Beauty, or borrow a Shilling of P— *W*—.[3]

But to proceed. After a reasonable Time, if your Guest intends staying with you the whole Evening, and declines the Bottle, you may propose Play, Walking, or any other Amusement; but these are to be but barely mentioned, and offered to his Choice with all Indifference on your Part. What Person can be so dull as not to perceive in *Agyrtes* a Longing to pick your Pockets? or in *Alazon*, a Desire to satisfy his own Vanity in shewing you the Rarities of his House and Gardens? When your Guest offers to go, there should be no Solicitations to stay, unless for the whole Night, and that no farther than to give him a moral Assurance of his being welcome so to do: no Assertions that he shan't go yet; no laying on violent Hands; no private Orders to Servants, to delay providing the Horses or Vehicles; like *Desmophylax*, who never suffers any one to depart from his House without entitling him to an Action of false Imprisonment.

Let us now consider a little the Part which the Visitor himself is to act. And first, he is to avoid the two Extremes of being too early, or too late, so as neither to surprize his Friend unawares or unprovided, nor detain him too long in Expectation. *Orthrius*, who hath nothing to do, disturbs your Rest in a Morning; and the frugal *Chronophidus*, lest he should waste some Minutes of his precious Time, is sure to spoil your Dinner.

The Address at your Arrival should be as short as possible, especially when you visit a Superior; not imitating *Phlenaphius*, who would stop his Friend in the Rain, rather than omit a single Bowe.

Be not too observant of trifling Ceremonies, such as rising, sitting, walking first in or out of the Room, except with one greatly your Superior; but when such a one offers you Precedence, it is uncivil to refuse it: Of which I will give you the following

---

1 he ambiguity of Fielding's attitudes toward Prudence is perhaps exhibited in the fact that he here employs the name 'Sophronus' (from σώφρων, discreet, prudent, moderate) for a watchful, selfish kind of prudence, and below (p. 144) for benevolent discretion.

2 On the bottleneck at Temple Bar, see *Tatler*, 137 and *Spectator*, 498.

3 On Peter Walter, see below, p. 193, and above, p. 67.

Instance. An *English* Nobleman being in *France*, was bid by *Lewis* XIV. to enter his Coach before him, which he excused himself from; the King then immediately mounted, and ordering the Door to be shut, drove on, leaving the Nobleman behind him.[1]

Never refuse any Thing offered you out of Civility, unless in Preference of a Lady, and that no oftner than once; for nothing is more truly Good Breeding, than to avoid being troublesome. Though the Taste and Humour of the Visitor is to be chiefly considered, yet is some Regard likewise to be had to that of the Master of the House; for otherwise your Company will be rather a Penance than a Pleasure. *Methusus* plainly discovers his Visit to be paid to his sober Friend's Bottle; nor will *Philopasus* abstain from Cards, though he is certain they are agreeable only to himself; whilst the slender *Leptines* gives his fat Entertainer a Sweat, and makes him run the Hazard of breaking his Wind up his own Mounts.

If Conveniency allows your staying longer than the Time proposed, it may be civil to offer to depart, lest your Stay may be incommodious to your Friend: but if you perceive the contrary, by his Solicitations, they should be readily accepted; without tempting him to break these Rules we have above laid down for him; causing a Confusion in his Family, and among his Servants, by Preparations for your Departure. Lastly, when you are resolved to go, the same Method is to be observed which I have prescribed at your Arrival. No tedious Ceremonies of taking Leave: not like *Hyperphylus*, who bowes and kisses, and squeezes by the Hand as heartily, and wishes you as much Health and Happiness, when he is going a Journey home of ten Miles, from a common Acquaintance, as if he was leaving his nearest Friend or Relation on a Voyage to the *East-Indies*.

Having thus briefly considered our Reader in the Circumstance of a private Visit, let us now take him into a public Assembly, where, as more Eyes will be on his Behaviour, it cannot be less his Interest to be instructed. We have indeed already formed a general Picture of the chief Enormities committed

---

[1] Fielding seems to have heard an inverted version of the anecdote in which Lord Stair, at Louis's invitation, mounted into the coach before him, shocking the French court but winning Louis's approval. See Baron Ferdinand Rothschild, *Personal Characteristics from French History* (1896), p. 59; Henry Kett, ed., *Flowers of Wit* (1814), i. 176.

on these Occasions, we shall here endeavour to explain more particularly the Rules of an opposite Demeanour, which we may divide into three Sorts, *viz.* our Behaviour to our Superiours, to our Equals, and to our Inferiours.[1]

In our Behaviour to our Superiours, two Extremes are to be avoided, namely, an abject and base Servility, and an impudent and encroaching Freedom. When the well-born *Hyperdulus* approaches a Nobleman in any public Place, you would be persuaded he was one of the meanest of his Domestics: his Cringes fall little short of Prostration; and his whole Behaviour is so mean and servile, that an Eastern Monarch would not require more Humiliation from his Vassals.[2] On the other Side; *Anaschyntus*, whom fortunate Accidents, without any Pretensions from his Birth, have raised to associate with his Betters, shakes my Lord Duke by the Hand, with a Familiarity savouring not only of the most perfect Intimacy, but the closest Alliance. The former Behaviour properly raises our Contempt, the latter our Disgust. *Hyperdulus* seems worthy of wearing his Lordship's Livery; *Anaschyntus* deserves to be turned out of his Service for his Impudence. Between these two is that golden Mean, which declares a Man ready to acquiesce in allowing the Respect due to a Title by the Laws and Customs of his Country, but impatient of any Insult, and disdaining to purchase the Intimacy with, and Favour of a Superior, at the Expence of Conscience or Honour.[3] As to the Question, Who are our Superiours? I shall endeavour to ascertain them, when I come, in the second Place, to mention our Behaviour to our Equals. The first Instruction on this Head, being carefully to consider who are such: Every little Superiority of Fortune or Profession being too apt to intoxicate Men's Minds, and elevate them in their own Opinion, beyond their

[1] The conventional *divisio*; and in Fielding's society a realistic one. Lord Chesterfield censured a person (sometimes taken to have been Dr. Johnson) who, being 'absolutely ignorant of the several gradations of familiarity or respect, . . . is exactly the same to his superiors, his equals, and his inferiors; and therefore, by a necessary consequence, absurd to two of the three' (*Letters to His Son*, ed. Strachey-Calthrop, ii. 120). For the *reductio ad absurdum*, however, cf. Lord Froth's measured bows in *Guardian*, 137.

[2] The standard instance (even from antiquity) of despotism; Addison's allegory of Liberty, in *Tatler*, 161, describes Tyranny as 'dressed in an Eastern Habit'. Cf. *Amelia*, III. iv; and the *Journal of a Voyage to Lisbon*, 27 and 30 June.

[3] Cf. *Tatler*, 204: 'The highest Point of good Breeding, if any one can hit it, is to show a very nice Regard to your own Dignity; and with that, in your Heart express your Value for the Man above you.'

Merit or Pretensions. Men are superior to each other in this our Country by Title, by Birth, by Rank in Profession, and by Age; very little, if any, being to be allowed to Fortune, though so much is generally exacted by it, and commonly paid to it. Mankind never appear to me in a more despicable Light, than when I see them, by a simple as well as mean Servility, voluntarily concurring in the Adoration of Riches, without the least Benefit or Prospect from them. Respect and Deference are perhaps justly demandable of the obliged, and may be, with some Reason at least, from Expectation, paid to the Rich and Liberal from the Necessitious: but that Men should be allured by the glittering of Wealth only, to feed the insolent Pride of those who will not in Return feed their Hunger; that the sordid Niggard should find any Sacrifices on the Altar of his Vanity, seems to arise from a blinder Idolatry, and a more bigotted and senseless Superstition, than any which the sharp Eyes of Priests have discovered in the human Mind.

All Gentlemen, therefore, who are not raised above each other by Title, Birth, Rank in Profession, Age, or actual Obligation, being to be considered as Equals, let us take some Lessons for their Behaviour to each other in public, from the following Examples; in which we shall discern as well what we are to elect, as what we are to avoid. *Authades* is so absolutely abandoned to his own Humour, that he never gives it up on any Occasion. If *Seraphina* herself, whose Charms one would imagine should infuse Alacrity into the Limbs of a Cripple sooner than the *Bath* Waters, was to offer herself for his Partner, he would answer, *He never danced*, even though the Ladies lost their Ball by it. Nor doth this Denial arise from Incapacity; for he was in his Youth an excellent Dancer, and still retains sufficient Knowledge of the Art, and sufficient Abilities in his Limbs to practice it; but from an Affectation of Gravity, which he will not sacrifice to the eagerest Desire of others. *Dyskolus* hath the same Aversion to Cards; and though competently skilled in all Games, is by no Importunities to be prevailed on to make a third at *Ombre*, or a fourth at Whisk and *Quadrille*. He will suffer any Company to be disappointed of their Amusement, rather than submit to pass an Hour or two a little disagreeably to himself. The Refusal of *Philautus* is not so general: he is very ready to engage, provided you will indulge him in his favourite Game, but it is impossible to perswade him to any other. I should add, both these are Men of Fortune, and the Consequences of Loss or Gain, at the Rate they are desired to engage, very trifling and inconsiderable to them.

The Rebukes these People sometimes meet with, are no more equal to their Deserts than the Honour paid to *Charistus*, the Benevolence of whose Mind scarce permits him to indulge his own Will, unless by Accident. Though neither his Age nor Understanding incline him to dance, nor will admit his receiving any Pleasure from it, yet would he caper a whole Evening, rather than a fine young Lady should lose an Opportunity of displaying her Charms by the several genteel and amiable Attitudes which this Exercise affords the skilful of that Sex. And though Cards are not adapted to his Temper, he never once baulked the Inclinations of others on that Account.

But as there are many who will not in the least Instance mortify their own Humour to purchase the Satisfaction of all Mankind, so there are some who make no Scruple of satisfying their own Pride and Vanity, at the Expence of the most cruel Mortification of others. Of this Kind is *Agroicus*, who seldom goes to an Assembly, but he affronts half his Acquaintance, by overlooking, or disregarding them.

As this is a very common Offence, and indeed much more criminal, both in its Cause and Effect, than is generally imagined, I shall examine it very minutely; and I doubt not but to make it appear, that there is no Behaviour (to speak like a Philosopher) more contemptible, nor, in a civil Sense, more detestable than this.[1]

The first Ingredient in this Composition is PRIDE, which, according to the Doctrine of some, is the universal Passion.[2] There are others who consider it as the Foible of great Minds;[3] and others again, who will have it to be the very Foundation of Greatness;[4] and perhaps it may of that Greatness which we have

---

[1] See the analysis in *Covent-Garden Journal*, 61, which also derives Contempt from a mixture of Pride and Ill-nature.

[2] Cf. Edward Young, *Love of Fame, The Universal Passion* (1725–8). Arthur Murphy meant this work when he said, 'A witty Satirist has called Pride the Universal Passion . . .' (*Gray's-Inn Journal*, 1756, ii. 34). Hobbes (see following notes) and Mandeville (cf. *Amelia*, III. v) could also have been in Fielding's mind.   [3] e.g., Milton, *Lycidas*, 70–1.

[4] Cf. Aristotle's portrait of the Magnanimous Man (esp. *Nic. Eth.* IV. iii. 18 and 22). But Fielding may be thinking of Hobbes.

endeavoured to expose in many Parts of these Works: but to real Greatness, which is the Union of a good Heart with a good Head, it is almost diametrically opposite, as it generally proceeds from the Depravity[1] of both, and almost certainly from the Badness of the latter. Indeed, a little Observation will shew us, that Fools are the most addicted to this Vice; and a little Reflection will teach us, that it is incompatible with true Understanding. Accordingly we see, that while the wisest of Men have constantly lamented the Imbecility and Imperfection of their own Nature, the meanest and weakest have been trumpeting forth their own Excellencies, and triumphing in their own Sufficiency.

PRIDE may, I think, be properly defined; *the Pleasure we feel in contemplating our own superior Merit, on* comparing *it with that of others*.[2] That it arises from this supposed Superiority is evident: for however great you admit a Man's Merit to be, if all Men were equal to him, there would be no Room for Pride: now if it stop here, perhaps there is no enormous Harm in it, or at least, no more than is common to all other Folly; every Species of which is always liable to produce every Species of Mischief: Folly I fear it is; for should the Man estimate rightly on this Occasion, and the Ballance should fairly turn on his Side in this particular Instance; should he be indeed a greater Orator, Poet, General; should he be more wise, witty, learned, young, rich, healthy, or in whatever Instance he may excel one, or many, or all; yet, if he examine himself thoroughly, will he find no Reason to abate his Pride? Is the Quality, in which he is so eminent, so generally or justly esteemed; Is it so entirely his own? Doth he not rather owe his Superiority to the Defects of others, than to his own Perfection? Or, lastly, Can he find in no Part of his Character, a Weakness which may counterpoise this Merit, and which as justly, at least, threatens him with Shame, as this entices him to Pride? I fancy, if such a Scrutiny was made,

---

[1] Cf. Addison's attack on Man's pride, 'a Passion which rises from the Depravity of his Nature' (*Guardian*, 153; 5th edn., 1729, ii. 262). The censuring of Pride, was, of course, an Augustan commonplace.

[2] Cf. Hobbes, *Human Nature*, IX. i: 'Glory, or internal gloriation or triumph of the mind, is the passion which proceedeth from the imagination or conception of our *own power* above the power of him that contendeth with us; ... and this passion, of them whom it displeaseth, is called *pride*; by them whom it pleaseth, it is termed a *just valuation* of himself' (*English Works*, ed. Molesworth, iv. 40–1).

(and nothing so ready as good Sense to make it) a proud Man would be as rare, as in Reality he is a ridiculous Monster. But suppose a Man, on this Comparison, is (as may sometimes happen) a little partial to himself, the Harm is to himself, and he becomes only ridiculous from it. If I prefer my Excellence in Poetry to *Pope* or *Young*:[1] if an inferior Actor should, in his Opinion, exceed *Quin* or *Garrick*;[2] or a Sign-Post Painter set himself above the inimitable *Hogarth*;[3] we become only ridiculous by our Vanity; and the Persons themselves, who are thus humbled in the Comparison, would laugh with more Reason than any other. PRIDE therefore, hitherto, seems an inoffensive Weakness only, and entitles a Man to no worse an Appellation than that of a FOOL: but it will not stop here; though FOOL be perhaps no desirable Term, the proud Man will deserve worse: He is not contented with the Admiration he pays himself; he now becomes ARROGANT, and requires the same Respect and Preference from the World; for Pride, though the greatest of Flatterers, is by no means a profitable Servant to itself; it resembles the Parson of the Parish more than the 'Squire, and lives rather on the Tithes, Oblations, and Contributions it collects from others, than on its own Demesne. As Pride therefore is seldom without Arrogance, so is this never to be found without Insolence. The arrogant Man must be insolent, in order to attain his own Ends: and to convince and remind Men of the Superiority he affects, will naturally, by ill Words, Actions, and Gestures, endeavour to throw the despised Person at as much Distance as possible from him. Hence proceeds that supercilious Look, and all those visible Indignities with which Men behave in public, to those whom they fancy their Inferiors. Hence the very notable Custom of deriding and often denying the nearest Relations, Friends, and Acquaintance, in Poverty and Distress; left we should anywise be levelled with the Wretches we despise, either in their own Imagination, or in the Conceit of any who should behold Familiarities pass between us.

But besides Pride, Folly, Arrogance, and Insolence, there is another Simple (which Vice never willingly leaves out of any Composition) and that is Ill-nature. A Good-natured Man may

---

[1] See above, p. 78.   [2] See above, p. 53.
[3] William Hogarth (1697–1764), whom Fielding never tired of praising. See the *Champion*, 10 June 1740, the Preface to *Joseph Andrews*, and *Tom Jones, passim*.

indeed (provided he is a Fool) be proud, but arrogant and insolent
he cannot be; unless we will allow to such a still greater Degree
of Folly, and Ignorance of human Nature; which may indeed
entitle them to Forgiveness, in the benign Language of Scripture,
because *they know not what they do*.[1]

For when we come to consider the Effect of this Behaviour
on the Person who suffers it, we may perhaps have Reason to
conclude, that Murder is not a much more cruel Injury. What
is the Consequence of this Contempt? or indeed, What is the
Design of it, but to expose the Object of it to Shame? a Sensation
as uneasy, and almost intolerable, as those which arise from the
severest Pains inflicted on the Body: a Convulsion of the Mind
(if I may so call it) which immediately produces Symptoms of
universal Disorder in the whole Man; which hath sometimes
been attended with Death itself, and to which Death hath, by
great Multitudes, been with much Alacrity preferred.[2] Now,
what less than the highest Degree of Ill-nature can permit a Man
to pamper his own Vanity at the Price of another's Shame?
Is the Glutton, who, to raise the Flavour of his Dish, puts some
Bird or Beast to exquisite Torment, more cruel to the Animal,
than this our proud Man to his own Species?[3]

This Character then is a Composition made up of those odious
contemptible Qualities, Pride, Folly, Arrogance, Insolence, and
Ill-nature. I shall dismiss it with some general Observations,
which will place it in so ridiculous a Light, that a Man must
hereafter be possessed of a very considerable Portion, either
of Folly or Impudence, to assume it.

First, it proceeds on one grand Fallacy: for whereas this
Wretch is endeavouring, by a supercilious Conduct, to lead the
Beholder into an Opinion of his Superiority to the despised

---

[1] Luke 23: 24.
[2] Cf. Seneca, *Ad Helviam*, xiii. 8: 'Scio quosdam dicere contemptu nihil esse gravius,
mortem ipsis potiorem videri'; Burton, *Anat. Melancholy*, i. 2. 3. 6; and Robert South:
'Some have been struck with Phrenzy and Distraction, and some with Death itself upon
the sudden Attack of an intolerable confounding *Shame*: The Sense of which has at once
bereaved them of all their other Senses, and they have given up the *Ghost* and their *Credit*
together' (*Sermons*, 6th edn., 1727, iv. 107–8).
[3] See the like image in the *Champion*, 13 March 1740; cf. *Tatler*, 148, and Pope, in
Guardian, 61: 'But if our *Sports* are destructive, our *Gluttony* is more so, and in a more
inhuman manner. *Lobsters roasted alive, Pigs whipt to Death, Fowls sowed up*, are Testi-
monies of our outrageous Luxury' (5th edn., 1729, i. 261); Swift, *Gulliver's Travels*, i.
vii; George Cheyne, *The English Malady* (1733), p. 50.

Person, he inwardly flatters his own Vanity with a deceitful Presumption, that this his Conduct is founded on a general pre-conceived Opinion of this Superiority.

Secondly, This Caution to preserve it, plainly indicates a Doubt, that the Superiority of our own Character is very slightly estab-lished;[1] for which Reason we see it chiefly practiced by Men who have the weakest Pretensions to the Reputation they aim at: and indeed, none was ever freer from it than that noble Person whom we have already mentioned in this Essay,[2] and who can never be mentioned but with Honour, by those who know him.

Thirdly, This Opinion of our Superiority is commonly very erroneous. Who hath not seen a General behaving in this super-cilious Manner to an Officer of lower Rank, who hath been greatly his Superior in that very Art, to his Excellence in which the General ascribes all his Merit. Parallel Instances occur in every other Art, Science, or Profession.

Fourthly, Men who excel others in trifling Instances, fre-quently cast a supercilious Eye on their Superiors in the highest. Thus the least Pretensions to Pre-eminence in Title, Birth, Riches, Equipage, Dress, &c. constantly overlook the most noble Endowments of Virtue, Honour, Wisdom, Sense, Wit, and every other Quality which can truly dignify and adorn a Man.[3]

Lastly, The lowest and meanest of our Species are the most strongly addicted to this Vice. Men who are a Scandal to their Sex, and Women who disgrace Human Nature: for the basest Mechanic[4] is so far from being exempt, that he is generally the most guilty of it. It visits Ale-Houses and Gin-Shops, and whistles in the empty Heads of Fidlers, Mountebanks, and Dancing-Masters.

To conclude a Character, on which we have already dwelt longer than is consistent with the intended Measure of this Essay: This Contempt of others is the truest Symptom of a base and a bad Heart. While it suggests itself to the Mean and the Vile, and tickles their little Fancy on every Occasion, it never enters the great and good Mind, but on the strongest Motives;

[1] Cf. *Covent-Garden Journal*, 59.
[2] i.e. Chesterfield.
[3] Cf. *Guardian*, 153, on 'the Vanity of those imaginary Perfections that swell the Heart of Man, and of those little supernumerary Advantages, whether in Birth, Fortune, or Title, which one Man enjoys above another . . .' (5th edn., 1729, ii. 263).
[4] 'A low or vulgar fellow' (*OED*, citing Fielding's *Intriguing Chambermaid*, II. ix).

nor is it then a welcome Guest, affording only an uneasy Sensation, and brings always with it a Mixture of Concern and Compassion.

We will now proceed to inferior Criminals in Society. *Theoretus* conceiving that the Assembly is only met to see and admire him, is uneasy unless he engrosses the Eyes of the whole Company. The Giant doth not take more Pains to be view'd;[1] and as he is unfortunately not so tall, he carefully deposits himself in the most conspicuous Place: nor will that suffice, he must walk about the Room, though to the great Disturbance of the Company; and if he can purchase general Observation, at no less Rate will condescend to be ridiculous; for he prefers being laughed at, to being taken little Notice of.

On the other Side, *Dusopius* is so bashful, that he hides himself in a Corner; he hardly bears being looked at, and never quits the first Chair he lights upon, lest he should expose himself to public View. He trembles when you bowe to him at a Distance; is shocked at hearing his own Voice, and would almost swoon at the Repetition of his Name.

The audacious *Anedes*, who is extremely amorous in his Inclinations, never likes a Woman, but his Eyes ask her the Question; without considering the Confusion he often occasions to the Object: he ogles and languishes at every pretty Woman in the Room. As there is no Law of Morality which he would not break to satisfy his Desires, so is there no Form of Civility which he doth not violate to communicate them. When he gets Possession of a Woman's Hand, which those of stricter Decency never give him but with Reluctance, he considers himself as its Master. Indeed there is scarce a Familiarity which he will abstain from, on the slightest Acquaintance, and in the most publick Place. *Seraphina* herself can make no Impression on the rough Temper of *Agroicus*; neither her Quality, nor her Beauty, can exact the least Complacence from him; and he would let her lovely Limbs ach,[2] rather than offer her his Chair: while the gentle *Lyperus* tumbles over Benches, and overthrows Tea-Tables, to take up a Fan or a Glove: he forces you as a good Parent doth his Child, for your own Good: he is absolute Master of a Lady's

---

[1] London was seldom without giants on display. Perhaps this one is to be identified with Cajanus, the Swedish giant, of *Journey from This World to the Next*, I. ix. He was exhibited in London and Oxford throughout 1742. [2] Cf. p. 15 for spelling.

Will, nor will allow her the Election of standing or sitting in his Company. In short, the impertinent Civility of *Lyperus* is as troublesome, tho' perhaps not so offensive as the brutish Rudeness of *Agroicus*.[1]

Thus we have hinted at most of the common Enormities committed in publick Assemblies, to our Equals; for it would be tedious and difficult to enumerate all: nor is it needful; since from this Sketch we may trace all others, most of which, I believe, will be found to branch out from some of the Particulars here specified.

I am now, in the last Place, to consider our Behaviour to our Inferiors: in which Condescension[2] can never be too strongly recommended: for as a Deviation on this Side is much more innocent than on the other, so the Pride of Man renders us much less liable to it. For besides that we are apt to over-rate our own Perfections, and undervalue the Qualifications of our Neighbours, we likewise set too high an Esteem on the Things themselves, and consider them as constituting a more essential Difference between us than they really do. The Qualities of the Mind do, in reality, establish the truest Superiority over one another; yet should not these so far elevate our Pride, as to inflate us with Contempt, and make us look down on our Fellow Creatures, as on Animals of an inferior Order: but that the fortuitous Accident of Birth, the Acquisition of Wealth, with some outward Ornaments of Dress, should inspire Men with an Insolence capable of treating the rest of Mankind with Disdain, is so preposterous, that nothing less than daily Experience could give it Credit.

If Men were to be rightly estimated, and divided into subordinate Classes, according to the superior Excellence of their several Natures, perhaps the lowest Class of either Sex would be properly assigned to those two Disgracers of the human Species, common called[3] a Beau, and a fine Lady: For if we rate Men by the Faculties of the Mind, in what Degree must these stand? Nay, admitting the Qualities of the Body were to give the Preeminence, how many of those whom Fortune hath placed in the lowest Station, must be ranked above them? If Dress is their only Title, sure even the Monkey, if as well dressed, is on as high a

---

[1] Cf. Montaigne, I. xiii: 'I have seen some People rude, by being over-civil, and troublesome in their Courtesie' (trans. Cotton, 3rd edn., 1700, i. 71); see the *Champion*, 15 March 1740.   [2] See above, p. 126 and n.

[3] The quasi-adverbial use of 'common' has the sanction of Shakespeare (*As You Like It*, I. iii. 117.)

Footing as the Beau.—But perhaps I shall be told, they challenge their Dignity from Birth: That is a poor and mean Pretence to Honour, when supported with no other. Persons who have no better Claim to Superiority, should be ashamed of this; they are really a Disgrace to those very Ancestors from whom they would derive their Pride,[1] and are chiefly happy in this, that they want the very moderate Portion of Understanding which would enable them to despise themselves.

And yet, who so prone to a contemptuous Carriage as these! I have myself seen a little female Thing *which* they have called My Lady, of no greater Dignity in the order of Beings than a Cat, and of no more Use in Society than a Butterfly; whose Mien would not give even the Idea of a Gentlewoman, and whose Face would cool the loosest Libertine; with a Mind as empty of Ideas as an Opera, and a Body fuller of Diseases than an Hospital. I have seen this *Thing* express Contempt to a Woman who was an Honour to her Sex, and an Ornament to the Creation.

To confess the Truth, there is little Danger of the Possessor's ever undervaluing this Titular Excellence. Not that I would withdraw from it that Deference which the Policy of Government hath assigned it. On the contrary, I have laid down the most exact Compliance with this Respect, as a Fundamental in Good-Breeding; nay, I insist only that we may be admitted to pay it; and not treated with a Disdain even beyond what the Eastern Monarchs shew to their Slaves. Surely it is too high an Elevation, when instead of treating the lowest human Creature, in a Christian Sense, as our Brethren; we look down on such as are but one Rank, in the Civil Order, removed from us, as unworthy to breathe even the same Air, and regard the most distant Communication with them as an Indignity and Disgrace offered to ourselves. This is considering the Difference not in the Individual, but in the very Species; a Height of Insolence impious in a Christian Society, and most absurd and ridiculous in a trading Nation.[2]

---

[1] The theme of Juvenal's *Eighth Satire* ('Stemmata quid faciunt?'); cf. Pope, *Essay on Man*, iv. 209–16; and Samuel Butler: 'A Degenerate Noble: Or, One that is proud of his Birth, Is like a Turnep, there is nothing good of him, but that which is under-ground . . .' (*Genuine Remains*, 1759, ii. 76). See George M. Vogt, 'Gleanings for the History of a Sentiment: Generositas Virtus, non Sanguis', *JEGP*, xxiv (1925), 102–24.

[2] Cf. Burton, *Anat. Melancholy*, i. 2. 3. 10: 'He loathes and scorns his inferior . . .; insults over all such as are under him, as if he were of another *species* . . .' (ed. Shilleto,

I have now done with my first Head, in which I have treated of Good-Breeding, as it regards our Actions. I shall, in the next Place, consider it with respect to our Words; and shall endeavour to lay down some Rules, by observing which our well-bred Man may, in his Discourse as well as Actions, contribute to the Happiness and Well-being of Society.

Certain it is, that the highest Pleasure which we are capable of enjoying in Conversation, is to be met with only in the Society of Persons whose Understanding is pretty near on an Equality with our own:[1] nor is this Equality only necessary to enable Men of exalted Genius, and extensive Knowledge, to taste the sublimer Pleasures of communicating their refined Ideas to each other; but it is likewise necessary to the inferior Happiness of every subordinate Degree of Society, down to the very lowest. For Instance; we will suppose a Conversation betwen *Socrates*, *Plato*, *Aristotle*, and three Dancing-Masters. It will be acknowledged, I believe, that the Heel Sophists would be as little pleased with the Company of the Philosophers, as the Philosophers with theirs.

It would be greatly therefore for the Improvement and Happiness of Conversation, if Society could be formed on this Equality: but as Men are not ranked in this World by the different Degrees of their Understanding, but by other Methods, and consequently all Degrees of Understanding often meet in the same Class, and must *ex necessitate* frequently converse together, the Impossibility of accomplishing any such *Utopian* Scheme very plainly appears.[2] Here therefore is a visible but unavoidable Imperfection in Society itself.

But as we have laid it down as a Fundamental, that the Essence of Good-Breeding is to contribute as much as possible to the Ease and Happiness of Mankind, so will it be the Business of our well-bred Man to endeavour to lessen this Imperfection to his utmost, and to bring Society as near to a Level at least as he is able.

i. 320); Mr. Bickerstaff, in *Tatler*, 256, will not let his jury of 'Men of Honour' punish severely a merchant lacking in respect for 'the Cadet of a very ancient Family . . . [because] such Penalties might be of ill Consequence in a Trading Nation'. Cf. Fielding's pointed note to his burlesque of Juvenal (line 333, above p. 109); and see the letter from 'Paul Traffick' in *Covent-Garden Journal*, 43.

[1] Cf. Milton, *Paradise Lost*, viii. 383–4: 'Among unequals what society / Can sort, what harmony or true delight?' (p. 211; in *Poetical Works*, 1695).

[2] Cf. Burton, *Anat. Melancholy*, 'Democritus to the Reader': '*Utopian* parity is a kind of government to be wished for rather than effected' (ed. Shilleto, i. 113).

Now there are but two Ways to compass this, *viz.* by raising the lower, and by lowering what is higher.

Let us suppose then, that very unequal Company I have before mentioned met: the former of these is apparently impracticable. Let *Socrates*, for Instance, institute a Discourse on the Nature of the Soul, or *Plato* reason on the native Beauty of Virtue, and *Aristotle* on his occult Qualities.—[1] What must become of our Dancing-Masters? Would they not stare at one another with Surprize? and, most probably, at our Philosophers with Contempt? Would they have any Pleasure in such Society? or would they not rather wish themselves in a Dancing-School, or a Green-Room at the Play-House?[2] What therefore have our Philosophers to do, but to lower themselves to those who cannot rise to them?

And surely there are Subjects on which both can converse. Hath not *Socrates* heard of Harmony?[3] Hath not *Plato*, who draws Virtue in the Person of a fine Woman,[4] any Idea of the Gracefulness of Attitude? and hath not *Aristotle* himself written a Book on Motion?[5] In short, to be a little serious, there are many Topics on which they can at least be intelligible to each other.

How absurd then must appear the Conduct of *Cenodoxus*, who having had the Advantage of a liberal Education, and having made a pretty good Progress in Literature, is constantly advancing learned Subjects in common Conversation? He talks of the Classics before the Ladies; and of *Greek* Criticisms among fine Gentlemen. What is this less than an Insult on the Company, over whom he thus affects a Superiority, and whose Time he sacrifices to his Vanity?

[1] Cf. Hobbes' attack on the 'Aristotelity' of the universities: 'as when they attribute many effects to *occult qualities*; that is, qualities not known to them; and therefore also, as they think, to no man else' (*Leviathan*, IV. xlvi; *English Works*, ed. Molesworth, iii. 679–80); cf. John Smith, *Select Discourses* (1660), I. ii (p. 15); John Eachard, *Grounds and Occasions of the Contempt of the Clergy* (1685 edn.), pp. 32–3; Swift, *Gulliver's Travels*, II. iii; Leibniz (translated) on Newton's 'attraction': ''Tis a Chimerical Thing, a Scholastick *occult Quality*' (*A Collection of Papers, Which Passed between . . . Mr. Leibnitz, and Dr. Clarke*, 1717, p. 273); John Hildrop, *Free Thoughts upon the Brute Creation* (1742), p. 5; Samuel Butler, *Genuine Remains* (1759), ii. 468.

[2] Retiring-room for the actors: cf. Fielding, *Pasquin* (1736), i: 'Sir, the Prompter, and most of the Players, are drinking tea in the *Green-Room*.'

[3] See, e.g., Plato, *Symposium*, 187 a–e; *Phaedo*, xxxv–xxxvi (85 b–87 c); *Republic*, III. xvii–xviii (410–12), IV. viii–ix (430–2), IV. xvi (441–3).   [4] See below, p. 173.

[5] Presumably *De motu animalium*, though Fielding may have the *Physica* in mind.

Wisely different is the amiable Conduct of *Sophronus*; who, though he exceeds the former in Knowledge, can submit to discourse on the most trivial Matters, rather than introduce such as his Company are utter Strangers to. He can talk of Fashions and Diversions among the Ladies; nay, can even condescend to Horses and Dogs with Country Gentlemen. This Gentleman, who is equal to dispute on the highest and abstrusest Points, can likewise talk on a Fan, or a Horse-Race; nor had ever any one, who was not himself a Man of Learning, the least Reason to conceive the vast Knowledge of *Sophronus*, unless from the Report of others.

Let us compare these together. *Cenodoxus* proposes the Satisfaction of his own Pride from the Admiration of others; *Sophronus* thinks of nothing but their Amusement. In the Company of *Cenodoxus*, every one is rendered uneasy, laments his own want of Knowledge, and longs for the End of the dull Assembly: With *Sophronus* all are pleased, and contented with themselves in their Knowledge of Matters which they find worthy the Consideration of a Man of Sense. Admiration is involuntarily paid the former; to the latter it is given joyfully. The former receives it with Envy and Hatred; the latter enjoys it as the sweet Fruit of Good-Will. The former is shunned, the latter courted by all.

This Behaviour in *Cenodoxus* may, in some Measure, account for an Observation we must have frequent Occasion to make: That the Conversation of Men of very moderate Capacities is often preferred to that with Men of superior Talents: In which the World act more wisely than at first they may seem; for besides that Backwardness in Mankind to give their Admiration, what can be duller, or more void of Pleasure than Discourses on Subjects above our Comprehension! It is like listning to an unknown Language; and if such Company is ever desired by us, it is a Sacrifice to our Vanity, which imposes on us to believe that we may by these Means raise the general Opinion of our own Parts and Knowledge, and not from that cheerful Delight which is the natural Result of an agreeable Conversation.

There is another very common Fault, equally destructive of this Delight, by much the same Means; though it is far from owing its Original to any real Superiority of Parts and Knowledge: This is discoursing on the Mysteries of a particular Profession, to which all the rest of the Company, except one or two, are utter Strangers. Lawyers are generally guilty of this Fault, as they are more confined to the Conversation of one another; and I have known a very agreeable Company spoilt, where there have been two of these Gentlemen present, who have seemed rather to think themselves in a Court of Justice, than in a mixed Assembly of Persons, met only for the Entertainment of each other.

But it is not sufficient that the whole Company understand the Topic of their Conversation; they should be likewise equally interested in every Subject not tending to their general Information or Amusement; for these are not to be postponed to the Relation of private Affairs, much less of the particular Grievance or Misfortune of a single Person. To bear a Share in the Afflictions of another is a Degree of Friendship not to be expected in a common Acquaintance; nor hath any Man a Right to indulge the Satisfaction of a weak and mean Mind by the Comfort of Pity, at the Expence of the whole Company's Diversion. The inferior and unsuccessful Members of the several Professions are generally guilty of this Fault; for as they fail of the Reward due to their great Merit, they can seldom refrain from reviling their Superiors, and complaining of their own hard and unjust Fate.

Farther; as a Man is not to make himself the Subject of the Conversation, so neither is he to engross the whole to himself.[1] As every Man had rather please others by what he says, than be himself pleased by what they say; or, in other Words, as every Man is best pleased with the Consciousness of pleasing; so should all have an equal Opportunity of aiming at it. This is a Right which we are so offended at being deprived of, that though I remember to have known a Man reputed a good Companion, who seldom opened his Mouth in Company, unless to swallow his Liquor; yet I have scarce ever heard that Appellation given to a very talkative Person, even when he hath been capable of entertaining, unless he hath done this with Buffoon'ry, and made the rest amends, by partaking of their Scorn, together with their Admiration and Applause.

A well-bred Man therefore will not take more of the Discourse than falls to his Share: nor in this will he shew any violent

[1] Cf. *Spectator*, 428: 'It is an impertinent and unreasonable Fault in Conversation, for one Man to take up all the Discourse.'

Impetuosity of Temper, or exert any Loudness of Voice, even in arguing: for the Information of the Company, and the Conviction of his Antagonist, are to be his apparent Motives; not the Indulgence of his own Pride, or an ambitious Desire of Victory; which latter if a wise Man should entertain, he will be sure to conceal with his utmost Endeavour: since he must know, that to lay open his Vanity in public, is no less absurd than to lay open his Bosom to an Enemy, whose drawn Sword is pointed against it: for every Man hath a Dagger in his Hand, ready to stab the Vanity of another, wherever he perceives it.[1]

Having now shewn, that the Pleasure of Conversation must arise from the Discourse being on Subjects levelled to the Capacity of the whole Company; from being on such in which every Person is equally interested; from every one's being admitted to his Share in the Discourse; and lastly, from carefully avoiding all Noise, Violence, and Impetuosity; it might seem proper to lay down some particular Rules for the Choice of those Subjects which are most likely to conduce to the cheerful Delights proposed from this social Communication: but as such an Attempt might appear absurd, from the infinite Variety, and perhaps too dictatorial in its Nature, I shall confine myself to rejecting those Topics only which seem most foreign to this Delight, and which are most likely to be attended with Consequences rather tending to make Society an Evil, than to procure us any Good from it.[2]

And First, I shall mention that which I have hitherto only endeavoured to restrain within certain Bounds, namely, Arguments: but which if they were entirely banished out of Company, especially from mixed Assemblies, and where Ladies make Part of the Society, it would, I believe, promote their Happiness: they have been sometimes attended with Bloodshed, generally with Hatred from the conquered Party towards his Victor; and scarce ever with Conviction. Here I except jocose Arguments, which often produce much Mirth; and serious Disputes between Men of Learning (when none but such are present) which tend to the Propagation of Knowledge, and the Edification of the Company.

---

[1] See *Spectator*, 255; cf. La Rochefoucauld, *Maxims*, ccclxxxix: 'The thing that makes other Peoples Vanity insupportable to us, is, that it shocks our own' (trans. 1706, p. 159).

[2] On the topics inappropriate to conversation or to jest, see, among many prescribers, Isaac Barrow's sermon, 'Against Foolish Talking and Jesting' (*Theological Works*, ed. A. Napier, ii. 1–35), and Bacon's essay, 'Of Discourse'.

An Essay on Conversation 147

Secondly, Slander; which, however frequently used, or however savory to the Palate of Ill-nature, is extremely pernicious. As it is often unjust, and highly injurious to the Person slandered; and always dangerous, especially in large and mixed Companies; where sometimes an undesigned Offence is given to an innocent Relation or Friend of such Person, who is thus exposed to Shame and Confusion, without having any Right to resent the Affront. Of this there have been very tragical Instances; and I have myself seen some very ridiculous ones, but which have given great Pain, as well to the Person offended, as to him who hath been the innocent Occasion of giving the Offence.

Thirdly; all general Reflections on Countries,[1] Religions, and Professions, which are always unjust. If these are ever tolerable, they are only from the Persons who with some Pleasantry ridicule their own Country. It is very common among us to cast Sarcasms on a neighbouring Nation,[2] to which we have no other Reason to bear an Antipathy, than what is more usual than justifiable, because we have injured it: But sure such general Satire is not founded on Truth: for I have known Gentlemen of that Nation possessed with every good Quality which are to be wished in a Man, or required in a Friend. I remember a Repartee made by a Gentleman of this Country,[3] which though it was full of the severest Wit, the Person to whom it was directed, could not resent, as he so plainly deserved it. He had with great Bitterness inveighed against this whole People; upon which, one of them who was present, very cooly answered, *I don't know, Sir, whether I have not more Reason to be pleased with the Compliment you pay my Country, than to be angry with what you say against it; since by your abusing us all so heavily, you have plainly implied you are not of it.* This exposed the other to so much Laughter, especially as he was not unexceptionable in his Character, that I believe he was sufficiently punished for his ill-manner'd Satire.

Fourthly; Blasphemy, and irreverent mention of Religion. I will not here debate what Compliment a Man pays to his own Understanding, by the Profession of Infidelity; it is sufficient to

---

[1] Cf. Pope's note on the two lines omitted from the *Essay on Criticism*, 'as containing a *National Reflection*, which in his stricter judgment he could not but disapprove, on any People whatever' (Twickenham edn., i. 301); Quintilian, *Inst. orat.* VI. iii. 34; Sir Thomas Browne, *Religio Medici*, II. iv; *Spectator*, 435.
[2] Probably Ireland: cf. the *Champion*, 29 January and 29 March 1740.
[3] Not identified.

my Purpose, that he runs a Risque of giving the cruellest Offence to Persons of a different Temper: for if a Loyalist would be greatly affronted by hearing any Indecencies offered to the Person of a temporal Prince, how much more bitterly must a Man, who sincerely believes in such a Being as the Almighty, feel any Irreverence, or Insult shewn to his Name, his Honour, or his Institution? And notwithstanding the impious Character of the present Age, and especially of many among those whose more immediate Business it is to lead Men, as well by Example as Precept, into the Ways of Piety, there are still sufficient Numbers left, who pay so honest and sincere a Reverence to Religion, as may give us a reasonable Expectation of finding one at least of this Stamp in every large Company.

A fifth Particular to be avoided is Indecency. We are not only to forbear the repeating such Words as would give an immediate Affront to a Lady of Reputation; but the raising any loose Ideas tending to the Offence of that Modesty, which if a young Woman hath not something more than the Affectation of, she is not worthy the Regard even of a Man of Pleasure, provided he hath any Delicacy in his Constitution. How inconsistent with Good-Breeding it is to give Pain and Confusion to such, is sufficiently apparent; all Double-Entendres, and obscene Jests, are therefore carefully to be avoided before them. But suppose no Ladies present, nothing can be meaner, lower, and less productive of rational Mirth, than this loose Conversation. For my own Part, I cannot conceive how the Idea of Jest or Pleasantry came ever to be annexed to one of our highest and most serious Pleasures. Nor can I help observing, to the Discredit of such Merriment, that it is commonly the last Resource of impotent Wit, the weak Strainings of the lowest, silliest, and dullest Fellows in the World.

Sixthly; You are to avoid knowingly mentioning any thing which may revive in any Person the Remembrance of some past Accident; or raise an uneasy Reflection on a present Misfortune, or corporeal Blemish. To maintain this Rule nicely, perhaps requires great Delicacy; but it is absolutely necessary to a well-bred Man. I have observed numberless Breaches of it; many, I believe, proceeding from Negligence and Inadvertency; yet I am afraid some may be too justly imputed to a malicious Desire of triumphing in our own superior Happiness and Perfections:

now when it proceeds from this Motive, it is not easy to imagine any thing more criminal.

Under this Head I shall caution my well-bred Reader against a common Fault, much of the same Nature; which is mentioning any particular Quality as absolutely essential to either Man or Woman, and exploding all those who want it. This renders every one uneasy, who is in the least self-conscious of the Defect. I have heard a *Boor* of Fashion declare in the Presence of Women remarkably plain, that Beauty was the chief Perfection of that Sex; and an Essential, without which no Woman was worth regarding. A certain Method of putting all those in the Room, who are but suspicious of their Defect that way, out of Countenance.

I shall mention one Fault more, which is, not paying a proper Regard to the present Temper of the Company, or the Occasion of their meeting, in introducing a Topic of Conversation, by which as great an Absurdity is sometimes committed, as it would be to sing a Dirge at a Wedding, or an Epithalamium at a Funeral.

Thus I have, I think, enumerated most of the principal Errors which we are apt to fall into in Conversation; and though perhaps some Particulars worthy of Remark may have escaped me, yet an Attention to what I have here said, may enable the Reader to discover them. At least I am persuaded, that if the Rules I have now laid down were strictly observed, our Conversation would be more perfect, and the Pleasure resulting from it purer, and more unsullied, than at present it is.

But I must not dismiss this Subject without some Animadversions on a particular Species of Pleasantry, which though I am far from being desirous of banishing from Conversation, requires, most certainly, some Reins to govern, and some Rule to direct it. The Reader may perhaps guess, I mean Raillery; to which I may apply the Fable of the Lap-Dog and the Ass:[1] for while in some Hands it diverts and delights us with its Dexterity and Gentleness; in others, it paws, dawbs, offends, and hurts.

The End of Conversation being the Happiness of Mankind, and the chief Means to procure their Delight and Pleasure; it

---

[1] Cf. *Fables, of Æsop and Other Eminent Mythologists . . . By Sir Roger L'Estrange* (1669), pp. 15–16 (Fable XV: 'An Asse and a Whelp'). Warnings against the misuse of raillery extend from Aristotle (*Nic. Eth.* IV. viii. 7) and Cicero (*De officiis,* I. xxix. 103–4) to the *Spectator* (422). Cf. Shaftesbury, *Sensus Communis,* I. iii; Swift, 'Hints towards an Essay on Conversation' (*Prose Works,* ed. Davis, iv. 91).

follows, I think, that nothing can conduce to this End, which tends to make a Man uneasy and dissatisfied with himself, or which exposes him to the Scorn and Contempt of others. I here except that Kind of Raillery therefore, which is concerned in tossing Men out of their Chairs, tumbling them into Water,[1] or any of those handicraft Jokes which are exercised on those notable Persons, commonly known by the Name of Buffoons; who are contented to feed their Belly at the Price of their Br—ch, and to carry off the Wine and the P—ss of a Great Man together. This I pass by, as well as all Remarks on the Genius of the Great Men themselves, who are (to fetch a Phrase from School, a Place not improperly mentioned on this Occasion) great DABS[2] at this kind of Facetiousness.

But leaving all such Persons to expose Human Nature among themselves, I shall recommend to my well-bred Man, who aims at Raillery, the excellent Character given of *Horace* by *Persius*.

> *Omne vafer vitium ridenti Flaccus amico*
> *Tangit, et admissus circum Præcordia ludit.*
> *Callidus excusso Populum suspendere naso.*[3]

Thus excellently rendered by the late ingenious Translator of that obscure Author.

> *Yet cou'd shrewd* Horace, *with disportive Wit,*
> *Rally his Friend, and tickle while he bit:*
> *Winning Access, he play'd around the Heart,*
> *And gently touching, prick'd the tainted Part.*
> *The Crowd he sneer'd; but sneer'd with such a Grace,*
> *It pass'd for downright Innocence of Face.*[4]

The Raillery which is consistent with Good-Breeding, is a gentle Animadversion on some Foible; which while it raises a Laugh in the rest of the Company, doth not put the Person rallied out of Countenance, or expose him to Shame and Contempt. On the contrary, the Jest should be so delicate, that the Object of it should be capable of joining in the Mirth it occasions.

---

[1] Cf. *Joseph Andrews*, III. vii.

[2] School-boy slang for 'adept'; cf. Arthur Murphy on one who 'was a great dab at the Multiplication Table' (*Works*, 1786, v. 311).

[3] *Sat.* i. 116–18; applied in a like context to Charles, Earl of Dorset, by Prior in the dedication to his *Poems*, 1709 (*Lit. Works*, ed. Wright-Spears, i. 250).

Dr. Thomas Brewster (see above, p. 119), *The Satires of Persius, Translated into English Verse . . . Satire the First* (1741), p. 24.

All great Vices therefore, Misfortunes, and notorious Blemishes of Mind or Body, are improper Subjects of Raillery. Indeed, a Hint at such is an Abuse and Affront is sure to give the Person (unless he be one shameless and abandoned) Pain and Uneasiness, and should be received with Contempt, instead of Applause, by all the rest of the Company.

Again; the Nature and Quality of the Person are to be considered. As to the first, some Men will not bear any Raillery at all. I remember a Gentleman who declared, *He never made a Jest, nor would ever take one.*[1] I do not indeed greatly recommend such a Person for a Companion; but at the same Time, a well-bred Man, who is to consult the Pleasure and Happiness of the whole, is not at Liberty to make any one present uneasy. By the Quality, I mean the Sex, Degree, Profession, and Circumstances; on which Head I need not be very particular. With Regard to the two former, all Raillery on Ladies and Superiors should be extremely fine and gentle; and with respect to the latter, any of the Rules I have above laid down, most of which are to be applied to it, will afford sufficient Caution.

Lastly. A Consideration is to be had of the Persons before whom we rally. A Man will be justly uneasy at being reminded of those Railleries in one Company, which he would very patiently bear the Imputation of in another. Instances on this Head are so obvious, that they need not be mentioned. In short, the whole Doctrine of Raillery is comprized in this famous Line.

QUID *de* QUOQUE *viro et* CUI *dicas sæpe caveto.*
Be cautious WHAT *you say,* OF WHOM *and* TO WHOM.[2]

And now methinks I hear some one cry out, that such Restrictions are, in Effect, to exclude all Raillery from Conversation: and, to confess the Truth, it is a Weapon from which many Persons will do wisely in totally abstaining; for it is a Weapon which doth the more Mischief, by how much the blunter it is. The sharpest Wit therefore is only to be indulged the free Use of it; for no more than a very slight Touch is to be allowed; no hacking, nor bruising, as if they were to *hew a Carcase for Hounds,* as *Shakespear* phrases it.[3]

---

[1] The gentleman is unidentified; cf. Col. Bath's maxim, in *Amelia,* 'never to give an Affront nor ever to take one'.
[2] Cf. Horace, *Epist.* I. xviii. 68, with 'videto' for 'caveto'.
[3] *Julius Caesar,* II. i. 174.

Nor is it sufficient that it be sharp, it must be used likewise with the utmost Tenderness and Good-nature: and as the nicest Dexterity of a Gladiator is shewn in being able to hit without cutting deep,[1] so is this of our Rallier, who is rather to tickle than wound.

True Raillery indeed consists either in playing on Peccadillo's, which, however they may be censured by some, are not esteemed as really Blemishes in a Character in the Company where they are made the Subject of Mirth; as too much Freedom with the Bottle, or too much Indulgence with Women, &c.

Or, Secondly, in pleasantly representing real good Qualities in a false Light of Shame, and bantering them as ill ones. So Generosity may be treated as Prodigality; Œconomy as Avarice; true Courage as Fool-Hardiness; and so of the rest.

Lastly; in ridiculing Men for Vices and Faults which they are known to be free from. Thus the Cowardice of *A—le*, the Dulness of *Ch—d*, the Unpoliteness of *D—ton*, may be attacked without Danger of Offence; and thus *Lyt—n* may be censured for whatever Vice or Folly you please to impute to him.[2]

And however limited these Bounds may appear to some, yet, in skilful and wittty Hands, I have known Raillery, thus confined, afford a very diverting, as well as inoffensive Entertainment to the whole Company.

I shall conclude this Essay with these two Observations, which I think may be clearly deduced from what hath been said.

First, That every Person who indulges his Ill-nature or Vanity, at the Expence of others; and in introducing Uneasiness, Vexation, and Confusion into Society, however exalted or high-titled he may be, is thoroughly ill-bred.

Secondly, That whoever, from the Goodness of his Disposition or Understanding, endeavours to his utmost to cultivate the Good-humour and Happiness of others, and to contribute to the Ease and Comfort of all his Acquaintance, however low in Rank Fortune may have placed him, or however clumsy he may be in his Figure or Demeanour, hath, in the truest Sense of the Word, a Claim to Good-Breeding.

[1] Cf. James Ralph on the gladiators in Rome: 'an *Academy* [was] establish'd for instructing them in the Art of cutting Throats cleverly and decently' (*The Touchstone*, 1728, Essay VII, p. 215). Cf. Dryden's preface to the *Satires* of Juvenal and Persius (1693), sig. L1ᵛ.

[2] Argyle, Chesterfield, Dodington, and Lyttelton. Cf. like compliments in the *Champion*, 29 January 1740, and in *Of True Greatness*, above, pp. 25 and 29.

AN ESSAY

ON THE KNOWLEDGE OF THE

Characters of Men.[1]

I have often thought it a melancholy Instance of the great Depravity[2] of Human Nature, that whilst so many Men have employed their utmost Abilities to invent Systems, by which the artful and cunning Part of Mankind may be enabled to impose on the rest of the World; few or none should have stood up the Champions of the innocent and undesigning, and have endeavoured to arm them against Imposition.[3]

Those who predicate of Man in general, that he is an Animal of this or that Disposition, seem to me not sufficiently to have studied Human Nature;[4] for that immense Variety of Characters so apparent in Men even of the same Climate,[5] Religion, and Education, which gives the Poet a sufficient Licence, as I apprehend, for saying, that

Man differs more from Man, than Man from Beast,[6]

could hardly exist, unless the Distinction had some original Foundation in Nature itself. Nor is it perhaps a less proper

---

[1] Fielding's reference to Pope's *Letters* (see p. 176 n. 3) must date after 1735, when the earliest editions appeared (the 'authorized' edition of 1737 has, however, the same reading for the passage that Fielding adapts). A number of parallels to observations made in the *Champion* during the period 1739–40 (see notes, *passim*) might suggest that Fielding was working on this essay at about the same time.

[2] 'Depravity' did not normally carry the theological overtones of original sin until mid century (cf. *OED*); it meant simply corruption or perversion (*depravatio*). Cf. Cicero, *Tusc. Disp.* III. i. 2; *Tatler*, 230 (by Swift); *Guardian*, 153; but also, Prior, 'Predestination', 29–30: 'Whence rises this depravity of thought / Was it from mine or my forefathers fault ?' (*Lit. Works*, ed. Wright-Spears, i. 560). Cf. below, p. 215.

[3] Cf. Proverbs 1: 4: 'To give subtility to the simple, to the young man knowledge and discretion.'

[4] Cf. Locke, *Essay Concerning Human Understanding*, III. vi. 27; Sir William Temple, 'An Essay upon the Original and Nature of Government' (*Works*, 1757, i. 38–9).

[5] Cf. the *Champion*, 15 December 1739. See J. W. Johnson, ' "Of Differing Ages and Climes" ', *JHI*, xxi (1960), 465–80.

[6] John Wilmot, Earl of Rochester, 'Satyr [against Mankind]', 224 (*Poems on Several Occasions*, 1680, p. 13). Cited also in the *Champion*, 15 December 1739; the *Jacobite's Journal*, 42 (17 September 1748). Cf. Sir Charles Sedley, *Bellamira, or the Mistress* (1687), II. i; Locke, *Essay*, IV. xx. 5. The phrase is ultimately from Plutarch, *Bruta animalia ratione uti*, 992e; and it was doubtless given greater currency by Montaigne (*Essays*, I. xlii and II. i; trans. Cotton, 3rd edn., 1700, i. 439 and ii. 214).

Predicament[1] of the Genius of a Tree, that it will flourish so many Years, loves such a Soil, bears such a Fruit, &c. than of Man in general, that he is good, bad, fierce, tame, honest, or cunning.

This original Difference will, I think, alone account for that very early and strong Inclination to Good or Evil, which distinguishes different Dispositions in Children, in their first Infancy; in the most un-informed Savages, who can be thought to have altered their Nature by no Rules, nor artfully acquired Habits;[2] and lastly, in Persons who from the same Education, &c. might be thought to have directed Nature the same Way; yet, among all these, there subsists, as I have before hinted, so manifest and extreme a Difference of Inclination or Character, that almost obliges us, I think, to acknowledge some unacquired, original Distinction, in the Nature or Soul of one Man, from that of another.[3]

Thus, without asserting in general, that Man is a deceitful Animal; we may, I believe, appeal for Instances of Deceit to the Behaviour of some Children and Savages. When this Quality therefore is nourished and improved by Education, in which we are taught rather to conceal Vices, than to cultivate Virtues; when it hath sucked in the Instruction of Politicians, and is instituted in the *Art of thriving*, it will be no Wonder that it should grow to that monstrous Height to which we sometimes see it arrive. This *Art of thriving*[4] being the very Reverse of that Doctrine of the Stoics; by which Men were taught to consider themselves as Fellow-Citizens of the World, and to labour jointly for the common Good, without any private Distinction of their own:[5] Whereas *This*, on the contrary, points out to every Individual

---

1 'That which is predicated or asserted'; a quality (*OED*). Cf. La Rochefoucauld (?), *Maximes supprimées*, 594: 'Chaque talent dans les hommes de même que chaque arbre, a ses propriétés et ses effets qui lui sont tous particuliers' (*Maximes*, ed. H. A. Grubbs, p. 116).

2 Cf. Locke, *Essay*, I. i. 27, though in a different context.

3 See Aristotle, *Hist. animalium*, VIII. i. 2; Montaigne, III. ii: 'Natural inclinations are much assisted and fortified by Education, but they seldom alter and overcome their Institution' (trans. Cotton, 3rd edn., 1700, iii. 36). Locke, in *Some Thoughts Concerning Education* (1693), sects. 100–2 *et passim*, takes for granted a kind of innate predisposition of 'constitution' or 'temper' or 'native propensities'.

4 The type of 'chrematistic' or acquisitive art that Aristotle declared to be non-natural and without bounds (*Polit.* I. iii. 10–20). Cf. *Amelia*, ix. 5. There were indeed numerous handbooks such as that by Thomas Powell, called *The Art of Thriving, or the Plaine Path-Way to Preferment* (1635).

5 See Cicero, *De finibus*, III. xix. 64, and IV. iii. 7: 'mundum hunc omnem oppidum esse nostrum'; Epictetus, *Discourses*, I. xix; Marcus Aurelius, vi. 44 *et passim*.

his own particular and separate Advantage, to which he is to sacrifice the Interest of all others; which he is to consider as his *Summum Bonum*, to pursue with his utmost Diligence and Industry, and to acquire by all Means whatever.[1] Now when this noble End is once established, Deceit must immediately suggest itself as the necessary Means: for as it is impossible that any Man endowed with rational Faculties, and being in a State of Freedom, should willingly agree, without some Motive of Love or Friendship, absolutely to sacrifice his own Interest to that of another; it becomes necessary to impose upon him, to persuade him, that his own Good is designed, and that he will be a Gainer by coming into those Schemes, which are, in Reality, calculated for his Destruction. And this, if I mistake not, is the very Essence of that excellent Art, called *The Art of Politics*.[2]

Thus while the crafty and designing Part of Mankind, consulting only their own separate Advantage, endeavour to maintain one constant Imposition on others, the whole World becomes a vast Masquerade, where the greatest Part appear disguised under false Vizors and Habits; a very few only shewing their own Faces, who become, by so doing, the Astonishment and Ridicule of all the rest.

But however cunning the Disguise be which a Masquerader wears: however foreign to his Age, Degree, or Circumstance, yet if closely attended to, he very rarely escapes the Discovery of an accurate Observer; for Nature, which unwillingly submits to the Imposture, is ever endeavouring to peep forth and shew herself;[3] nor can the Cardinal, the Friar, or the Judge, long conceal the Sot, the Gamester, or the Rake.

In the same Manner will those Disguises which are worn on the greater Stage, generally vanish, or prove ineffectual to impose the assumed for the real Character upon us, if we employ sufficient Diligence and Attention in the Scrutiny. But as this Discovery is of infinitely greater Consequence to us; and as perhaps all are not equally qualified to make it, I shall venture to set down some few Rules, the Efficacy (I had almost said Infallibility) of which, I have myself experienced. Nor need any Man be ashamed of

---

[1] Cf. Burton, *Anat. Melancholy*, 'Democritus to the Reader': 'Our *summum bonum* is commodity, and the goddess we adore *Dea Moneta* . . .' (ed. Shilleto, i. 69).

[2] Cf. *Jonathan Wild*, II. v.

[3] See above, 'To John Hayes', 37–8 and n.

wanting or receiving Instructions on this Head; since that open Disposition, which is the surest Indication of an honest and upright Heart, chiefly renders us liable to be imposed on by Craft and Deceit, and principally disqualifies us for this Discovery.[1]

Neither will the Reader, I hope, be offended, if he should here find no Observations entirely new to him. Nothing can be plainer, or more known, than the general Rules of Morality, and yet thousands of Men are thought well employed in reviving our Remembrance, and enforcing our Practice of them. But though I am convinced there are many of my Readers whom I am not capable of instructing on this Head, and who are indeed fitter to give than receive Instructions, at least from me, yet this Essay may perhaps be of some Use to the young and unexperienced, to the more open, honest and considering Part of Mankind, who, either from Ignorance or Inattention, are daily exposed to all the pernicious Designs of that detestable Fiend, Hypocrisy.

I will proceed therefore, without further Preface, to those Diagnostics which Nature, I apprehend, gives us of the Diseases of the Mind, seeing she takes such Pains to discover those of the Body. And first, I doubt whether the old Adage of *Fronti nulla Fides*, be generally well understood: The Meaning of which is commonly taken to be, that *no Trust is to be given to the Countenance*. But what is the Context in *Juvenal*?

> —*Quis enim non vicus abundat*
> *Tristibus obscœnis?*[2]
> —*What Place is not filled with*
> *austere Libertines?*

Now that an austere Countenance is no Token of Purity of Heart, I readily concede. So far otherwise, it is perhaps rather a Symptom of the contrary. But the Satyrist surely never intended by these Words, which have grown into a Proverb, utterly to depreciate an Art on which so wise a Man as *Aristotle* hath thought proper to compose a Treatise.[3]

The Truth is, we almost universally mistake the Symptoms which Nature kindly holds forth to us; and err as grossly as

---

[1] Cf. Martial, XII. li: 'Semper homo bonus tiro est'; Plato, *Republic*, III. xvi (409 a–b); Machiavelli, *The Prince*, chap. xv. This was one of Fielding's abiding convictions: see the *Champion*, 21 February 1740.

[2] Juvenal, *Sat.* ii. 8. Quoted as the motto of the *Champion*, 11 December 1739.

[3] The *Physiognomonica*, probably spurious. Cf. Sir Thomas Browne on this 'acute, and singular Book of Physiognomy' (*Religio Medici*, II. ii; 8th edn., 1685, p. 34).

a Physician would, who should conclude that a very high Pulse is a certain Indication of Health; but sure the Faculty would rather impute such a Mistake to his deplorable Ignorance, than conclude from it, that the Pulse could give a skilful and sensible Observer no Information of the Patient's Distemper.

In the same Manner, I conceive, the Passions of Men do commonly imprint sufficient Marks on the Countenance;[1] and it is owing chiefly to want of Skill in the Observer, that Physiognomy is of so little Use and Credit in the World.

But our Errors in this Disquisition would be little wondered at, if it was acknowledged, that the few Rules which generally prevail on this Head are utterly false, and the very Reverse of Truth. And this will perhaps appear, if we condescend to the Examination of some Particulars. Let us begin with the Instance given us by the Poet above, of Austerity; which, as he shews us, was held to indicate a Chastity or Severity of Morals, the contrary of which as himself shews us, is true.

Among us, this Austerity, or Gravity of Countenance, passes for Wisdom with just the same Equity of Pretension. My Lord *Shaftsbury* tells us, that *Gravity is of the Essence of Imposture*.[2] I will not venture to say, that it certainly denotes Folly, though I have known some of the silliest Fellows in the World very eminently possessed of it. The Affections which it indicates, and which we shall seldom err in suspecting to lie under it, are Pride, Ill-nature, and Cunning. Three Qualities which when we know to be inherent in any Man, we have no Reason to desire any further Discovery to instruct us, to deal as little and as cautiously with him as we are able.

But though the World often pays a Respect to these Appearances which they do not deserve; they rather attract Admiration

---

[1] Cf. *Tatler*, 248: '. . . the Ideas which most frequently pass through our Imaginations, leave Traces of themselves in our Countenances'; *Spectator*, 86: 'Every Passion gives a particular Cast to the Countenance and is apt to discover itself in some Feature or other'; Robert South, 'Of the Base Sins of Falsehood and Lying' (*Sermons*, 6th edn., 1727, i. 495). On the background of attitudes toward physiognomy, see Richard D. Loewenberg, 'The Significance of the Obvious: an Eighteenth Century Controversy on Psychosomatic Principles', *Bull. Hist. Med.* x (1941), 666–79; Carroll Camden, 'The Mind's Construction in the Face', in *Renaissance Studies in Honor of Hardin Craig* (Stanford, 1941), pp. 208–20.

[2] *A Letter Concerning Enthusiasm*, ii (*Characteristicks*, 6th edn., 1737, i. 11). Cf. La Rochefoucauld, *Maxims*, cclvii: 'Gravity is an Affectation of the Body, put on to conceal the defects of the Mind' (trans. 1706, p. 109).

than Love, and inspire us rather with Awe than Confidence. There is a Countenance of a contrary Kind, which hath been called a Letter of Recommendation;[1] which throws our Arms open to receive the Poison, divests us of all kind of Apprehension, and disarms us of all Caution: I mean that glavering,[2] sneering Smile, of which the greater Part of Mankind are extremely fond, conceiving it to be the Sign of Good-Nature; whereas this is generally a Compound of Malice and Fraud, and as surely indicates a bad Heart, as a galloping Pulse doth a Fever.

Men are chiefly betrayed into this Deceit, by a gross but common Mistake of Good-Humour for Good-Nature. Two Qualities so far from bearing any Resemblance to each other, that they are almost Opposites. Good-Nature is that benevolent and amiable Temper of Mind which disposes us to feel the Misfortunes, and enjoy the Happiness of others; and consequently pushes us on to promote the latter, and prevent the former; and that without any abstract Contemplation on the Beauty of Virtue, and without the Allurements or Terrors of Religion.[3] Now Good-Humour is nothing more than the Triumph of the Mind, when reflecting on its own Happiness, and that perhaps from having compared it with the inferior Happiness of others.[4]

If this be allowed, I believe we may admit that glavering Smile, whose principal Ingredient is Malice, to be the Symptom of Good-Humour. And here give me Leave to define this Word Malice, as I doubt whether it be not in common Speech so often confounded with Envy, that common Readers may not have very distinct Ideas between them. But as Envy is a Repining at the Good of others, compared with our own, so Malice is a

---

[1] Cf. *Tom Jones*, VIII. x; *Amelia*, IX. v; and see the *Spectator*, 144 and 221. See Diogenes Laertius, v. xviii (on Aristotle): 'Beauty he declared to be a greater recommendation than any letter of introduction. Others attribute this definition to Diogenes' (trans. R. D. Hicks, Loeb Library). A fragment from Ovid, *Epist. ex Ponto*, II. viii. 53–4, became proverbial: 'Auxilium non leve vultus habet'; and Publilius Syrus, in his *Sententiae*, has: 'Formosa facies muta commendatio est' (ed. R. A. H. Bickford-Smith, p. 12).

[2] Deceitful, flattering; *OED* cites South (*Sermons*, 1717, vi. 121): 'Some slavish, glavering flattering Parasite'. Fielding uses the word four times in this essay.

[3] Fielding believed that the image of future rewards and punishments was necessary to morality (e.g., the *Champion*, 22 January 1740; Dr. Harrison's argument in *Amelia*, XII. v), but that Good-nature was independent of these considerations. This was not unorthodox: cf. *A Sermon Preached before the Right Honourable the Lord Mayor . . . By Thomas [Herring] Lord Bishop of Bangor* (1739), pp. 5–6.

[4] Hence to be equated with Hobbes' 'Glory, or internal gloriation': see above, p. 135 n. 2.

rejoicing at their Evil, on the same Comparison.¹ And thus it appears to have a very close Affinity to that malevolent Disposition, which I have above described under the Word Good-Humour: for nothing is truer than the Observation of *Shakespear*;

*—A Man may smile, and smile, and be a Villain.*²

But how alien must this Countenance be to that heavenly Frame of Soul, of which *Jesus Christ* himself was the most perfect Pattern; of which blessed Person it is recorded, that he never was once seen to laugh, during his whole Abode on Earth.³ And what indeed hath Good-Nature to do with a smiling Countenance? It would be like a Purse in the Hands of a Miser, which he could never use. For admitting, that laughing at the Vices and Follies of Mankind is entirely innocent, (which is more perhaps than we ought to admit) yet surely their Miseries and Misfortunes are no Subjects of Mirth: And with these, *Quis non vicus abundat?*⁴ the World is so full of them, that scarce a Day passes without inclining a truly good-natured Man rather to Tears than Merriment.

Mr. *Hobbes* tells us, that Laughter arises from Pride,⁵ which is far from being a good-natured Passion. And though I would not severely discountenance all Indulgence of it, since Laughter, while confined to Vice and Folly, is no very cruel Punishment on the Object, and may be attended with good Consequences to him; yet we shall, I believe, find, on a careful Examination into its Motive, that it is not produced from Good-Nature. But this is one of the first Efforts of the Mind, which few attend to, or indeed are capable of discovering; and however Self-Love may

---

¹ Cf. *Covent-Garden Journal*, 14, citing Cicero, who, in *Tusc. Disp.* IV. vii. 16, places *invidentia* (*invidia*) under the head of *aegritudo*, a grieving, and *malevolentia* under *voluptas*, where it is defined as 'laetans malo alieno'. See Mandeville, *Fable of the Bees*, 'Remark N' (6th edn., 1732, pp. 139 ff.).

² Cf. *Hamlet*, I. iii. 54.

³ Cf. John Donne, 'A Lent-Sermon Preached before the King' (*Sermons*, ed. Potter-Simpson, iii. 221): 'that melancholick man, who was never seen to laugh in all his life'; Giles Fletcher, 'Christs Victorie on Earth', st. xii; Sir Thomas Browne, *Pseudodoxia epidemica* (1646), VII. xvi; *Spectator*, 381; *The New Help to Discourse* (8th edn., 1721), p. 47. Ernst Curtius derives this teaching from St. John Chrysostom (*European Literature and the Latin Middle Ages*, p. 420).

⁴ See the citation from Juvenal, above, p. 156. Cf. Seneca, *Ad Polybium*, iv. 2: 'Omnis agedum mortalis circumspice, larga ubique flendi et adsidua materia est.'

⁵ Hobbes, *Human Nature*, IX. xiii (*English Works*, ed. Molesworth, iv. 45–7); *Leviathan*, I. vi (ibid., iii. 46). Cf. Quintilian, *Inst. orat.* VI. iii. 7–8; Cicero, *De oratore*, II. lviii. 236.

make us pleased with seeing a Blemish in another which we are ourselves free from, yet Compassion on the first Reflection of any Unhappiness in the Object, immediately puts a Stop to it in good Minds. For Instance; suppose a Person well drest should tumble in a dirty Place in the Street; I am afraid there are few who would not laugh at the Accident: Now what is this Laughter other than a convulsive Extasy, occasioned by the Contemplation of our own Happiness, compared with the unfortunate Person's! a Pleasure which seems to savour of Ill-nature: but as this is one of those first, and as it were, spontaneous Motions of the Soul,[1] which few, as I have said, attend to, and none can prevent; so it doth not properly constitute the Character. When we come to reflect on the Uneasiness this Person suffers, Laughter, in a good and delicate Mind, will begin to change itself into Compassion; and in Proportion as this latter operates on us, we may be said to have more or less Good-Nature: but should any fatal Consequence, such as a violent Bruise, or the breaking of a Bone, attend the Fall, the Man who should still continue to laugh, would be entitled to the basest and vilest Appellation with which any Language can stigmatize him.

From what hath been said, I think we may conclude, that a constant, settled, glavering, sneering Smile in the Countenance, is so far from indicating Goodness, that it may be with much Confidence depended on as an Assurance of the contrary.

But I would not be understood here to speak with the least Regard to that amiable, open, composed, cheerful Aspect, which is the Result of a good Conscience, and the Emanation of a good Heart; of both which it is an infallible Symptom; and may be the more depended on, as it cannot, I believe, be counterfeited, with any reasonable Resemblance, by the nicest Power of Art.

Neither have I any Eye towards that honest, hearty, loud Chuckle, which shakes the Sides of Aldermen and 'Squires, without the least Provocation of a Jest; proceeding chiefly from a full Belly; and is a Symptom (however strange it may seem) of a very gentle and inoffensive Quality, called Dulness, than

---

[1] See *Tom Jones*, XI. iii, on 'secret spontaneous Emotions of the Soul'; cf. Seneca, *De ira*, II. ii. 1; Montaigne, *Apology for Raimond de Sebonde*, on 'vehement Agitations . . . which surprize the Soul on a sudden, without giving it leisure to recollect it self' (*Essays*, trans. Cotton, 3rd edn., 1700, ii. 391); Steele, *The Lying Lover* (1703), Epilogue. That such 'reflex actions' do not properly constitute one's 'Character' is a significant aspect of Fielding's conception of human nature.

which nothing is more risible: for as Mr. *Pope*, with exquisite
Pleasantry, says;

—*Gentle Dulness ever loves a Joke.*[1]

i.e. one of her own Jokes. These are sometimes performed by
the Foot; as by leaping over Heads, or Chairs, or Tables, Kicks
in the B——ch, *&c.* sometimes by the Hand; as by Slaps in the
Face, pulling off Wigs, and infinite other Dexterities, too tedious
to particularize: sometimes by the Voice; as by hollowing,
huzzaing, and singing merry (*i.e.* dull) Catches, by *merry* (*i.e.*
dull) Fellows.[2]

Lastly; I do by no means hint at the various Laughs, Titters,
Tehes, *&c.* of the Fair Sex, with whom indeed this Essay hath
not any thing to do; the Knowledge of the Characters of Women
being foreign to my intended Purpose; as it is in Fact a Science,
to which I make not the least Pretension.

The Smile or Sneer which composes the Countenance I have
above endeavour'd to describe, is extremely different from all
these: but as I have already dwelt pretty long on it, and as my
Reader will not, I apprehend, be liable to mistake it, I shall wind
up my Caution to him against this Symptom, in Part of a Line
of *Horace*:

—*Hic niger est; hunc tu caveto.*[3]

There is one Countenance, which is the plainest Instance of
the general Misunderstanding of that Adage, *Fronti nulla Fides.*
This is a fierce Aspect, which hath the same Right to signify
Courage, as Gravity to denote Wisdom, or a Smile Good-Nature;
whereas Experience teaches us the contrary, and it passes among
most Men for the Symptom only of a Bully.

But I am aware, that I shall be reminded of an Assertion which
I set out with in the Beginning of this Essay, *viz. That Nature
gives us as sure Symptoms of the Diseases of the Mind as she doth of
those of the Body.* To which what I have now advanced may seem
a Contradiction. The Truth is, Nature doth really imprint
sufficient Marks in the Countenance, to inform an accurate and
discerning Eye: but as such is the Property of few, the Generality

[1] *Variorum Dunciad*, ii. 30; rev. (1743), ii. 34.
[2] Cf. the concluding section of *Tatler*, 45.
[3] *Serm.* I. iv. 85: 'That man is black of heart; of him beware' (trans. H. R. Fairclough, Loeb Library).

of Mankind mistake the Affectation for the Reality:[1] for as Affectation always over-acts her Part, it fares with her as with a Farcical Actor on the Stage, whose monstrous over-done Grimaces are sure to catch the Applause of an insensible Audience; while the truest and finest Strokes of Nature, represented by a judicious and just Actor, pass unobserved and disregarded. In the same Manner, the true Symptoms being finer, and less glaring, make no Impression on our Physiognomist; while the grosser Appearances of Affectation are sure to attract his Eye, and deceive his Judgment. Thus that sprightly and penetrating Look, which is almost a certain Token of Understanding; that cheerful, composed Serenity, which always indicates Good-Nature; and that fiery Cast of the Eyes, which is never unaccompanied with Courage, are often over-looked: while a formal, stately, austere Gravity; a glavering, fawning Smile, and a strong Contraction of the Muscles, pass generally on the World for the Virtues they only endeavour to affect.

But as these Rules are, I believe, none of them without some Exceptions; as they are of no Use but to an Observer of much Penetration: Lastly, as a more subtle Hypocrisy will sometimes escape undiscovered from the highest Discernment; let us see if we have not a more infallible Guide to direct us to the Knowledge of Men; one more easily to be attained, and on the Efficacy of which we may with the greatest Certainty rely.

And surely the Actions of Men seem to be the justest Interpreters of their Thoughts, and the truest Standards by which we may judge them.[2] *By their Fruits you shall know them,*[3] is a Saying of great Wisdom, as well as Authority. And indeed this is so certain a Method of acquiring the Knowledge I contend for, that at first Appearance, it seems absolutely perfect, and to want no manner of Assistance.

There are, however, two Causes of our Mistakes on this Head; and which lead us into forming very erroneous Judgments of Men, even while their Actions stare us in the Face, and as it were hold a Candle to us, by which we may see into them.

[1] Cf. the *Champion*, 4 March 1740.
[2] Cf. Sophia's argument, *Tom Jones*, XVIII. xii. See Locke, *Essay*, I. ii. 3; Samuel Clarke, 'How to Judge of Moral Actions', in *Sermons on Several Subjects* (7th edn., 1749), iii. 82.
[3] Matt. 7: 16 and 20.

The first of these is when we take their own Words against their Actions.[1] This (if I may borrow another Illustration from Physic) is no less ridiculous, than it would be in a learned Professor of that Art, when he perceives his light-headed Patient is in the utmost Danger, to take his Word that he is well. This Error is infinitely more common than its extream Absurdity would persuade us was possible. And many a credulous Person hath been ruined by trusting to the Assertions of another, who must have preserved himself, had he placed a wiser Confidence in his Actions.

The Second is an Error still more general. This is when we take the Colour of a Man's Actions not from their own visible Tendency, but from his public Character: when we believe what others say of him, in Opposition to what we see him do? How often do we suffer ourselves to be deceived, out of the Credit of a Fact, or out of a just Opinion of its Heinousness, by the reputed Dignity or Honesty of the Person who did it? How common are such Ejaculations as these? 'O 'tis impossible HE should be guilty of any such Thing! HE must have done it by Mistake; HE could not design it. I will never believe any Ill of HIM. So good a Man, &c.!' when in Reality, the Mistake lies only in his Character. Nor is there any more simple, unjust, and insufficient Method of judging Mankind, than by public Estimation, which is oftner acquired by Deceit, Partiality, Prejudice, and such like, than by real Desert. I will venture to affirm, that I have known some of *the best sort of Men in the World,* (to use the vulgar Phrase,) who would not have scrupled cutting a Friend's Throat; and *a Fellow whom no Man should be seen to speak to,* capable of the highest Acts of Friendship and Benevolence.

Now it will be necessary to divest ourselves of both these Errors, before we can reasonably hope to attain any adequate Knowledge of the true Characters of Men. Actions are their own best Expositors; and though Crimes may admit of alleviating Circumstances, which may properly induce a Judge to mitigate the Punishment; from the Motive, for Instance, as Necessity may lessen the Crime of Robbery, when compared to Wantonness or Vanity; or from some Circumstance attending the Fact itself, as robbing a Stranger, or an Enemy, compared with committing it on a Friend or Benefactor; yet the Crime is still

[1] Cf. Cicero, *Tusc. Disp.* III. xx. 48: 'Quid verba audiam, cum facta videam?'

164 *Miscellanies*

Robbery, and the Person who commits it is a Robber; though he should pretend to have done it with a good Design, or the World should concur in calling him an honest Man.

But I am aware of another Objection which may be made to my Doctrine, *viz.* admitting that the Actions of Men are the surest Evidence of their Character, that this Knowledge comes too late; that it is to caution us against a Highwayman after he hath plundered us, or against an Incendiary, after he hath fired our House.

To which I answer, That it is not against Force, but Deceit, which I am here seeking for Armour; against those who can injure us only by obtaining our good Opinion.[1] If therefore I can instruct my Reader from what sort of Persons he is to withhold this Opinion, and inform him of all, or at least the principal Arts by which Deceit proceeds to ingratiate itself with us, by which he will be effectually enabled to defeat its Purpose, I shall have sufficiently satisfied the Design of this Essay.

And here, the first Caution I shall give him is against FLATTERY, which I am convinced no one uses, without some Design on the Person flattered. I remember to have heard of a certain Nobleman,[2] who though he was an immoderate Lover of receiving Flattery himself, was so far from being guilty of this Vice to others, that he was remarkably free in telling Men their Faults. A Friend, who had his Intimacy, one Day told him; He wondered that he who loved Flattery better than any Man living, did not return a little of it himself, which he might be sure would bring him back such plentiful Interest. To which he answered, Though he admitted the Justness of the Observation, he could never think of giving away what he was so extremely covetous of. Indeed, whoever knows any thing of the Nature of Men, how greedy they are of Praise, and how backward in bestowing it on others; that it is a Debt seldom paid, even to the greatest Merit, 'till we are compelled to it, may reasonably conclude, that this Profusion, this voluntary throwing it away on those who do not

[1] This was the reason that the Lilliputians gave for looking upon Fraud as a greater crime than Theft, for 'Honesty hath no Fence against superior Cunning' (Swift, *Gulliver's Travels*, I. vi). Cf. Addison's desire that, through his papers, 'the Virtuous and the Innocent may know in Speculation what they could never arrive at by Practice, and by this means avoid the Snares of the Crafty, the Corruptions of the Vicious, and the Reasonings of the Prejudiced' (*Spectator*, 245). See *Amelia*, VIII. ix.

[2] Not identified.

deserve it, proceeds, as *Martial* says of a Beggar's Present, from some other Motive than Generosity or Good-will.[1]

But indeed there are few whose Vanity is so foul a Feeder, to digest Flattery, if undisguised: It must impose on us, in order to allure us: Before we can relish it, we must call it by some other Name; such as, a just Esteem of, and Respect for our real Worth; a Debt due to our Merit, and not a Present to our Pride.[2]

Suppose it should be really so, and we should have all those great or good Qualities which are extolled in us; yet considering, as I have said above, with what Reluctance such Debts are paid, we may justly suspect some Design in the Person who so readily and forwardly offers it us. It is well observed, That we do not attend, without Uneasiness, to Praises in which we have no Concern,[3] much less shall we be eager to utter and exaggerate the Praise of another, without some Expectation from it.

A Flatterer therefore is a just Object of our Distrust, and will, by prudent Men, be avoided.

Next to the Flatterer is the Professor, who carries his Affection to you still farther; and on a slight or no Acquaintance, embraces, hugs, kisses, and vows the greatest Esteem for your Person, Parts, and Virtues. To know whether this Friend is sincere, you have only to examine into the Nature of Friendship, which is always founded either on Esteem or Gratitude, or perhaps on both.[4] Now Esteem, admitting every Requisite for its Formation present, and these are not a few, is of very slow Growth; it is an involuntary Affection, rather apt to give us Pain than Pleasure, and therefore meets with no Encouragement in our Minds, which it creeps into by small and almost imperceptible Degrees: And perhaps, when it hath got an absolute Possession of us, may require some other Ingredient to engage our Friendship to its own Object. It appears then pretty plain, that this Mushroom Passion here mentioned, owes not its Original to

---

[1] *Epigrammata*, VIII. xxxviii.

[2] Cf. Cicero, *De amicitia*, xxvi. 97; La Rochefoucauld, *Maxims*, clii: 'If we did not Flatter our selves, the Flattery of others cou'd never hurt us' (trans. 1706, p. 63; cf. cxliv, p. 60 and cccxxix, p. 138); and *Tatler*, 208: 'The Reason that there is such a general Outcry amongst us against Flatterers, is, that there are so very few good ones.'

[3] Cf. Mandeville, *Fable of the Bees*: '. . . nothing is more tiresome to us than the Repetition of Praises we have no manner of Share in' (Remark N; 6th edn., 1732, p. 148). See *Spectator*, 238 and 256.

[4] Cf. Cicero, *De amicitia*, xxvii. 100; *Tom Jones*, vi. 1.

Esteem. Whether it can possibly flow from Gratitude, which may indeed produce it more immediately, you will more easily judge: for though there are some Minds whom no Benefits can inspire with Gratitude; there are more, I believe, who conceive this Affection without even a supposed Obligation. If therefore you can assure yourself it is impossible he should imagine himself obliged to you, you may be satisfied that Gratitude is not the Motive to his Friendship. Seeing then that you can derive it from neither of these Fountains, you may well be justified in suspecting its Falshood; and if so, you will act as wisely in receiving it into your Heart, as he doth who knowingly lodges a Viper in his Bosom, or a Thief in his House. FORGIVE THE ACTS OF YOUR ENEMIES hath been thought the highest Maxim of Morality; FEAR THE PROFESSIONS OF YOUR FRIENDS, is perhaps the wisest.[1]

The Third Character against which an open Heart should be alarmed, is a PROMISER,[2] one who rises another Step in Friendship. The Man who is wantonly profuse of his Promises ought to sink his Credit as much as a Tradesman would by uttering great Numbers of Promissory Notes, payable at a distant Day. The truest Conclusion in both Cases is, that neither intend, or will be able to pay. And as the latter most probably intends to cheat you of your Money, so the former at least designs to cheat you of your Thanks; and it is well for you, if he hath no deeper Purpose, and that Vanity is the only evil Passion to which he destines you a Sacrifice.

I would not be here understood to point at the Promises of political Great Men, which they are supposed to lie under a Necessity of giving in great Abundance, and the Value of them is so well known, that few are to be imposed on by them. The Professor I here mean, is he who on all Occasions is ready, of his own Head, and unasked, to promise Favours. This is such another Instance of Generosity, as his who relieves his Friend in

1 Cf. Matt. 5: 44; Luke 6: 27, 35. See Ecclus. 6: 6–13; Mic. 7: 5. On false friends as a greater danger than declared foes, see Cicero, *In C. Verrem*, II. i. 15; Lucian's epigram in the Greek Anthology (Loeb Library, iv. 20); Sir Thomas More's epigram, 'De Ficto Amico' (*Latin Epigrams*, ed. L. Bradner and C. A. Lynch, pp. 9–10); Wycherley, *Plain Dealer*, conclusion of Act I; Prior, *Solomon*, iii. 77–8; Lord Lansdowne, 'Ode: On the Present Corruption of Mankind', st. iv (*Genuine Works*, 1736, i. 141–3). Cf. *Tom Jones*, III. iv.
2 Cf. the empty Promiser in *Joseph Andrews*, II. xvi.

Distress, by a Draught on *Aldgate* Pump.[1] Of these there are several Kinds: some who promise what they never intend to perform; others who promise what they are not sure they can perform; and others again, who promise so many, that like Debtors, being not able to pay all their Debts, they afterwards pay none.

The Man who is inquisitive into the Secrets of your Affairs, with which he hath no concern, is another Object of your Caution.[2] Men no more desire another's Secrets, to conceal them, than they would another's Purse, for the Pleasure only of carrying it.

Nor is a Slanderer less wisely to be avoided, unless you chuse to feast on your Neighbour's Faults, at the Price of being served up yourself at the Tables of others: for Persons of this Stamp are generally impartial in their Abuse. Indeed it is not always possible totally to escape them; for being barely known to them is a sure Title to their Calumny; but the more they are admitted to your Acquaintance, the more you will be abused by them.[3]

I fear the next Character I shall mention, may give Offence to the grave Part of Mankind; for whose Wisdom and Honesty I have an equal Respect; but I must, however, venture to caution my open-hearted Reader against a Saint. No honest and sensible Man will understand me here, as attempting to declaim against Sanctity of Morals. The Sanctity I mean is that which flows from the Lips, and shines in the Countenance. It may be said, perhaps, that real Sanctity may wear these Appearances; and how shall we then distinguish with any Certainty, the true from the fictitious? I answer, That if we admit this to be possible, yet as it is likewise possible that it may be only counterfeit; and as in Fact it is so Ninety Nine Times in a Hundred; it is better that one real Saint should suffer a little unjust Suspicion, than that Ninety Nine Villains should impose on the World, and be enabled to perpetrate their Villainies under this Mask.

[1] A Mercantile Phrase for a bad Note. [Fielding's note.] For the proverb, see Lean's *Collectanea*, i. 136–7.

[2] Cf. Horace, *Epist.* I. xviii. 69: 'Percontatorem fugito, nam garrulus idem est'; Robert South: 'For most certain it is, that no Man enquires into another Man's concerns, or makes it his Business to acquaint himself with his Privacies, but with a design to do him some shrewd Turn or other' (*Sermons*, 6th edn., 1727, v. 397–8).

[3] Cf. *Champion*, 6 March 1740; *Covent-Garden Journal*, 14; *Tom Jones*, XI. i. In the closing pages of *A Charge to the Grand Jury*, Fielding cites Coke, Pulton (*De pace*), Demosthenes, Aristotle's *Politics*, and Scripture against slander and libelling.

But, to say the Truth; a sour, morose, ill-natured, censorious Sanctity, never is, nor can be sincere. Is a Readiness to despise, to hate, and to condemn, the Temper of a Christian? Can he who passes Sentence on the Souls of Men with more Delight and Triumph than the Devil can execute it, have the Impudence to pretend himself a Disciple of one who died for the Sins of Mankind?[1] Is not such a Sanctity the true Mark of that Hypocrisy which in many Places of Scripture, and particularly in the twenty third Chapter of St. *Matthew*, is so bitterly inveighed against?

As this is a most detestable Character in Society; and as its Malignity is more particularly bent against the best and worthiest Men, the sincere and open-hearted, whom it persecutes with inveterate Envy and Hatred, I shall take some Pains in the ripping it up,[2] and exposing the Horrors of its Inside, that we may all shun it; and at the same Time will endeavour so plainly to describe its Outside, that we shall hardly be liable, by any Mistake, to fall into its Snares.

With Regard then to the Inside (if I am allowed that Expression) of this Character, the Scripture-writers have employed uncommon Labour in dissecting it. Let us hear our Saviour himself, in the Chapter above-cited. *It devours Widows Houses; it makes its Proselytes two-fold more the Children of Hell; it omits the weightier Matters of the Law, Judgment, Mercy, and Faith; it strains off a Gnat,*[3] *and swallows a Camel; it is full of Extortion and Excess.*[4] St. *Paul*, in his first Epistle to *Timothy*, says of them, That *they speak Lies, and their Conscience is seared with a red hot Iron.*[5] And in many Parts of the Old Testament, as in *Job*; *Let the Hypocrite reign not, lest the People be ensnared:*[6] And *Solomon* in his Proverbs; *An Hypocrite with his Mouth destroyeth his Neighbour.*[7]

---

[1] Cf. the *Champion*, 5 and 19 April 1740.

[2] A favourite phrase with Robert South, e.g.: 'That which has provoked me thus to rip up, and expose to you their nauseous and ridiculous way of addressing to God ...' (*Sermons*, 6th edn., 1727, ii. 160–1).

[3] So is the *Greek*, which the Translators have mistaken: They render it, *strain at a Gnat*, i.e. struggle in swallowing, whereas, in Reality, the *Greek* Word is, to strain through a Cullender; and the Idea is, that though they pretend their Consciences are so fine, that a Gnat is with Difficulty strained through them, yet they can, if they please, open them wide enough to admit a Camel. [Fielding's note.] On this reading, see Daniel Scott, *A New Version of St. Matthew's Gospel* (1741), p. 155.

[4] Cf. Matt. 23: 24.   [5] 1 Tim. 4: 2.

[6] Job 34: 30.   [7] Prov. 11: 9.

In these several Texts, most of the Enormities of this Character are described: but there is one which deserves a fuller Comment, as pointing at its very Essence: I mean the thirteenth Verse of the twenty third Chapter of St. *Matthew*, where *Jesus* addresses himself thus to the *Pharisees*: *Hypocrites; for ye shut up the Kingdom of Heaven against Men; for ye neither go in yourselves, neither suffer ye them that are entring to go in.*

This is an admirable Picture of sanctified Hypocrisy, which will neither do Good itself, nor suffer others to do it. But if we understand the Text figuratively, we may apply it to that censorious Quality of this Vice, which as it will do nothing honestly to deserve Reputation, so is it ever industrious to deprive others of the Praises due to their Virtues. It confines all Merit to those external Forms which are fully particularized in Scripture; of these it is itself a rigid Observer; hence it must derive all Honour and Reward in this World; nay, and even in the next, if it can impose on itself so far as to imagine itself capable of cheating the Almighty, and obtaining any Reward there.[1]

Now a Galley-Slave, of an envious Disposition, doth not behold a Man free from Chains, and at his Ease, with more Envy than Persons in these Fetters of Sanctity view the rest of Mankind; especially such as they behold without them *entring into the Kingdom of Heaven*. These are indeed the Objects of their highest Animosity, and are always the surest Marks of their Detraction. Persons of more Goodness than Knowledge of Mankind, when they are calumniated by these Saints, are, I believe, apt to impute the Calumny to an Ignorance of their real Character; and imagine if they could better inform the said Saints of their innate Worth, they should be better treated by them; but alas, this is a total Mistake: the more Good a sanctified Hypocrite knows of an open and an honest Man, the more he envies and hates him, and the more ready he is to seize or invent an Opportunity of detracting from his real Merit.[2]

---

[1] Of many like comments, cf. Samuel Clarke's: '. . . . *such* persons, as under pretence of *Sanctity* and a *Form* of Godliness, or with great zeal for certain *Rites* and *Ceremonies* and *Appearances* of Religion, either cheat and defraud men in their *dealings* without Truth and Justice, or corrupt mens manners. . . . Our Saviour has given us a never-failing Rule, to discover this hypocrisy: *By their* Fruits, says he, *ye shall know them* . . .' ('Of the Several Sorts of Hypocrisy', *Sermons on Several Subjects*, 7th edn., 1749, x. 148–9).

[2] Cf. Bacon, *Essays*, ix: 'A man that hath no virtue in himself, ever *envieth* virtue in others' (1701 edn., p. 19); La Rochefoucauld, *Maxims*, xxix: 'The ill we do exposes us not

But envy is not their only Motive of Hatred to Good-Men; they are eternally jealous of being seen through, and consequently exposed by them. A Hypocrite in Society lives in the same Apprehension with a Thief, who lies concealed in the midst of the Family he is to rob: for this fancies himself perceived when he is least so; every Motion alarms him; he fears he is discovered, and is suspicious that every one who enters the Room, knows where he is hid, and is coming to seize him.[1] And thus, as nothing hates more violently than Fear, many an innocent Person, who suspects no Evil intended him, is detested by him who intends it.

Now in destroying the Reputation of a virtuous and good Man, the Hypocrite imagines he hath disarmed his Enemy of all Weapons to hurt him; and therefore this sanctified Hypocrisy is not more industrious to conceal its own Vices, than to obscure and contaminate the Virtues of others. As the Business of such a Man's Life is to procure Praise, by acquiring and maintaining an undeserved Character; so is his utmost Care employed to deprive those who have an honest Claim to the Character himself affects only, of all the Emoluments which could otherwise arise to them from it.[2]

The Prophet *Isaiah* speaks of these People, where he says, *Woe unto them who call Evil Good, and Good Evil; that put Darkness for Light, and Light for Darkness*, &c.[3] In his Sermon on which Text, the witty Dr. *South* hath these Words.—Detraction *is that killing poisonous Arrow, drawn out of the Devil's Quiver, which is always flying about, and doing Execution in the Dark: Against which* no Virtue is a Defence, no Innocence a Security. *It is a Weapon forged in Hell, and formed by that prime Artificer and Engineer, the Devil; and none but that Great God, who knows all Things, and can do all Things, can protect the* best *of Men against it.*[4]

so much to Persecution and Hatred as our good qualities' (trans. 1706, p. 14); Tacitus, *Annals*, IV. xxxiii. See Fielding's *Covent-Garden Journal*, 21, and Mr. Wilson on vanity in *Joseph Andrews*, III. iii.

[1] On the fears of those who live in a mask (*sub persona*), cf. Seneca, *De tranqu. animi*, xvii. 1.

[2] Cf. Seneca, *De vita beata*, xix. 2.

[3] Isa. 5: 20. South preached four sermons on this text.

[4] South, *Sermons* (6th edn., 1727), ii. 353, 356-7. Also quoted by Fielding in the *Champion*, 6 March 1740.

To these likewise *Martial* alludes in the following Lines.

Ut bene loquatur Sentiatque Mamercus,
Efficere nullis, Aule, Moribus possis.[1]

I have been somewhat diffusive in the censorious Branch of this Character, as it is a very pernicious one; and (according to what I have observed) little known and attended to. I shall not describe all its other Qualities. Indeed there is no Species of Mischief which it doth not produce. For, not to mention the private Villanies it daily transacts, most of the great Evils which have affected Society, Wars, Murders, and Massacres,[2] have owed their Original to this abominable Vice; which is the Destroyer of the Innocent, and Protector of the Guilty; which hath introduced all manner of Evil into the World, and hath almost expelled every Grain of Good out of it. Doth it not attempt to cheat Men into the Pursuit of Sorrow and Misery, under the Appearance of Virtue, and to frighten them from Mirth and Pleasure, under the Colour of Vice, or, if you please, SIN? Doth it not attempt to gild over that poisonous Potion, made up of Malevolence, Austerity, and such cursed Ingredients, while it embitters the delightful Draught of innocent Pleasure with the nauseous Relish of Fear and Shame?

No wonder then that this malignant cursed Disposition, which is the Disgrace of Human Nature, and the Bane of Society, should be spoke against with such remarkable Bitterness, by the benevolent Author of our Religion, particularly in the thirty third Verse of the above cited Chapter of St. *Matthew.*

YE SERPENTS, YE GENERATION OF VIPERS, HOW CAN YE ESCAPE THE DAMNATION OF HELL?[3]

Having now dispatched the Inside of this Character, and, as I apprehend, said enough to make any one avoid, I am sure

---

[1] *Epigrammata*, v. xxviii. 1–2: 'There is no virtue, Aulus, by which you could induce Mamercus to speak and think kindly of you' (trans. W. C. A. Ker, Loeb Library). Cited by Fielding as epigraph to the *Champion*, 6 March 1740.

[2] Perhaps an echo of Nathaniel Lee: 'Yet there I'll stay and fix my Imagination, / On all their Mischiefs, Murders, Massacres . . .' (*Constantine the Great*, v. ii; *Dramatick Works*, 1734, ii. 71); but cf. also Defoe, *Jure Divino* (1706), Book II, p. 18. This kind of expansive general indictment is a mannerism of South, e.g., on the mistaken naming of good and evil: 'All, or most of the Miseries and Calamities which afflict Mankind, and turn the World upside down, have been conceived in, and issued from the fruitful Womb of this one villanous Artifice' (*Sermons*, 6th edn., 1727, vi. 112).

[3] Matt. 23: 33. Cf. Matt. 3: 7, 12: 34; Luke 3: 7.

sufficient to make a Christian detest it, nothing remains but to examine the Outside, in order to furnish honest Men with sufficient Rules to discover it. And in this we shall have the same divine Guide, whom we have in the former Part followed.

First then, beware of that sanctified Appearance, *that whited Sepulchre, which looks beautiful outward, and is within full of all Uncleanness. Those who can make clean the Outside of the Platter, but within are full of Extortion and Excess.*[1]

Secondly, Look well to those *who bind heavy Burdens, and grievous to be born, and lay them on Mens Shoulders; but they themselves will not move them with one of their Fingers.*[2]

These heavy Burdens (says *Burkit*) *were Counsels and Directions, Rules and Canons, Austerities and Severities, which the Pharisees introduced and imposed upon their Hearers.*[3] This requires no further Comment: for, as I have before said, these Hypocrites place all Virtue, and all Religion, in the Observation of those *Austerities and Severities*, without which the truest and purest Goodness will never receive their Commendation: but how different this Doctrine is from the Temper of Christianity, may be gathered by that Total of all Christian Morality, with which *Jesus* sums up the excellent Precepts delivered in his divine Sermon: Therefore *do unto all Men as ye would they should do unto you*: For this is the Law and the Prophets.[4]

Thirdly, Beware of all Ostentation of Virtue, Goodness, or Piety. By this Ostentation I mean that of the Countenance and the Mouth, or of some external Forms. And this, I apprehend, is the Meaning of *Jesus*, where he says, *They do their Works to be seen of Men*, as appears by the Context; *They make broad their Philacteries, and enlarge the Borders of their Garments.*[5] These *Philacteries* were certain Scrowls of Parchment, whereon were written the ten Commandments, and particular Parts of the *Mosaic* Law, which they ostentatiously wore on their Garments, thinking by that Ceremony to fulfil the Precept delivered to them in a Verse of *Deuteronomy*, though they neglected to fulfil the Laws they wore thus about them.

---

[1] Conflation of Matt. 23: 27 and 25 (cf. Luke 11: 39).

[2] Matt. 23: 4; Luke 11: 46.

[3] William Burkitt, *Expository Notes with Practical Observations on the New Testament* (7th edn., 1719), sig. I2ᵛ.

[4] Cf. Matt. 7: 12.

[5] Matt. 23: 5. Fielding goes on to paraphrase Burkit, sig. I2ᵛ. See Deut. 6: 8.

Another Instance of their Ostentation was—*making long Prayers*, i.e. (says *Burkett*) *making long Prayers* (or perhaps pretending to make them) *in the Temples and Synagogues for Widows, and thereupon persuading them to give bountifully to the Corban, or the common Treasure of the Temple, some Part of which was employed for their Maintenance. Learn*, 1. *It is no* NEW *Thing for designing Hypocrites to cover the foulest Transgression with the Cloak of Religion. The Pharisees make long Prayers a Cover for their Covetousness.* 2. *That to make use of Religion in Policy for worldly Advantage sake, is the Way to be damned with a Vengeance for Religion sake.*[1]

Again says *Jesus—in paying Tithe of Mint and Anise and Cummin, while they omit the weightier Matters of the Law, Judgment, Mercy, and Faith.*[2] By which we are not to understand (nor would I be understood so to mean) any Inhibition of paying the Priest his Dues; but, as my Commentator observes, *an Ostentation of a precise keeping the Law in smaller Matters, and neglecting weightier Duties. They paid Tythe of Mint, Anise, and Cummin* (*i.e.* of the minutest and most worthless Things) *but at the same Time omitted Judgment, Mercy, and Faith; that is, just Dealing among Men, Charity towards the Poor, and Faithfulness in their Promises and Covenants one with another. This, says our Saviour, is* TO STRAIN AT *a Gnat, and swallow a Camel: A proverbial Expression, intimating, that some Persons pretend great Niceness and Scrupulosity about small Matters, and none, or but little, about Duties of the greatest Moment. Hence, Note, That Hypocrites lay the greatest Stress upon the least Matters in Religion, and place Holiness most in these Things where God places it least. Ye Tythe Mint, &c.* but neglect the weightier Matters of the Law. *This is indeed the Bane of all Religion and true Piety, to prefer Rituals and human Institutions before divine Commands, and the Practice of Natural Religion.* THUS TO DO IS A CERTAIN SIGN OF GROSS HYPOCRISY.[3]

Nothing can, in Fact, be more foreign to the Nature of Virtue, than Ostentation. It is truly said of Virtue, that could Men behold her naked, they would be all in Love with her.[4] Here it

---

[1] Burkitt, sig. I3. Cf. Matt. 23: 14, Mark 12: 40, Luke 20: 47, the latter cited in the *Champion*, 29 March 1740.

[2] Matt. 23: 23.   [3] Burkitt, sig. I3–I3ᵛ.

[4] Attributed to Plato in the *Champion*, 24 January 1740, and the dedication of *Tom Jones*; cf. above, p. 143. The idea of nakedness seems to be Fielding's own, though 'naked virtue', like naked truth, is perhaps proverbial. Plato's declaration that virtue (or wisdom), if she could be seen in a physical image, would awaken admiration (*Phaedrus*, 250 d) was

is implied, that this is a Sight very rare or difficult to come at; and indeed there is always a modest Backwardness in true Virtue to expose her naked Beauty. She is conscious of her innate Worth, and little desirous of exposing it to the publick View. It is the Harlot Vice who constantly endeavours to set off the Charms she counterfeits, in order to attract Men's Applause, and to work her sinister Ends by gaining their Admiration and their Confidence.[1]

I shall mention but one Symptom more of this Hypocrisy; and this is a Readiness to censure the Faults of others. *Judge not*, says *Jesus, lest you be judged.*[2]—And again; *Why beholdest thou the Mote that is in thy Brother's Eye, but considerest not the Beam that is in thine own Eye?*[3] On which the abovementioned Commentator rightly observes, *That those who are most censorious of the lesser Infirmities of others, are usually most notoriously guilty of far greater Failings themselves.*[4] This sanctified Slander is, of all, the most severe, bitter, and cruel; and is so easily distinguished from that which is either the Effect of Anger or Wantonness, and which I have mentioned before, that I shall dwell no longer upon it.

And here I shall dismiss my Character of a sanctified Hypocrite, with the honest Wish which *Shakespeare* hath launched forth against an execrable Villain:

—*That Heaven would put in every honest Hand a Whip,*
To lash the Rascal naked through the World.[5]

I have now, I think, enumerated the principal Methods by which Deceit works its Ends on easy, credulous, and open Dispositions; and have endeavoured to point out the Symptoms by which they may be discovered: but while Men are blinded by Vanity and Self-Love, and while artful Hypocrisy knows how to adapt itself to their Blind-sides, and to humour their Passions, it will be difficult for honest and undesigning Men to escape the Snares of Cunning and Imposition;[6] I shall therefore recommend one more certain Rule, and which, I believe, if duly attended to,

often repeated: see Cicero, *De officiis*, I. v. 15, and *De finibus*, ii. 16. 52 (and cf. Seneca, *Epist. mor.* cxv. 6); Rabelais, II. xviii; Bacon, *Advancement of Learning*, II. xviii. 3. Cf. Dryden, *Hind and the Panther*, 33–4.
1 Cf. the *Champion*, 4 March 1740. 2 Matt. 7: 1; cf. Luke 6: 37.
3 Matt. 7: 3; Luke 6: 41. 4 Burkitt, sig. C4v.
5 Cf. *Othello*, IV. ii. 141–3.
6 Cf. Ovid, *Remedia amoris*, 686: 'Dum sibi quisque placet, credula turba sumus.'

would, in a great measure, extirpate all Fallacy out of the World; or must at least so effectually disappoint its Purposes, that it would soon be worth no Man's while to assume it, and the Character of Knave and Fool would be more apparently (what they are at present in Reality) allied, or united.

This Method is, carefully to observe the Actions of Men with others, and especially with those to whom they are allied in Blood, Marriage, Friendship, Profession, Neighbourhood, or any other Connection: nor can you want an Opportunity of doing this; for none but the weakest of Men would rashly and madly place a Confidence which may very materially affect him in any one, on a slight or no Acquaintance.

Trace then the Man proposed to your Trust, into his private Family and nearest Intimacies. See whether he hath acted the Part of a good Son, Brother, Husband, Father, Friend, Master, Servant, &c. if he hath discharged these Duties well, your Confidence will have a good Foundation;[1] but if he hath behaved himself in these Offices with Tyranny, with Cruelty, with Infidelity, with Inconstancy, you may be assured he will take the first Opportunity his Interest points out to him, of exercising the same ill Talents at your Expence.

I have often thought Mankind would be little liable to Deceit (at least much less than they are) if they would believe their own Eyes, and judge of Men by what they actually see them perform towards those with whom they are most closely connected: Whereas how common is it to persuade ourselves, that the undutiful, ungrateful Son, the unkind, or barbarous Brother; or the Man who is void of all Tenderness, Honour, or even Humanity, to his Wife or Children, shall nevertheless become a sincere and faithful Friend! But how monstrous a Belief is it, that the Person whom we find incapable of discharging the nearest Duties of Relation, whom no Ties of Blood or Affinity can bind; nay, who is even deficient in that Goodness which Instinct infuses into the brute Creation;[2] that such a Person should have a sufficient Stock of Virtue to supply the arduous Character of Honour and Honesty. This is a Credulity so absurd that it admits of no Aggravation.

[1] Cf. Dr. Harrison's character of Booth (*Amelia*, III. vii). See St. Augustine, *De civ. dei*, XIX. xiv.

[2] The *storgé* celebrated by all the physico-theologians. See John Ray, *The Wisdom of God Manifested in the Works of the Creation* (10th edn., 1735), p. 121 *et passim*; *Spectator*, 120 and 121.

Nothing indeed can be more unjustifiable to our Prudence, than an Opinion that the Man whom we see act the Part of a Villain to others, should on some minute Change of Person, Time, Place, or other Circumstance, behave like an honest and just Man to ourselves.[1] I shall not here dispute the Doctrine of Repentance, any more than its Tendency to the Good of Society; but as the Actions of Men are the best Index to their Thoughts, as they do, if well attended to and understood, with the utmost Certainty demonstrate the Character; and as we are not so certain of the Sincerity of the Repentance, I think we may with Justice suspect, as least so far as to deny him our Confidence, that a Man whom we once knew to be a Villain, remains a Villain still.

And now let us see whether these Observations, extended a little further, and taken into public Life, may not help us to account for some Phœnomena which have lately appeared in this Hemisphere:[2] For as a Man's good Behaviour to those with whom he hath the nearest and closest Connection is the best Assurance to which a Stranger can trust for his honest Conduct in any Engagement he shall enter into with him; so is a worthy Discharge of the social Offices of a private Station, the strongest Security which a Man can give of an upright Demeanour in any public Trust, if his Country shall repose it in him; and we may be well satisfied, that the most popular Speeches, and most plausible Pretences of one of a different Character, are only gilded Snares to delude us, and to sacrifice us, in some manner or other, to his own sinister Purposes. It is well said in one of Mr. *Pope's* Letters; 'How shall a man love five Millions, who could never love a single Person?'[3] If a Man hath more Love than what centers in himself, it will certainly light on his Children, his Relations, Friends, and nearest Acquaintance. If he extends it farther, what is it less than general Philanthropy, or Love to Mankind?[4] Now as a good Man loves his Friend better than

---

[1] Cf. above, 'To a Friend on the Choice of a Wife', 189–90.

[2] Probably a reference to the cut-throat scramble for places by the 'Patriot' Opposition after the fall of Walpole in February 1742 (cf. *The Opposition: A Vision*, 1741).

[3] *Letters of Mr. Alexander Pope* (1737), p. 95; Pope says 'twenty thousand People'. The manuscript reading, followed by George Sherburn, is 'a hundred thousand men' (*Corr. of Alexander Pope*, i. 357).

[4] Cf. the *Champion*, 27 March 1740. Bacon, in his essay 'Of Goodness, and Goodness of Nature', associated Good-nature with *philanthropia* (*Essays*, 1701 edn., p. 30); Dryden, in the preface to Sir Henry Sheers's translation of Polybius (1693–8), speaks of 'This *Philanthropy* (which we have not a proper word in English to express) . . .' (sig. B5ᵛ).

a common Acquaintance; so Philanthropy will operate stronger
towards his own Country than any other: but no Man can have
this general Philanthropy who hath not private Affection, any
more than he who hath not Strength sufficient to lift ten Pounds,
can at the same Time be able to throw a hundred Weight over
his Head. Therefore the bad Son, Husband, Father, Brother,
Friend; in a Word, the bad Man in private can never be a sincere
Patriot.

In *Rome* and *Sparta* I agree it was otherwise: for there Patriotism, by Education, became a Part of the Character. Their
Children were nursed in Patriotism, it was taught them at an
Age when Religion in all Countries is first inculcated.¹ And as
we see Men of all Religions ready to lay down their Lives for
the Doctrines of it (which they often do not know, and seldom
have considered) so were these *Spartans* and *Romans* ready with
as implicit Faith to die for their Country. Though the private
Morals of the former were very depraved, and the latter were the
public Robbers of Mankind.²

Upon what Foundation their Patriotism then stood, seems
pretty apparent, and perhaps there can be no surer. For I apprehend, if twenty Boys were taught from their Infancy to believe,
that the *Royal-Exchange* was the Kingdom of Heaven; and consequently inspired with a suitable Awe for it; and lastly, instructed
that it was great, glorious, and god-like to defend it; nineteen
of them would afterwards cheerfully sacrifice their Lives to its
Defence; at least it is impossible that any of them would agree,
for a paultry Reward, to set it on Fire; not even though they
were Rogues and Highwaymen in their Disposition.³ But if you
were admitted to chuse twenty of such Dispositions at the Age
of Manhood, who had never learnt any thing of its Holiness,
contracted any such Awe, nor imbibed any such Duty, I believe
it would be difficult to bring them to venture their Lives in its
Cause; nor should I doubt, could I perswade them of the Security

---

¹ Cf. *Tatler*, 183: 'In the *Grecian* and *Roman* Nations they were wise enough to keep
up this great Incentive [publick Spirit], and it was impossible to be in the Fashion without
being a Patriot.'
² Cf. Burton, *Anat. Melancholy*, 'Democritus to the Reader': '. . . and as those old
Romans robbed all the cities of the world, to set out their bad sited *Rome* . . .' (ed. Shilleto,
i. 20). See Tacitus, *Agricola*, xxx ('raptores orbis').
³ Cf. Locke, *Essay*, II. xxxiii. 17. Fielding may be gently mocking such eulogiums on
the Royal Exchange as Addison's in *Spectator*, 69.

of the Fact, of bribing them to apply the Firebrand to any Part of the Building I pleased.

But a worthy Citizen of *London*, without borrowing any such Superstition from Education, would scarce be tempted by any Reward, to deprive the City of so great an Ornament, and what is so useful and necessary to its Trade; at the same Time to endanger the Ruin of Thousands, and perhaps the Destruction of the whole.

The Application seems pretty easy, That as there is no such Passion in Human Nature as Patriotism, considered abstractedly, and by itself, it must be introduced by Art,[1] and that while the Mind of Man is yet soft and ductile, and the unformed Character susceptible of any arbitrary Impression you please to make on it: or, Secondly, it must be founded on Philanthropy, or universal Benevolence; a Passion which really exists in some Natures, and which is necessarily attended with the excellent Quality above-mentioned: for as it seems granted, that the Man cannot love a Million who never could love a single Person; so will it, I apprehend, appear as certain, that he who could not be induced to cheat or to destroy a single Man, will never be prevailed on to cheat or to destroy many Millions.

Thus I have endeavoured to shew the several Methods by which we can propose to get any Insight into the Characters of those with whom we converse, and by which we may frustrate all the Cunning and Designs of Hypocrisy. These Methods I have shewn to be three-fold, *viz.* by the Marks which Nature hath imprinted on the Countenance, by their Behaviour to ourselves, and by their Behaviour to others. On the first of these I have not much insisted, as liable to some Incertainty; and as the latter seem abundantly sufficient to secure us, with proper Caution, against the subtle Devices of Hypocrisy, though she be the most cunning as well as malicious of all the Vices which have ever corrupted the Nature of Man.

But however useless this Treatise may be to instruct, I hope it will be at least effectual to alarm my Reader; and sure no honest undesigning Man can ever be too much on his Guard against the Hypocrite, or too industrious to expose and expel him out of Society.

[1] Cf. Bolingbroke, *Letters on the Study and Use of History* (2 vols., 1752), Letter II: 'But surely the love of our country is a lesson of reason, not an institution of nature. Education and habit, obligation and interest, attach us to it, not instinct' (i. 32).

AN ESSAY ON
NOTHING.[1]

The INTRODUCTION

It is surprizing, that while such trifling Matters employ the masterly Pens of the present Age, the great and noble Subject of this Essay should have passed totally neglected; and the rather, as it is a Subject to which the Genius of many of those Writers who have unsuccessfully applied themselves to Politics, Religion, &c. is most peculiarly adapted.[2]

Perhaps their Unwillingness to handle what is of such Importance, may not improperly be ascribed to their Modesty; though they may not be remarkably addicted to this Vice on every Occasion. Indeed I have heard it predicated of some, whose Assurance in treating other Subjects hath been sufficiently notable, that they have blushed at this. For such is the Awe with which this Nothing inspires Mankind, that I believe it is generally apprehended of many Persons of very high Character among us, that were Title, Power, or Riches to allure them, they would stick at it.[3]

But whatever be the Reason, certain it is, that except a hardy Wit in the Reign of *Charles* II. none ever hath dared to write on this Subject.[4] I mean openly and avowedly; for it must be confessed, that most of our modern Authors, however foreign the Matter which they endeavour to treat may seem at their first setting out, they generally bring the Work to this in the End.

[1] A passing allusion to the *Love Elegies* of James Hammond, published in November 1742, with a preface by the Earl of Chesterfield (see p. 185 n. 2), suggests that the *Essay on Nothing* was composed after that date; but the reference could be merely an inserted compliment.

[2] Fielding adopts throughout his essay Swift's ironic approach to 'the Moderns' in *A Tale of a Tub.*

[3] The phrase, 'to stick at nothing', meaning to be unscrupulous, dates from at least the early seventeenth century (*OED*). Cf. Pope's note to the *Variorum Dunciad* (ii. 264 ff.): 'The three chief qualifications of Party-writers; to stick at nothing . . .' (Twickenham edn., v. 133 n).

[4] John Wilmot, Earl of Rochester, 'Upon Nothing', in *Poems on Several Occasions* (1680), pp. 51–4. In point of fact, there had been many treatments of 'Nothing', from Joannes Passerati's Latin poem, *Nihil*, in the sixteenth century, up to 'The Elogy of Nothing, Dedicated to No Body', published as by one T. Trifler in 1742 (*Gent. Mag.*, p. 392).

I hope, however, this Attempt will not be imputed to me as an Act of Immodesty; since I am convinced there are many Persons in this Kingdom, who are persuaded of my Fitness for what I have undertaken. But as talking of a Man's Self is generally suspected to arise from Vanity, I shall, without any more Excuse or Preface, proceed to my Essay.

SECT. I.

Of the Antiquity of NOTHING.

There is nothing falser than that old Proverb, which (like many other Falsehoods) is in every one's Mouth;

Ex Nihilo nihil Fit.[1]

Thus translated by *Shakespeare*, in *Lear*.

Nothing can come of Nothing.[2]

Whereas in Fact, from Nothing proceeds every Thing. And this is a Truth confessed by the Philosophers of all Sects: the only Point in Controversy between them being, whether Something made the World out of Nothing, or Nothing out of Something. A Matter not much worth debating at present, since either will equally serve our Turn. Indeed the Wits of all Ages seem to have ranged themselves on each Side of this Question, as their Genius tended more or less to the Spiritual or Material Substance. For those of the more spiritual Species have inclined to the former, and those whose Genius hath partaken more of the chief Properties of Matter, such as Solidity, Thickness, &c. have embraced the latter.[3]

---

[1] Cf. *Tom Jones*, VII. ii. The ultimate source of this proverbial expression is uncertain, but cf. Lucretius, *De rerum nat.* i. 155–6; Aristotle, *Physica*, I. iv. 2–3, and *Metaphysica*, IV. v. 4–7. The orthodox theological treatment of the maxim can be seen in Barrow's sermon on the 'Maker of Heaven and Earth', which argues that, whereas it is valid with reference to the creations of art, it is not to be extended to doubting the creation of the universe out of nothing by God (*Theological Works*, ed. Napier, v. 364–6).

[2] *King Lear*, I. i. 92; cf. also I. iv. 146.

[3] i.e. the neo-Epicureans, and materialists like Hobbes. Cf. Locke, *Essay*, IV. x. 15, on the materialists: 'But allow it [the creation of matter] to be by some other way [than by thought] which is above our conception, it must still be creation; and these men must give up their great maxim, *Ex nihilo nil fit*' (ed. Fraser, ii. 318). Blackmore presents the Lucretian creed in *Creation*, iii. 127–8: 'To parent matter things their being owe, / Because from nothing no productions flow' (*Poetical Works* [Cooke's edn., n.d.], p. 81.)

But whether Nothing was the *Artifex* or *Materies* only, it is plain in either Case, it will have a Right to claim to itself the Origination of all Things.

And farther, the great Antiquity of Nothing is apparent from its being so visible in the Accounts we have of the Beginning of every Nation. This is very plainly to be discovered in the first Pages, and sometimes Books of all general Historians;[1] and indeed, the Study of this important Subject fills up the whole Life of an Antiquary, it being always at the Bottom of his Enquiry, and is commonly at last discovered by him with infinite Labour and Pains.

SECT. II.
Of the Nature of NOTHING.

Another Falsehood which we must detect in the Pursuit of this Essay, is an Assertion, *That no one can have an Idea of* NOTHING: But Men who thus confidently deny us this Idea, either grossly deceive themselves, or would impose a downright Cheat on the World: for so far from having none, I believe there are few who have not many Ideas of it; though perhaps they may mistake them for the Idea of something.

For Instance; is there any one who hath not an Idea of immaterial Substance?—Now what is immaterial Substance, more than *Nothing*?[2] But here we are artfully deceived by the Use of Words: For were we to ask another what Idea he had of immaterial Matter, or unsubstantial Substance, the Absurdity of affirming it to be Something, would shock him, and he would immediately reply, it was *Nothing*.

Some Persons perhaps will say then, we have no Idea of it: but as I can support the contrary by such undoubted Authority,

[1] Cf. Bolingbroke on the lack of authentic historical evidence concerning 'the first ages' ('Reflections on the state of ancient History', *Letters on the Study and Use of History*, 2 vols., 1752, i. 71 ff.). Most of the classic historians make this complaint.

[2] The Author would not be here understood to speak against the Doctrine of Immateriality, to which he is a hearty Well-wisher; but to point at the Stupidity of those, who instead of immaterial *Essence*, which would convey a rational Meaning, have substituted immaterial *Substance*, which is a Contradiction in Terms. [Fielding's note.] Fielding follows Hobbes in limiting substance to *body*. The whole question was a subject of hot debate between Locke and Stillingfleet, and later, Clarke, Henry Dodwell, and Anthony Collins. Shaftesbury dismissed the controversy as mere school-philosophy, 'delusive and infatuating' (*Characteristicks*, 6th edn., 1737, i. 289–90).

I shall, instead of trying to confute such idle Opinions, proceed to shew, First, what Nothing is; Secondly, I shall disclose the various Kinds of Nothing; and lastly, shall prove its great Dignity, and that it is the End of every thing.

It is extremely hard to define Nothing in positive Terms, I shall therefore do it in Negative.[1] Nothing then is not Something. And here I must object to a third Error concerning it, which is, that it is in no Place; which is an indirect way of depriving it of its Existence; whereas indeed it possesses the greatest and noblest Place on this Earth, *viz.* the human Brain. But indeed this Mistake hath been sufficiently refuted by many very wise Men; who having spent their whole Lives in the Contemplation and Pursuit of Nothing, have at last gravely concluded—*That there is Nothing in this World.*

Farther; as Nothing is not Something, so every thing which is not Something, is Nothing; and wherever Something is not, Nothing is: a very large Allowance in its Favour, as must appear to Persons well skilled in human Affairs.[2]

For Instance; when a Bladder is full of Wind, it is full of Something; but when that is let out, we aptly say, there is Nothing in it.

The same may be as justly asserted of a Man as of a Bladder. However well he may be bedawbed with Lace, or with Title, yet if he have not Something in him, we may predicate the same of him as of an empty Bladder.

But if we cannot reach an adequate Knowledge of the true Essence of Nothing, no more than we can of Matter, let us, in Imitation of the Experimental Philosophers, examine some of its Properties or Accidents.[3]

And here we shall see the infinite Advantages which Nothing hath over Something: for while the latter is confined to one Sense, or two perhaps at the most, Nothing is the Object of them all.

[1] Cf. Cowley's 'Ode of Wit': 'What is it then, which like the *Power Divine* / We only can by *Negatives* define ?' (*Miscellanies*, p. 3, in *Works*, 1668). Cf. John Donne's 'Negative Love', 10–12.

[2] Fielding might almost be echoing Sir Thomas Browne on the Creation (*Religio Medici*, I. xxxv): 'that is, a production of something out of nothing; and what is that? Whatsoever is opposite to something, or more exactly, that which is truly contrary unto God.... God being all things, is contrary unto nothing, out of which were made all things, and so nothing became something; and *Omneity* informed *Nullity* into an Essence' (8th edn., 1685, p. 19).

[3] Cf. Locke, *Essay*, IV. xii. 9 *et passim*.

For First; Nothing may be seen, as is plain from the Relation of Persons who have recovered from high Fevers; and perhaps may be suspected from some (at least) of those who have seen Apparitions, both on Earth, and in the Clouds. Nay, I have often heard it confessed by Men, when asked what they saw at such a Place and Time, that they saw Nothing. Admitting then that there are two Sights, *viz.* a first and second Sight, according to the firm Belief of some, Nothing must be allowed to have a very large Share of the first; and as to the second, it hath it all entirely to itself.

Secondly; Nothing may be heard: of which the same Proofs may be given, as of the foregoing. The *Argive*, mentioned by *Horace*, is a strong Instance of this.

> —*Fuit haud ignobilis Argis*
> *Qui se credebat miros acedire Tragædos*
> *In vacuo lætos sessor, Plausorque Theatro.*[1]

That Nothing may be tasted and smelt, is not only known to Persons of delicate Palates and Nostrils. How commonly do we hear, that such a Thing smells or tastes of Nothing? The latter I have heard asserted of a Dish compounded of five or six savory Ingredients. And as to the former, I remember an elderly Gentlewoman who had a great Antipathy to the Smell of Apples; who upon discovering that an idle Boy had fastened some mellow Apple to her Tail, contracted a Habit of smelling them, whenever that Boy came within her Sight, though there were then none within a Mile of her.[2]

Lastly, Feeling; and sure if any Sense seems more particularly the Object of Matter only, which must be allowed to be Something, this doth. Nay, I have heard it asserted (and with a Colour of Truth) of several Persons, that they can feel nothing but a Cudgel. Notwithstanding which, some have felt the Motions of the Spirit;[3] and others have felt very bitterly the Misfortunes of their Friends, without endeavouring to relieve them. Now these seem two plain Instances, that Nothing is an Object of this Sense. Nay, I have heard a Surgeon declare, while he was cutting off a Patient's Leg, that *he was sure he felt nothing.*

---

[1] *Epist.* II. ii. 128–30: 'Once at Argos there was a man of some rank, who used to fancy that he was listening to wonderful tragic actors, while he sat happy and applauded in the empty theatre' (trans. H. R. Fairclough, Loeb Library).

[2] Cf. Locke, on association of ideas (*Essay*, II. xxxiii).

[3] Cf. Swift, *A Discourse Concerning the Mechanical Operation of the Spirit* (1704).

Nothing is as well the Object of our Passions as our Senses. Thus there are many who love Nothing, some who hate Nothing, and some who fear Nothing, &c.

We have already mentioned three of the Properties of a Noun, to belong to Nothing; we shall find the fourth likewise to be as justly claim'd by it: and that Nothing is as often the Object of the Understanding, as of the Senses.[1]

Indeed some have imagined, that Knowledge, with the Adjective *human* placed before it, is another Word of Nothing. And one of the wisest Men in the World declared, he knew nothing.[2]

But without carrying it so far, this I believe may be allowed, that it is at least possible for a Man to know Nothing. And whoever hath read over many Works of our ingenious Moderns, with proper Attention and Emolument, will, I believe, confess, that if he understands them right, he understands *Nothing*.

This is a Secret not known to all Readers; and want of this Knowledge hath occasioned much puzzling; for where a Book, or Chapter, or Paragraph, hath seemed to the Reader to contain Nothing, his Modesty hath sometimes persuaded him, that the true Meaning of the Author hath escaped him, instead of concluding, as in Reality the Fact was, that the Author, in the said Book, &c. did truly, and *bona Fide*, mean Nothing. I remember once, at the Table of a Person of great Eminence,[3] and one no less distinguished by Superiority of Wit than Fortune, when a very dark Passage was read out of a Poet, famous for being so sublime, that he is often out of the Sight of his Reader,[4] some Persons present declared they did not understand the Meaning. The Gentleman himself, casting his Eyes over the Performance, testified a Surprize at the Dulness of his Company; seeing Nothing could, he said, possibly be plainer than the Meaning of the Passage which they stuck at. This set all of us to puzzling again; but with like Success; we frankly owned we could not find it out, and desired he would explain it.— Explain it! said the Gentleman, why he means NOTHING.

1 Cf. the opening words of the Eton Latin Grammar: 'A Noun is the Name of a Thing that may be seen, felt, heard or understood' (*A Short Introduction to Grammar*, 1720, p. 1).

2 Socrates: see Plato, *Apology* 20 a–23 b; *Republic*, I. x–xi (336 b–338 a); Diogenes Laertius, ii. 32. Cf. Montaigne: 'The wisest Man that ever was, being asked what he knew, made answer, *He knew this, that he knew nothing*' (*Essays*, trans. Cotton, 3rd edn., 1700, ii. 274).

3 Perhaps Dodington: the example of his wit would serve.

4 Sir Richard Blackmore ?—or Milton ?

An Essay on Nothing
185

In Fact, this Mistake arises from a too vulgar Error among Persons unacquainted with the Mystery of Writing, who imagine it impossible that a Man should sit down to write without any Meaning at all; whereas in Reality, nothing is more common: for, not to Instance in myself, who have confessedly sat down to write this Essay, with Nothing in my Head, or, which is much the same Thing, to write about Nothing; it may be incontestably proved, *ab Effectu*,[1] that Nothing is commoner among the Moderns. The inimitable Author of a Preface to the Posthumous Eclogues of a late ingenious young Gentleman, says,—There are Men who sit down to write what they think, and others to think what they shall write.[2] But indeed there is a third, and a much more numerous Sort, who never think either before they sit down, or afterwards; and who when they produce on Paper what was before in their Heads, are sure to produce Nothing.

Thus we have endeavoured to demonstrate the Nature of Nothing, by shewing First, definitively, *what it is not*; and Secondly, by describing *what it is*. The next Thing therefore proposed, is to shew its various Kinds.

Now some imagine these several Kinds differ in Name only. But without endeavouring to confute so absurd an Opinion, especially as these different Kinds of Nothing occur frequently in the best Authors, I shall content myself with setting them down, and leave it to the Determination of the distinguishing Reader, whether it is probable, or indeed possible, that they should all convey one and the same Meaning.

These are, Nothing *per se* Nothing; Nothing at all; Nothing in the least; Nothing in Nature; Nothing in the World; Nothing in the whole World; Nothing in the whole universal World. And perhaps many others, of which we say—*Nothing*.

---

[1] Argument from the effect; cf. Pope, *Essay on Criticism*, i. 79: '*It self unseen*, but in th' *Effects*, remains' (Twickenham edn., i. 248).

[2] The Earl of Chesterfield, preface to *Love Elegies*, by James Hammond, published in November 1742 (*London Mag.*, p. 572), with title-page date of 1743. On Hammond, a young disciple of Chesterfield, see Horace Walpole to Mann, 10 June 1742 (*Yale Edition of the Corr.* xvii. 451); Hammond died June 1742. Chesterfield's preface actually says only: '. . . he sat down to write what he thought, not to think what he should write; 'twas Nature, and Sentiment only that dictated to a real Mistress, not youthful and poetic Fancy, to an imaginary one' (*Love Elegies*, 1743 [publ. 1742], sig. A2).

SECT. III.

Of the Dignity of NOTHING; *and an Endeavour to prove, that it is the End as well as Beginning of all Things.*

NOTHING contains so much Dignity as NOTHING. Ask an infamous worthless Nobleman (if any such be) in what his Dignity consists? It may not be perhaps consistent with his Dignity to give you an Answer; but suppose he should be willing to condescend so far, what could he in Effect say? Should he say he had it from his Ancestors, I apprehend a Lawyer would oblige him to prove, that the Virtues to which this Dignity was annexed, descended to him.[1] If he claims it as inherent in the Title, might he not be told, that a Title originally implied Dignity, as it implied the Presence of those Virtues to which Dignity is inseparably annexed; but that no Implication will fly in the Face of downright positive Proof to the contrary. In short, to examine no farther, since his Endeavour to derive it from any other Fountain would be equally impotent, his Dignity arises from Nothing, and in Reality is Nothing. Yet, that this Dignity really exists; that it glares in the Eyes of Men, and produces much Good to the Person who wears it, is, I believe, incontestable.

Perhaps this may appear in the following Syllogism.

The Respect paid to Men on account of their Titles, is paid at least to the Supposal of their superior Virtues and Abilities, or it is paid to *Nothing*.

But when a Man is a notorious Knave or Fool, it is impossible there should be any such Supposal.

The Conclusion is apparent.[2]

Now that no Man is ashamed of either paying or receiving this Respect, I wonder not, since the great Importance of Nothing seems, I think, to be pretty apparent: but that they should deny the Deity worshipped, and endeavour to represent Nothing as Something, is more worthy Reprehension. This is a Fallacy extremely common. I have seen a Fellow, whom all the World knew to have Nothing in him, not only pretend to Something

[1] Cf. above, p. 141.
[2] Cf. Young, *Love of Fame*, i. 145–6: 'Titles are marks of *honest* men, and *wise*; / The Fool, or Knave that wears a Title, lies' (2nd edn., 1728, p. 12).

himself; but supported in that Pretension by others who have been less liable to be deceived. Now whence can this proceed, but from their being ashamed of Nothing? A Modesty very peculiar to this Age.

But notwithstanding all such Disguise and Deceit, a Man must have very little Discernment, who can live long in Courts, or populous Cities, without being convinced of the great Dignity of Nothing; and though he should, through Corruption or Necessity, comply with the vulgar Worship and Adulation, he will know to what it is paid, namely to *Nothing*.

The most astonishing Instance of this Respect, so frequently paid to Nothing, is when it is paid (if I may so express myself) to Something less than Nothing; when the Person who receives it is not only void of the Quality for which he is respected, but is in Reality notoriously guilty of Vices directly opposite to the Virtues, whose Applause he receives. This is, indeed, the highest Degree of Nothing, or, (if I may be allowed the Word) the *Nothingest* of all Nothings.

Here it is to be known, that Respect may be aimed at Something, and really light on Nothing. For Instance; when mistaking certain Things called Gravity, Canting, Blustring, Ostentation, Pomp, and such like, for Wisdom, Piety, Magnanimity, Charity, True Greatness, &c., we give to the former the Honour and Reverence due to the latter. Not that I would be understood so far to discredit my Subject, as to insinuate that Gravity, Canting, &c. are really Nothing; on the contrary, there is much more Reason to suspect, (if we judge from the Practice of the World) that Wisdom, Piety, and other Virtues, have a good Title to that Name. But we do not, in Fact, pay our Respect to the former, but to the latter: In other Words, we pay it to that which is not, and consequently pay it to Nothing.

So far then for the Dignity of the Subject on which I am treating. I am now to shew, that Nothing is the End as well as Beginning of all Things.

That every thing is resolvable, and will be resolved into its first Principles, will be, I believe, readily acknowledged by all Philosophers.[1] As therefore we have sufficiently proved the World

[1] Cf. Dryden on the 'four prolifick Principles': 'All Things are mix'd of these, which all contain, / And into these are all resolv'd again . . .' ('Of the Pythagorean Philosophy' [from Ovid, *Metam.* xv], 374–5; *Works*, 1701, III. ii. 516, 517); Donne, 'The Dissolution',

came from Nothing, it follows, that it will likewise end in the same: but as I am writing to a Nation of Christians, I have no need to be prolix on this Head; since every one of my Readers, by his Faith, acknowledges that the World is to have an End, *i.e.* is to come to Nothing.

And as Nothing is the End of the World, so is it of every thing in the World. Ambition, the greatest, highest, noblest, finest, most heroic and godlike of all Passions, what doth it end in?—Nothing. What did *Alexander*, *Cæsar*, and all the rest of that heroic Band, who have plundered, and massacred so many Millions,[1] obtain by all their Care, Labour, Pain, Fatigue, and Danger?— Could they speak for themselves, must they not own, that the End of all their Pursuit was Nothing? Nor is this the End of private Ambition only. What is become of that proud Mistress of the World,—the *Caput triumphati Orbis?* that *Rome*, of which her own Flatterers so liberally prophesied the Immortality, In what hath all her Glory ended? surely in Nothing.[2]

Again, What is the End of Avarice? Not Power, or Pleasure, as some think, for the Miser will part with a Shilling for neither: not Ease or Happiness; for the more he attains of what he desires, the more uneasy and miserable he is. If every Good in this World was put to him, he could not say he pursued one. Shall we say then, he pursues Misery only? that surely would be contradictory to the first Principles of Human Nature.[3] May we not therefore, nay, must we not confess, that he aims at Nothing? especially if he be himself unable to tell us what is the End of all this Bustle and Hurry, this watching and toiling, this Self-Denial, and Self-Constraint!

1–2: 'Shee'is dead; And all which die / To their first Elements resolve' (*Poems*, ed. Grierson, i. 64); South: 'Consider with thy self, how great and glorious a Being that must needs be, that raised so vast and beautiful a Fabrick, as this of the World out of Nothing, with the breath of his Mouth, and can and will, with the same, reduce it to Nothing again . . .' (*Sermons*, 6th edn., 1727, ii. 98); Swift, on 'The Learned Æolists' and Wind (*Tale of a Tub*, sect. viii).

1 See below, *A Dialogue between Alexander and Diogenes.*

2 Cf. Ovid, *Amores*, I. xv. 26. See *Spectator*, 146, 'on the Vanity and transient Glory of this habitable World': 'All the Vanities of Nature, all the Works of Art, all the Labours of Men, are reduced to Nothing. . . . *Rome* it self, eternal *Rome*, the great City, the Empress of the World . . . what is become of her now?'

3 See Cicero, *Tusc. Disp.* IV. vi. 12: 'natura enim omnes ea, quae bona videntur, sequuntur fugiuntque contraria'; *De finibus*, III. xix. 63; Seneca, *Epist. mor.* cxxi. 17; Aristotle, *Nic. Eth.* I. vii. 5–8; Montaigne, *Essays*, I. xix (trans. Cotton, 3rd edn., 1700, i. 92).

It will not, I apprehend, be sufficient for him to plead, that his Design is to amass a large Fortune, which he never can nor will use himself, nor would willingly quit to any other Person; unless he can shew us some substantial Good which this Fortune is to produce, we shall certainly be justified in concluding, that his End is the same with that of Ambition.

The Great Mr. *Hobbes* so plainly saw this, that as he was an Enemy to that notable immaterial Substance[1] which we have here handled, and therefore unwilling to allow it the large Province we have contended for, he advanced a very strange Doctrine, and asserted truly,—That in all these grand Pursuits, the Means themselves were the End proposed,[2] *viz.* to Ambition, Plotting, Fighting, Danger, Difficulty, and such like:—To Avarice, Cheating, Starving, Watching, and the numberless painful Arts by which this Passion proceeds.

However easy it may be to demonstrate the Absurdity of this Opinion, it will be needless to my Purpose, since if we are driven to confess that the Means are the only End attained,—I think we must likewise confess, that the End proposed is absolutely Nothing.

As I have here shewn the End of our two greatest and noblest Pursuits, one or other of which engages almost every Individual of the busy Part of Mankind,[3] I shall not tire the Reader with carrying him through all the rest, since I believe the same Conclusion may be easily drawn from them all.

I shall therefore finish this Essay with an Inference, which aptly enough suggests itself from what hath been said: seeing that such is its Dignity and Importance, and that it is really the End of all those Things which are supported with so much Pomp and Solemnity, and looked on with such Respect and Esteem, surely it becomes a wise Man to regard Nothing with the utmost Awe and Adoration; to pursue it with all his Parts and Pains; and to sacrifice to it his Ease, his Innocence, and his present Happiness.

---

[1] e.g., in the *Leviathan*, I. iv, v, xii; III. xxxiv (*English Works*, ed. Molesworth, iii. 27, 32, 96–7, 381, 393); and *An Answer to . . . Dr. Bramhall* (ed. cit. iv. 306–14, 349, 383).

[2] See *Leviathan*, I. xi; and *Human Nature*, VII. iv and vi (*English Works*, iii. 85–6; and iv. 32 and 33).

[3] Cf. *Covent-Garden Journal*, 69: 'And yet these two [Avarice and Ambition] are the great Business which the World espouses; to the Pursuit of which it assigns the Appellation of Wisdom; and to which, if we will attain that Honour, we must sacrifice all the real Enjoyments of Life.' Cf. Aristotle, *Polit.* II. vi. 19.

To which noble Pursuit we have this great Incitement, that we may assure ourselves of never being cheated or deceived in the End proposed. The Virtuous, Wise, and Learned may then be unconcerned at all the Changes of Ministries and of Government;[1] since they may be well satisfied, that while Ministers of State are Rogues themselves, and have inferior Knavish Tools to bribe and reward; true Virtue, Wisdom, Learning, Wit, and Integrity, will most certainly bring their Possessors—Nothing.

[1] Perhaps an allusion to the fall of Walpole in February 1742, and the undignified scramble for places that ensued.

SOME

P A P E R S

P R O P E R to be Read before the

R———L S O C I E T Y,

Concerning the

Terrestrial C H R Y S I P U S,

GOLDEN - FOOT or GUINEA;

A N

INSECT, or VEGETABLE, resembling the P O L Y P U S, which hath this
surprising Property, That being cut into
several Pieces, each Piece becomes a
perfect Animal, or Vegetable, as complete as that of which it was originally
only a Part.

———————————

COLLECTED

By PETRUS GUALTERUS,

But not Published till after His Death.

PHILOSOPHICAL TRANSACTIONS

For the YEAR 1742–3

The CONTENTS

Several Papers *relating to the* Terrestrial CHRYSIPUS, GOLDEN-FOOT, *or* GUINEA, *an* Insect, *or* Vegetable, *which has this surprising* Property, *that being cut into several Pieces, each Piece lives, and in a short time becomes as perfect an Insect, or Vegetable, as that of which it was originally only a Part.*

Abstract of *Part* of a Letter from the *Heer Rottenscrach* in *Germany*,[1] communicating Observations on the CHRYSIPUS.[2]

Sir,

Some time since died here of Old-Age, one Petrus Gualterus,[3] *a Man well known in the Learned World, and famous for nothing so much as for an extraordinary Collection which he had made of the* Chrysipi, *an Animal or Vegetable; of which I doubt not but there are* still some *to be found in* England: *However, if that should be difficult, it may be easy to send some over to you; as they are at present very plentiful in these Parts.*[4] *I can answer for the Truth of the Facts contained in the Paper I send you, as there is not one of them but what I have seen repeated above twenty times, and I wish others*

---

[1] The two title-pages, the prefatory letter, and the report parody a specific issue of the *Philosophical Transactions* of the Royal Society, viz., No. 467 (for 13 and 21 January 1743), an account of experiments made upon the freshwater polyp by the great Swiss naturalist, Abraham Trembley (1710–84). See Appendix D. This issue was published 28 January 1743 (*Daily Advertiser* of that date); and Fielding's burlesque was published soon after, 16 February 1743, without the 'Postscript' added in the *Miscellanies*. Hence it must have been written within a space of two weeks.

[2] In the original, a letter from William Bentinck to Martin Folkes, the President of the Royal Society, commenting upon Trembley's experiments conducted in The Hague.

[3] An obvious Latinizing of Peter Walter (1664 ?–1746), the wealthy scrivener who stood as a model for Fielding's Peter Pounce in *Joseph Andrews* (and cf. *Jonathan Wild*, II. vii). Satirized by Swift, Pope, and Fielding's friend, Sir Charles Hanbury Williams, among others, Peter Walter was for the age the very type of the avaricious trickster. See the *Champion*, 31 May 1740, and above, pp. 67 and 130. For an anecdote on Fielding 'teazing Peter Walters' see W. B. Coley, 'Henry Fielding and the Two Walpoles', *PQ*, xlv (1966), 169–70.

[4] The familiar charge that George II 'steadily pursued' the interests of Hanover, rather than those of England. See the pamphlet by Chesterfield and Edmund Waller, *The Case of the Hanover Forces in the Pay of Great Britain*, 1742. Horace Walpole quoted, in a letter to Mann on 2 November 1741, an abusive ballad on 'a Famous Balancing Captain' (i.e. George II), of which the second stanza read:

> This Captain he takes, in a *gold*-ballasted Ship,
> Each summer to *Terra Damnosa* a trip,
> For which he begs, borrows, scrapes all he can get,
> And runs his poor *Owners* most vilely in debt.

(*Yale Edition of the Corr.* xvii. 187.) Swift had added a dry marginal note, some years before, to Addison's account of the rise of Hanover in *Freeholder*, 9 : 'It is indeed grown considerable by draining of England' (*Prose Works*, ed. Davis, v. 252). Fielding carried on the attack in a pamphlet that has much in common with this satire on the Royal Society, *An Attempt towards a Natural History of the Hanover Rat* (1744).

may be encouraged to try the Experiments over again, and satisfy themselves of the Truth by their own Eyes. The Accounts of the Chrysipi, *as well as the Collection itself, were found in the Cabinet of the abovementioned* Petrus, *after his Death: for he could never be prevailed on to communicate a Sight of either while alive. I am, Sir,* &c.

The Figure of the TERRESTRIAL CHRYSIPUS *sticking to a Finger.*[1]

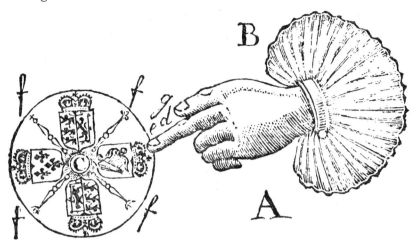

Observations and Experiments upon the TERRESTRIAL CHRYSIPUS, *or* GUINEA, *by Mynheer* Petrus Gualterus.

Translated from the FRENCH *by* P.H.I.Z. C.G.S.[2]

The Animal in question is a terrestrial Vegetable or Insect,[3] of which mention is made in the *Philosophical Transactions* for several Years, as may be seen in No. ooo. Art. oooo. and No. oo. Art. oo2. and No.—Art. 18.

This Animal or Vegetable is of a rotund, orbicular or round Form, as represented in the Figure annexed. In which *A.* denotes the Ruffle. *B.* the Hand. *G.* the Thumb of that Hand. *D.* the Finger. *E.* the Part of that Finger to which the CHRYSIPUS sticks. *F.f.f.f.* Four Tubes, representing the *Πέος,*[4] or *Man's Staff,*

---

[1] The 'Terrestrial Chrysipus' of the diagram is the guinea coined under Anne, after the union of England and Scotland in 1707. It pictures the shields of Ireland, France, and (at top and bottom) of England and Scotland impaled, arranged about the Star of the Garter at the centre (replaced by 'C' here), and four sceptres in saltire.

[2] Fielding's jest of 'P.H.I.Z.' (cf. *Tatler*, 230 and Swift's *Polite Conversation* for attacks upon this abbreviation of 'physiognomy') replaces the initials of Philip Henry Zollman in the original. The initials 'C.G.S' in place of those for Fellow of the Royal Society are unexplained (perhaps Covent Garden Society, or the like ?).

[3] The terminological vagueness reflects that of the period: Réaumur, after all, called the starfish an insect (*Mémoires pour servir à l'histoire des insectes*, 1734–42, i. 57).

[4] See *Philos. Transact.* concerning the *Arbor Vitæ, anno* 1732. [Fielding's note.] Fielding's reference has not been traced; it is presumably just a bawdy pun.

mentioned by *Galen* in his Treatise *de Usu Partium*; and by *Aristotle*, in that little Book called his Ἀρχίβιβλίον, or *Master-Piece*.[1] The τὸ θηλυκόν, or *Woman's Pipe*, an oblong perforated Substance, to which the said Πέη directly tend, is represented by the Letter *C*. *The Mouth of the* Chrysipus *is in this anteriour Middle, it opens into the Stomach, which takes up the whole Length of the Body*. The whole Body forms but one Pipe, a sort of Gut which can be opened but at one end, *i.e.* at Letter *C*.

The Size of the Body of a *Chrysipus* varies according to its different Species.

I know two Species only, differing in Extent almost one half; which, for Distinction sake, I call the *Whole Chrysipus*, and the *Hemi-Chrysipus*. The latter of these is by no means so valuable as the former. The Length of the Πέη differ likewise in proportion to the different Size or Extension of these two.

The Πέη of those of a modern Growth are so imperfect and invisible to the naked Eye, that it is much to be feared the Species will soon be entirely lost among us: And indeed in *England*, they are observed of late to be much rarer than formerly, especially in the Country, where at present there are very few of them to be found:[2] but at the same time it is remarked, that in some Places of the Continent, particularly in a certain Part of *Germany*, they are much plentier; being to be found in great Numbers, where formerly there were scarce any to be met with.

I have not, after the minutest Observation, been able to settle with any degree of certainty, whether this be really an Animal or a Vegetable, or whether it be not strictly neither, or rather both. For as I have by the Help of my Microscope discovered some of its Parts to resemble those of a Lion; I have at other times taken notice of something not unlike the *Flower de Luce*.[3] Not to repeat those Parts above-mentioned, which bear great Analogy to the Ἀιδοῖα[4] of the Human Body. On their Extremities (if

---

[1] Galen's famous *De usu partium* is a legitimate work, of course, but the other is Fielding's joke, a somewhat 'underground' book called *Aristotle's Master-Piece; or, The Secrets of Generation Displayed in All the Parts Thereof. . . . Very Necessary for All Midwives, Nurses, and Young-Married Women* (1694).

[2] Probably alluding to the so-called 'Country Party' of the Opposition, as opposed to the 'Court Party' of the Hanoverians.

[3] The lion, of course, in the shield of England on the guinea; the *fleur de luce* in that of France.

[4] The privy parts, pudenda.

they are not very old) may be seen certain Letters forming the Names of several of our Kings; whence I have been almost inclined to conclude, that these are the Flowers mentioned by *Virgil*, and which appear to have been so extremely scarce in his Time.

> *Dic quibus in terris inscripti nomina Regum*
> *Nascuntur flores.*

Particularly as he adds,

> —*Et Phyllida solus habeto.*[1]

Of which we shall take notice hereafter, when we come to speak of its Properties. What hath principally dissuaded me from an Opinion of its being an Animal, is, that I could never observe any Symptoms of voluntary Motion: But indeed the same may be said of an Oyster, which I think is not yet settled by the Learned to be *absolutely* a Vegetable.[2]

But though it hath not, or seems not to have any progressive Motion of its own, yet is it very easy to communicate a Motion to it. Indeed some Persons have made them fly all over the Town with great Velocity.

What is said of the *Polypus*, in a late excellent Paper communicated to the Royal Society, is likewise applicable to the *Chrysipus*.[3]

'They make use of their progressive Motion, when communicated to them, to place themselves conveniently, so as to catch their Prey. They are voracious Animals; their Πέη are so many Snares which they set for Numbers of small *Insects*. As soon as any of them touches one of the Πέη, it is caught.'

But then it differs from the *Polypus* in the Consequence: for instead of making the *Insect* its Prey, it becomes itself a Prey to

---

[1] *Eclogues*, iv. 106–7: 'Tell me in what land spring up flowers with royal names written thereon—and have Phyllis to yourself' (trans. H. R. Fairclough, Loeb Library). The flower is the hyacinth: cf. *Tom Jones*, XVI. iii.

[2] The position of the Oyster in the Great Chain of Being had been ambiguous. Bacon said: 'The participles or confiners between plants and living creatures, are such chiefly as are fixed, and have no local motion of remove, though they have a motion in their parts; such as are oisters, cockles, and such like' (*Sylva Sylvarum*, cent. VII, sect. 609; *Works*, 1753, i. 215). See Locke on the line between animal and vegetable (*Essay*, III. vi. 12), ultimately from Aristotle, *Hist. animalium*, VIII. i. 2–3. By Fielding's time, the oyster was fairly well defined as of the animal kingdom (see, e.g., Chambers's *Cyclopaedia*, 5th edn., 1741–3, s.v. 'Animal').

[3] Fielding's citations may be compared with Appendix D.

it; and instead of conveying an Insect twice as large as its own
Mouth into it, in imitation of the *Polypus*, the poor *Chrysipus*
is itself conveyed into the *Loculus* or Pouch of an *Insect* a thousand
times as large as itself. Notwithstanding which, this wretched
Animal (for so I think we may be allowed to call it) is so eager
after its Prey, that if the *Insect* (which seldom happens) makes
any Resistance, it summons other *Chrysipi* to its Aid, which in
the end hardly ever fail of subduing it, and getting into its
Pouch.

The Learned *Gualterus* goes on in these Words: 'A *Chrysipus*,
by the simple Contact of my own Finger, has so closely attached
itself to my Hand, that by the joint and indefatigable Labour of
several of my Friends, it could by no means be sever'd, or made
to quit its Hold.'

As to the Generation of the *Chrysipus*, it differs from all other
Animals or Vegetables whatever: for though it seems the best
supplied for this natural Function, Nature having provided each
Female Part with four Male ones, which one would think
sufficient; yet it may be said, as of the *Polypus*, they have no
distinguished Place by which they bring forth their Young.

Gualterus judiciously remarks:[1] 'I have (says he) some of them,
that have greatly *multiplied under my Eyes*, and of which I might
almost say, that they have produced Young-ones from all the
exterior Parts of their Body.

'I have learned by a *continual Attention* to the two Species of
them, that all the Individuals of these Species produce Young-
ones.

'I have for Sixty Years had under my Eye Thousands of
them; and though I have OBSERVED THEM CONSTANTLY, AND
WITH ATTENTION, so as to watch them Night and Day, I never
observed any thing like the common Animal-Copulation.

'I tried at first two of them; but these I found would not
produce a compleat *Chrysipus*; at least I had reason to think
the Operation would be so slow, that I must have waited some
Years for its Completion. Upon this, I tried a Hundred of them
together; by whose marvellous Union (whether it be, that they
mix Total, like those Heavenly Spirits mentioned by *Milton*,[2] or
by any other Process not yet revealed to human Wit) they were

---

[1] Vid. Remarks on the *Polypus*, pag. 6. [Fielding's note.]
[2] *Paradise Lost*, viii. 626–9.

found in the Year's End to produce three, four, and sometimes five complete *Chrysipi*. I have indeed often made them in that Space produce Ten or Twenty; but this hath been by some held a dangerous Experiment, not only to the Parent *Chrysipi* themselves, which have by these means been utterly lost and destroyed, but even to the Philosopher who hath attempted it: For as some curious Persons have, by Hermetic Experiments, endangered the Loss of their Teeth, so we, by a too intense Application to this *Chrysipean* Philosophy, have been sometimes found to endanger our Ears.'[1] He then proceeds[2] thus:

'Another Fact, which I have observed, has proved to me, that they have the Faculty of multiplying, before they are sever'd from their Parent. I have seen a *Chrysipus*, still adhering, bring forth Young-ones; and those Young-ones themselves have also brought forth others. Upon Supposition, that perhaps there was some *Copulation between the Parent and Young-ones*, whilst they were yet united; or between the Young-ones coming from the Body of the same Parent: I made divers Experiments, to be sure of the Fact; but not one of those Experiments ever led me to any thing that could give the Idea of a Copulation.'

I now proceed to the Singularities resulting from the Operation I have tried upon them.

A *Chrysipus* of the larger kind may be divided into one and twenty Substances, (whether Animal or Vegetable we determine not) every Substance being at least as large as the original *Chrysipus*. These may again be subdivided, each of them into twenty four; and what is very remarkable, every one of these Parts is heavier, and rather larger than the first *Chrysipus*. The only Difference in this Change, is that of the Colour; for the first Sort are yellow, the second white, and the third resemble the Complexion and Substance of many human Faces.

These subdivided Parts are by some observed to lose in a great degree their adherescent Quality: Notwithstanding which, *Gualterus* writes, that, from the minutest Observations upon his own Experience, they all adhered with equal Tenacity to his own Fingers.

---

[1] The penalty for exceeding the allowable rate of usury, fixed at 5 per cent by the statute of 12 Anne c. 16 (1713), did not apparently include loss of the offender's ears; but Fielding doubtless had in mind the old story that Peter Walter had narrowly escaped losing an ear for forgery (cf. Pope, *Epilogue to the Satires*, ii. 57; Twickenham edn., iv. 315 and n.).

[2] *Remarks*, Pag. 7. [Fielding's note.]

The Manner of dividing a *Chrysipus* differs, however, greatly from that of the *Polypus*; for whereas we are taught in that excellent Treatise abovementioned,[1] that

'If the Body of a *Polypus* is cut into two Parts transversly, each of those Parts becomes a complete *Polypus*: On the very Day of the Operation, the first Part, or anterior End of the *Polypus*, that is, the Head, the Mouth, and the Arms; this Part, I say, lengthens itself, it creeps, and eats.

'The second Part, *which has no Head, gets one*; a Mouth forms itself, at the anterior End; and shoots forth Arms. This Reproduction comes about more or less quickly, according as the Weather is more or less warm. In Summer, I have seen Arms begin to sprout out twenty-four Hours after the Operation, and *the new Head perfected in every respect in a few Days*.

'Each of those Parts, thus become a perfect *Polypus*, performs absolutely all its Functions. It creeps, it eats, it grows, and it multiplies; *and all that*, as much as a *Polypus* which never had been cut.

'In whatever Place the Body of a *Polypus* is cut, whether in the Middle, or more or less near the Head, or the posterior Part, the Experiment has always the same Success.

'If a *Polypus* is cut transversly, at the same Moment, into three or four Parts, they all equally become so many complete ones.

'The Animal is too small to be cut at the same time into a great Number of Parts; *I therefore did it successively*. I first cut a *Polypus* into four Parts, and let them grow; next, I cut those Quarters again; and at this rate I proceeded, *till I had made fifty out of one single one*: And here I stopp'd, for there would have been *no End of the Experiment*.

'I have now actually by me several Parts of the same *Polypus*, cut into Pieces above a Year ago; since which time, they have produced a great Number of Young-ones.

'*A Polypus may also be cut in two, lengthways. Beginning by the Head, one first splits the said Head, and afterwards the Stomach*: The *Polypus* being in the Form of a Pipe, each Half of what is thus cut lengthways forms a Half-pipe; the anterior Extremity of which is terminated by the half of the Head, the half of the Mouth, and Part of the Arms. It is not long before the two Edges of those Half-pipes close, after the Operation: They

[1] See *Polypus*, pag. 8, 9, 10. [Fielding's note.]

generally begin at the posterior Part, and close up by degrees to the anterior Part. *Then, each Half-pipe becomes a Whole-one, complete*: A Stomach is formed, in which nothing is wanting; and *out of each Half-mouth a Whole-one is formed also.*

'I have seen all this done in less than an Hour; and that the *Polypus*, produced from each of those Halves, at the End of that time did not differ from the Whole-ones, except that it had fewer Arms; but in a few Days more grew out.

'I have cut a *Polypus*, lengthways, between Seven and Eight in the Morning; and between Two and Three in the Afternoon, *each of the Parts has been able to eat a Worm as long as itself.*

'If a *Polypus* is cut lengthways, beginning at the Head, and the Section is not carried quite through; the Result is, a *Polypus* with two Bodies, two Heads, and one Tail. Some of those Bodies and Heads may again be cut, lengthways, soon after. In this manner I have *produced a* Polypus *that had seven Bodies, as many Heads, and one Tail.* I afterwards, at once, cut off the seven Heads of this new *Hydra*: Seven others grew again; *and the Heads, that were cut off, became each a complete* Polypus.

'I cut a *Polypus*, transversly, into two Parts: I put these two Parts close to each other again, and they reunited where they had been cut. The *Polypus*, thus reunited, eat the Day after it had undergone this Operation: It is since grown, and has multiplied.

'*I took the posterior Part of one* Polypus, *and the anterior of another, and I have brought them to reunite in the same manner as the foregoing.* Next Day, the *Polypus that resulted*, eat: It has continued well these two Months, since the Operation: It is grown, and has put forth Young-ones, from each of the Parts of which it was formed. The two foregoing Experiments do not always succeed; it often happens, that the two Parts will not join again.

'In order to comprehend the Experiment I am now going to speak of, one should recollect, that the whole Body of a *Polypus* forms only one Pipe, a sort of Gut, or Pouch.

'*I have been able to turn that Pouch, that Body of the* Polypus, INSIDE-OUTWARDS; AS ONE MAY TURN A STOCKING.

'I have several by me, that have remained turned in this manner; THEIR INSIDE IS BECOME THEIR OUTSIDE, AND THEIR OUTSIDE THEIR INSIDE: They eat, they grow, and they multiply, as if they had never been turned.'

Now in the Division and Subdivision of our *Chrysipus*, we are forced to proceed in quite a different manner; namely, by the Metabolic or Mutative, not by the Schystic or Divisive. Some have indeed attempted this latter Method; but, like that great Philosopher the Elder *Pliny*, they have perished in their Disquisitions, as he did, by Suffocation.[1] Indeed there is a Method called the *Kleptistic*,[2] which hath been preferred to the Metabolic: But this too is dangerous; the Ingenious *Gualterus* never carried it farther than the Metabolic, contenting himself sometimes to divide the original *Chrysipus* into twenty-two Parts, and again to subdivide these into twenty-five; but this requires great Art.

It can't be doubted but that Mr. *Trembley* will, in the Work he is pleased to promise us, give some Account of the Longevity of the *Polypus*. As to the Age of the *Chrysipus*, it differs extremely; some being of equal Duration with the Life of Man, and some of scarce a Moment's Existence. The best Method of preserving them, is, I believe, in Bags or Chests, in large Numbers; for they seldom live long when they are alone. The Great *Gualterus* says, he thought he could never put enough of them together. If you carry them in your Pockets singly, or in Pairs, as some do, they will last a very little while, and in some Pockets not a Day.

We are told of the *Polypus*,[3] 'That they are to be look'd for in such Ditches whose Water is stock'd with small Insects. Pieces of Wood, Leaves, aquatic Plants, in short, every thing is to be taken out of the Water, that is met with at the Bottom, or on the Surface of the Water, on the Edges, and in the Middle of the Ditches. What is thus taken out, must be put into a Glass of clear Water, and these Insects, if there are any, will soon discover themselves; especially if the Glass is let stand a little, without moving it: for thus the Insects, which contract themselves when they are first taken out, will again extend themselves when they are at Rest, and become thereby so much the more remarkable.'

[1] See the Younger Pliny's *Epistles*, Bk. VI, epist. xvi.

[2] i.e., stealing (from κλέπτης, a thief), which is here contrasted with the gradual increase obtained safely by usury ('metabolic': μεταβολή, a change), or the clipping of coins ('schystic': σχίζειν, to split). Clipping or counterfeiting coins was an offense of high treason, punishable by death.

[3] *Polypus*, pag. 1, 2. [Fielding's note.]

The *Chrysipus* is to be look'd for in Scrutores,[1] and behind Wainscotes in old Houses. In searching for them, particular Regard is to be had to the Persons who inhabit, or have inhabited in the same Houses, by observing which Rule, you may often prevent throwing away your Labour. They love to be rather with old than young Persons, and detest Finery so much, that they are seldom to be found in the Pockets of laced Clothes,[2] and hardly ever in gilded Palaces. They are sometimes very difficult to be met with, even though you know where they are, by reason of *Pieces of Wood*, *Iron*, &c. which must be removed away before you can come at them. There are, however, several sure Methods of procuring them, which are all ascertained in a Treatise on that Subject, composed by *Petrus Gualterus*, which, now he is dead, will shortly see the Light.

I come now, in the last Place, to speak of the Virtues of the *Chrysipus*; In these it exceeds not only the *Polypus*, of which not one single Virtue is recorded, but all other Animals and Vegetables whatever. Indeed I intend here only to set down some of its chief Qualities; for to enumerate all, would require a large Volume.

First, then, A single *Chrysipus* stuck on to the Finger, will make a Man talk for a full Hour, nay will make him say whatever the Person who sticks it on desires: And again, if you desire Silence, it will as effectually stop the most loquacious Tongue.[3] Sometimes, indeed, one or two, or even twenty, are not sufficient; but if you apply the proper Number, they seldom or never fail of Success: It will likewise make Men blind or deaf, as you think proper; and all this without doing the least Injury to the several Organs.

Secondly, It hath a most miraculous Quality of turning Black into White, or White into Black. Indeed it hath the Powers of the Prismatic Glass, and can, from any Object, reflect what Colour it pleases.[4]

Thirdly, It is the strongest Love-Powder in the World, and hath such Efficacy on the Female Sex, that it hath often produced

---

[1] Variant spelling of 'Scrutoires' (see *OED*). Cf. p. 115, l. 410.

[2] Cf. *Jonathan Wild*, I. xi: 'as empty Pockets as are to be found in any laced Coat in the Kingdom'.   [3] Cf. Fielding's note to *The Vernoniad*, 163.

[4] See Newton's *Opticks* (1704), Bk. I, pt. ii (though, of course, Newton does not say that the prism can reflect what colour it pleases). Cf. Pope, *Essay on Criticism*, ii. 311–12; Twickenham edn., i. 274.

Love in the finest Women to the most worthless and ugly, old and decrepit of our Sex.

To give the strongest Idea in one Instance, of the salubrious Quality of the *Chrysipus*; It is a Medicine which the Physicians are so fond of taking themselves, that few of them care to visit a Patient, without swallowing a Dose of it.

To conclude; *Facts like these I have related, to be admitted,* require the most convincing Proofs. *I venture to say, I am able to produce such Proofs.* In the mean time, I refer my curious Reader to the Treatise I have above mentioned, which is not yet published, and perhaps never may.[1]

POSTSCRIPT.

Since I composed the above Treatise, I have been informed, that these Animals swarm in *England* all over the Country, like the Locusts, one in SEVEN Years;[2] and like them too, they generally cause much Mischief, and greatly ruin the Country in which they have swarmed.

---

[1] For the syntax, cf. Swift, *Intelligencer*, 3 (1728): 'I am glad to hear there are no weightier Objections . . . and I wish there never may' (*Prose Works*, ed. Davis, xii. 36); South: 'the late times (which we are not thoroughly recovered from yet, and perhaps never shall) . . .' (*Sermons*, 6th edn., 1727, v. 31); *Tom Jones*, VII. iii.

[2] i.e. at election time.

THE FIRST

OLYNTHIAC

OF *DEMOSTHENES*[1]

The ARGUMENT[2]

Olynthus *was a powerful free City of* Thrace, *on the Confines of* Macedonia. *By certain alluring Offers,* Philip *had tempted them into an Alliance with him, the Terms of which were a joint War against the* Athenians, *and if a Peace, a joint Peace. The* Olynthians, *some time after, becoming jealous of his growing Power, detach themselves from his Alliance, and make a separate Peace with the* Athenians. Philip, *exclaiming against this, as a Breach of their former Treaty, and glad of an Opportunity, which he had long been seeking, immediately declares War against them, and besieges their City. Upon this, they dispatch an Embassy to* Athens, *for Succour. The Subject of this Embassy coming to be debated among the* Athenians, Demosthenes *gives his Sentiments in the following Oration.*[3]

No Treasures, O *Athenians*, can, I am confident, be so desirable in your Eyes, as to discover what is most advantageous to be done for this City, in the Affair now before you. And since it is of so important a Nature, the strictest Attention should be given to all those who are willing to deliver their Opinions: for not only the salutary Councils which any one may have premeditated, are to be heard and received; but I consider it as peculiar to your Fortune and good Genius, that many Things, highly expedient,

---

[1] There is no evidence for the date or causes of this translation, but it seems likely that Fielding intended to exploit the political situation in the late 1730s, when the war-party of the Opposition was whipping up sentiment against Spain. The piece seems not to have been published at that time, however.
[2] For the background of the Olynthiac orations, see G. L. Cawkwell, 'The Defence of Olynthus', *Classical Quarterly*, N.S. xii (1962), 122–40; and Werner Jaeger, *Demosthenes: The Origin and Growth of His Policy* (1938), pp. 125–49.
[3] The text that Fielding employed for this translation was presumably that in his personal library, *Demosthenis et Æschinis principum graeciae oratorum opera* (Frankfurt, 1604), in which the Greek text was paralleled by the Latin translation of Hieronymus Wolfius. The Latin phrasing of Wolfius occasionally influences Fielding's rendering.

may suggest themselves to the Speakers, even extemporarily, and without Premeditation; and then you may easily, from the whole, collect the most useful Resolutions. The present Occasion wants only a Tongue to declare, that the Posture of these Affairs requires your immediate Application, if you have any Regard for your Preservation. I know not what Disposition we all entertain; but my own Opinion is, that we vote a Supply of Men to the *Olynthians*, and that we send them immediately; and thus by lending them our Assistance now, we shall prevent the Accidents which we have formerly felt, from falling again on us. Let an Embassy be dispatched, not only to declare these our Intentions, but to see them executed. For my greatest Apprehension is, that the artful *Philip*, who well knows to improve every Opportunity, by Concessions, where they are most convenient, and by Threats, which we may believe him capable of fulfilling, at the same time objecting our Absence to our Allies, may draw from the whole some considerable Advantage to himself. This however, O *Athenians*, will give some Comfort, that the very particular Circumstance which adds the greatest Strength to *Philip*, is likewise favourable to us. In his own Person he unites the several Powers of General, of King, and of Treasurer; he presides absolutely in all Councils, and is constantly at the Head of his Army. This indeed will contribute greatly to his Successes in the Field, but will have a contrary Effect, with Regard to that Truce which he is so desirous to make with the *Olynthians*; who will find their Contention not to be for Glory, nor for the Enlargement of Dominion: the Subversion or Slavery of their Country is what they fight against. They have seen in what Manner he hath treated those *Amphipolitans*, who surrendered their City to him; and those *Pydnæans*, who received him into theirs: and indeed, universally, a Kingly State is, in my Opinion, a Thing in which Republics will never trust; and above all, if their Territories border on each other. These Things therefore, O *Athenians*, being well known to you, when you enter on this Debate, your Resolutions must be for War, and to prosecute it with as much Vigour as you have formerly shewn on any Occasion. You must resolve to raise Supplies with the utmost Alacrity; to muster yourselves; to omit nothing: for no longer can a Reason be assigned, or Excuse alledged, why you should decline what the present Exigency requires. For the *Olynthians*, whom with such universal Clamours you have formerly insisted on our fomenting against *Philip*, are now embroiled with him by meer Accident; and this most advantageously for you; since had they undertaken the War at your Request, their Alliance might have been less stable, and only to serve a present Turn: but since their Animosity arises from Injuries offered to themselves, their Hostility will be firm; as well on Account of their Fears, as of their Resentment. The Opportunity which now offers is not, O *Athenians*, to be lost, nor should you suffer what you have already often suffered. For had we, when we returned from succouring the *Eubæans*; when *Hierax* and *Stratrocles* from the *Amphipolitans*, in this very Place, besought you to sail to their Assistance, and to receive their City into your Protection; had we then consulted our own Interest with the same Zeal with which we provided for the Safety of the *Eubæans*, we had then possessed ourselves of *Amphipolis*, and escaped the Troubles which have since perplexed us. Again, when we were first acquainted with the Sieges of *Pydna*, *Potidæa*, *Methone*, *Pagasæ*, and others, (for I will not waste Time in enumerating all) had we then assisted only one of these with proper Vigour, we should have found *Philip* much humbler, and easier to be dealt with: whereas now, by constantly pretermitting the Opportunities when they presented themselves, and trusting in Fortune for the good Success of future Events, we have encreased the Power, O *Athenians*, of *Philip* ourselves, and have raised him higher than any King of *Macedonia* ever was. Now then an Opportunity is come. What is it? why this which the *Olynthians* have of their own Accord offered to this City; nor is it inferior to any of those we have formerly lost. To me, O *Athenians*, it appears, that if we settle a just Account with the Gods, notwithstanding all Things are not as they ought to be, they are entitled to our liberal Thanksgivings. For as to our Losses in War, they are justly to be set down to our own Neglect: but that we formerly suffered not these Misfortunes, and that an Alliance now appears to ballance these Evils, if we will but accept it: this, in my Opinion, must be referred to the Benevolence of the Gods. But it happens as in the Affair of Riches, of which, I think, it is proverbially said, that if a Man preserves the Wealth he attains, he is greatly thankful to Fortune; but if he insensibly consumes it, his Gratitude to Fortune is consumed at the same Time. So in public

Affairs: if we make not a right Improvement of Opportunities, we forget the Good offered us by the Gods: for from the final Event, we generally form our Judgments of all that preceded. It is therefore highly necessary, O *Athenians*, to take effectual Care, that by making a right Use of the Occasion now offered us, we wipe off the Stains contracted by our former Conduct: for should we, O *Athenians*, desert these People likewise, and *Philip* be enabled to destroy *Olynthus*, will any Man tell me what afterwards shall stop his future Progress, wherever he desires to extend it? But consider, O *Athenians*, and see, by what Means this *Philip*, once so inconsiderable, is now become so great. He first became Master of *Amphipolis*, secondly of *Pydna*, next of *Potidea*, and then of *Methone*. After these Conquests, he turned his Arms towards *Thessaly*, where having reduced *Phera*, *Pagasæ*, *Magnesia*, he marched on to *Thrace*. Here, after he had dethroned some Kings, and given Crowns to others, he fell sick. On a small Amendment of Health, instead of refreshing himself with Repose, he fell presently on the *Olynthians*. His Expeditions against the *Illyrians*, the *Pæonians*, against *Arymba*, and who can recount all the other Nations, I omit. But should any Man say, Why therefore do you commemorate these Things to us now? my Answer is, That you may know, O *Athenians*, and sensibly perceive these two Things. First, how pernicious it is to neglect the least Article of what ought to be done; and, secondly, that you may discern the restless Disposition of *Philip* to undertake, and his Alacrity to execute: whence we may conclude, he will never think he hath done enough, nor indulge himself in Ease. If then his Disposition be to aim still at greater and greater Conquests, and ours to neglect every brave Measure for our Defence; consider, in what Event we can hope these Things should terminate! Good Gods! is there any of you so infatuated, that he can be ignorant that the War will come home to us, if we neglect it? And if this should happen, I fear, O *Athenians*, that we shall imitate those who borrow Money at great Usury, who for a short Affluence of present Wealth, are afterwards turned out of their original Patrimony. So we shall be found to pay dearly for our Sloth, and by giving our Minds entirely up to Pleasure, shall bring on ourselves many and grievous Calamities, against our Will shall be at last reduced to a Necessity of Action, and to contend even for our own Country. Perhaps some one may object, that to find Fault is easy, and within any Man's Capacity; but to advise proper Measures to be taken in the present Exigency, is the Part of a Counsellor. I am not ignorant, O *Athenians*, that not those who have been the first Causes of the Misfortune, but those who have afterwards delivered their Opinions concerning it, fall often under your severe Displeasure, when the Success doth not answer their Expectations. Be that as it will, I do not so tender my own Safety, that from any Regard to that, I should conceal what I imagine may conduce to your Welfare.

The Measures you are to take are, in my Opinion, two. First, to preserve the *Olynthian* Cities, by sending a Supply of Men to their Assistance; Secondly, to ravage the Country of the Enemy; and this by attacking it both by Sea and Land. If either of these be neglected, I much fear the Success of your Expedition: for should he, while you are wasting his Territories, by submitting to suffer this, take *Olynthus*; he will be easily able to return Home, and defend his own. On the other Hand, if you only send Succours to the *Olynthians*; when *Philip* perceives himself safe at Home, he will sit down before *Olynthus*, and employing every Artifice against the Town, will at length master it. We must therefore assist the *Olynthians* with numerous Forces, and in two several Places. This is my Advice concerning the manner of our assisting them. As for the Supply of Money to be raised; you have a Treasury, O *Athenians*, you have a Treasury fuller of Money, set apart for Military Uses, than any other City of *Greece*: this Fund you may apply according to your Pleasure, on this Occasion: if the Army be supplied this Way, you will want no Tax: If not, you will hardly find any Tax sufficient. What? says some one, Do you move to have this Fund applied to the Army? Not I truly; I only suggest that an Army should be levied; that this Fund should be applied to it; that those who do their Duty to the Public, should receive their Reward from it; whereas in celebrating the public Festivals, much is received by those who do nothing for it.

As to the rest, I think, all should contribute, largely if much wanted, less if little. Money is wanted, and without it, nothing which is necessary to be done can be performed. Others propose other Means of raising it; of which do you fix on that which seems most advantageous, and apply yourselves to your Preservation, while you have an Opportunity: for you ought to consider and weigh well the Posture in which *Philip's* Affairs now stand: for it appears to me, that no Man, even though he hath not examined them with much Accuracy, can imagine them to be in the fairest Situation. He would never have entered into this War, had he thought it would have been protracted. He hoped, at his very Entrance, to have carried all Things before him, which Expectation hath deceived him. This therefore, by falling out contrary to his Opinion, hath given him the first Shock, and much dejected him. Then the Commotions in *Thessaly*: for these are by Nature the most perfidious of Mortals, and have always proved so; as such he hath now sufficiently experienced them. They have decreed to demand *Pagasæ* of him, and to forbid the fortifying *Magnesia*. I have moreover heard it said, that the *Thessalians* would no longer open their Ports to him, nor suffer his Fleets to be victualled in their Markets; for that these should go to the Support of the Republics of *Thessaly*, and not to the Use of *Philip*. But should he be deprived of these, he will find himself reduced to great Streights to provide for his Auxiliaries. And further; Can we suppose that *Pæonia* and *Illyria*, and all the other Cities, will chuse rather to be Slaves than free, and their own Masters? They are not inured to Bondage, and the Man is, as they say, prone to Insolence; which is indeed very credible; for unmerited Success entirely perverts the Understanding in weaker Minds; whence it is often more difficult to retain Advantages, than it was to gain them. It is our Parts then, O *Athenians*, to take Advantage of this Distress of *Philip*, to undertake the Business with the utmost Expedition; not only to dispatch the necessary Embassies, but to follow them with an Army, and to stir up all his other Enemies against him: for we may be assured of this, that had *Philip* the same Opportunity, and the War was near our Borders, he would be abundantly ready to invade us. Are you not then ashamed through Fear to omit bringing that on him, when you have an Opportunity, which he, had he that Opportunity, would surely bring on you? Besides, let none of you be ignorant, that you have now your Option, whether you shall attack him Abroad, or be attacked by him at Home: for if the *Olynthians*, by your Assistance, are preserved, the Kingdom of *Philip* will be by your Forces invaded, and you may then retain you own Dominions, your own City in Safety; but should *Philip* once Master the *Olynthians*, who would oppose his March hither? The *Thebans?* Let me not be thought too bitter, if I say, they would be ready to assist him against us. The *Phocians?* they are not able to save themselves, unless you, or some one else, will assist them. But my Friend, says one, *Philip* will have no Desire to invade us—I answer, it would surely be most absurd, if what he imprudently now threatens us with, he would not, when he conveniently could, perform. As to the Difference, whether the War be here or there, there is, I think, no need of Argument: for if it was necessary for you to be thirty Days in the Field within your own Territories, and to sustain your Army with your own Product, supposing no Enemy there at the same Time; I say, the Losses of your Husbandmen, who supply those Provisions, would be greater than the whole Expence of the preceding War. But if an actual War should come to our Doors, what Losses must we then expect? Add to this, the Insults of the Enemy, and that which to generous Minds is not inferior to any Loss, the Disgrace of such an Incident. It becomes us all therefore, when we consider all these Things, to apply our utmost Endeavours to expel this War from our Borders: the Rich, that for the many Things they possess, parting with a little, they may secure the quiet Possession of the rest: the young Men, that having learnt Experience in the Art of War, at *Philip's* Expence, in his Country, they may become formidable Defenders of their own: the Orators, that they may be judicially vindicated in the Advice they have given to the Republick; since according to the Success of the Measures taken in Consequence of their Opinions, so you will judge of the Advisers themselves. May this Success be happy, for the Sake of every one.

OF THE REMEDY OF
AFFLICTION
For the LOSS of our FRIENDS[1]

It would be a strange Consideration (saith *Cicero*)[2] that while so many excellent Remedies have been discovered for the several Diseases of the human Body, the Mind should be left without any Assistance to alleviate and repel the Disorders which befal it. The contrary of this he asserts to be true, and prescribes Philosophy to us, as a certain and infallible Method to asswage and remove all those Perturbations which are liable to affect this nobler Part of Man.

Of the same Opinion were all those wise and illustrious Antients, whose Writings and Sayings on this Subject have been transmitted to us.[3] And when *Seneca* tells us, that *Virtue* is sufficient to subdue all our Passions, he means no other (as he explains it in many Parts of his Works) than *that exalted divine Philosophy*, which consisted not in vain Pomp, or useless Curiosity, nor even in the Search of more profitable Knowledge, but in acquiring solid lasting Habits of Virtue, and ingrafting them into our Character.[4] It was not the bare knowing the right Way, but the

---

[1] The allusion below to the death of a daughter is surely to the death of his own child, Charlotte, who died in March 1742 (see pp. xv–xvi). Fielding's assertion that many of the remedies offered here for the alleviation of grief 'have this uncommon Recommendation, that I have tried them upon myself with some Success' could refer both to this loss and to the earlier death of his father in June 1741.

[2] *Tusc. Disp.* III. i. 1.

[3] Fielding's essay follows very closely the traditional topics of the classical *consolatio*, represented by such works as Cicero's *Tusculan Disputations* (i and iii), Seneca's *De consolatione ad Marciam*, *Ad Polybium*, and *Epistulae morales* (lxiii, xcviii, xcix), and Plutarch's *Consolatio ad Apollonium*. Cf. Montaigne: 'Would I fortifie my self against the fear of Death ? It must be at the Expence of *Seneca*: Would I extract Consolation for my self, or my Friend ? I borrow it from him, or *Cicero*' (*Essays*, I. xxiv; trans. Cotton, 3rd edn., 1700, i. 199). Montaigne's essays, 'That Men Are Not to Judge of Our Happiness Till after Death' and 'That to Study Philosophy, is to Learn to Die' (I. xviii and xix) were very much in Fielding's mind in this work. Almost all of the topics touched on by Fielding appear in contemporary treatises of consolation, e.g. Simon Patrick, 'A Consolatory Discourse to Prevent Immoderate Grief for the Death of our Friends', in *The Heart's Ease* (3rd edn., 1671).

[4] e.g., *De ira*, II. xi. 3–6 *et passim*; *Epist. mor.* xvi. The phrase on philosophy is Cicero's: 'illa praestans et divina sapientia' (*Tusc. Disp.* III. xiv. 30).

constant and steady walking in it, which those glorious Writers recommended and dignified by the august Names of *Philosophy* and *Virtue*; which two Words, if they did not always use in a synonimous Sense, yet they all agreed in this, that Virtue was the Consummation of true Philosophy.

Now that this Supreme Philosophy, this Habit of Virtue, which strengthened the Mind of a *Socrates*, or a *Brutus*, is really superior to every Evil which can attack us, I make no doubt: but in Truth, this is to have a sound, not a sickly Constitution. With all proper Deference therefore to such great Authorities, they seem to me to assert no more, than that Health is a Remedy against Disease:[1] for a Soul once possessed of that Degree of Virtue, which can without Emotion look on Poverty, Pain, Disgrace, and Death, as Things indifferent: A Soul, as *Horace* expresses it,

Totus teres atque rotundus.[2]

or, according to *Seneca, which derives all its Comfort from* WITHIN, *not from* WITHOUT: which can look down on all the ruffling Billows of Fortune, as from a Rock on Shore, we survey a tempestuous Sea, with Unconcern;[3] such a Soul is surely in a State of Health, which no Vigour of Bodily Constitution can resemble.

And as this Health of the Mind exceeds that of the Body in Degree, so doth it in Constancy or Duration. In the latter, the Transition from perfect Health to Sickness is easy, and often sudden; whereas the former being once firmly established in the robust State above described, is never afterwards liable to be shocked by any Accident, or Impulse of Fortune.

It must be confessed indeed, that those great Masters have pointed out the Way to this Philosophy, and have endeavoured to allure and perswade others into it: but as it is certain, that few of their Disciples have been able to arrive at its Perfection; nay, as several of the Masters themselves have done little Honour to their Precepts, by their Examples,[4] there seems still great

---

[1] Cf. Matt. 9: 12: 'They that be whole need not a physician, but they that are sick.' See Seneca, *De tranqu. animi.* xi. 1; Montaigne, *Apology for Raimond de Sebonde* (*Essays*, trans. Cotton, 3rd edn., 1700, ii. 360). Cf. the *Champion*, 2 February 1740.
[2] *Serm.* II. vii. 86: 'a whole, smoothed and rounded'.
[3] e.g., *Epist. mor.* lxvi. 6, lxxii. 4–5; *De vita beata,* iii. 1, viii. 3. Cf. *Epist. mor.* xli. 4; and for the image, see Lucretius, *De rerum nat.* ii. 1–5.
[4] Cf. Sir Thomas Browne, *Relig. Med.* i. lv (8th edn., 1685, p. 29); Seneca anticipated this objection (*De vita beata,* xix. 3).

Occasion for a mental Physician,[1] who should consider the human Mind (as is often the Case of the Body) in too weak and depraved a Situation to be restored to firm Vigour and Sanity, and should propose rather to palliate and lessen its Disorders, than absolutely to cure them.[2]

To consider the whole Catalogue of Diseases, to which our Minds are liable, and to prescribe proper Remedies for them all, would require a much longer Treatise than what I now intend; I shall confine myself therefore to one only, and to a particular Species of that one, *viz.* to *Affliction for the Death of our Friends*.

This is a Malady to which the best and worthiest of Men are chiefly liable. It is, like a Fever, the Distemper of a rich and generous Constitution.[3] Indeed we may say of those base Tempers, which are totally incapable of being affected with it, what a witty Physician of the last Age[4] said of a shattered and rotten Carcase, that they are not worth preserving.

For this Reason the calm Demeanor of *Stilpo* the Philosopher, who, when he had lost his Children at the taking *Megara* by *Demetrius*, concluded, *he had lost nothing, for that he carried all which was his own about him*,[5] hath no Charms for me. I am more apt to impute such sudden Tranquility, at so great a Loss, to Ostentation or Obduracy, than to consummate Virtue. It is rather wanting the Affection, than conquering it. To overcome the Affliction arising from the Loss of our Friends, is great and

[1] Fielding speaks of 'Tully or Aristotle' as mental physicians in *Amelia*, IV. v.

[2] Cf. Seneca, *Epist. mor.* xciv. 24; Montaigne, *Apol. for Raimond de Sebonde,* on precepts of consolation: 'Where they cannot cure the Wound, they are content to palliate and benumb it' (*Essays,* trans. Cotton, 3rd edn., 1700, ii. 264).

[3] Cf. George Lyttelton, defending Cicero's grief at the death of Tullia: 'Great minds are most sensible of such losses; and the sentiments of humanity and affection are usually most tender, where in every other respect there is the greatest strength of reason' (*Observations on the Life of Cicero,* in *The Works,* 1774, pp. 26–7); *Spectator,* 22: 'It is like that Grief which we have for the Decease of our Friends: It is no Diminution, but a Recommendation of humane Nature, that in such Incidents Passion gets the better of Reason; and all we can think to comfort ourselves, is impotent against half what we feel.'

[4] Not identified. Perhaps Fielding had in mind the vigorous polemic of Dr. Edward Baynard (b. 1641), *Of Cold Baths,* appended to Sir John Floyer's *Psychrolousia* (1702). He cited the former in the *Champion* (6 December 1739); and the choleric Baynard has a number of passages in this vein: 'But for a Brainless, Unthinking Animal to outlive his Substance, and become the Jest and Contempt . . . of those Land *Leviathans* that have swallow'd him up alive, his own Whore's, Pimps and Bawds, &c. . . .' (3rd edn., 1709, p. 373).

[5] See Seneca, *De constantia sap.* v. 6; *Epist. mor.* ix. 18–19; Montaigne, I. xxxviii (trans. Cotton, 3rd edn., 1700, i. 377).

praise-worthy; but it requires some Reason and Time. This sudden unruffled Composure is owing to meer Insensibility; to a Depravity of the Heart, not Goodness of the Understanding.

But in a Mind of a different Cast, in one susceptible of a tender Affection, Fortune can make no other Ravage equal to such a Loss. It is tearing the Heart, the Soul from the Body; not by a momentary Operation, like that by which the most cruel Tormentors of the Body soon destroy the Subject of their Cruelty; but by a continued, tedious, though violent Agitation: the Soul having this double unfortunate Superiority to the Body; that its Agonies, as they are more exquisite, so they are more lasting.

If however this Calamity be not in a more humane Disposition to be presently or totally removed, an Attempt to lessen it is, however, worth our Attention. He who could reduce the Torments of the Gout to one Half or a Third of the Pain, would, I apprehend, be a Physician in much Vogue and Request; and surely, some palliative Remedies are as much worth our seeking in the mental Disorder; especially if this latter should (as appears to me who have felt both) exceed the former in its Anguish a hundred fold.

I will proceed therefore, without further Apology, to present my Reader with the best Prescriptions I am capable of furnishing; many of which have this uncommon Recommendation, that I have tried them upon myself with some Success.[1] And if *Montagne* be right in his Choice of a Physician, who had himself had the Disease which he undertook to cure,[2] I shall at least have that Pretension to some Confidence and Regard.

And first, by way of Preparative: while we yet enjoy our Friends, and no immediate Danger threatens us of losing them, nothing can be wholsomer than frequent Reflections on the Certainty of this Loss, however distant it may then appear to us: for if it be worth our while to prepare the Body for Diseases which may possibly (or at most probably) attack us; how much more necessary must it seem to furnish the Mind with every Assistance to encounter a Calamity, which our own Death only,

[1] Presumably on the death of his father in June 1741, and of his daughter, Charlotte (see below, p. 224).

[2] *Essays*, III. xiii ('Of Experience'), trans. Cotton, 3rd edn., 1700, iii. 492. Cf. Plato, *Republic*, III. xvi (408 d–e).

or the previous Determination of our Friendship, can prevent from happening to us.[1]

It hath been mentioned as one of the first Ingredients of a *wise* Man, that nothing befals him entirely unforeseen, and unexpected. And this is surely the principal Means of taking his Happiness or Misery out of the Hands of Fortune.[2] Pleasure or Pain, which sieze us unprepared, and by Surprize, have a double Force, and are both more capable of subduing the Mind, than when they come upon us looking for them, and prepared to receive them. That Pleasure is heighten'd by long Expectation, appears to me a great though vulgar Error. The Mind, by constant Premeditation on either, lessens the Sweetness of the one, and Bitterness of the other. It hath been well said of Lovers, who for a long time procrastinate and delay their Happiness, that they have loved themselves out before they come to the actual Enjoyment:[3] this is as true in the more ungrateful Article of Affliction. The Objects of our Passions, as well as of our Appetites, may be, in great measure, devoured by Imagination; and Grief, like Hunger, may be so palled and abated by Expectation, that it may retain no Sharpness when its Food is set before it.

The Thoughts which are to engage our Consideration on this Head, are too various, and many of them too obvious to be enumerated: the principal are surely, First, the Certainty of the Dissolution of this Alliance, however sweet it be to us, or however closely the Knot be tied. Secondly, the extreme Shortness of its Duration, even at the best. And, Thirdly, the many Accidents by which it is daily and hourly liable of being brought to an End.

Had not the wise Man frequently meditated on these Subjects, he would not have cooly answered the Person who acquainted him with the Death of his Son—I KNEW *I had begot a Mortal*.[4] Whereas by the Behaviour of some on these Occasions, we might be almost induced to suspect they were disappointed

---

[1] The *praemeditatio futurorum*: see Cicero, *Tusc. Disp.* III. xiv. 29; Seneca, *De consolatione ad Marciam*, ix. 5; Plutarch, *Consolatio ad Apollonium*, 112d.

[2] Cf. Cicero, *Tusc. Disp.* IV. xvii. 37; *De officiis*, I. xxiii. 81; Seneca, *De const. sap.* xix. 3; *De tranq. animi*, xi. 6–12 and xiii. 3; *Epist. mor.* lxxvi. 35.

[3] Congreve's Heartwell says (not quite the same point): 'You young, termagant flashy Sinners are cloy'd with the Preparative, and what you mean for a Whet, turns the Edge of your puny Stomachs' (*The Old Bachelor*, I. iv; *Works*, 5th edn., 1730, i. 13).

[4] See Seneca, *Ad Polyb.* xi. 2; attributed to Anaxagoras by Cicero, *Tusc. Disp.* III. xiv. 30; to Xenophon, by Diogenes Laertius, ii. 55.

in their Hopes of their Friend's Immortality; that something uncommon, and beyond the general Fate of Men, had happened to them. In a Word, that they had flattered their Fondness for their Children and Friends as enthusiastically as the Poets have their Works, which

> —*nec Jovis Ira nec Ignis,*
> *Nec poterit Ferrum, nec edax abolere vetustas.*[1]

Nor is there any Dissuasive from such Contemplation: It is no Breach of Friendship, nor Violence of Paternal Fondness; for the Event we dread and detest, is not by these Means forwarded, as simple Persons think their own Death would be by making a Will.[2] On the contrary, the sweetest and most rapturous Enjoyments are thus promoted and encouraged: for what can be a more delightful Thought than to assure ourselves, after such Reflections, that the Evil we apprehend, and which might so probably have happened, hath been yet fortunately escaped. If it be true, that the Loss of a Blessing teaches us its true Value,[3] will not these Ruminations on the Certainty of losing our Friends, and the Incertainty of our Enjoyment of them, add a Relish to the present Possession? Shall we not, in a Word, return to their Conversation, after such Reflections, with the same Eagerness and Extasy, with which we receive those we love into our Arms, when we first wake from a Dream which hath terrified us with their Deaths?

Thus then we have a double Incentive to these Meditations; as they serve as well to heighten our present Enjoyment, as to lessen our future Loss, and to fortify us against it. I shall now proceed to give my Reader some Instructions for his Conduct, when this dreadful Catastrophe hath actually befallen him.

And here I address myself to common Men, and who partake of the more amiable Weaknesses of Human Nature; not to those elevated Souls whom the Consummation of Virtue and Philosophy hath raised to a divine Pitch of Excellence, and placed beyond the Reach of human Calamity: for which Reason I do not expect this Loss shall be received with the Composure of *Stilpo*. Nay,

---

[1] Ovid, *Metam.* xv. 871–2: 'which neither the wrath of Jove, nor fire, nor sword, nor the gnawing tooth of time shall ever be able to undo' (trans. F. J. Miller, Loeb Library).

[2] See Montaigne, *Essays*, I. xix (trans. Cotton, 3rd edn., 1700, i. 97).

[3] Cf. Thomas Fuller, *Gnomologia: Adagies and Proverbs* (1732), p. 36 (No. 989): 'Blessings are not valued, till they are gone.'

I shall not regard Tears, Lamentations, or any other Indulgence to the first Agonies of our Grief on so dreadful an Occasion, as Marks of Effeminacy; but shall rather esteem them as the Symptoms of a laudable Tenderness, than of a contemptible Imbecility of Heart.

However, though I admit the first Emotions of our Grief to be so far irresistible, that they are not to be instantly and absolutely overcome, yet we are not, on the other Side, totally to abandon ourselves to them.[1] Wisdom is our Shield against all Calamity, and This we are not cowardly to throw away, though some of the sharper Darts of Fortune may have pierced us through it. The Mind of a wise Man may be ruffled and disordered, but cannot be subdued:[2] in the former it differs from the Perfection of the Deity; in the latter, from the abject Condition of a Fool.

With whatever Violence our Passions at first attack us, they will in Time subside. It is then that Reason is to be called to our Assistance, and we should use every Suggestion which it can lend to our Relief; our utmost Force being to be exerted to repel and subdue an Enemy when he begins to retreat: This indeed, one would imagine, should want little or no Persuasion to recommend it; inasmuch as we all naturally pursue Happiness and avoid Misery.[3]

There are, however, two Causes of our Unwillingness to hearken to the Voice of Reason on this Occasion. The first is, a foolish Opinion, that Friendship requires an exorbitant Affliction of us; that we are thus discharging our Duty to the Dead, and offering (according to the Superstition of the Ancients) an agreeable Sacrifice to their Manes:[4] the other, and perhaps the commoner Motive is, the immediate Satisfaction we ourselves feel in this Indulgence; which, though attended with very dreadful Consequences, gives the same present Relief to a tender Disposition, that Air or Water brings to one in a high Fever.

---

[1] Cf. Cicero, *Tusc. Disp.* III. vi. 12; Seneca, *Ad Polyb.* xviii. 5–6; Plutarch, *Ad Apoll.* 102 c. As Seneca says, we may weep but we must not wail: 'Lacrimandum est, non plorandum' (*Epist. mor.* lxiii. 1).

[2] Cf. the description of Allworthy, *Tom Jones*, VI. iii.

[3] See above, pp. 122 and 188.

[4] Cf. *Tatler*, 181: 'some Sages have thought it pious to preserve a certain Reverence for the Manes of their deceased Friends . . .'. See Cicero, *Tusc. Disp.* III. xxvi. 61–2; Seneca, *Epist. mor.* lxiii. 2.

Now what can possibly, on the least Examination, appear more absurd than the former of these? When the Grave, beyond which we can enter into no Engagement with one another, hath dissolved all Bonds of Friendship between us, and removed the Object of our Affection far from the Reach of any of our Offices; Can any thing be more vain and ridiculous, than to nourish an Affliction to our own Misery, by which we can convey neither Profit nor Pleasure to our Friend! But I shall not dwell on an Absurdity so monstrous in itself, that the bare first Mention throws it in a Light, which no Illustration nor Argument can heighten.

And as to the Second, it is, as I have said, like those Indulgencies, which however pleasant they may be to the Distemper, serve only to encrease it, and for which we are sure to pay the bitterest Agonies in the End. Nothing can indeed betray a weaker or more childish Temper of Mind than this Conduct; by which, like Infants, we reject a Remedy, if it be the least distasteful; and are ready to receive any grateful Food, without regarding the Nourishment which at the same Time we contribute to the Disease.

Without staying therefore longer to argue with such, I shall first recommend to my Disciple or Patient, of another Complexion, carefully to avoid all Circumstances which may revive the Memory of the Deceased, whom it is now his Business to forget as fast, and as much as possible; whereas, such is the Perverseness of our Natures, we are constantly endeavouring, at every Opportunity, to recal to our Remembrance the Words, Looks, Gestures, and other Particularities of a Friend. One carries about with him the Picture; a second the Hair; and others, some little Gift or Token of the Dead, as a Memorial of their Loss. What is all this less than being Self-Tormentors, and playing with Affliction?[1] Indeed Time is the truest and best Physician on these Occasions; and our wisest Part is to lend him the utmost Assistance we can: whereas by pursuing the Methods I have here objected to, we withstand with all our Might the Aid and Comfort which that great Reliever of human Misery so kindly offers us.

---

[1] Fielding here departs from the normal topics of the *consolatio*: the classical texts recommend solacing oneself with remembrances of one's friend. Montaigne, like Fielding, argues that this 'would rather be a greater torment' (*Apol. for Raimond de Sebonde*, *Essays*, trans. Cotton, 3rd edn., 1700, ii. 262).

Diversions of the lightest Kind have been recommended as a Remedy for Affliction: but for my Part, I rather conceive they will encrease than diminish it; especially where Music is to make up any Part of the Entertainment: for the Nature of this is to soothe or inflame, not to alter our Passions. Indeed I should rather propose such Diversions by way of Trial than of Cure: for when they can be pursued with any good Effect, our Affliction is, I apprehend, very little grievous or dangerous.[1]

To say the Truth, the Physic for this, as well as every other mental Disorder, is to be dispensed to us by Philosophy and Religion. The former of these Words (however unhappily it hath contracted the Contempt of the pretty Gentlemen and fine Ladies) doth surely convey to those who understand it, no very ridiculous Idea. Philosophy, in its purer and stricter Sense, means no more than the Love of Wisdom; but in its common and vulgar Acceptation it signifies, the Search after Wisdom; or often, Wisdom itself: For to distinguish between Wisdom and Philosophy (says a great Writer) is rather Matter of vain Curiosity, than of real Utility.[2]

Now from this Fountain (call it by which of the Names we please) may be drawn the following Considerations.

First, the Injustice of our Complaint, who have been only obliged to fulfil the Condition on which we first received the Good, whose Loss we deplore, *viz.* that of parting with it again. We are Tenants at Will to Fortune, and as we have advanced no Consideration on our Side, can have no Right to accuse her Caprice in determining our Estate.[3] However short-lived our Possession hath been, it was still more than she promised, or we could demand. We are already obliged to her for more than we can pay; but, like ungrateful Persons, with whom one Denial effaces the Remembrance of an Hundred Benefits, we forget what we have already received; and rail at her, because she is not pleased to continue those Favours, which of her own Free-Will she hath so long bestowed on us.

[1] So Cicero, against Epicurus (*Tusc. Disp.* III. xviii. 43). Cf. *Spectator*, 163.

[2] Not identified; but this is a commonplace, from Cicero ('nec quicquam aliud est philosophia . . . praeter studium sapientiae') and Seneca (e.g. *Epist. mor.* lxxxix), to Bacon and Shaftesbury. Cf. *Spectator*, 196: 'It is a lamentable Circumstance, that Wisdom, or, as you call it, Philosophy, should furnish Ideas only for the Learned. . . .'

[3] Cf. Cicero, *Tusc. Disp.* I. xxxix. 93; Seneca, *Ad Marc.* x. 1–4; Plutarch, *Ad Apoll.* 116 a–b.

Again, as we might have been called on to fulfil the Condition of our Tenure long before, so, sooner, or later, of Necessity we must have done it. The longest Term we could hope for is extremely short, and compared by *Solomon* himself to the Length of a Span.¹ Of what Duration is this Life of Man computed? A Scrivener who sells his Annuity² at fourteen Years and a half, rejoices in his Cunning, and thinks he hath outwitted you, at least half a Year in the Bargain.

But who will insure these fourteen Years? No Man. On the contrary, how great is the Premium for insuring you one? And great as it is, he who accepts it is often a Loser.

I shall not go into the hackneyed Common-place of the numberless Avenues to Death: a Road almost as much beaten by Writers, as those Avenues to Death are by Mankind: *Tibullus* sums 'em up in half a Verse.

—*Leti mille repente viæ.*³

Surely no Accident can befal our Friend which should so little surprize us; for there is no other which he may not escape. In Poverty, Pain, or other Instances, his Lot may be harder than his Neighbours. In this the happiest and most miserable, the greatest and lowest, richest and poorest of Mankind share all alike.

It is not then, it cannot be Death itself (which is a Part of Life) that we lament should happen to our Friend, but it is the Time of his dying. We desire not a Pardon, we desire a Reprieve only. A Reprieve, for how long? *Sine Die.*⁴ But if he could escape this Fever, this Small-Pox, this Inflammation of the Bowels, he may live twenty Years. He may so: but it is more probable he will not live ten: it is very possible, not one. But suppose he should have twenty, nay thirty Years to come. In Prospect, it is true,

¹ Perhaps the Book of Wisdom 15:9 Cf. Ps. 39: 6, in the Book of Common Prayer: 'Behold, thou hast made my days as it were a span long.' Cf. Cicero, *Tusc. Disp.* i. xxxix. 94; Seneca, *Ad Marc.* xxi. 1; Plutarch, *Ad Apoll.* 113 c–e.

² Among other meanings, a scrivener was one who 'received money to place out at interest, and who supplied those who wanted to raise money on security' (*OED*); 'Annuity': 'An investment of money, whereby the investor becomes entitled to receive a series of equal annual payments . . .' (*OED*).

³ Tibullus, i. iii. 50: 'a thousand ways of sudden death' (trans. J. P. Postgate, Loeb Library). Cf. Seneca, *Phoen.* i. i. 151; Montaigne, *Essays*, ii. iii (trans. Cotton, 3rd edn., 1700, ii. 30); Browne, *Religio Medici*, i. xliv; Milton, *Paradise Lost*, xi. 467–9; Swift, dedication to Prince Posterity, in *A Tale of a Tub*; *Guardian*, 136 (5th edn., 1729, ii. 202).

⁴ Without appointing a day.

the Term seems to have some Duration; but cast your Eyes backwards, and how contemptible the Span appears: for it happens in Life (however pleasant the Journey may be) as to a weary Traveller, the Plain he is yet to pass extends itself much larger to his Eye than that which he hath already conquered.

And suppose Fortune should be so generous to indulge us in the Possession of our Wish, and give us this twenty Years longer Possession of our Friend, should we be then contented to resign? Or shall we not, in Imitation of a Child who desires its Mamma to stay five Minutes, and it will take the Potion, be still as unwilling as ever? I am afraid the latter will be the Case; seeing that neither our Calamity, nor the Child's Physic becomes less nauseous by the Delay.

But admitting this Condition to be never so hard, will not Philosophy shew us the Folly of immoderate Affliction? Can all our Sorrow mend our Case? Can we wash back our Friend with our Tears, or waft him back with our Sighs and Lamentations?[1] It is a foolish Mean-spiritedness in a Criminal, to blubber to his Judge when he knows he shall not prevail by it; and it is natural to admire those more who meet their Fate with a decent Constancy and Resignation. Were the Sentences of Fate capable of Remission; could our Sorrows or Sufferings restore our Friends to us, I would commend him who out-did the fabled *Niobe* in weeping:[2] but since no such Event is to be expected; since *from that Bourne no Traveller returns*,[3] surely it is the Part of a wise Man, to bring himself to be content in a Situation which no Wit or Wisdom, Labour or Art, Trouble or Pain, can alter.

And let us seriously examine our Hearts, whether it is for the Sake of our Friends, or ourselves, that we grieve.[4] I am ready to agree with a celebrated *French* Writer; that *the Lamentation expressed for the Loss of our dearest Friends, is often, in Reality, for ourselves; that we are concerned at being less happy, less easy, and of less Consequence than we were before; and thus the Dead enjoy the Honour of those Tears which are truly shed on Account of the Living*:

[1] Cf. Seneca, *Ad Marc.* vi. 1–2; Plutarch, *Ad Apoll.* 105 f. Thus Shakespeare, *All's Well that Ends Well*, I. i. 64–5: 'Moderate lamentation is the Right of the Dead, excessive grief the enemy to the Living' (*Works*, 1733, ii. 361); so Claudius to Hamlet, I. ii. 87 ff.

[2] See Ovid, *Metam.* vi. 146–312.

[3] *Hamlet*, III. i. 79–80.

[4] Cf. Cicero to Titius, *Ad fam.* v. xvi. 4; Seneca, *Ad Polyb.* ix. 1; *Ad Marc.* xii. 1; Plutarch, *Ad Apoll.* 111 e.

concluding,—that *in these Afflictions Men impose on themselves.*[1] Now if on the Enquiry this should be found to be our Case, I shall leave the Patient to seek his Remedy elsewhere; having first recommended to him, an Assembly, a Ball, an Opera, a Play, an Amour, or, if he please, all of them, which will very speedily produce his Cure. But, on the contrary, if after the strictest Examination, it should appear (as I make no doubt is sometimes the Case) that our Sorrow arises from that pure and disinterested Affection which many Minds are so far from being capable of entertaining, that they can have no Idea of it: in a Word, if it be manifest that our Tears are justly to be imputed to our Friend's Account, it may be then worth our while to consider the Nature and Degree of this Misfortune which hath happened to him: and if, on duly considering it, we should be able to demonstrate to ourselves, that this supposed dreadful Calamity should exist only in Opinion, and all its Horrors vanish, on being closely and nearly examined; then, I apprehend, the very Foundation of our Grief will be removed, and it must, of necessary Consequence, immediately cease.

I shall not attempt to make an Estimate of Human Life, which to do in the most concise Manner, would fill more Pages than I can here allow it; nor will it be necessary for me, since admitting there was more real Happiness in Life than the wisest Men have allowed; as the weakest and simplest will be ready to confess that there is much Evil in it likewise; and as I conceive every impartial Man will, on casting up the whole, acknowledge that the latter is more than a Ballance for the former, I apprehend it will appear sufficiently for my Purpose, that Death is not that King of Terrors, as he is represented to be.

Death is nothing more than the Negation of Life. If therefore Life be no general Good, Death is no general Evil. Now if this be a Point in Judgment, who shall decide it? Shall we prefer the Judgment of Women and Children, or of wise Men? If of the latter, shall I not have all their Suffrages with me? *Thales*, the chief of the Sages, held Life and Death as Things indifferent. *Socrates*, the greatest of all the Philosophers, speaks of Death as of a Deliverance. *Solomon*, who had tasted all the Sweets of Life, condemns the whole as Vanity and Vexation: and *Cicero* (to name no more) whose Life had been a very fortunate one, assures

[1] La Rochefoucauld, *Maxims*, ccxxxiii (trans. 1706, pp. 97–8).

us in his Old Age, that *if any of the Gods would frankly offer him to renew his Infancy, and live his Life over again, he would strenuously refuse it.*[1]

But if we will be hardy enough to fly in the Face of these and numberless other such Authorities; if we will still maintain that the Pleasures of Life have in them something truly solid, and worthy our Regard and Desire, we shall not, however, be bold enough to say, that these Pleasures are lasting, certain, or the Portion of many among us. We shall not, I apprehend, insure the Possession of them to our Friend, nor secure him from all those Evils, which, as I have before said, none have ever denied the real Existence of: nor shall we surely contend, that he may not more likely have escaped the latter, than have been deprived of the former.[2]

I remember the most excellent of Women, and tenderest of Mothers,[3] when, after a painful and dangerous Delivery, she was told she had a Daughter, answering; *Good God! have I produced a Creature who is to undergo what I have suffered!* Some Years afterwards, I heard the same Woman, on the Death of that very Child, then one of the loveliest Creatures ever seen, comforting herself with reflecting, that *her Child could never know what is was to feel such a Loss as she then lamented.*

In Reality, she was right in both Instances: and however Instinct, Youth, a Flow of Spirits, violent Attachments, and above all, Folly may blind us, the Day of Death is (to most People at least) a Day of more Happiness than that of our Birth, as it puts an End to all those Evils which the other gave a Beginning to. So just is that Sentiment of *Solon*, which *Cræsus* afterwards experienced the Truth of, and which is couched in these Lines.

> —*ultima Semper*
> *Expectanda Dies Homini, dicique beatus*
> *Ante obitum nemo, postremaque funera debet.*[4]

If therefore Death be no Evil, there is certainly no Reason

[1] Thales: Diog. Laert. i. 35–6; Socrates: *Phaedo*, 66 b–67 d; Solomon: Eccles. 1: 14 *et passim* (cf. Prior's *Solomon*); Cicero: through Cato the Elder, *De senectute*, xxiii. 83.

[2] Cf. Cicero to Titius, *Ad fam.* v. xvi. 3; and Servius Sulpicius to Cicero, *Ad fam.* IV. v. 3–5; Plutarch, *Ad Apoll.* 113 f–114 c.

[3] Charlotte Fielding, whose daughter Charlotte had been born in April 1736 and had died in March 1742.

[4] Ovid, *Metam.* iii. 135–7, with 'supremaque' for 'postremaque': 'man's last day must ever be awaited, and none be counted happy till his death, till his last funeral rites are paid' (trans. F. J. Miller, Loeb Library). On Solon and Croesus, see Herodotus, Book I.

why we should lament its having happened to our Friend: but if there be any whom neither his own Observation, nor what *Plato* hath advanced in his Apology for *Socrates*, in his *Crito*, and his *Phædon*;[1] or *Cicero*, in the first and third Books of his *Tusculan* Questions; or *Montagne*, (if he hath a Contempt for the Ancients) can convince, that Death is not an Evil worthy our Lamentation, let such a Man comfort himself, that the Evil which his Friend hath suffered, he shall himself shortly have his Share in. As nothing can be a greater Consolation to a delicate Friendship than this, so there is nothing we may so surely depend on. A few Days may, and a few Years most infallibly will bring this about, and we shall then reap one Benefit from the Cause of our present Affliction, that we are not then to be torn from the Person we love.

These are, I think, the chief Comforts which the Voice of human Philosophy can administer to us on this Occasion. Religion goes much farther, and gives us a most delightful Assurance, that our Friend is not barely no Loser, but a Gainer by his Dissolution; that those Virtues and good Qualities which were the Objects of our Affection on Earth, are now become the Foundation of his Happiness and Reward in a better World.

Lastly; It gives a Hope, the sweetest, most endearing, and ravishing, which can enter into a Mind capable of, and inflamed with, Friendship. The Hope of again meeting the beloved Person, of renewing and cementing the dear Union in Bliss everlasting. This is a Rapture which leaves the warmest Imagination at a Distance. *Who can conceive* (says *Sherlock*, in his Discourse on Death) *the melting Caresses of two Souls in Paradice?*[2] What are all the Trash and Trifles, the Bubbles, Bawbles and Gewgaws of this Life, to such a Meeting? This is a Hope which no Reasoning shall ever argue me out of, nor Millions of such Worlds as this should purchase: nor can any Man shew me its absolute Impossibility, 'till he can demonstrate that it is not in the Power of the Almighty to bestow it on me.[3]

---

[1] *Apology*, 39 e–42; *Crito*, conclusion; *Phaedo*, 64 a–68 b *et passim*.

[2] William Sherlock, *Practical Discourse Concerning Death* (1689), pp. 85–6: 'Our imperfect Conceptions of God in this World, cannot help us to guess what the Joys of Heaven are; we know not how the sight of God, how the thoughts of him, will peirce our Souls, with what extasies and raptures we shall sing the Song of the Lamb, with what melting affections perfect Souls shall embrace, what glories and wonders we shall there see and know. . . .'

[3] Cf. Cicero, *Tusc. Disp.* I. xi. 24 and I. xxxii. 18; and *De senectute*, xxiii. 84–5.

A DIALOGUE

BETWEEN

ALEXANDER THE GREAT

AND

DIOGENES THE CYNIC[1]

ALEXANDER

What Fellow art thou, who darest thus to lie at thy Ease in our Presence, when all others, as thou seest, rise to do us Homage? Dost thou not know us?[2]

DIOGENES

I cannot say I do: But by the Number of thy Attendants, by the Splendor of thy Habit; but, above all, by the Vanity of thy Appearance, and the Arrogance of thy Speech, I conceive thou mayst be *Alexander* the Son of *Philip.*

ALEXANDER

And who can more justly challenge thy Respect, than *Alexander*, at the Head of that victorious Army, who hath performed such wonderful Exploits, and under his Conduct hath subdued the World?[3]

DIOGENES

Who? why the Taylor who made me this old Cloak.

[1] No date of composition can be offered for this dialogue; but Fielding had also roughly handled its two characters in the poem *Of True Greatness*, published in January 1741, as 'writ several Years ago'.

[2] The major accounts of this celebrated meeting (which is generally placed at Corinth in 336 B.C.) are those of Cicero, *Tusc. Disp.* v. xxxii. 92; Valerius Maximus, *Dictorum factorumque memorabilium*, IV. iii, Ext. 4; Dio Chrysostom, *Fourth Discourse*; Plutarch, *Alexander*, xiv; Arrian, *Anabasis*, VII. ii. 1–2; and Diogenes Laertius, vi. 32, 38, 60, 68. See Fielding's poetic commentary upon Diogenes and Alexander in *Of True Greatness*, 55-98; and cf. the *Champion*, 28 February 1740.

[3] This is an Anachronism: for *Diogenes* was of *Sinope*, and the Meeting between him and *Alexander* fell out while the latter was confederating the *Grecian* States in the *Peloponnese* before his *Asiatic* Expedition: But that Season would not have furnished sufficient Matter for this Dialogue; we have therefore fixed the Time of it at the Conqueror's Return from *India*. [Fielding's note.]

ALEXANDER

Thou art an odd Fellow, and I have a Curiosity to know thy Name.

DIOGENES

I am not ashamed of it: I am called *Diogenes*; a Name composed of as many and as well sounding Syllables as *Alexander*.

ALEXANDER

Diogenes, I rejoyce at this Encounter. I have heard of thy Name, and been long desirous of seeing thee; in which Wish, since Fortune hath accidentally favoured me, I shall be glad of thy Conversation a-while: And that thou likewise may'st be pleased with our Meeting, ask me some Favour; and as thou knowest my Power, so shalt thou experience my Will to oblige thee.

DIOGENES

Why then, *Alexander the Great*, I desire thee to stand from between me and the Sun;[1] whose Beams thou hast with-held from me some Time, a Blessing which it is not in thy Power to recompence the Loss of.

ALEXANDER

Thou hast a very shallow Opinion of my Power indeed; and if it was a just one, I should have travelled so far, undergone so much, and conquered so many Nations, to a fine Purpose truly.

DIOGENES

That is not my Fault.

ALEXANDER

Dost thou not know that I am able to give thee a Kingdom?

DIOGENES

I know thou art able, if I had one, to take it from me; and I shall never place any Value on that which such as thou art can deprive me of.[2]

---

[1] This famous anecdote appears in all the authorities cited above.
[2] Cf. Seneca, *De benef.* v. iv. 4 and vi. 1.

ALEXANDER

Thou dost speak vainly in Contempt of a Power which no other Man ever yet arrived at. Hath the *Granicus* yet recovered the bloody Colour with which I contaminated its Waves? Are not the Fields of *Issus* and *Arbela* still white with human Bones? Will *Susa* shew no Monuments of my Victory? Are *Darius* and *Porus* Names unknown to thee?[1] Have not the Groans of those Millions reached thy Ears, who but for the Valour of this Heart, and the Strength of this Arm, had still enjoyed Life and Tranquillity? Hath then this Son of *Jupiter*,[2] this Conqueror of the World, adored by his Followers, dreaded by his Foes, and worshipped by All, lived to hear his Power contemned, and the Offer of his Favour slighted, by a poor Philosopher, a wretched Cynic, whose Cloak appears to be his only Possession!

DIOGENES

I retort the Charge of Vanity on thyself, proud *Alexander*; for how vainly dost thou endeavour to raise thyself on the Monuments of thy Disgrace! I acknowledge, indeed, all the Exploits thou hast recounted, and the Millions thou hast to thy eternal Shame destroyed. But is it hence thou wouldst claim *Jupiter* for thy Father? Hath not then every Plague or pestilential Vapour the same Title?[3] If thou art the Dread of Wretches to whom Death appears the greatest of Evils, is not every mortal Disease the same? And if thou hast the Adoration of thy servile Followers, do they offer thee more, than they are ready to pay to every Tinsel Ornament, or empty Title? Is then the Fear or Worship of Slaves of so great Honour, when at the same time thou art the Contempt of every brave honest Man, tho', like me, an old Cloak should be his only Possession?

---

[1] The battles of the River Granicus, Issus, and Arbela were Alexander's major triumphs over Darius (Plutarch, *Alexander*, xvi, xx, xxxi–xxxiii; Arrian, *Anabasis*, I. xiii–xv, II. vi–xi, III. viii ff.); Susa, the winter capital of the Persian kings; Porus, the Indian king defeated by Alexander at the River Hydaspes (Plutarch, lx; Arrian, V. viii ff.).

[2] On Alexander's claim to be the son of Jupiter Ammon, see Plutarch, xxvii–xxviii; Arrian, IV. ix. 9; Quintus Curtius, VI. ix. 18–19 and xi. 5 ff. Lucian has some sport with the idea in *Dial. mortuorum*, xiii–xiv (the first, a dialogue between Diogenes and Alexander). Cf. the *Champion*, 17 November 1739.

[3] Cf. Seneca, *Nat. quaest.* iii, Praef. 5; Milton, *Paradise Lost*, xi. 694–7; Young, *Love of Fame*, vii. 47–52.

ALEXANDER

Thou seemest, to my Apprehension, to be ignorant, that in professing this Disregard for the Glory I have so painfully atchieved, thou art undermining the Foundation of all that Honour, which is the Encouragement to, and Reward of, every thing truly great and noble: For in what doth all Honour, Glory, and Fame consist, but in the Breath of that Multitude, whose Estimation with such ill-grounded Scorn thou dost affect to despise. A Reward which hath ever appeared sufficient to inflame the Ambition of high and exalted Souls; tho' from their Meanness, low Minds may be incapable of tasting, or rather, for which Pride from the Despair of attaining it may inspire thee to feign a false and counterfeit Disdain. What other Reward than this have all those Heroes proposed to themselves, who rejecting the Enjoyments which Ease, Riches, Pleasure, and Power, have held forth to them in their native Country, have deserted their Homes, and all those Things which to vulgar Mortals appear lovely or desirable, and in Defiance of Difficulty and Danger, invaded and spoiled the Cities and Territories of others; when their Anger hath been provoked by no Injury, nor their Hope inspired by the Prospect of any other Good than of this very Glory and Honour, this Adoration of Slaves, which thou, from having never tasted its Sweets, hast treated with Contempt.

DIOGENES

Thy own Words have convinced me, (stand a little more out of the Sun, if you please) that thou hast not the least Idea of true Honour.[1] Was it to depend on the Suffrages of such Wretches, it would indeed be that contemptible Thing which you represent it to be estimated in my Opinion: But true Honour is of a different Nature; it results from the secret Satisfaction of our own Minds, and is decreed us by Wise Men and the Gods; it is the Shadow of Wisdom and Virtue, and is inseparable from them: Nor is it either in thy Power to deserve, nor in that of thy Followers to bestow. As for such Heroes as thou hast named, who, like thyself, were born the Curses of Mankind,[2] I readily

[1] All the traditional topics on this question can be found in Timothy Hooker's exhaustive series of epistles, *An Essay on Honour* (1741).

[2] Contemporary English attacks on the 'criminal conqueror' liked to find parallels between Alexander and Caesar, on the one hand, and Louis XIV and Charles XII on the other. The Opposition (e.g. *Craftsman*, 320, 19 August 1732), with an eye on Walpole,

agree they pursue another kind of Glory, even that which thou hast mentioned, the Applause of their Slaves and Sycophants; in this Instance indeed their Masters, since they bestow on them the Reward, such as it is, of all their Labours.

ALEXANDER

However, as you would persuade me you have so clear a Notion of my Honour, I would be glad to be on a Par with you, by conceiving some Idea of yours; which I can never obtain of the Shadow, till I have some clearer Knowledge of the Substance, and understand in what your Wisdom and Virtue consist.

DIOGENES

Not in ravaging Countries, burning Cities, plundering and massacring Mankind.

ALEXANDER

No, rather in biting and snarling at them.

DIOGENES

I snarl at them because of their Vice and Folly; in a word, because there are among them many such as Thee and thy Followers.

ALEXANDER

If thou wouldst confess the Truth, Envy is the true Source of all thy Bitterness; it is that which begets thy Hatred, and from Hatred comes thy Railing: Whereas the Thirst of Glory only is my Motive. I hate not those whom I attack, as plainly appears by the Clemency I shew to them when they are conquered.

DIOGENES

Thy Clemency is Cruelty.[1] Thou givest to one what thou hast by Violence and Plunder taken from another: And in so doing,

often argued, like John Gay, that the distinction between 'a Publick Robber' and Alexander was that '*Alexander* the great was more successful. That's all' (Gay, *Polly*, III. xi). Cf. Fielding, the *Champion*, 4 March 1740. To Pope, Alexander was 'Macedonia's madman' (*Essay on Man*, iv. 220), and to Thomson, 'The Macedonian vulture' (*Liberty*, ii. 479). Such epithets, of course, occur as early as Lucan's *Pharsalia*, x. 20–52. And cf. Augustine, *De civ. dei*, IV. iv.

[1] See Fielding's angry comment on Alexander's 'clemency' in *Jonathan Wild*, I. i.

thou only raisest him to be again the Mark of Fortune's Caprice, and to be tumbled down a second Time by thyself, or by some other like thee. My Snarling is the Effect of my Love; in order, by my Invectives against Vice, to frighten Men from it, and drive them into the Road of Virtue.

ALEXANDER

For which Purpose thou hast forsworn Society, and art retired to preach to Trees and Stones.[1]

DIOGENES

I have left Society, because I cannot endure the Evils I see and detest in it.[2]

ALEXANDER

Rather because thou canst not enjoy the Good thou dost covet in it. For the same Reason I have left my own Country, which afforded not sufficient Food for my Ambition.

DIOGENES

But I come not, like thee, abroad to rob and plunder others. Thy Ambition hath destroyed a Million, whereas I have never occasioned the Death of a single Man.

---

[1] The force of this retort lies, of course, in the assumption that man is a social animal (see above, p. 119). As Hobbes (*Leviathan*, I. xiii) had said, and as all the classical political philosophers insisted, Justice and Injustice are qualities that relate only to men in society, not in solitude. Lyttelton made the same point in Dialogue XXX (Plato and Diogenes) of his *Dialogues of the Dead*: 'He, who can mistake a brutal pride and savage indecency of manners for freedom, may naturally think that the being in a court (however virtuous one's conduct, however free one's language there) is slavery. But I was taught by my great master, the incomparable Socrates, that the business of true philosophy is to consult and promote the happiness of society. She must not therefore be confined to a *tub* or a *cell*' (*Works*, 1774, pp. 530–1). See also Fénelon, *Les avantures de Télémaque* (Paris, 1699), xiv; 1743 edn., p. 243.

[2] Diogenes was normally represented, in classic texts and in the Renaissance, as a staunch moralist and an admirable man: see Farrand Sayre, *Diogenes of Sinope* (Baltimore, 1938), and John L. Lievsay, 'Some Renaissance Views of Diogenes the Cynic', in *Joseph Quincy Adams: Memorial Studies*, ed. McManaway *et al.*, pp. 447–55; but by the late seventeenth century this view was modified by an emphasis upon his snarling envy. See, e.g., Samuel Parker the Younger, *Sylva* (1701), pp. 113–14; Samuel Wesley, 'The Dog', *Poems on Several Occasions* (1736), p. 150; Bonnell Thornton, *Drury-Lane Journal* (coll. edn., 1752), p. 93.

ALEXANDER

Because thou hast not been able: but thou hast done all within thy Power, by cursing and devoting to Destruction almost as many as I have conquered. Come, come, thou art not the poor-spirited Fellow thou wouldst appear. There is more Greatness of Soul in thee than at present shines forth. Poor Circumstances are Clouds which often conceal and obscure the brightest Minds. Pride will not suffer thee to confess Passions which Fortune hath not put it in thy Power to gratify. It is therefore that thou deniest Ambition: for hadst thou a Soul as capacious as mine, I see no better Way which thy humble Fortune would allow thee of feeding its Ambition, than what thou hast chosen: for when alone in this Retreat which thou hast chosen, thou may'st contemplate thy own Greatness.[1] Here no stronger Rival will contend with thee; nor can the hateful Objects of superior Power, Riches, or Happiness, invade thy Sight. But, be honest and confess, had Fortune placed thee at the Head of a *Macedonian* Army.—

DIOGENES

Had Fortune placed me at the Head of the World, it could not have raised me in my own Opinion. And is this mighty Soul, which is, it seems, so much more capacious than mine, obliged at last to support its Superiority on the Backs of a Multitude of armed Slaves?[2] And who in Reality have gained these Conquests, and gathered all these Lawrels, of which thou art so vain? Hadst thou alone past into *Asia*, the Empire of *Darius* had still stood unshaken. But tho' *Alexander* had never been born, who will say the same Troops might not, under some other General, have done as great, or perhaps greater Mischiefs? The Honour therefore, such as it is, is by no means justly thy own. Thou usurpest the whole, when thou art, at most, entitled to an equal Share only. It is not then *Alexander*, but *Alexander* and his Army are superior to *Diogenes*. And in what are they his Superiors? In brutal Strength—in which they would be again excelled by an equal Number of Lions, or Wolves, or Tygers. An Army

---

[1] Cf. Sir Thomas Browne: '*Diogenes* I hold to be the most vain-glorious man of his time, and more ambitious in refusing all Honours, than *Alexander* in rejecting none' (*Religio Medici*, I. lv; 8th edn., 1685, p. 29).

[2] Cf. Dio Chrysostom, *Fourth Discourse*, 8.

which would be able to do as much more Mischief than themselves, as they are than *Diogenes*.

ALEXANDER

Then thy Grief broke forth. Thou hatest us because we can do more Mischief than thyself. And in this I see thou claimest the Precedence over me; that I make use of others as the Instruments of my Conquests, whereas all thy Railery and Curses against Mankind, proceed only out of thy own Mouth. And if I alone am not able to conquer the World, thou alone art able to curse it.

DIOGENES

If I desired to curse it effectually, I have nothing more to do, than to wish thee long Life and Prosperity.

ALEXANDER

But then thou must wish well to an Individual, which is contrary to thy Nature, who hatest all.

DIOGENES

Thou art mistaken. Long Life, to such as thee, is the greatest of Curses: for, to mortify thy Pride effectually, know there is not in thy whole Army, no, nor among all the Objects of thy Triumph, one equally miserable with thyself: For if the Satisfaction of violent Desires be Happiness, and a total Failure of Success in most eager Pursuits, Misery, (which cannot, I apprehend, be doubted) what can be more miserable, than to entertain Desires which we know never can be satisfied? And this a little Reflection will teach thee is thy own Case: For what are thy Desires? not Pleasure; with that *Macedonia* would have furnished thee. Not Riches; for capacious as thy Soul is, if it had been all filled with Avarice, the Wealth of *Darius* would have contented it. Not Power; for then the Conquest of *Porus*, and the extending thy Arms to the farthest Limits of the World,[1] must have satisfied thy Ambition. Thy Desire consists in nothing certain, and therefore with nothing certain can be gratified. It is as restless as Fire, which still consumes whatever comes in its Way, without determining where to stop. How contemptible must thy own Power

---

[1] Which was then known to the *Greeks*. [Fielding's note.]

appear to thee, when it cannot give thee the Possession of thy
Wish; but how much more contemptible thy Understanding,
which cannot enable thee to know certainly what that Wish is?[1]

ALEXANDER

I can at least comprehend thine, and can grant it. I like thy
Humour, and will deserve thy Friendship. I know the *Athenians*
have affronted thee, have contemned thy Philosophy, and suspected thy Morals.[2] I will revenge thy Cause on them. I will lead
my Army back, and punish their ill Usage of thee. Thou thyself
shalt accompany us; and when thou beholdest their City in
Flames, shalt have the Triumph of proclaiming, that thy just
Resentment hath brought this Calamity on them.

DIOGENES

They do indeed deserve it at my Hands; and tho' Revenge
is not what I profess, yet the Punishment of such Dogs may be
of good Example. I therefore embrace thy Offer: but let us not
be particular, let *Corinth* and *Lacedæmon* share the same Fate.
They are both the Nests of Vermin only, and Fire alone will
purify them. Gods! what a Delight it will be to see the Rascals,
who have so often in Derision call'd me a snarling Cur, roasting
in their own Houses.

ALEXANDER

Yet, on a second Consideration, would it not be wiser to
preserve the Cities, especially *Corinth*, which is so full of Wealth,
and only massacre the Inhabitants?

DIOGENES

D—n their Wealth, I despise it.

ALEXANDER

Well then, let it be given to the Soldiers; as the Demolition
of it will not encrease the Punishment of the Citizens, when we
have cut their Throats.

---

[1] Cf. Cicero, *Tusc. Disp.* v. xxxii. 92; Dio Chrysostom, *Sixth Discourse*, 1–7.
[2] See Farrand Sayre, *Diogenes of Sinope*, p. 81.

DIOGENES

True—Then you may give some of it to the Soldiers: but as the Dogs have formerly insulted me with their Riches, I will, if you please, retain a little—perhaps a Moiety, or not much more, to my own Use. It will give me at least an Opportunity of shewing the World, I can despise Riches when I possess them, as much as I did before in my Poverty.

ALEXANDER

Art not thou a true Dog? Is this thy Contempt of Wealth? This thy Abhorrence of the Vices of Mankind? To sacrifice three of the noblest Cities of the World to thy Wrath and Revenge! And hast thou the Impudence to dispute any longer the Superiority with me, who have it in my Power to punish my Enemies with Death, while thou only canst persecute with evil Wishes.

DIOGENES

I have still the same Superiority over thee, which thou dost challenge over thy Soldiers. I would have made thee the Tool of my Purpose. But I will discourse no longer with thee; for I now despise and curse thee more than I do all the World besides. And may Perdition seize thee, and all thy Followers.

Here some of the Army would have fallen upon him, but Alexander *interposed.*

ALEXANDER

Let him alone. I admire his Obstinacy; nay, I almost envy it.— Farewell, old Cynic; and if it will flatter thy Pride, be assured, I esteem thee so much, that *was I not* Alexander, *I could desire to be* Diogenes.

DIOGENES

Go to the Gibbet, and take with thee as a Mortification; that *was I not* Diogenes, *I could almost content myself with being* Alexander.[1]

---

[1] See Diogenes Laertius, vi. 32; Plutarch, *Alex.* xiv. 1–3.

AN INTERLUDE

BETWEEN

Jupiter, *Juno*, *Apollo*, and *Mercury*.

Which was originally intended as an

INTRODUCTION to a COMEDY,

CALLED,

JUPITER'S *Descent on Earth*[1]

SCENE I

JUPITER, JUNO

Jupiter. Pray be pacified.[2]

Juno. It is intolerable, insufferable, and I never will submit to it.

Jupiter. But, my Dear.

Juno. Good Mr. *Jupiter*, leave off that odious Word: You know I detest it. Use it to the Trollop *Venus*, and the rest of your Sluts. It sounds most agreeable to their Ears, but it is nauseous to a Goddess of strict Virtue.

Jupiter. Madam, I do not doubt your Virtue.

Juno. You don't? That is, I suppose, humbly insinuating that others do: But who are their Divinities? I would be glad to know who they are; they are neither *Diana*, nor *Minerva*, I am well assured; both of whom pity me; for they know your Tricks; they can neither of them keep a Maid of Honour for you. I desire you will treat me with Good-Manners at least.[3] I should have had

---

[1] Nothing is known of this comedy. The most likely date for the *Interlude* would seem to be in the years 1736–7, when Fielding was managing the Little Theatre in the Haymarket; the burlesque treatment of mythological characters was also a feature of Fielding's *Tumble-Down Dick* in 1736 and *Eurydice* in 1737.

[2] The opening and some of the other material in this scene between Jupiter and Juno repeat the dialogue of the first scene in Fielding's *Good-Natured Man* (posthumously titled *The Fathers*); he apparently stole from himself some material he did not expect to publish in play form.

[3] A phrase repeated by Mrs. Boncour in *The Fathers*, I. i; Laetitia in *Jonathan Wild*, III. viii; and Mrs. James in *Amelia*, XI. i.

that, if I had married a Mortal, tho' he had spent my Fortune, and lain with my Chamber-Maids, as you suffer Men to do with Impunity, highly to your Honour be it spoken.

Jupiter. Faith! Madam, I know but one Way to prevent them, which is, by annihilating Mankind; and I fancy your Friends below, the Ladies, would hardly thank you for obtaining that Favour at my Hands.

Juno. I desire you would not reflect on my Friends below; it is very well known, I never shewed any Favour, but to those of the purest, unspotted Characters. And all my Acquaintance, when I have been on the Earth, have been of that Kind: for I never return a Visit to any other.

Jupiter. Nay, I have no Inclination to find Fault with the Women of the Earth; you know I like them very well.[1]

Juno. Yes, the Trollops of the Earth, such as *Venus* converses with. You never shew any Civility to my Favourites, nor make the Men do it.

Jupiter. My Dear, give me Leave to say, your Favourites are such, that Man must be new made before he can be brought to give them the Preference: For when I moulded up the Clay of Man, I put not one Ingredient in to make him in Love with Ugliness, which is one of the most glaring Qualities in all your Favourites, whom I have ever seen; and you must not wonder, while you have such Favourites, that the Men slight them.

Juno. The Men slight them! I'd have you know, Sir, they slight the Men; and I can, at this Moment, hear not less than a Thousand railing at Mankind.

Jupiter. Ay, as I hear at this Instant several grave black Gentlemen railing at Riches, and enjoying them, or at least coveting them, at the same Time.[2]

Juno. Very fine! very civil! I understand your Comparison.— Well, Sir, you may go on giving an Example of a bad Husband,

---

[1] Cf. Defoe's indignant lines on Jove: 'His rampant Vices the Creation Vex, / And make one General Whore of either Sex'; to which the note is added: '*Danae, Calisto, Alcmena, Semele, Leda, Antiope, Europa,* and innumerable others, where [*sic*] his Whores; whom he Debauched, some by one Method, some by another' (*Jure Divino,* 1706, Book I, p. 9). Defoe continues: 'And *Juno*'s made the *Billingsgate* o' th' Sky', with the note: 'The Wife of *Jupiter* Jealous of him, as well she might, Quarrelling with him or his Whores, and therefore represented Clamorous. *Tantaene animis Coelestibus irae?* Virgil' (Book I, p. 10).

[2] Cf. Pope's version of Donne, *Sat.* ii. 81: 'Not more of Simony beneath black Gowns' (Twickenham edn., iv. 141); and Fielding's note to *The Vernoniad,* 244.

but I will not give the Example of a tame Wife; and if you will not make Men better, I will go down to the Earth, and make Women worse; that every House may be too hot for a Husband, as I will shortly make Heaven for you.

Jupiter. That I believe you will—but if you begin your Project of making Women worse, I will take *Hymen*, and hang him; for I will take some Care of my Votaries, as well as you of yours.

SCENE II

Enter APOLLO

Apollo. Mr. *Jupiter*, Good-morrow to you.

Jupiter. *Apollo*, how dost thou?—You are a wise Deity, *Apollo*; prithee will you answer me one Question?

Apollo. To my best Ability.

Jupiter. You have been much conversant with the Affairs of Men, What dost thou think the foolishest Thing a Man can do?

Apollo. Turn Poet.

Jupiter. That is honest enough, as it comes from the God of Poets: But you have miss'd the Mark; for certainly, the foolishest Thing a Man can do, is to marry.

Apollo. Fie! What is it then in a God? who, besides that he ought to be wiser than Man, is tied for ever by his Immortality, and has not the Chance which you have given to Man, of getting rid of his Wife.

Jupiter. *Apollo*, thy Reproof is just; but let us talk of something else: for when I am out of the hearing my Wife, I beg I may never hear of her.

Apollo. Have you read any of those Books I brought you, just sent me by my Votaries upon Earth?

Jupiter. I have read them all.—The Poem is extremely fine, and the Similes most beautiful.—There is indeed one little Fault in the Similes.

Apollo. What is that?

Jupiter. There is not the least Resemblance between the Things compared together.

Apollo. One Half of the Simile is good, however.[1]

[1] Cf. *Jonathan Wild*, I. xiv: 'one Part of my Simile is sufficiently apparent, (and indeed, in all these Illustrations one Side is generally much more apparent than the other). . . .'

Jupiter. The Dedications please me extremely, and I am glad to find there are such excellent Men upon Earth.—There is one whom I find two or three Authors agree to be much better than any of us in Heaven are.[1] This Discovery, together with my Wife's Tongue, has determined me to make a Trip to the Earth, and spend some Time in such God-like Company. *Apollo,* will you go with me?

Apollo. I would with all my heart, but I shall be of Disservice to you; for when I was last on Earth, tho' I heard of these People, I could not get Admission to any of them; you had better take *Plutus*[2] with you, he is acquainted with them all.

Jupiter. Hang him, proud Rascal, of all the Deities he is my Aversion; I would have kick'd him out of Heaven long ago, but that I am afraid, if he was to take his Residence entirely upon the Earth, he would foment a Rebellion against me.

Apollo. Your Fear has too just a Ground, for the God of Riches has more Interest there, than all the other Gods put together: Nay, he has supplanted us in all our Provinces; he gives Wit to Men I never heard of, and Beauty to Women *Venus* never saw—Nay, he ventures to make free with *Mars* himself; and sometimes, they tell me, puts Men at the Head of Military Affairs, who never saw an Enemy, nor of whom an Enemy ever could see any other than the Back.[3]

Jupiter. Faith! it is surprizing, that a God whom I sent down to Earth when I was angry with Mankind, and who has done them more Hurt than all the other Deities, should ingratiate himself so far into their Favour.

Apollo. You may thank yourself, you might have made Man wiser if you would.

Jupiter. What, to laugh at? No, *Apollo,* believe me, Man far outdoes my Intention; and when I read in those little Histories called Dedications, how excellent he is grown, I am eager to be with him, that I may make another Promotion to the Stars; and here comes my Son of Fortune to accompany us.

[1] Probably George II. In Jove's determination to visit earth, Fielding doubtless intends a reverse parody of Ovid, *Metam.* I. 210 ff.

[2] Cf. Fielding's translation, with William Young, of the *Plutus* of Aristophanes. On Plutus, symbol of Wealth, see Hesiod, *Theogony,* 969–74, and Diodorus Siculus, v. xlix. 4 and lxxvii. 1–2.

[3] Among many such complaints in Fielding, cf. *Amelia,* XI. ii.

SCENE III

MERCURY, JUPITER, APOLLO

[MERCURY *kneels*.]

Mercury. Pray, Father *Jupiter*, be pleased to bless me.

Jupiter. I do, my Boy. What Part of Heaven, pray, have you been spending your Time in?

Mercury. With some Ladies of your Acquaintance, *Apollo*. I have been at Blind-man's-buff with the Nine Muses: But before we began to play, we had charming Sport between Miss *Thally* and one of the Poets: Such a Scene of Courtship or Invocation as you call it. *Say, O Thalia*, cries the Bard; and then he scratches his Head: And then, *Say, O Thalia*, again; and repeated it an hundred times over; but the devil a Word would she say.

Apollo. She's a humoursome little Jade, and if she takes it into her Head to hold her Tongue, not all the Poets on Earth can open her Lips.

Jupiter. I wish *Juno* had some of her Frolicks, with all my Heart.

Mercury. No, my Mother-in-law[1] is of a Humour quite contrary—

Jupiter. Ay; for which Reason I intend to make an Elopement from her, and pay a short Visit to our Friends on Earth. Son *Mercury*, you shall along with me.

Mercury. Sir, I am at your Disposal: But pray, what is the Reason of this Visit?

Jupiter. Partly my Wife's Temper, and partly some Informations I have lately received, of the prodigious Virtue of Mankind; which if I find as great as represented, I believe I shall leave Madam *Juno* for Good-and-all, and live entirely amongst Men.

Mercury. I shall be glad to be introduced by you into the Company of these virtuous Men; for I am quite weary of the little Rogues you put me at the Head of. The last time I was on the Earth, I believe I had three Sets of my Acquaintance hang'd in one Year's Revolution, and not one Man of any reputable Condition among them; there were indeed one or two condemned,

---

[1] Hermes' mother was, of course, Maia.

but, I don't know how, they were found to be honest at last. And I must tell you, Sir, I will be God of Rogues no longer, if you suffer it to be an establish'd Maxim, that no Rich Man can be a Rogue.

Jupiter. We'll talk of that hereafter. I'll now go put on my travelling Cloaths, order my Charge, and be ready for you in half an Hour.

SCENE IV

APOLLO, MERCURY

Mercury. Do you know the true Reason of this Expedition?

Apollo. The great Virtue of Mankind, he tells us.

Mercury. The little Virtue of Womankind rather—Do you know him no better, than to think he would budge a Step after human Virtue: Besides, Where the devil should he find it, if he would?

Apollo. You have not read the late Dedications of my Votaries.

Mercury. Of my Votaries, you mean: I hope you will not dispute my Title to the Dedications, as the God of Thieves. You make no Distinction, I hope, between robbing with a Pistol and with a Pen.

Apollo. My Votaries Robbers, Mr. *Mercury?*

Mercury. Yes, Mr. *Apollo*; did not my Lord Chancellor *Minos*[1] decree me the Lawyers for the same Reason? Would not he be a Rogue who should take a Man's Money for persuading him he was a Lord or a Baronet, when he knew he was no such Thing? Is not he equally such, who picks his Pocket by heaping Virtues on him which he knows he has no Title to? These Fellows prevent the very Use of Praise, which while only the Reward of Virtue, will always invite Men to it; but when it is to be bought, will be despised by the True Deserving, equally with a Ribbon or a Feather, which may be bought by any one in a Milliner's or a Minister's Shop.[2]

Apollo. Very well! At this Rate you will rob me of all my Panegyrical Writers.

[1] The mythical Cretan king, judge of the shades in the underworld (Homer, *Od.* xi. 568; Plato, *Apol.* 41 a). Cf. *A Journey from This World to the Next*, I. vii, and *The Author's Farce* (rev. edn.), III. i. The text reads 'Midos' (see Textual Notes); this could scarcely be an error for 'Midas', whose story is irrelevant in this context.

[2] Cf. Swift, *Gulliver's Travels*, I. iii.

242Miscellanies

Mercury. Ay, and of your Satirical Writers too, at least a great many of 'em; for unjust Satire is as bad as unjust Panegyrick.

Apollo. If it is unjust indeed—But, Sir, I hope you have no Claim to my Writers of Plays, Poems, which have neither Satire nor Panegyrick in 'em.

Mercury. Yes, Sir, to all who are Thieves and steal from one another.

Apollo. Methinks, Sir, you should not reflect thus on Wits to me, who am the God of Wit.

Mercury. Hey-day, Sir, nor you on Thieves, to me who am the God of Thieves. We have no such Reason to quarrel about our Votaries, they are much of the same Kind: For as it is a Proverb, That all Poets are poor:[1] so is it a Maxim, That all poor Men are Rogues.

Apollo. Sir, Sir, I have Men of Quality that write.

Mercury. Yes, Sir, and I have Men of Quality that rob; but neither are the one Poets, or the other Rogues: For as the one can write without Wit, so can the other rob without Roguery. They call it Privilege, I think;[2] *Jupiter* I suppose gave it them; and instead of quarrelling with one another, I think it would be wiser in us to unite in a Petition to my Father that he would revoke it, and put them on a Footing with our other Votaries.

Apollo. It is in vain to petition him any thing against Mankind at present, he is in such Good-humour with them; if they should sour his Temper, at his Return perhaps he may be willing to do us Justice.

Mercury. It shall be my Fault if he is not in a worse Humour with them; at least, I will take care he shall not be deceived: And that might happen; for Men are such Hypocrites, that the

---

[1] Cf. Marlowe, *Hero and Leander*, i. 469–71; and Burton, *Anat. Melancholy*, i. 2. 3. 15: 'Poetry and Beggary are *gemelli*, twin-born brats, inseparable companions' (ed. Shilleto, i. 350).

[2] '*Privilege of Parliament*, the immunities enjoyed by either house of parliament, or by individual members, as such; as freedom of speech, freedom from arrest in civil matters, the power of committing persons to prison; similarly of other legislative assemblies; so *privilege of peerage, of peers*' (*OED*). Cf. Otway, *Venice Preserv'd*, I. i, where Pierre, having beaten an old lustful Senator, says:

> The Matter was complain'd of in the Senate,
> I summon'd to appear, and censur'd basely,
> For violating something they call *Privilege* . . .

(*Works*, 1768, iii. 234).

greatest Part deceive even themselves, and are much worse than they think themselves to be.

Apollo. And *Jupiter* you know, tho' he is the greatest, is far from being the wisest of the Gods.

Mercury. His own Honesty makes him the less suspicious of others; for, except in regard to Women, he is as honest a Fellow as any Deity in all the *Elysian Fields*: But I shall make him wait for me—Dear Mr. *Apollo*, I am your humble Servant.

Apollo. My dear *Mercury*, a good Journey to you; at your Return, I shall be glad to drink a Bottle of Nectar with you.

Mercury. I shall be proud to kiss your Hands.

The End of the FIRST VOLUME.

APPENDICES

APPENDIX A

OF / TRUE GREATNESS. / An EPISTLE to / The RIGHT HONOURABLE / GEORGE DODINGTON, Esq; / By HENRY FIELDING, Esq; / . . . LONDON: / Printed for C. CORBET, at *Addison's Head* against St. *Dunstan's* / Church, in *Fleetstreet*. 1741.

THE PREFACE

THIS Poem was writ several Years ago, and comes forth now with a very few Additions or Alterations. It could be so properly addressed to no other as to that illustrious Person[1] from whose Conduct and Conversation I actually borrowed the first Hint of the Subject.

It may be perhaps wondered at, that I should chuse a Time, when the public Appetite relishes nothing but Scandal, to publish what is so entirely void of any such Seasoning; and this may seem more strange, when I aver it becomes public almost against the Consent of him to whom it is addressed, whom no Man will be ever paid for praising, nor (which is more surprizing) *by himself* for abusing, from a Fear of being abused again. The true Reason therefore that the World *now* (or perhaps ever) sees this Poem is, that I feel any Calumny thrown on one for whom I have so perfect a Respect much more than he himself, whose Contempt of the dirty *Effluvia* of Malice or Folly, makes no inconsiderable Part of his great Character.[2] This Superiority to Scandal, as it argues an uncommon Dignity in the Mind, so is it most especially necessary at present, when nothing else will defend us against a Set of Ruffians, hired in Disguise and the Dark to butcher the best and worthiest Characters; a Circumstance I have the Honour to know very particularly, since I have fallen severely under their Lash for refusing to be of their Number.

But however base and barbarous such Intentions may be, they have not been executed with perfect Policy: The Arrows by aiming too high have missed what was in their Reach. If they had contented themselves with falling on such as had no Defence but in their Innocence, the Malice might have been effectual; but these were not sufficient Incense to *Baal*;[3] it was not an adequate Retaliation of a little Ridicule and Satyr against some of the

---

[1] On Bubb Dodington, see above, p. 19 and n.

[2] Dodington had been severely handled by the press for following the Duke of Argyle into the ranks of the Opposition; in the famous political print, *The Motion*, which appeared in February 1741, a month after Fielding's poem, Dodington was portrayed as a carriage-dog at Argyle's feet (see M. Dorothy George, *English Political Caricature*, Oxford, 1959, i. 89 and Plate 26).

[3] Jer. 7: 9, among other passages.

most pernicious Vermin that ever infected a Common-Wealth, to vent their Scurrility on such as were barely innocent. An *Argyle*, a *Chesterfield*, a *Dodington*, a *Pulteney*,[1] a *Lyttleton*, the brightest Characters must be sullied in Revenge; but alas! the Reverse of their Design hath happened, instead of blackening such Characters, their Ink hath contracted a Whiteness from them, and ever since whitens all those it is cast on.

For my own Part, I may truly say, I have had more of this Whitening than my Share, or than I believe was ever before applied to one of my very little Consequence in the World. Indeed, I have been often so little conscious of the Merit, that if they had not laid violent Hands on some Letters of my Name, I should not have known for whom the Picture was designed; for besides the Imputation of Vices (particularly Ingratitude)[2] which my Nature abhors, as much at least as any one Man breathing, I have been often censured for Writings which I never saw till published, and which if I had known them, and could have prevented it, never should have been published.[3] I can truly say I have not to my Knowledge, ever personally reflected on any Man breathing, not even One, who has basely injured me, by misrepresenting an Affair which he himself knows, if thoroughly disclosed, would shew him in a meaner Light than he hath been yet exposed in.[4]

But to talk of himself is rarely excusable in a Writer, and never but in one, who is otherwise a Man of Consequence; and, tho' I have been obliged with Money to silence my Productions, professedly and by Way of Bargain given me for that Purpose, tho' I have been offered my own Terms to exert my Talent of Ridicule (as it was called) against some Persons (dead and living) whom I shall never mention but with Honour, tho' I have drawn my Pen in Defence of my Country, have sacrificed to it the Interest of myself and Family, and have been the standing Mark of honourable Abuse for so doing; I cannot yield to all these Persuasions to arrogate to myself a Character of more Consequence than (what in spite of the whole World I shall ever enjoy in my own Conscience) of a Man who hath readily done all the Good in his little Power to Mankind, and never did, or had even the least Propensity to do, an Injury to any one Person.

---

[1] At this date William Pulteney was still a hero to the Opposition; see above, Introduction, p. xiv.

[2] In the pamphlet by 'Marforio' called *An Historical View of the . . . Political Writers in Great Britain,* published in October 1740, the editor of the *Champion,* 'one F—ng, Son to a General Officer of that Name' was cited as 'a strong Instance of Ingratitude to the Ministry, as he lies under the strongest Obligations to Sir R—rt W—le' (p. 49).

[3] Cf. the like complaint in the preface to the *Miscellanies,* above, p. 14.

[4] This also seems to be a reaction to the *Historical View,* above, which declared that Fielding had once been rescued by Walpole 'when he was arrested in a Country-Town'; and that 'Soon after he libelled him personally in a Satyr . . .' (pp. 49–50).

APPENDIX B

(See p. 56 n.)

[From *The Gentleman's Magazine*, viii (December 1738), p. 653]

To Sir R. W——LE.

SIR,
    WHILE at helm of state you ride,
The nation's envy, and its pride;
While foreign courts with wonder gaze,
And justly all your counsels praise,
Which in contempt of *faction's* force,   5
Steer, tho' oppos'd, a steady course;
Wou'd you not wonder, SIR, to view
Your BARD as great a man as you,
And yet the sequel proves it true.
You know, SIR, certain ancient fellows,   10
Philosophers, and others, tell us,
That no alliance e'er between
Greatness and *happiness* is seen;
If so, may heav'n still deny
To YOU to be as great as *I.*   15
Besides, we're taught it does behove us
To think those greater who're above us;
Another instance of my glory,
Who live above you twice two story;
And from my garret can look down,   20
As from an hill, on half the town.
Greatness by *poets* still is painted
With many followers acquainted;
This, too, does in my favour speak,
Your levee is but twice a week;   25
From mine I can exclude but one day,
My door is quiet on a *sunday.*
The distance, too, at which they bow,
Does my superior greatness shew;
Familiar you to admiration   30
May be approach'd by half the nation;
While I, like great *Mogul* of *Indo,*
Am never seen but at a window.
The family that dines the latest,

Is in our street esteem'd the greatest;   35
But greater him we surely call
Who hardly deigns to dine at all.
If with my greatness you're offended,
The fault is easily amended;
You have it, SIR, within your power   40
To bring your humble servant lower.

F——G

Collation (substantive only) with text of the poem in Robert Dodsley's *A Collection of Poems in Six Volumes*, 1758, v. 117–18.

[title]; A LETTER to Sir ROBERT WALPOLE. By the late HENRY FIELDING, 1 helm; the ~   2 The; Our   8 as great a man as; a greater man than 16 does; doth   17 greater; better   31 half; all   32 of; in   41 bring; take   [signature omitted]

APPENDIX C

[From *The Champion*, No. 84 (27 May 1740), p. 1]

The following Verses were writ some Years ago, / by one of the Family of the *Vinegars*, on a / Half-penny; which a young Lady gave to a / Beggar, and the Author purchased at the Price of Half a Crown.

> DEAR, pretty, little fav'rite Ore,
> Which once enlarg'd MARIA's Store;
> Not for the Treasures yet untold,
> Of W[ALPOL]E's Self shouldst thou be sold;
> Not for the larger, mighty Mass,
> Which Misers wish or M[arlboroug]h has;
> Not for what INDIA sends to SPAIN,
> Nor all the Riches of the Main.
> Possessing thee I ask no more,
> Possessing thee I can't be poor;
> None can be richer, unless he
> Who owns the Fair who once had thee.
> Thee while alive my Breast shall have,
> My Hand shall grasp thee in the Grave;
> Nor shalt thou be to PETER giv'n,
> 'Tho he should keep me out of Heav'n.[1]

[1] Alluding to the Roman Catholick Custom of Peter-Pence. [Fielding's note.]

APPENDIX D

PHILOSOPHICAL TRANSACTIONS

For *Thursday, January* 13. and *Thursday, January* 21. 1742–3.

The CONTENTS

Several Papers *relating to the* Fresh-water POLYPUS, *an* Insect, *which has this surprising* Property, *that being cut into several Pieces, each Piece lives, and in a short time becomes as perfect an Insect, as that of which it was originally only a Part.*

Abstract of Part of a Letter from the Honourable William Bentinck, *Esq;* F.R.S. *to* Martin Folkes, *Esq;* Pr.R.S. *communicating the following Paper from Mons.* Trembley, *of the* Hague.

SIR, *Hague, Jan.* 15. N.S. 1743.
    What I here send you inclos'd will, I hope, answer the Queries of your last Letter. Mr. *Trembley*, the Gentleman who has made the Observations on the Insects, has drawn this Extract from his Journal: And I can answer for the Truth of the Facts therein contained, as there is not one of them but what I have seen repeated above Twenty times. I send you the Paper in *French*, not having had Time to translate it. I wish others may be encouraged to try the Experiments over-again, and satisfy themselves of the Truth, by their own Eyes. The Insects may certainly be found in *England*, if carefully lookt for, especially by such as are accustomed to such Enquiries. However, if that should be found difficult, it may be easy to send some over to you: And Mr. *Trembley* will give Directions how to keep and feed them; for he makes himself a *Point d'honneur* of being communicative, and concealing nothing of what he knows about them. If therefore you have any Doubt, or want any further Information, please only to write to me, or to him, and you shall be sure of an Answer, by the first Opportunity. I pray to be kindly remembred—*&c.*

The Figure of the Fresh-water Polypus, *sticking to a Twig.*

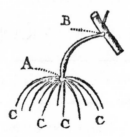

Observations and Experiments upon the Fresh-water P O L Y P U S, *by Monsieur* Trembley, *at the* Hague. *Translated from the* French *by* P.H.Z. *F.R.S.*

The Animal in question is an aquatick Insect, of which mention is made in the *Philosophical Transactions* for the Year 1703. No. 283. *Art.* IV. *pag.* 1307, and No. 288. *Art.* I. *pag.* 1494.

It is represented in the Figure annexed. Its Body *AB.* which is pretty slender, has on its anterior Extremity *A.* several Horns *AC.* which serve it instead of Legs and Arms, and which are yet slenderer than the Body. The Mouth of the *Polypus* is in that anterior Extremity; it opens into the Stomach, which takes up the whole Length of the Body *AB.* This whole Body forms but one Pipe; a sort of a Gut, which can be open'd at both Ends.

The Length of the Body of a *Polypus* varies according to its different Species, and according to many other Circumstances, to be mentioned hereafter. / [p. 4]

I know two Species, of which I have seen some Individuals extend their Bodies to the Length of an Inch and a half; but this is uncommon. Few are generally found above 9 or 10 Lines long; and even these are of the larger Kind.

The Body of the *Polypus* can contract itself, so as not to be above a Line, or thereabouts, in Length.

Both in contracting and extending itself, it can stop at any Degree imaginable, between that of the greatest Extension, and of the greatest Contraction.

The Length of the Arms of the *Polypus* differs also according to the several Species: Those of one of the Species that I know, can be extended to the Length of seven Inches at least.

The Number of Legs or Arms is not always the same in the same Species. One seldom sees in a *Polypus*, come to its full Growth, fewer than six.

The same may be said of the Extension, and of the Contraction of the Arms, which I have said concerning the Body.

The Body and the Arms admit of Inflexion in all their Parts, and that in all manner of Ways.

From the different Degrees of Extension, Contraction, and Inflexion, which the Body and the Arms of the *Polypus* admit of, results a great Variety of Figures, which they can form themselves into.

These Insects do not swim, they crawl upon all the Bodies they meet with in the Water, upon the Ground, upon Plants, upon Pieces of Wood, &c.

Their most common Position is, to fix themselves by their posterior End *B.* to something, and so stretch their Body and Arms forwards into the Water. / [p. 5]

They make use of their progressive Motion, to place themselves conveniently, so as to catch their Prey. They are voracious Animals: Their Arms extended into the Water, are so many Snares which they set for Numbers of small Insects that are swimming there. As soon as any of them touches one of the Arms, it is caught.

The *Polypus* being seized of a Prey, conveys it to his Mouth, by contracting or bending his Arm. If the Prey be strong enough to make Resistance, he makes use of several Arms.

A *Polypus* can master a Worm twice or thrice as long as himself. He seizes it, he draws it to his Mouth, and what is more, swallows it whole.

If the Worm comes endways to the Mouth, he swallows it by that End; if not, he makes it enter double into his Stomach, and the Skin of the *Polypus* gives way. The Size of the Stomach extends itself so as to take in a much larger Bulk than that of the *Polypus* itself, before it swallowed that Worm. The Worm is forced to make several Windings and Folds in the Stomach but does not keep there long alive; the *Polypus* sucks it, and after having drawn from it what serves for his Nourishment, he voids the Remainder by his Mouth, and these are his Excrements. According as the Weather is more or less hot, the *Polypus* eats more or less, oftener or less often.

They grow in Proportion to what they eat; they can bear to be whole Months without eating, but then they waste in Proportion to their Fasting.

The Observations related in the *Philosophical Transactions*, principally concern the Manner in / [p. 6] which these insects multiply. What is there said of them, is true and exact. The more one searches into the Manner how a *Polypus* comes from the Body of its Parent, the more evidently is one persuaded, that it is done by a true Vegetation.

There is not on the Body of a *Polypus* any distinguished Place, by which they bring forth their Young. I have some of them, that have greatly multiplied under my Eyes, and of which I might almost say, that they have produced young ones, from all the exterior Parts of their Body.

A *Polypus* does not always put forth a single young one at a time; it is a common thing to find those which produce five or six: I have kept some which have put forth nine or ten at the same Time, and when one dropt off, another came in its Place.

These Insects seem so many Stems from which issue many Branches. I have learned by a continual Attention to two Species of them, that all the Individuals of these Species produce young ones.

I have for two Years had under my Eye thousands of them; and though I have observed them constantly, and with Attention, I never observed any thing like Copulation.

Upon Supposition, that this Copulation is perform'd in some secret Manner: I tried at first to be sure it had not Place between two of them, after they were severed from the Body of their Parent. To this end, I took young ones, the Moment they came from the Parent, which was alone in a Glass; or I even parted them with Scissars: Each of these young ones I put into perfect Solitude, I fed them every one separately in a Glass; they all multiplied, not only / [p. 7] themselves, but also their Offsprings, which from Generation to Generation, as far as the Seventh, were all confined to Solitude with the same Precaution.

Another Fact, which I have observed, has proved to me, that they have the Faculty of multiplying, before they are severed from their Parent. I have seen a *Polypus*, still adhering, bring forth young ones; and those young ones themselves have also brought forth others. Upon Supposition, that perhaps there was some Copulation between the Parent and young ones, whilst they were yet united; or between the young ones coming from the Body of the same Parent; I made divers Experiments, to be sure of the Fact; but not one of those Experiments ever led me to any thing that could give the Idea of a Copulation.

The *Polypus* multiplies more or less, as he is more or less fed, and as the Weather is more or less warm. If plenty of Food, and a sufficient Degree of Warmth concur, they multiply prodigiously.

I now proceed to the Singularities resulting from the Operations I have tried upon them.

If the Body of a *Polypus* is cut into two Parts transversly, each of those Parts becomes a complete *Polypus*. On the very Day of the Operation, the first Part, or anterior End of the *Polypus*, that is, the Head, the Mouth, and the Arms; this Part, I say, lengthens itself, it creeps, and eats.

The second Part, which has no Head, gets one; a Mouth forms itself, at the anterior End; and shoots forth Arms. This Reproduction comes about more or less quickly, according as the Weather is more or less warm. In Summer, I have seen Arms begin to / [p. 8] sprout out 24 Hours after the Operation, and the new Head perfected in every respect in a few Days.

Each of those Parts, thus become a perfect *Polypus*, performs absolutely all its Functions. It creeps, it eats, it grows, and it multiplies; and all that, as much as a *Polypus* which never had been cut.

In whatever Place the Body of a *Polypus* is cut, whether in the Middle, or more or less near the Head, or the posterior Part, the Experiment has always the same Success.

If a *Polypus* is cut transversly, at the same Moment, into three or four Parts, they all equally become so many complete ones.

The Animal is too small to be cut at the same time into a great Number of Parts; I therefore did it successively. I first cut a *Polypus* into four Parts, and let them grow; next, I cut those Quarters again; and at this rate I proceeded, till I had made 50 out of one single one: And here I stopp'd, for there would have been no End of the Experiment.

I have now actually by me several Parts of the same *Polypus*, cut into Pieces above a Year ago; since which time, they have produced a great Number of young ones.

A *Polypus* may also be cut in two, lengthways. Beginning by the Head, one first splits the said Head, and afterwards the Stomach: The *Polypus* being in the Form of a Pipe, each Half of what is thus cut lengthways forms a Half-pipe; the anterior Extremity of which is terminated by the half of the Head, the half of the Mouth, and Part of the Arms. It is not long before the two Edges of those Half-pipes close, after the Operation: They generally begin at the / [p. 9] posterior Part, and close up by degrees to the anterior Part. Then, each Half-pipe becomes a Whole-one, complete: A Stomach is formed, in which nothing is wanting; and out of each Half-mouth a Whole-one is formed also.

I have seen all this done in less than an Hour; and that the *Polypus*, produced from each of those Halves, at the End of that time did not differ from the Whole-ones, except that it had fewer Arms; but in a few Days more grew out.

I have cut a *Polypus*, lengthways, between Seven and Eight in the Morning; and between Two and Three in the Afternoon, each of the Parts has been able to eat a Worm as long as itself.

If a *Polypus* is cut lengthways, beginning at the Head, and the Section is not carried quite through; the Result is, a *Polypus* with two Bodies, two Heads, and one Tail. Some of those Bodies and Heads may again be cut, lengthways, soon after. In this manner I have produced a *Polypus* that had seven Bodies, as many Heads, and one Tail. I afterwards, at once, cut off the seven Heads of this new *Hydra*: Seven others grew again; and the Heads, that were cut off, became each a complete *Polypus*.

I cut a *Polypus*, transversly, into two Parts: I put these two Parts close to each other again, and they reunited where they had been cut. The *Polypus*, thus reunited, eat the Day after it had undergone this Operation: It is since grown, and has multiplied.

I took the posterior Part of one *Polypus*, and the anterior of another, and I have brought them to reunite in the same manner as the foregoing: Next

Day, the *Polypus* that resulted, eat: It has continued well these / [p. 10] two Months, since the Operation: It is grown, and has put forth young ones, from each of the Parts of which it was formed. The two foregoing Experiments do not always succeed; it often happens, that the two Parts will not join again.

In order to comprehend the Experiment I am now going to speak of, one should recollect, that the whole Body of a *Polypus* forms only one Pipe, a sort of Gut, or Pouch.

I have been able to turn that Pouch, that Body of the *Polypus*, inside-outwards; as one may turn a Stocking.

I have several by me, that have remained turned in this manner; their Inside is become their Outside, and their Outside their Inside: They eat, they grow, and they multiply, as if they had never been turned.

Facts like these I have related, to be admitted, require the most convincing Proofs. I venture to say, I am able to produce such Proofs.

They arise from the Detail of my Experiments, from the Precautions I have taken to avoid all Uncertainties, from the Care I have used to repeat the same Experiment several times, from the Assiduity and Attention with which I have observed them.

All this would require a Discussion too long to be here related.

I might also appeal to the Quality and the Number of the Persons who have been Witnesses to these Facts; as well of those who have seen *me* observe, as of those who have observed *themselves*.

For Brevity-sake, I have omitted several curious and material Facts. / [p. 11]

If any Persons in *England* shall be desirous to make Observations on the *Polypus*, and to repeat my Experiments; I hope I shall be able to send some over, in case they shall not be found there.

They are to be look'd for in such Ditches whose Water is stock'd with small Insects. Pieces of Wood, Leaves, aquatic Plants, in short, every thing is to be taken out of the Water, that is met with at the Bottom, or on the Surface of the Water, on the Edges, and in the Middle of the Ditches. What is thus taken out, must be put into a Glass of clear Water, and these Insects, if there are any, will soon discover themselves; especially if the Glass is let stand a little, without moving it; for thus the Insects, which contract themselves when they are first taken out, will again extend themselves when they are at Rest, and become thereby so much the more remarkable.

In order to feed them, one must know how to provide one's self with Insects fit for their Food.

If that is thought necessary, I will point out the Means I make use of for that Purpose.

I am ready to impart to every one who shall desire to make Observations on these Animals, all the Means and Contrivances I have used; to enable them to practise the same, and to judge of them.

I shall set forth all these Means and Contrivances in the History of the *Polypus*, which I am now at work upon. But if, before its Publication, any Informations should be desired, I again repeat, that I shall be ready and willing to furnish them.

TEXTUAL APPENDICES

ABBREVIATIONS

W   Wesleyan edition.
M   *Miscellanies,* 1st edition 1743.
1741   *Of True Greatness,* 1st edition 1741.
1743   *Some Papers Proper to be Read before the R—l Society,*
       1st edition 1743.

APPENDIX I

List of Substantive Emendations

19   *om.*] M; THE PREFACE . . . Person 1741 (see Appendix A).
25.3   *H—cote*] M; *G—schal* 1741.
29.26   *om.*] M; *FINIS* 1741.
204.12 ff. *POSTSCRIPT* . . . swarmed] M; *FINIS* 1743.
223.11   Tears] W; Fears M.
228.4   *Arbela*] W; *Artela* M.
234.20   often] W; only M.
241.22   *Minos*] W; *Midos* M.

[NOTE. The following individual title-pages in M have been cancelled in
W: *Of True Greatness; An Essay on Conversation; An Essay on the Knowledge of the Characters of Men; An Essay on Nothing; The First Olynthiac of
Demosthenes; Of the Remedy of Affliction for the Loss of Our Friends;* and
A Dialogue between Alexander the Great and Diogenes the Cynic. The title-
page for *Some Papers Proper to be Read before the R—l Society* has been
kept, as integral to the text; and the material contained on the title-page of
An Interlude between Jupiter, Juno, Apollo, and Mercury has been inserted
in place of the second title.]

APPENDIX II

List of Accidentals Emendations

4.4	*Essay on*] W; Essay on M.
12.18	*Iliad*] W; Iliad M.
23.24	him, and *Seneca*,] M; him and *Seneca* 1741.
23.26	Occasion, he can] M; Occasion he, can 1741.
24.15	Name,] M; ~ₐ 1741.
26.23	succeed,] M; ~ₐ 1741.
36.19	Brutus'] W; ~ₐ M.
47.20	Stock,] W; ~. M.
47.23	Hence, should] W; Hence should, M.
49.14	Friend sure knows,] W; Friend, sure knows M.
50.2	blind,] W; ~. M.
58.2	Ascendance.] W; ~ₐ M.
58.5	in] W; *in* M.
59.7	Lie?] W; ~, M.
100.21	[Tres rugae subeant et se cutis arida laxet] W; *om.* M.
101.7	away.] W; ~? M.
113.33	tickle,] W; ~ₐ M.
136.12	Appellation] W; Appellati-/tion M.
137.21	Species?] W; ~. M.
154.24	This] W; *This* M.
156.14	open,] W; ~ₐ M.
158.5	glavering,] W; ~ₐ M.
162.6	judicious] W; judi-/dicious M.
162.12	cheerful,] W; ~ₐ M.
162.15	glavering,] W; ~ₐ M.
168.7	Mankind?] W; ~. M.
168.9	against?] W; ~. M.
171.21	Shame?] W; ~. M.
199.24	Substances,] W; ~ₐ 1743, M.
201.4	*Whole-one*] M; *whole-one* 1743.
202.10	twenty-two] W; twenty two 1743.
208.9	wherever] W; where-/ever M.
208.16	fell] W; fill M.
208.19	*Pæonians*,] W; ~ₐ M.
211.8	think,] W; ~ₐ M.
224.31	*postremaque*] W; *posttremaque* M.
228.10	Tranquillity?] W; ~. M.
241.23	Reason?] W; ~. M.
248.4	alas] W; alass 1741.
248.13	least] W; lest 1741.

APPENDIX III

Word-Division

1. *End-of-the-Line Hyphenation in the Wesleyan Edition*

[NOTE. The following compounds, hyphenated at the eud of the line in the Wesleyan edition, are hyphenated within the line in the copy-text. Hyphenated compounds in which both elements are capitalized are not included.]

127.25	high-	flown
140.33	Pre-	eminence
148.36	well-	bred
152.28	high-	titled
164.13	with-	hold
198.26	Young-	ones
258.8	inside-	outwards

2. *End-of-the-Line Hyphenation in the Copy-Text*

[NOTE. The following compounds, or possible compounds, are hyphenated at the end of the line in the copy-text. The form in which they have been given in the Wesleyan edition, as listed below, represents the usual practice of the copy-text in so far as it may be ascertained from other appearances.]

122.29	presupposes		176.32	Mankind
126.5	overlook		186.5	Nobleman
127.12	Mankind		194.4	abovementioned
140.15	undervalue		199.14	Young-ones
142.6	Well-being		207.32	Thanksgivings
145.11	postponed		221.7	outwitted
147.2	Ill-nature		225.10	Friendship
152.26	Ill-nature		234.6	Friendship
156.14	Mankind		237.5	Mankind
158.6	Mankind		240.10	Courtship
159.17	good-natured		242.24	Good-humour
164.7	Highwayman		257.21	Whole-one
165.31	Friendship		257.26	Whole-ones
174.30	Blind-sides			

3. *Special Cases*

[NOTE. The following compounds, or possible compounds, are hyphenated at the end of the line in both the Wesleyan edition and the copy-text.]

138.2	pre-	conceived	232.3	poor-	spirited
176.15	Hemi-	sphere			

APPENDIX IV

Historical Collation

19.   *om.*] THE PREFACE . . . Person 1741 (see Appendix A).
25.3   *H—cote*] *G—schal* 1741.
29.26   *om.*] *FINIS* 1741.
201.16   *seven*] *several* M.
204.12 ff. *POSTSCRIPT* . . . swarmed] *FINIS* 1743.
223.11   Tears] Fears M.
228.4   *Arbela*] *Artela* M.
234.20   often] only M.
241.22   *Minos*] *Midos* M.

APPENDIX V

Bibliographical Description of Miscellanies, by Henry Fielding, Volume One.

(1) *Miscellanies*, 'First Edition' (coarse and fine paper).

General Title: MISCELLANIES, | BY | *Henry Fielding* Esq; | In THREE VOLUMES. | ['*vase*' *ornament*] | *LONDON:* Printed for the AUTHOR: | And sold by A. MILLAR, opposite to | *Catharine-Street*, in the *Strand.* | MDCCXLIII.

Volume Title: MISCELLANIES, | BY | *Henry Fielding* Esq; | VOL. I. | ['*rabbit*' *ornament*] | *LONDON:* | Printed for the AUTHOR: | And sold by A. MILLAR, opposite to | *Catharine-Street*, in the *Strand.* | MDCCXLIII.

Collation: 8vo: πA(8 leaves) a(5 leaves) b–c⁸ d 1. 2, 3 A–Y⁸ Z1, $4 (–B4, T4, X2) signed, 209 leaves, pp. [*26*] *i* ii–xxxvii *xxxviii, 1–3* 4–115 *116* 117–178 *179–180* 181–227 *228–230* 231–251 *252–254* 255 *256* 257–277 *278–280* 281–294 *295–296* 297–322 *323–324* 325–340 *341–342* 343–354 (misnumbering xxxiii–xxxvii as xxxi, xxviii, xxix, xxvi, xxvii; 255 as 254).

Contents: πA1: general title (verso blank). πA2: volume title (verso blank). πA3: 'LIST OF SUBSCREBERS' [*sic*]. p. i [b 1]: 'PREFACE.' p. 1 [A1]: 'OF TRUE GREATNESS.' p. 15: 'OF GOOD-NATURE.' p. 20: 'LIBERTY.' p. 26: 'TO A FRIEND ON THE CHOICE of a WIFE.' p. 36: 'TO *JOHN HAYES*, Esq;' p. 38: [shorter poems]. p. 72: 'JUVENALIS SATYRA SEXTA.' p. 73: 'PART OF *Juvenal*'s Sixth SATIRE, MODERNIZED IN BURLESQUE VERSE.' p. 114: 'TO Miss H—AND at *Bath*.' p. 115: 'AN ESSAY ON CONVERSATION.' p. 179: 'AN ESSAY ON THE KNOWLEDGE OF THE Characters of Men.' p. 229: 'AN ESSAY ON *NOTHING*.' p. 253: 'SOME PAPERS PROPER to be Read before the R—L SOCIETY.' p. 279: 'THE FIRST OLYNTHIAC OF *DEMOSTHENES*.' p. 295: 'OF THE REMEDY OF AFFLICTION For the LOSS of our FRIENDS.' p. 323: 'A DIALOGUE BETWEEN ALEXANDER THE GREAT AND DIOGENES THE CYNIC.' p. 341: 'AN INTERLUDE BETWEEN *Jupiter, Juno, Apollo,* and *Mercury*.' (Pp. xxxviii, 2, 116, 180, 228, 230, 252, 254, 256, 278, 280, 296, 324, 342 blank.)

Running-Titles: 'LIST of Subscribers' πA3ᵛ–a5ᵛ; 'Preface' pp. ii–xxxvii. (No running-titles in text.)

Copies examined: Coarse-paper (demy): Princeton University (Ex 3738. 1743); Houghton Library (*EC7. F460. 743ma); University of Pennsylvania (EC7. F4605. B743m); Peabody Library (828. F459. 1743); fine-paper (royal): Houghton Library (*EC7. F460. 743m); Yale University (Fielding Coll. C743Ac).

(2) *Miscellanies*, 'Second Edition' (coarse paper)

General Title: MISCELLANIES, | BY | *Henry Fielding* Esq; | In Three Volumes. | The Second Edition. | ['*vase*' ornament] | *LONDON:* | Printed for A. Millar, opposite to | *Catharine-Street*, in the *Strand*. | MDCCXLIII.

Volume Title: MISCELLANIES, | BY | *Henry Fielding* Esq; | VOL. I. | The Second Edition. | ['*rabbit*' ornament] | *LONDON:* | Printed for A. Millar, opposite to | *Catharine-Street*, in the *Strand*. | MDCCXLIII.

Collation: 8vo: *a*² b–c⁸ d1. 2, 3 A–Y⁸ Z1, \$4 (–B4, T4, X2) signed, 198 leaves, pp. [*4*] *i* (rest as in 'First Edition').

Contents: a1: general title (verso blank). a2: volume title (verso blank). p. i [b1]: 'Preface.' (rest as in 'First Edition').

Running-Titles: 'Preface.' pp. ii–xxxvii. (No running-titles in text.)

Copies examined: Houghton Library (*EC7. F460. 743mb); Yale University (Fielding Coll. C743b).

(3) *Of True Greatness*, First edition, separately published.

Title: OF | TRUE GREATNESS. | An EPISTLE to | The Right Honourable | *GEORGE DODINGTON*, Esq; | [*rule*] | By HENRY FIELDING, *Esq*; | [*rule*] | [*ornament*] | [*double rule*] | *LONDON:* | Printed for C. Corbet, at *Addison's Head* against *St. Dunstan's* | Church, in *Fleetstreet*. 1741. | [Price One Shilling.]

Collation: fol: π² A–C², \$1 signed, 8 leaves, pp. *1–3* 4–16.

Contents: p. 1: title. p. 2: blank. p. 3: 'THE PREFACE.' p. 5: 'OF TRUE GREATNESS.'

Running-titles: none.

Copies examined: Houghton Library (*fEC7. F460. 7410); Yale University (Fielding Coll. 741n).

(4) *Some Papers Proper to be Read before the R—l Society*, First Edition, separately published.

Title: SOME | PAPERS | Proper to be Read before the | R—L SOCIETY, | Concerning the | Terrestrial Chrysipus, | GOLDEN-FOOT or GUINEA; | AN | INSECT, or VEGETABLE, resem- | bling the Polypus, which hath this sur- | prising Property, That being cut into several | Pieces, each Piece becomes a perfect Animal, | or Vegetable, as complete as that of which it | was originally only a Part. | [*rule*] | COLLECTED | *By PETRUS GUALTERUS,* | But not Published till after His Death. | [*double rule*] | *LONDON:* | Printed for J. Roberts, near the *Oxford-Arms,* | in *Warwick-Lane.* 1743. | [Price Sixpence.]

Collation: 4to: A–D⁴, $2 (–A1) signed, 16 leaves, pp. *1–4* 5–31.

Contents: p. 1: title. p. 2: blank. p. 3: 'The CONTENTS'. p. 4: blank p. 5: 'Abstract of *Part* of a Letter. . . .' p. 7: '*Observations and Experiments upon the* Terrestrial Chrysipus. . . .'

Running-titles: none.

Copies examined: Princeton University (Ex 3738. 386); Houghton Library (*EC7. F460. 743s); Yale University (Fielding Coll. 743s).

INDEX OF NAMES AND PLACES

IN INTRODUCTION, TEXT, APPENDICES, AND NOTES

(Fielding's own notes distinguished by an asterisk)

A., D., *Whole Art of Converse*, xxxiv.

Accius, Roman actor, in Juvenal, 92.

Account of the Life of Mrs. Susannah Maria Cibber, 89 n.

Adams, Joseph Quincy, 231 n.

Addison, Joseph, 91 n.; *The Campaign*, 23 n., quoted: 35 n., 41 n.; *Cato*, 41 n., 53, 53 n., 64 n., quoted: 39 n.; *Freeholder*, 193 n.; *Guardian*, quoted: 135 n. (see also *Guardian*); *Letter from Italy*, quoted: 40 n., opening imitated by F, 54 n.; *Poem to His Majesty*, 23 n., quoted: 32 n., 41 n.; *Spectator*, xli n., 177 n., quoted: 164 n. (see also *Spectator*); *Tatler*, quoted: 126 n., 132 n. (see also *Tatler*); trans. of Virgil's *Fourth Georgic*, quoted: 55 n.

Adlerfeld, Gustaf, *Military History of Charles XII*, trans. by F, xii.

Aelian (Claudius Aelianus), *Variae historiae*, 105 n.

Aemilian Bridge, in Juvenal, 88.

Aeneas, 105. *See also* Virgil, *Aeneid*.

Aeschines, 205 n.

Aesop, *Fables*, 149, 149 n.

Aganippe, nymph of Helicon, 69 n.

Agincourt, battle of, 41, 41 n.

Agrippa I, king of Judah, 103 n.

Agrippa II, 103, 103 n.

A— House, 77.

Akenside, Mark, *A British Philippic*, xlii n.

Alcmena, and Jupiter, 62, 62 n., 237 n.

Aldgate Pump, 167, *167 n.

Alexander the Great, xl–xli, xl n., xli n.(3), 226 ff., *226 n., 228 n.(2); English attacks on, xli n., 23 n., 229 n., 230 n.; F's censure of, xli n., 21, 22, 188. *See also* F's *Dialogue between Alexander the Great and Diogenes the Cynic*.

Allen, Ralph, F's patron, xvi, xvi n., xlviii, 36 n., 91 n.

Ambrosius, Roman flute-player, in Juvenal, 94.

Amory, Hugh, xliv n.

Amphion, king of Thebes, 104, 105, *105 n.

Amphipolis, in Demosthenes' oration, 206, 207, 208.

Anacreon, 72 n.; Anacreontics, xxviii, 70 n.

Anaxagoras, 216 n.

Andrew, Sarah, of Lyme Regis, 3 n., 85 n.

Anne, queen of England, 85, 111 n., 195 n., 199 n.

Antiochus, tutor of Cicero, xviii n.

Antiope, and Jupiter, 237 n.

Aphrodite, *see* Venus.

Apollo, 104, *105 n., 236, 238 ff. *See also* F's *Interlude*.

Apollodorus, *Bibliotheca*, 60 n., 62 n., 71 n.

Apulia, Italy, *103 n.

Arachne, 69, 69 n., 70 n.

Arbela, battle of, 228, 228 n.

Arbuthnot, Dr. John, *History of John Bull*, 81 n., quoted: 64 n.

Archigenes, Roman physician, in Juvenal, 110.

Arcturus, star, 118, 118 n.

Argos, 183 n.; Argive, 183.

Argus Panoptes, 71, 71 n.

Argyle (Argyll), John Campbell, 2nd Duke of, 25 n., 29 n.; compliment to, 25, 28, 152, 248; leader of Opposition, xiii, xiii n., 247 n.

Aristides, xxxiii n.

Aristophanes, xvii, xxxix. *See also* F's trans. of *Plutus*.

Aristotle, 142, 143(2), 143 n., 158 n., 196; as a 'mental physician', 214 n.; *De motu animalium*, 143 n.; *Historia animalium*, 154 n., 197 n.; *Metaphysics*, 180 n.; *Nicomachean Ethics*, 134 n., 149 n., 188 n., quoted: 20 n., 122 n.; *Physics*, 143 n., 180 n.; *Physiognomonica* (attrib.), 156, 156 n.; *Politics*, 38 n., 119 n., 154 n., 167 n., 189 n.

Aristotle's Master-Piece, 196, 196 n.

Arlington Street, 57, *57 n.

Armada, the Spanish, 115.

Armstrong, John, *Art of Preserving Health*, 30 n.

Arrian (Flavius Arrianus), *Anabasis Alexandri*, 226 n., 227 n., 228 n.(3).

Art of Complaisance, by 'S. C.', xxxiv.

Art of Pleasing in Conversation, see Ortigue.

Arymba, in Demosthenes' oration, 208.

Asia, associated with tyranny, 132, 132 n., 141; expedition of Alexander into, *226 n. *See also* China, India, Persia.

Astraea, 86, 87, 87 n.

Asylus, Roman gladiator, in Juvenal, 112.

Athena (Pallas), 39. *See also* Minerva.

Athenian Sport, 66 n.

Athens, 234; Demosthenes' appeal to, against Philip, 205 ff.

Audra, Émile, *see* Pope.

Augustine, *see* St. Augustine.

Ault, Norman, *see* Pope.

Austrian Succession, War of the, 40 n., 93 n.

Avery, Emmett L., 54 n.

Baal, 247.

Bacon, Sir Francis, 220 n.; *Advancement of Learning*, 174 n.; *Essays*, 146 n., 176 n., quoted: 52 n., 56 n., 122 n., 169 n.; *Sylva Sylvarum*, quoted: 197 n.

Baker, John R., xxxix n.

Baker, Sheridan, vii.

Balguy, John, divine, *The Law of Truth*, quoted: 32 n.

Ballad on George II, quoted: 193 n.

Barber, John, printer, 66 n.

Barbeyrac, Jean, political philosopher, 32 n.

Barnard, Sir John, lord mayor, 25, 25 n.

Barrow, Isaac, sermons: 'Against Foolish Talking and Jesting', 146 n.; 'Maker of Heaven and Earth', 180 n.

Bartholomew Fair, 93, 93 n.

Bateson, F. W., xxxii n. *See also* Pope.

Bath, Earl of, *see* William Pulteney.

Bath, 91, 118.

Bathyllus, Roman dancer, in Juvenal, 92, 93.

Battestin, Martin C., vii, xiii n.(2), xxx n., xxxi n.

Battles, *see* Agincourt, Arbela, Blenheim, Crécy, Granicus, Hydaspes, Issus, Malplaquet.

Bavius, Roman poetaster, 64, 64 n.

Bayle, Pierre, *Dictionary*, 23 n., 103 n.

Baynard, Dr. Edward, *Of Cold Baths*, quoted: 214 n.

Baynton, family of, 113, 113 n.

Beard, John, singer, 95, 95 n.

Bear-Garden, at Hockley-in-the-Hole, 99, 99 n.

Beauchamp, George Seymour, 1st Baron, 7 n.

Bellegarde, Jean Baptiste Morvan de, *Reflexions upon Ridicule*, xxxiv, quoted: xxxv n.

Bennet, Miss (of Salisbury ?), 71, 71 n.

Bentinck, William, F.R.S., 193 n., 253.

Bentley, Richard, classical scholar, 64, 64 n.

Berenice, daughter of Agrippa I, 102, 103, *103 n.

Berkeley, George, essay in *Guardian*, quoted: 122 n.

Bermondspit Hundred, Hampshire, 79 n.

Bernier, François, *History of the Late Revolution*, quoted: 58 n.

Bible, the, 32 n., 167 n.; O.T.: Deuteronomy, 172; Ecclesiastes, 224 n.; Ecclesiasticus, 166 n.; Isaiah, quoted: 170; Jeremiah, 247 n.; Job, quoted: xxxv n., 168; Micah, 166 n.; Proverbs, quoted: 153 n., 168; Psalms, *see* Book of Common Prayer; N. T.: Luke, 171 n., 172 n., 173 n., 174 n.(2), quoted: 124, 137, 166; Mark, 173 n.; Matthew, 35 n., *168 n., 171 n., 173 n., quoted: 124, 162, 166, 168, 171, 172(4), 173, 174(2), 213 n.; Timothy, quoted: 168.

Bickford-Smith, R. A. H., 158 n.

Billingsgate, 237 n.

Biscay, Bay of, 97.

Blackmore, Sir Richard, 184 n.; *Creation*, quoted: 180 n.

Blackstone, Sir William, *Commentaries*, 79 n.

Blackwall, Anthony, *An Introduction to the Classics*, xxxiv n.

Blenheim, battle of, 40 n., 41, 47.

Boas, George, 121 n.

Boheme, Anthony, actor, 64, 64 n.

Boileau, Nicolas, *Satire VIII*, 33 n.

Bolingbroke, Henry St. John, Viscount, 36 n.; *Letters on the Study and Use of History*, quoted: 178 n., 181 n.

Book of Common Prayer, Psalms in, quoted: 221 n.

Booth, Barton, actor, 27, 27 n., 53 n., 64, 64 n.

Boulton, William B., 111 n.

Bowers, Fredson, vii, li n., Textual Introduction, l–lv.

Bowyer, William, the younger, printer of F's *Miscellanies*, Vol. III.

Bowyer's Grammar, see Abel Boyer.

Boyce, Benjamin, xvi n., xxxviii n.

Boyer, Abel, *The Compleat French Master*, 107, 107 n.

Boyle, Robert, 49 n.

Bradner, Leicester, 166 n.

Brauer, George C., Jr., xxxiv n.

Bredvold, Louis I., xxxii n.

Brewster, Dr. Thomas, 118 n., 119 n.; compliment to, 118, 150; trans. *Satires of Persius*, 119 n., 150 n., quoted: 150.

Britannicus, son of empress Messalina, 100.

Brooke, Henry, *Gustavus Vasa*, xi.

Browne, J. P., edition of Fielding, xlix.

Browne, Sir Thomas, *Pseudodoxia epidemica*, 159 n.; *Religio Medici*, 147 n., 213 n., 221 n., quoted: 24 n., 156 n., 182 n., 232 n.

Brute, mythical king of Britain, 85, *85 n.

Brutus, Marcus Junius, xxxiii n., 12, 213.

Buckingham, George Villiers, 2nd Duke of, *The Rehearsal* (with others), 45 n.

Buckingham, John Sheffield, Duke of, *Julius Caesar*, quoted: 123, 123 n.

Budgell, Eustace, *Memoirs of the Late Earl of Orrery*, quoted: 49 n.

Burkitt, William, *Expository Notes on the New Testament*, 172 n., quoted: 172, 173(2), 174.

Burton, Robert, *Anatomy of Melancholy*, 21 n., 31 n., 137 n., quoted: 43 n., 45 n., 49 n., 60 n., 72 n., 141 n., 142 n., 155 n., 177 n., 242 n.

Butler, Samuel, 66, 66 n.; *Genuine Remains*, 143 n., quoted: 81 n., 141 n.; *Hudibras*, quoted: 51 n., 64 n., 117 n. *See also* F's 'Epitaph on Butler's Monument'.

Butt, John, *see* Pope.

C., S., *The Art of Complaisance*, xxxiv.

Caesar, Gaius Julius, 23, 188, 229 n.

Cajanus, the Swedish giant, 139 n.

Calisto, and Jupiter, 237 n.

Callistia: or The Prize of Beauty, 78 n.

Calthrop, Annette, 132 n.

Cambridge University, 51 n.

Camden, Carroll, 157 n.

Campania, Italy, 40.

Canopus, Egypt, 94, *94 n.

Canusium, Italy, in Juvenal, 102, *103 n.

Carew, Thomas, xxviii; poems: 'The Mistake', 118 n.; 'On a Damask-Rose', 60 n., quoted: 73 n.; 'A Prayer to the Wind', quoted: 72 n.; 'The Protestation', 69 n.; 'To A. L. Perswasions to Love', quoted: 61 n.

Caroline of Ansbach, queen of George II, xlii n.

Carpophorus, Roman actor, in Juvenal, 106.

Carteret, John, Baron (later Earl Granville), compliment to, 29; leader of Opposition, 29 n.; mistrusted by F's friends, xiv; not a subscriber to F's *Miscellanies*, xlviii.

Carthage, 104.

Castiglione, Baldassare, xxxiv.

Cato, Marcus Porcius, the Censor, 224 n.

Cato, Marcus Porcius, of Utica, *see* Addison, *Cato*.

Catullus, Gaius Valerius, xxviii, 72 n., *84 n., quoted: 73 n., 80 n.

Cawkwell, G. L., 205 n.

Cecropia (Attica), in Juvenal, 106.

Celsus, Roman jurist, in Juvenal, 110.

Ceres, 90, 90 n., 91, 91 n.

Cervantes Saavedra, Miguel de, xvii.

Chamberlayne, John, *Magna Britanniae Notitia*, 111 n.

Chambers, Ephraim, compiler, *Cyclopaedia*, 197 n., quoted: 79 n.

Champion, The, see Fielding.

Charles II, king of England, 57 n., 179.

Charles XII, king of Sweden, xxix, 229 n.

Charles Street, 99, 99 n.

Charteris, Francis, 67 n.

Chaucer, Geoffrey, xvii.

Cheapside, 25.

Chesterfield, Philip Dormer Stanhope, 4th Earl of, xiii, 12 n., 29 n.; compliment to, 29, 35, 126, 138, 152, 248; *Letters to His Son*, quoted: 132 n.; preface to James Hammond's *Love Elegies*, 179 n., quoted: 185, 185 n.; and Edmund Waller, *Case of the Hanover Forces in the Pay of Great Britain*, 193 n.

Chetwynd, William, licenser of the stage, 8, 8 n.

Cheyne, Dr. George, *The English Malady*, 137 n., quoted: 97 n.

Chinese, 127.

Chrysogonous, Roman singer, in Juvenal, 94.

Churchill, John, *see* Marlborough.

Churchill, Sarah, *see* Marlborough.

Cibber, Mrs. Susannah Maria, 89 n.

Cibber, Theophilus, 89 n., 95, 95 n.

Cicero, Marcus Tullius, 23, 214 n.; common moral and social aims with F, xviii ff.; on consolation, xxxviii, xxxviii n., 212 n., 214 n.; *De amicitia*, 165 n.(2); *De divinatione*, 119, 119 n.; *De finibus*, xviii n., 122 n., 154 n., 174 n., 188 n., quoted: 31 n., 120 n., 154 n.; *De inventione*, 80 n.; *De officiis*, 12 n., 33 n., 41 n., 119 n., 120 n., 149 n., 174 n., 216 n., quoted: 33 n., 220 n., parallel with F's *Miscellanies*, xviii–xxvii; *De oratore*, 159 n.; *De senectute*, 40 n., 225 n., quoted: 224; *Epistulae ad familiares*, xxxviii n., 222 n., 224 n.(2); *In C. Verrem*, 166 n.; *In Catilinam*, quoted: 39 n.; *Pro Caelio*, 85 n.; *Tusculan Disputations*, xxxviii n. 153 n., 212 n., 216 n.(3), 218 n.(2), 220 n.(2), 221 n., 225, 225 n., 226 n.,

Cicero (*cont.*):
227 n., 234 n., quoted: 159 n., 163 n., 188 n., 212, 212 n.
Cincinnatus, Lucius Quinctius, 39, 40 n.
Clarke, Samuel, divine, 181 n.; sermons: 'How to Judge of Moral Actions', 162 n.; 'Of the Several Sorts of Hypocrisy', quoted: 169 n. *See also* Leibniz.
Claudius, Roman emperor, 98.
Clerkenwell Green, 99 n.
Clifford, James L., vii.
Clive, Catherine (Kitty), actress, xlviii, 93, 93 n.
Clodia, sister of Publius Clodius Pulcher, *see* 'Lesbia'.
Clodius (Publius Clodius Pulcher), 85 n.
Cock, Christopher, auctioneer, 113, 113 n.
Cockman, Thomas, trans. Cicero's *De officiis*, xviii ff.
Codrus, poor poet, in Juvenal's *Satires*, 51, 51 n.
Codrus: or The Dunciad Dissected, *see* Elizabeth Thomas.
Coke, Sir Edward, jurist, 167 n.
Coleridge, Samuel Taylor, quoted: xvii.
Coley, William B., vii, xii n., xiii n., xvii n., 193 n.
Colie, Rosalie L., xxxix n.
Colline Gate, Rome, in Juvenal, 114.
Collins, Anthony, deist, 181 n.
Common Sense, xlii n.
Congreve, William, 19 n.; *The Old Bachelor*, quoted: 216 n.; 'To Sir R. Temple: Of Pleasing', quoted: 52 n.
Conversation of Gentlemen Considered, The, xxxiv.
Cooke edition of Blackmore, 180 n.
Coolidge, John S., xxiv n.
Corbet, C., printer, 247.
Corinth, 234; meeting of Alexander and Diogenes at, 226 n.; sack of, by Mummius, 60, 60 n.
Cornelia, mother of the Gracchi, 104, 104 n., 105 n. *See also* Gracchus.
Cornwall, 19, 19 n.
'Corruption Bill', 78, 78 n., 80 n.
Cotton, Charles, *Burlesque upon Burlesque*, xlii n.; *Scarronides, or Virgil Travestie*, quoted: 81 n., 95 n.; trans. Montaigne's *Essays*, *see* Montaigne.
Covent Garden, 99 n., 195 n.
Covent-Garden Journal, *see* Fielding.
Covent-Garden Theatre, 5 n.
Cowley, Abraham, xxviii; poems: 'Against Fruition', quoted: 44 n.; 'Against Hope', quoted: 49 n.; *Davideis*, quoted: 22 n., 56 n.; 'The Given Love', quoted: 60 n.; 'Love Undiscovered', quoted: 70 n.;

'Ode', quoted: 67 n.; 'Ode of Wit', quoted: 182 n.; 'The Thief', 82 n.
Cradock, Catherine, F's sister-in-law, xliv, xliv n., 76 n., 80, 80 n.
Cradock, Charlotte, *see* Charlotte Fielding.
Craftsman, The, 229 n.
Craig, Hardin, 157 n.
Crane, Ronald S., xxx n.
Crashaw, Richard, 'An Hymne of the Nativity', quoted: 20 n.
Crécy, battle of, 41, 41 n.
Creech, William, *Edinburgh Fugitive Pieces*, quoted: xlix.
Creighton, Charles, xvi n.
Crete, 241 n.
Croesus, king of Lydia, 224, 224 n.
Cross, Wilbur L., xii n.(2), xiii n.(2), xv n.(2), xliv n.(2), xlv n., 3 n., 6 n., 15 n., 47 n., 76 n., 85 n., 118 n.
Crowne, John, *Calisto*, xlii n.
Cumberland, Richard, the elder, 32 n.
Cupid, 70–2, 70 n., 72 n., 79.
Curtius, Ernst, 159 n.
Curtius Rufus, Quintus, *De rebus gestis Alexandri Magni*, 228 n.
Cynics, *see* Diogenes.
'Cynthia', of Propertius, 84, *84 n., 85, 85 n.
Cyprus, 40, 40 n., 79 n.
Cythera, 79 n.

Dacia, Roman province, in Juvenal, 106.
Daily Advertiser, xlvii n., xlviii n., 193 n.
Daily Gazetteer, xlii n.; F denies writing for, 14.
Daily Post, xlvi(2), xlvii(2), xlviii n.
Danae, and Jupiter, 60, 60 n., 237 n.
Darius, Persian emperor, 228, 228 n., 232, 233.
Davis, Herbert, xxxiii n. *See also* Swift.
De Castro, J. Paul, 53 n., 118 n.
Defoe, Daniel, *Jure Divino*, 171 n., quoted: 22 n., 38 n., 48 n., 237 n.; *Life of Jonathan Wild*, 8 n.; *Tour thro' Great Britain*, 19 n.; *True and Genuine Account of Jonathan Wild*, 8 n.; *The True-Born Englishman*, quoted: 77 n.
Delhi, India, 58 n.
Demetrius Poliorcetes, 214.
Demosthenes, xi, 167 n., 205 n.; used by Opposition against Walpole, xlii n., 205 n.; *First Olynthiac*, *86 n.; trans. by Fielding, 205–11; *see* F's *The First Olynthiac of Demosthenes*.
Dennis, John, critic, 64, 64 n.
Descartes, René, *Discours de la méthode*, 120 n.
Descent of the Heathen Gods, The, xlii n.

Diana, *105 n., 236.
Dio(n) Chrysostom, *Discourses*, 226 n., 227 n., 232 n., 234 n.
Diodorus Siculus, *Bibliotheca historica*, 239 n.
Diogenes, the Cynic, xl n., xli n.(3), 21, 21 n., 158 n., 226 ff., *226 n., 228 n., 231 n.; English attitudes toward, 231 n., 232 n. *See also* F's *Dialogue between Alexander the Great and Diogenes the Cynic*.
Diogenes Laertius, *Lives of the Philosophers*, 31 n., 184 n., 216 n., 224 n., 226 n., 227 n., 235 n., quoted: 158 n.
Dives, 34, 34 n.
Dodd, Henry P., 77 n.
Dodington, George, uncle of Bubb Dodington, 19 n.
Dodington, George Bubb, xiii, xiv, 19 n., 26 n., 184 n., 247 n.; compliment to, 152, 248; F's *Of True Greatness* addressed to, xiii, 19 ff., 247–8; *Epistle to Sir Robert Walpole*, quoted: 31 n.
Dodsley, Robert, compiler, *A Collection of Poems*: F's epistle to Walpole reprinted in, xlix, 56 n., 250 n.
Dodwell, Henry the elder, divine, 181 n.
Domitia Longinus, wife of Domitian, *95 n.
Domitian (Titus Flavius Domitianus), Roman emperor, *95 n.
Donne, John, 'The Dissolution', quoted: 188 n.; 'Negative Love', 182 n.; 'A Lent-Sermon Preached before the King', quoted: 159 n. *See also* Pope.
Dorset, Charles Sackville, Earl of, 150 n.; 'To All You Ladies', 67 n.
Draper, Richard, serjeant at law, 111, 111 n.
Draper, Thomas, 111 n.
Drury Lane Theatre, xlviii, 5 n., 6 n., 64 n., 93 n.(2).
Dryden, John, xxviii, 19 n., 24, 82. Plays: *Amphitryon*, xlii n.; *Aureng-Zebe*, quoted: 44 n.; *Cleomenes*, quoted: 20 n., 65 n.; *Conquest of Granada*, 37 n., quoted: 39 n.; *Marriage à la Mode*, quoted: 62 n.; *Princess of Cleves*, quoted: 49 n.; *Spanish Friar*, quoted: 117 n.; *Tyrannic Love*, quoted: 70 n. Poems: *Annus Mirabilis*, 36 n.; *Eleonora*, quoted: 26 n., 55 n., 75 n.; *Hind and the Panther*, 66 n., 174 n., quoted: 26 n.; *The Medal*, quoted: 117 n.; *Religio Laici*, quoted: 21 n., 33 n.; 'To My Honor'd Friend, Sir Robert Howard', 35 n. Prose: preface to Sir Henry Sheers's trans. of Polybius, quoted: 176 n. Translations: of Dufresnoy's *De arte graphica*, 52 n.; of

Juvenal and Persius, preface to, 152 n.; of Juvenal's *Satires*, quoted: 22 n., 91 n., 117 n., 124 n.; of Persius' *Satires*, quoted: 31 n.; of Ovid's *Metamorphoses* ('Of the Pythagorean Philosophy'), quoted: 33 n., 39 n., 87 n., 187 n.; of Virgil's *Aeneid*, 22 n., 37 n., quoted: 55 n., 80 n.; of Virgil's *Georgics*, 34 n., quoted: 24 n., 46 n.; of Virgil's *Eclogues* ('Pastorals'), 34 n.
Dudden, F. Homes, xv n., xliii n.
Dufresnoy, Charles Alphonse, *De arte graphica*, see Dryden.
Duncan, C. S., xl n.
Dutoit, Ernest, 69 n.

Eachard, John, *Grounds and Occasions of Contempt of the Clergy*, 143 n.
East Indies, 131.
East Stour, Dorset, xv, 68 n.
Echion, Roman singer, in Juvenal, 94.
Eddy, Donald D., liv.
Edward III, king of England, 41, 41 n.
Egypt, 94, *94 n., *95 n.
Eleusinian Mysteries, 90, 91; explicated by Warburton, *90 n., *91 n.
Elizabeth I, queen of England, 115.
Elysian Fields, 243.
England, xxxi, 127, 195 n., 196 n., 253; beauty's isle, 79; drained by Hanover, 193, 193 n., 196; election corruption in, 204; home of liberty, 40–1, 40 n.; Juvenal not applicable to ladies of, *117 n.; master of the sea, 68, 68 n.; old British virtues declining in, 115, 117.
'Enjoyment, The', 62 n.
Epictetus, *Discourses*, xxxiv n.
Epicurus, 119 n., 180 n., 220 n.
Erasmus, Desiderius, xviii n.; *Moriae encomium*, xxxix.
Eton, 76 n., 95 n.; Eton Latin Grammar, see William Lily.
Euboea, in Demosthenes' oration, 207.
Europa, and Jupiter, 237 n.
Eve, 55.
Excise Bill, 41 n.

Fabius Gurges, in Juvenal, 112.
Fairclough, H. R., 125 n., 161 n., 183 n., 197 n.
Falernia, Italy, in Juvenal, 102, *103 n.
'Fanny, Lord', see Hervey.
Farmer, John S., 65 n.
Farquhar, George, *The Recruiting Officer*, 26 n.
Fausan, Signor and Signora, dancers, 93, 93 n.
Favez, Charles, xxxviii n.

Fénelon, François de Salignac de la Mothe, *Avantures de Télémaque*, 34 n., 231 n., quoted: 39 n.; *Dialogues des morts*, xli n.

Fern, Sister Mary E., xxxviii n.

Fielding, Charlotte, daughter of HF, xv, xxxvii, xlv, 14, 14 n., 212 n., 215 n., 224, 224 n.

Fielding, Charlotte Cradock, wife of HF, xxvii, xliv, 7, 13, 13 n., 14, 59 n., 75 n.(2), 76 n., 80, 80 n., 224, 224 n.; poems to 'Celia' addressed to: 63–5, 70–2, 72–4, 74, 75(3).

Fielding, Edmund, father of HF, xv, xlv, 212 n., 215 n., 248 n.

Fielding, George, uncle of HF, xv.

FIELDING, HENRY: Works:

I. *Miscellanies*:
   circumstances of composition, xi–xvii: by subscription, xi; political element, xi–xiv; F's miscellaneous writing, xii–xv; personal circumstances, xv–xvi; date of composition, xlii–xlv; history of publication, xlvi–xlix.
   Preface to Miscellanies, in Volume I (text 3–15), xxvii n., xliv n., 248 n., quoted: xii n., xiv, xv, xvi, xvii, xix, xix n., xx n.(2), xxiii n.(2), xxvii, xxxi n., xxxiii n., xlii n., xlvii, xlviii, 85 n.
   Volume I: general introduction to, xi–xlix; textual introduction to, l–lv; contents of, xvii–xlii: moral and social concern, xvii; analogy with themes of Cicero's *De officiis*, xviii–xxvii: the *bona civitas*, xviii; necessity of moral instruction, xix–xxi; definition of greatness, xix; exemplification and rules, xx; cardinal virtues, xxii–xxvi; conversation and decorum, xxvi–xxvii.
   Poetry: xxvii–xxxiii, xxvii n., 3. 'Part of Juvenal's Sixth Satire, Modernized in Burlesque Verse' (text, 85–117; Latin text of Juvenal, 84–116), xxvii, xxxi n., liii, 3, 47 n., 142 n.; date of composition, xliv, xliv n., 85 n. Light Verse (texts, 53–82), xxvii–xxviii, 3; dates of composition, xliv–xlv, 53 ff.: 'Advice to the Nymphs of New S—m', 68–70; 'The Beggar', xxviii n., 61; 'The Cat and Fiddle', 77; 'A Description of U—n G—', 53–5, quoted: xxvii; 'Epigram' (That Kate weds), 76; 'Epigram' (When Jove), xxviii, 62; 'Another [Epigram]' (Miss Molly), 76; 'Epigram on One Who Invited Many Gentlemen', 67; 'Epitaph on Butler's Monument', 66; 'Another [Epitaph]', 66; 'Her Christian Name', see 'To Celia'; 'J—n W—ts at a Play',

63; 'On a Lady, Coquetting', 65; 'On the Same', 65; 'A Parody, from the First *Aeneid*', 80–1; 'The Price', see 'To Celia'; 'The Queen of Beauty', 77–80; 'The Question', see 'To Celia'; 'A Sailor's Song', 67–8; 'A Simile, from Silius Italicus', 81; 'Similes', see 'To Celia'; 'To Celia' (I hate the town), 63–5; 'To Celia, Occasioned by Her Apprehending', xxviii, 70–2; 'To the Same, On Her Wishing to Have a Lilliputian', xxviii, 60 n., 72–4; 'Similes, To the Same', 74; 'The Price, To the Same', 75; 'Her Christian Name, To the Same', 75; 'To the Same, Having Blamed Mr. Gay', 75; 'To Euthalia', xxviii, xxxiii n., 82; 'To Miss H—and at Bath', xliii n., 118; 'To the Right Honourable Sir Robert Walpole', xlix, li, 56–8: short version in *Gentleman's Magazine*, 56 n., 249–50 (Appendix B); 'To the Same', 59; 'To the Master of the Salisbury Assembly', 76; 'Written Extempore on a Halfpenny', li, 59–60: short version in *Champion*, li, 59 n., 251 (Appendix C). Verse-Essays, major convictions seen in, xxviii–xxxiii: *Liberty* (text, 36–41), xix n., xxx–xxxi; date of composition, xlv, 36 n., quoted: xxviii, xxxi; *Of Good-Nature* (text, 30–5), xxii n., xxiv n., xxix–xxx, xlix, 9 n., 37 n., 79 n.; date of composition, xlv, 30 n., quoted: xviii n., xix n., xxii n.(3), xxiv n., xxix, xxx; *Of True Greatness* (text, 19–29), xiii, xix n., xxiii n., xxviii–xxix, lv, 41 n., 45 n., 152 n., 226 n.(2); date of composition, xlv, 19 n., separate publication, xiii, li, 19 n., quoted: xiv; 'Preface' to (text, 247–8, Appendix A), xiii, li, quoted: 19 n.; *To a Friend on the Choice of a Wife* (text 42–50), xxvi n., xxxi–xxxii, 52 n., 176 n.; date of composition, xlv, 47 n.; *To John Hayes, Esq.* (text, 51–3), xxv n., xxxii–xxxiii, 155 n.; date of composition, xlv, 51 n., quoted: xxxii.
   Prose: concern for 'offices' of community in serious essays, xxxiii–xxxviii; variety of forms of satire, xxxviii–xlii; *A Dialogue between Alexander the Great and Diogenes the Cynic* (text, 226–35), xx n., xxiii n., xl–xli, 21 n., 188 n.; date of composition, xlv, 226 n., quoted: xxxiv n., xli; *An Essay on Conversation* (text, 119–52), xxvi n.(2), xxxiii–xxxv, xxxvii, xlix, 3–4, 118 n.; date of composition, xlv, 119 n., quoted: xviii n., xx n., xxi n.(2), xxiv n., xxv n., xxxiii, xxxiv; *An Essay on the Knowledge of the Charac-*

ters of Men (text, 153–78), xx n.(2), xxiii n., xxxv–xxxvii, xlix, 4; date of composition, xlv, 153 n., quoted: xxi n., xxv n.(3), xxvi n., xxxiii n.; *An Essay on Nothing* (text, 179–90), xvi, xxiii n., xxvi n., xxxviii–xxxix, xlviii, xlix; date of composition, xlv, 179 n.; *The First Olynthiac of Demosthenes* (text, 205–11), xlii; date of composition, xliii, xlv, 205 n.; *An Interlude between Jupiter, Juno, Apollo, and Mercury* (text, 236–43), xli–xlii, liii, liv; date of composition, xlv, 236 n., quoted: xlii; *Of the Remedy of Affliction for the Loss of Our Friends* (text, 212–25), xvi, xx n., xxiii n., xxxvii–xxxviii, xxxviii n.; date of composition, xlv, 212 n.; *Some Papers Proper to be Read before the R—l Society* (text, 191–204), xiv n., xxi, xxiii n., xxxix–xl, liv, lv, 15 n., 67 n.; date of composition, xlv, 193 n.; separate publication, xv, xliii, xlv, li, 193 n.

Volume II: xi, xi n.; *A Journey from This World to the Next*, xi, xi n., xiii n., xli n., xlvi, 4, 4 n., 23 n., 25 n., 69 n., 81 n., 91 n., 126 n., 139 n., 241 n.; date of composition, xliii, xliii n.; *Eurydice, or the Devil Henpeck'd*, xi, xi n., xliii n., 4, 4 n., 6 n., 236 n.; *The Wedding Day*, xi, xi n., xv, xliii n., 4–8, 4 n., 6 n., 7 n., 15 n., 93 n., 99 n.

Volume III: *The Life of Mr. Jonathan Wild the Great*, xi, xiii n., xvi, xxix n., xxxiii n., xxxvi n., xxxvii n.(2), xli n., xlvi, xlviii, 8–13, 10 n., 11 n., 53 n., 155 n., 193 n., 230 n., 236 n.; date of composition, xliii, quoted: xxxiii n., xxxv, 203 n., 238 n.

II. *Other Works*:
Prose-Fiction: *Amelia*, xix n., xxxii, xxxvi n.(2), xxxvii n.(2), 9 n., 27 n., 32 n., 41 n., 57 n., 132 n., 134 n., 154 n., 158 n.(2), 164 n., 175 n., 236 n., 239 n., quoted: xvi, 19 n., 151 n., 214 n.; *Jonathan Wild*, see *Miscellanies*; *Joseph Andrews*, xi, xiii n., xiv, xvi, xxiv n., xxxvi n.(3), xxxvii n., xxxviii n., xliii, 9 n., 15, 28 n., 51 n., 60 n., 62 n., 99 n. (2), 107 n., 113 n., 136 n., 150 n., 166 n., 170 n., 193 n., quoted: 45 n., 97 n.; *A Journey from This World to the Next*, see *Miscellanies*; *Shamela*, xiii; *Tom Jones*, xix n., xxii n., xxiii n.(2), xxiv n., xxx, xxx n.(3), xxxi n., xxxv n., xxxvi n., xxxvii n.(3), xxxviii n., xl n., 9 n.(2), 10 n., 27 n., 28 n., 30 n., 36 n., 39 n., 42 n., 49 n., 53 n., 65 n., 66 n., 95 n.,

118 n., 119 n., 136 n., 158 n., 162 n., 165 n., 166 n., 167 n., 173 n., 180 n., 197 n., 204 n., 218 n., quoted: xxxvii n., 59 n., 160 n.

Plays: *The Author's Farce*, 5 n., 54 n., 74 n., 241 n.; *The Coffee-House Politician (Rape upon Rape)*, xxiv n., 5 n.; *The Covent-Garden Tragedy*, 69 n., 101 n.; *Don Quixote in England*, 5 n., 64 n.; *Eurydice*, see *Miscellanies*; *Eurydice Hiss'd*, 63 n., 66 n.; *The Good-Natured Man* (posthumously titled *The Fathers*), xv, 6–7, 6 n., 236 n.(2); *The Grub-Street Opera*, 56 n.; *The Historical Register*, 67 n., 113 n.; *The Intriguing Chambermaid*, 93 n., quoted: 138 n.; *The Lottery*, 91 n.; *Love in Several Masques*, 5 n.(2); *The Miser*, 30 n.; *Miss Lucy in Town*, xiv, 6 n., 15, 15 n., 95 n., 99 n.; *The Modern Husband*, 5 n., 20 n., 56 n.; *An Old Man Taught Wisdom*, xiv, 6 n.; *Pasquin*, 63 n., quoted: 143 n.; *The Temple Beau*, xxiv n., xli n., 5 n., quoted: 26 n.; *Tom Thumb* (first version), 5 n., 56 n.; *The Tragedy of Tragedies; or Tom Thumb the Great*, 30 n., 64 n.(2); *Tumble-Down Dick*, 236 n.; *The Universal Gallant*, 6 n.; *The Wedding Day*, see *Miscellanies*.

Journals: *The Champion*, xii, xii n., xviii n., xx n., xxii n., xxiii n.(2), xxiv n., xxix n., xxx n., xxxi n., xxxvi n.(2), xxxvii n.(3), xxxix n., xl n., xli n., xliii, xlv(2), 9 n.(2), 23 n., 24 n., 27 n., 30 n., 49 n., 51 n., 54 n., 66 n., 89 n., 95 n., 99 n., 120 n., 125 n., 136 n., 137 n., 140 n., 147 n., 152 n., 193 n., 213 n., 214 n., 226 n., 228 n., 230 n., 248 n.; earlier version of lines from *Of Good-Nature* in, 35 n.; F's break with, xii n., xliii, 14; fragment of poem 'Written Extempore' in (text, 251, Appendix C), li, 59 n.; parallels with *Essay on the Knowledge of the Characters of Men*, 153 n.(3), 156 n.(2), 158 n., 162 n., 167 n., 168 n., 170 n., 171 n., 173 n.(2), 174 n., 176 n.; *The Covent-Garden Journal*, xxii n., xxx n., xxxv n., xxxvi n.(2), xl n., xli n., 15 n., 30 n., 32 n., 33 n., 53 n., 87 n., 124 n., 125 n., 134 n., 138 n., 142 n., 159 n., 167 n., 170 n., quoted: 189 n.; *The Jacobite's Journal*, xlviii, 30 n., 53 n., 153 n.; *The True Patriot*, xxii n., xxiii n., xli n., 9 n., 30 n., 32 n.

Miscellaneous Prose: *An Attempt towards a Natural History of the Hanover Rat*, 193 n.; *A Charge to the Grand Jury*, xx n., 167 n.; *A Clear State of the Case of Elizabeth Canning*, xxxvi n.; *The Crisis*,

FIELDING (*cont.*):
   a Sermon, xiii; *An Enquiry into the Causes of the Late Increase of Robbers*, xxxi n., 30 n., 127 n.; *A Full Vindication of the Duchess of Marlborough*, xiv, 15, 23 n., 31 n.; *The Journal of a Voyage to Lisbon*, xxix n., xxxv n., xxxvi n., 132 n.; *The Opposition, a Vision*, xiii, xiii n., 15, 176 n.; preface to the 2nd edn. of Sarah Fielding's *Adventures of David Simple*, 15 n.; letters contributed to her *Familiar Letters*, xl n.
   Poetry: *The Masquerade*, 3 n., 63 n., quoted: 65 n.; *The Vernoniad*, xiii, 3 n., 23 n., 24 n., 57 n., 64 n., 80 n., 118 n., 203 n., 237 n.
   Translation: of Adlerfeld's *Military History of Charles XII*, xii; of Ovid's *De amore* (*The Lovers Assistant*), 79 n.; of Aristophanes' *Plutus* (with William Young), xiv, xliv n., 15 n., *87 n., 91 n., 239 n., quoted: xiii n., 69 n., 87 n.
Fielding, Sarah, *see* Henry Fielding.
Figg, James, prize-fighter, 95, *95 n., 111 n.
Fink, Zera S., xxxi n.
Flanders, xliv n., 79, 91, 92 n.
Fleetwood, Charles, manager of Drury Lane Theatre, xlviii, 6–8, 6 n., 93, 93 n.
Fletcher, Giles, 'Christs Victorie on Earth', 159 n.
Flora, 46, *110 n.
Floralia, Roman festival, in Juvenal, 110, *110 n.
Florus, Lucius Annaeus, *Epitomae de Tito Livio*, quoted: 125.
Floyer, Sir John, *Psychrolousia*, 214 n.
Folkes, Martin, president of the Royal Society, 193 n., 253.
Fonseca, Christopher, quoted by Burton, 43 n.
Foss, Edward, 111 n.
France, 41, 68, 93 n., 107, *107 n., 117, 117 n., 127 n., 195 n., 196 n.; king of, 73. *See also* Louis XIV, Louis XV; French language, 58, 195, 253.
Fraser, Alexander C., 180 n.
Freeholder, The, 193 n.
Freind, Colonel, 91 n.
Friedman, Arthur, vii.
Fuller, Thomas, *Gnomologia*, quoted: 217 n.
Furies, *see* Tisiphone.
Fuzelier, Louis, *Momus Turn'd Fabulist*, xlii n.

Galen, *De usu partium*, 196, 196 n.
Garrick, David, xv, xlv, xlviii, 5 n., 6 n.,

15 n., 53 n.; acted in F's *The Wedding Day*, 5–7; compliment to, 51 n., 53, 136.
Garth, Samuel, 118 n.; *The Dispensary*, quoted: 69 n., 118 n.
'Gauls', *see* France.
Gay, John, xi, xxviii, 75, 75 n.; poems: 'Epistle to William Pulteney', quoted: 38 n., 75 n.; *Fables*, quoted: 21 n., 24 n., 25 n., 28 n.; 'A Journey to Exeter', quoted: 79 n.; 'Mr. Pope's Welcome from Greece', 25 n.; 'The Story of Arachne' (from Ovid), 70 n.; *Trivia*, quoted: 28 n., 32 n.; plays: *Polly*, xi, quoted: 230 n.; *The Wife of Bath*, 62 n. *See also* F's poem to Celia, 'Having Blamed Mr. Gay'.
Gazetteer, see *Daily Gazetteer*.
Gellius, Aulus, *Noctes Atticae*, 105 n.
General Evening Post, xlviii n.
Gentleman's Magazine, xlii n., 75 n., 103 n., 179 n.; version of F's first epistle to Walpole in, li, 56 n., 249–50 (Appendix B).
George I, king of England, 111 n.
George II, king of England, xlii n., 30 n., 78 n., 111 n., 193 n., 239 n. *See also* Hanover.
George, M. Dorothy, 247 n.
Germany, 69, 69 n., 79, 106, 117, 193, 196. *See also* Hanover, Prussia.
Giant, the, 139. *See also* Cajanus.
Glaphyrus, Roman singer, in Juvenal, 94.
Godden, G. M., xii n.
Godschall, Sir Robert, lord mayor, 25 n.
Golden, Morris, xxxvi n.
Golden Age, 33 n., 87 n.
Goldsmith, Oliver, *History of the Earth*, quoted: xlix; *Life of Richard Nash*, quoted: 54 n.
Goodman's Fields Theatre, 5 n., 51 n.
Gordon, Thomas, journalist, xli n., 64, 64 n.
Goths, xxxi, 40 n.; 'Gothick', 26.
Gough, J. W., 37 n.
Gould, Lady Sarah, F's grandmother, 68 n.
Gracchus, 'Cornelius', *104 n., *105 n. *See also* Cornelia.
Gracchus, Gaius Sempronius, 104, *104 n., *105 n.
Gracchus, Tiberius Sempronius, the elder, 104 n.
Gracchus, Tiberius Sempronius, the younger, 104, *104 n., *105 n.
Grafton, Charles Fitz-Roy, 2nd Duke of, 8 n.
Grainger, James, *Letters*, quoted: 81 n.
Grangaeus, Isaacus, *84 n.

Granicus, battle of the River, 228, 228 n.
Granville, George, *see* Lansdowne.
Granville, John, Lord, *see* Carteret.
Gray's Inn, 111 n.
Gray's-Inn Journal, see Murphy.
Greece, xxxi, 19, 40, 40 n., 86, *86 n., 87, *87 n., *107 n., *109 n., 177 n., *226 n., *233 n.; Greek language, 58, 106, 143, *168 n.
Greek Anthology, The, 166 n., quoted: 77 n.
Greene, Richard L., vii.
Greenland, 85.
Greg, Sir Walter, li n., lii.
Grenville, George, xiv n.
Grenville, Richard, letter quoted, xiv n.
Grierson, H. J. C., 188 n.
Grotius, Hugo (de Groot), 32 n.
Grubbs, H. A., 154 n.
Grub-Street Journal, 64, 64 n.
'Gualterus, Petrus', *see* Peter Walter.
Guardian, The, 132 n., 153 n., 221 n., quoted: 31 n., 73 n., 120 n., 122 n., 135 n., 137 n., 138 n. *See also* Addison, Berkeley, Pope, Steele.
Guazzo, Stefano, courtesy-writer, xxxiv.
Guicciardini, Francesco, 9 n.
Guildhall, London, 91, 91 n.
Guthkelch, A. C., xxxix n., 188 n.

Hadrian (Publius Aelius Hadrianus), Roman emperor, 59 n.
Haemus, Roman actor, in Juvenal, 106.
Hague, The, 81 n., 193 n., 253.
Haines, C. R., 21 n.
Hammond, Henry, *Paraphrase and Annotations upon the New Testament*, 124 n.
Hammond, James, 185 n.; *Love Elegies*, xlv, 179 n., 185, 185 n.
Hampden, family of, 113, 113 n.
Hampshire, 53 n., 79 n.; Hampshire Downs, 53 n.
Handel, George Frederick, 27, 27 n.; *Messiah*, 27 n.
Hannibal, of Carthage, 104, 114.
Hanover, *see* Germany; house of, in England, xiii n., xiv, 69 n., 193 n., 196 n. *See also* George I, George II.
Harecourt Pump, 69 n.
Harnham Hill, Salisbury, 69, 69 n.
Harrington, James, *Oceana*, 38 n.
Harris, James, philosopher, friend of F, 'Concerning Happiness: A Dialogue', xlv, 119 n., 122, *122 n., 123; *Hermes*, 122 n.; *Works*, 122 n.
Harris, James, Earl of Malmesbury, *see* Malmesbury.
Hayes, John, of Wolverhampton, Stafford-

shire, 51, 51 n. *See* F's verse-essay, *To John Hayes, Esq.*
Haymarket, 67 n., 236 n.
Haywood, Mrs. ('Mother'), bawd, 99, *99 n.
Hazen, Allen T., vii.
Heathcote, George, lord mayor, 25, 25 n.
Heathcote, Sir Gilbert, merchant, 25 n.
Helicon, 69.
Henley, Robert (later 1st Earl of Northington), 115, 115 n., 118 n.
Henley, William Ernest, edition of F's *Works*, xlix.
Henry V, king of England, 41, 41 n.
Henry VIII, king of England, 99, *99 n.
Herod, king of Chalcis, 103 n.
Herodotus, *History*, 224 n.
Herrick, Marvin T., xxiv n.
Herrick, Robert, poems: 'The Country Life', quoted: 20 n.; 'His Protestation to Perilla', 69 n.; 'On Himself', 118 n.
Herring, Thomas, Bishop of Bangor, *A Sermon before the Lord Mayor*, 158 n.
Hertford, Frances Seymour, Countess of, 7 n.
Hervey, John Hervey, Baron, 31 n., 107, 107 n.
Hesiod, *Theogony*, 40 n., 79 n., 239 n.
Hesperides, garden of the, 71, 71 n.
Heywood, John, 'A Fool Taken for Wise', quoted: 65 n.
Hicks, R. D., 158 n.
Hierax of Amphipolis, in Demosthenes' oration, 207.
Highgate Hill, 69 n.
Hildrop, John, *Free Thoughts upon the Brute Creation*, 143 n.
Hill, Aaron, xlviii.
Hillhouse, James T., 64 n.
Hippia (Eppia), wife of Fabricius Vejento, in Juvenal, 94, 95, *95 n., 96, *96 n., 97.
Hippocrates, *Airs, Waters, Places*, 118 n.
Historical View of Political Writers in Great Britain, by 'Marforio', anecdotes of F, 59 n., 248 n.(2).
History of Jack Connor, xlix.
Hoadly, Benjamin, Bishop of Winchester, 28, 28 n., 111 n.
Hoadly, Dr. Benjamin, 5 n., 111, 111 n.; *The Suspicious Husband*, 111 n.
Hobbes, Thomas, xviii n., xxxiii, 9 n., 30 n., 119 n., 134 n.(2), 159, 180 n., 181 n., 189; *An Answer to Dr. Bramhall*, 189 n.; *Human Nature*, 159 n., 189 n., quoted: 135 n., 158 n.; *Leviathan*, 159 n., 189 n.(2), 231 n., quoted: 143 n.
Hockley-in-the-Hole, 99 n., 111 n.
Hock Norton, Oxfordshire, 53 n.

Hogarth, William, 136 n.; compliment to, 136.

Holland, 79, 81, 81 n., 117, 127, 127 n. *See also* The Hague, Leyden.

Hollis, family of, 113, 113 n.

Homer, *Iliad*, 12, quoted: xxxv n.; *Odyssey*, 34 n., 241 n.

Homeric Hymn to Aphrodite, the Second, 79 n.

Honey-Suckle, The, 66 n.

Hooker, Timothy, *An Essay on Honour*, 229 n.

Horace (Quintus Horatius Flaccus), xxviii, xxxii, 51, 150; *Ars Poetica*, 11 n.; *Epistulae*, 51 n., 56 n., quoted: 48 n., 125, 125 n., 151, 167 n., 183; *Epodes*, quoted: 32 n.; *Odes (Carmina)*, 23 n., 25 n., 29 n., 33 n., 34 n., 36 n., 118 n.; trans. Charles Hanbury Williams, quoted: 79 n.; *Satires (Sermones)*, 51 n., quoted: 33 n., 161, 213.

Houghton, Norfolk, estate of Walpole, 57 n.

Howard, Catherine, wife of Henry VIII, 99 n.

Howard, Sir Robert, 35 n.

Hughes, Helen Sard, 8 n.

Hulse, Sir Edward, physician, 111, 111 n.

Huns, 40. *See also* Goths.

Husband, Jane (later Henley), 118, 118 n. *See* F's poem, 'To Miss H—and at Bath'.

Hyacinthus, 98.

Hydaspes, battle of the River, 228 n.

Hyde Park, 63 n., 113.

Hymen, 238.

Iberia, *see* Spain.

Illyria, in Demosthenes' oration, 208, 210.

India, 19, 58, 58 n., 73, 78, *226 n., 228 n., 249; meaning 'West Indies' (?), 60, 251.

Inns of Court, 13 n. *See also* Gray's Inn, Middle Temple.

Ionian Sea, 96.

Ireland, 147, 147 n., 195 n.

Iron Age, 86, 87.

Irus, beggar, 34, 34 n.

Irwin, William R., xxix n.

Iser, Wolfgang, xxxvi n.

Issus, battle of, 228, 228 n.

Italy, 40, 40 n., 78, *103 n., 117; Italian language, 58.

Izard, Mr., 'The Excuse', 75 n.

Jacobites, 63 n.

Jacobite's Journal, see Fielding.

Jaeger, Werner, 205 n.

James, Robert, *A Medicinal Dictionary*, 91 n.

Jenkins's Ear, War of, 40 n., 97 n.

Jesus Christ, 159, 168 ff. *See also* Bible.

Johnson, J. W., 153 n.

Johnson, Samuel, xlvii; *London*, 41 n., 63 n.

Jones, B. Maelor, xv n.

Jones, Richard Foster, xxxiv n.

Jones, William P., xl n.

Jonson, Ben, xxxix; *Epicoene*, 42 n.; *Volpone*, *85 n., 95 n.

Jortin, John, trans. epigram by Lucillius, 77 n.

Josephus, Flavius, *Antiquitates Judaicae*, 103 n.; *De bello Judaico*, 103 n.

Jove, *see* Jupiter.

Julian, the Apostate, Roman emperor, 4.

Junius, H., *Lexicon graeco-latinum*, 65 n.

Juno, 40, 40 n., 90, 236 ff. *See also* F's *Interlude*.

Jupiter (Jove), 60, 60 n., 62, 62 n., 71, 80, 86, *86 n., 87, 90, *91 n., 236 ff.; Jupiter Ammon, 228, 228 n. *See also* F's *Interlude*.

Jupiter and Io, xlii n.

Jupiter's Descent on Earth, unknown comedy, xli n., 236, 236 n.

Juvenal (Decimus Junius Juvenalis), *Satires*, xxvii, xxviii, 10 n., 31 n., 42 n., 47 n., 49 n., 51 n., 57 n., 63 n., 84 ff., 87 n., *95 n.(2), 156 n., quoted: 28 n., 29 n., 84 ff., 141 n., 156, 159; trans. Dryden, quoted: 22 n., 91 n., 124 n. *See also* F's 'Part of Juvenal's Sixth Satire, Modernized in Burlesque Verse'.

Kelley, Maurice, vii.

Kent, 115.

Ker, W. C. A., 171 n.

Kett, Henry, 131 n.

King, Joseph, creditor of F, xvi.

Kliger, Samuel, xxxi n., 40 n.

Lacedaemon, 234. *See also* Sparta.

Lagus, Egypt, 94, *94 n.

Landa, Louis A., vii.

Lansdowne, George Granville, Baron, 'Ode: On the Present Corruption of Mankind', 166 n., quoted: 41 n.; 'The Progress of Beauty', 118 n., quoted: 78 n.; 'To the Immortal Memory of Mr. Edmund Waller', 25 n.; *Genuine Works*, 118 n.

La Rochefoucauld, François de, xxxii, 9 n., 30 n., 51 n.; *Maximes*, 31 n., 42 n., 52 n.(2), quoted: 44 n., 51 n., 146 n., 157 n., 165 n., 169 n., 222–3; *Maximes supprimées*, quoted: 154 n.

Index

Latin language, 58, 106; Latin proverb, 156, 161, 180, 180 n.
Latinus, Roman actor, in Juvenal, 88, 89, *89 n.
Latona (Leto), 104, 105, *105 n.
'Leaden Age', 26, 26 n.
Lean, Vincent S., 167 n.
Leda, 92; and Jupiter, 237 n.
Lee, Nathaniel, *Constantine the Great*, quoted: 171 n.; 'To the Prince and Princess of Orange', quoted: 25 n.
Lee, Sir William, chief justice, 29 n.; compliment to, 29.
Leeward Islands, 105 n.
Leibniz, Gottfried Wilhelm, Baron von, *A Collection of Papers between Mr. Leibnitz and Dr. Clarke*, quoted: 143 n.
Lepidus, Marcus Aemilius, 112.
'Lesbia', of Catullus, 84, *84 n., 85, 85 n. *See* Clodia.
L'Estrange, Sir Roger, trans. *Fables of Aesop*, 149 n.
Lewis, Wilmarth S., xii n. *See also* Horace Walpole.
Lex Julia, 88, *88 n.
Leyden, Holland, 5 n., 81 n.
Licensing Act, xii, xlv, 26 n.
Lievsay, John L., 231 n.
Lily, William, compiler, Eton Latin grammar, 76, 76 n., quoted: 184 n.
Lincoln's-Inn Fields Theatre, 5 n., 54 n., 64 n.
Little Theatre in the Haymarket, 67 n., 236 n.
Livy (Titus Livius), *History*, 40 n.
Locke, John, 32 n., 82, 181 n.; *Essay Concerning Human Understanding*, 119 n., 120 n., 122 n., 153 n.(2), 154 n., 162 n., 177 n., 182 n., 183 n., 197 n., quoted: 180 n.; *Some Thoughts Concerning Education*, quoted: 123 n., 154 n.; *Two Treatises of Government*, xxxi, 36 n., 38 n.(2), 41 n., quoted: 37 n.(2), 39 n.
Loewenberg, Richard D., 157 n.
London, xxvii, 63, 139 n., 178, *et passim*. *See also* Aldgate pump, Arlington Street, Bartholomew Fair, Bear Garden, Charles Street, Cheapside, Clerkenwell Green, Covent Garden, Covent-Garden Theatre, Drury Lane Theatre, Goodman's Fields Theatre, Gray's Inn, Guildhall, Haymarket, Hockley-in-the-Hole, Hyde Park, Lincoln's-Inn Fields Theatre, Little Theatre in the Haymarket, The Mall, Marylebone Fields, Middle Temple, Newgate, Piccadilly, The Ring, Royal Exchange, Royal Society, St. James's Park, The Serpentine, Temple Bar, Thames, Westminster Abbey, Westminster Hall.
London Magazine, 185 n., quoted: 99 n.
Londonderry, Thomas Pitt, 1st Earl of, 105 n.
Louis XIV, king of France, xxix, 22 n., 229 n.; anecdote of, 131.
Louis XV, king of France, 103, 103 n.
Lubinus, Eilhardus, edition of Juvenal, *84 n.(2), *102 n., 104 n.
Lucan (Marcus Annaeus Lucanus), 36 n.; *Pharsalia*, 230 n.
Lucian of Samosata, xi, xvii, xxxviii, xl; *Dialogi mortuorum*, xl n., 228 n.; *Dialogi deorum*, xl n., xlii n.; *Laus muscae*, xxxix; epigram in the Greek Anthology, 166 n.
Lucillius, epigram in the Greek Anthology, quoted: 77 n.
Lucretius (Titus Lucretius Carus), xxviii; *De rerum natura*, xxxi, 33 n., 38 n.(3), 39 n., 44 n., 180 n., 213 n.
Lyme Regis, Dorsetshire, 3 n., 85 n.
Lynch, C. A., 166 n.
Lysander, Spartan naval commander, xxxiii n.
Lyttelton, George (later 1st Baron Lyttelton), xiv, xlv n., 29 n., 36 n., 47 n., 95, 95 n.; compliment to, 29, 152, 248; F's *Liberty* addressed to, xxx, 36 ff.; *Blenheim*, 23 n.; *Dialogues of the Dead*, quoted: 231 n.; *Letters from a Persian in England*, 24 n., 30 n., quoted: 37 n.; *Observations on the Life of Cicero*, quoted: 214 n.; (attrib.) *A Modest Apology for My Own Conduct*, quoted: xiv n.

Macedonia, *see* Philip of Macedon.
Machiavelli, Niccolò, 30 n.; *Discourses on Livy*, 38 n.; *The Prince*, 156 n.
Mack, Maynard, vii, xxxii n. *See also* Pope.
Macklin, Charles, actor, 7, 7 n.
Maecenas, Gaius, 27.
Magnesia, in Demosthenes' oration, 208, 210.
Mahomet (Mohammed), the Prophet, 23 n.
Mahomet II, Ottoman sultan, 22, 23 n.
Maia, mother of Hermes, 240 n.
Malcolm, James P., 73 n., 81 n.
Mall, The, 63, 93.
Malmesbury, James Harris, 1st Earl of, 122 n.
Malplaquet, battle of, 47 n.
Mandeville, Bernard, xviii n., 9 n., 30 n., 134 n.; *Fable of the Bees*, 33 n., 159 n., quoted: xxxiv n., 119 n., 165 n.

Mann, Horace, correspondent of Horace Walpole, 93 n., 185 n., 193 n.

Marcus Aurelius Antoninus, *Meditations*, 119 n., 154 n., quoted: 21 n.

'Marforio', see *Historical View*.

Mariana, Juan de, *General History of Spain*, 4 n.

Marlborough, John Churchill, 1st Duke of, 47, 47 n.; among F's personal heroes, 23 n.; tribute to, 23, 41.

Marlborough, Sarah, Duchess Dowager of, xiv, 31, 31 n., 60, 60 n., 251. *See also* F's *Full Vindication of the Duchess of Marlborough*.

Marlowe, Christopher, *Hero and Leander*, 61 n., 242 n.

Mars, 90, *91 n., 239.

Martial (Marcus Valerius Martialis), xxviii; *Epigrammata*, 57 n., 126 n., 171 n., quoted: 3, 29 n.(2), 50 n., 54 n., 59 n., 156 n., 165, 171.

Marylebone Fields, 95 n., 111 n.

Mason, John E., xxxiii n.

McKillop, Alan D., vii, xxxi n., xlviii n., 36 n.

McManaway, J. G., 231 n.

Mead, Dr. Richard, 60 n.

Megalesian games, in Juvenal, 92, *93 n.

Megara, city in Greece, 214.

Mercury, 236, 240 ff., 240 n. *See also* F's *Interlude*.

Messalina, Valeria, wife of emperor Claudius, 98, 100.

Metellus, Quintus Caecilius, 112.

Methone, in Demosthenes' oration, 207, 208.

Midas, 241 n.

Middle Temple, xii, xv, 51 n.

Miletus, Ionian city, in Juvenal, 116.

Millar, Andrew, publisher of F's *Miscellanies*, xlvi, xlvii, xlvii n., xlviii, l, 15 n.

Miller, F. J., 217 n., 224 n.

Miller, Henry K., xvii n., xxx n., xxxix n., xl n., xlvii n.

Miller, James, *The Universal Passion*, quoted: 42 n.

Milton, John, 94 n., 184 n.; *L'Allegro*, quoted: 118 n.; *Lycidas*, 134 n.; *Paradise Lost*, 22 n., 33 n., 34 n.(2), 37 n., 198, 221 n., 228 n., quoted: 29 n., 49 n., 142 n.; *Samson Agonistes*, 20 n., 22 n., 33 n., 48 n., quoted: 21 n.

Minerva, 69, 236. *See also* Athena.

Minos, mythical king of Crete, 241, 241 n.

Mitchell, Joseph, *Poems on Several Occasions*, 58 n., 66 n.

Mogul, the, of India, 58, 58 n., 69, 249.

Molesworth, Sir William, 135 n., 143 n., 159 n., 189 n.

Molière, Jean Baptiste Poquelin de, *Tartuffe*, xxxv.

Montagu, Charles (later Earl of Halifax), 82 n. *See also* Prior.

Montagu, George, correspondent of Horace Walpole, 103 n.

Montagu, Lady Mary Wortley, 5 n., 78 n., 82 n.; compliment to, 78, 82; 'Epithalamium', 76 n.; 'Unfinished Sketches of a Larger Poem', shares couplet with F, 81 n.

Montaigne, Michel de, *Essays* (incl. *Apology for Raimond de Sebonde*; trans. Charles Cotton), xxxii, xxxii n., 9 n., 120 n., 153 n., 188 n., 212 n., 213 n., 214 n., 215, 215 n., 217 n., 221 n., 225; quoted: 43 n., 51 n.(2), 52 n.(2), 140 n., 154 n., 160 n., 184 n., 212 n., 214 n., 219 n.

Montesquieu, Charles de Secondat, Baron de, *Lettres persanes*, 37 n.

Montfort, Henry Bromley, 1st Baron, 30 n.. 35 n.; compliment to, 35.

More, Sir Thomas, 'De ficto amico', 166n.

Motion, The, political print, 247 n.

Mummius, Lucius, Roman general, 60 n.

Murphy, Arthur, *Gray's-Inn Journal*, quoted: 134 n.; *Works*, quoted: 150 n.; edn. of F's *Works*, xlix, l; 'Essay on the Life and Genius of Henry Fielding', xii, quoted: xii n.; notes to Smart's *Hilliad*, quoted: xlviii.

Murray, A. T., xxxv n.

Murray, William (later 1st Earl of Mansfield), 115, 115 n.

Muses, the, 69.

Mythological allusions by F, see Alcmena, Amphion, Apollo, Arachne, Argus Panoptes, Astraea, Athena (Pallas), Ceres, Cupid, Danae, Diana, Elysian Fields, Flora, Furies, Golden Age, Hesperides, Hyacinthus, Hymen, Iron Age, Juno, Jupiter (Jove), Latona, Leda, Mars, Mercury, Minerva, Minos, Muses, Niobe, Orpheus, Parnassus, Pierians, Plutus, Saturn, Silver Age, Thalia, Tisiphone, Venus.

Napier, Alexander, 146 n., 180 n.

Nepos, Cornelius, xxix, xxxiii n.

Nero, Roman emperor, xxxiii n.

Netherlands, *see* Holland.

Newgate Prison, 10.

New Help to Discourse, The, 159 n.

New Sarum, *see* Salisbury.

Index

Newton, Sir Isaac, 82, 143 n.; *Opticks*, 203 n.
Nichol Smith, David, xxxix n., 188 n.
Nile River, 19 n., 94, *94 n., 117, 117 n.
Niobe, 104, 105, *105 n., 222.
Norfolk, 57 n.
Norfolk, Duke(s) of, 63, 63 n.
Nourse, John, bookseller, xv.
Noyes, Gertrude E., xxxiii n.
Nutley, manor of, Hampshire, 79 n.

Ogle, M. B., 70 n.
Oldenburg, H., translator, 58 n.
Oldfield, Anne, actress, 5, 5 n.
Oldham, John, 'A Satyr', 66 n.
Olynthus, city of Thrace, Demosthenes oration on, 205 ff.
Ombre, card-game, 133.
Opie, Iona, 77 n.
Opie, Peter, 77 n.
Opposition, the (to Walpole), xi, xiii n., xxxi n., 95 n., 196 n., 229 n., 247 n., 248 n.; F's contributions to, xi, xxx, xliii, 14; F's disillusionment with, xiii, xiii n.(2), xiv, 9 n., 53 n., 176 n., 190 n., 204 (*see also* Carteret, Pulteney); F's praise of leaders in, xiii (*see also* Argyle, Carteret, Chesterfield, Dodington, Hoadly, Lee, Lyttelton, Pitt, Pulteney); scramble for places, at fall of Walpole, 53 n., 176 n., 190 n.; subscribers to F's *Miscellanies*, xlviii; warparty in, xlii, xlii n., 205 n. *See also* Sir Robert Walpole and F's *The Opposition*.
Orford, Earl of, *57 n. *See also* Sir Robert Walpole.
Orleans, Duc d', Regent of France, 103 n.
Orpheus, 69 n., 77.
Ortigue, Pierre d', sieur de Vaumorière, *L'Art de plaire dans la conversation*, xxxiv, 123 n.
Osborn, James M., vii, xxxii n.
Otway, Thomas, plays: *Alcibiades*, 56 n.; *The Atheist*, quoted: 49 n.; *Don Carlos*, 56 n., 62 n., quoted: 20 n., 37 n.; *The Orphan*, quoted: 74 n.; *Venice Preserv'd*, quoted: 48 n., 242 n.
Ovid (Publius Ovidius Naso), xxviii, 54 n., 72 n.; *Amores*, 61 n., 74 n., 188 n., quoted: 34 n., 60 n., 72 n.; *Artis amatoriae, see* F's *The Lovers Assistant*; *Epistulae ex Ponto*, quoted: 158 n.; *Fasti*, *110 n.; *Heroides*, 118 n., quoted: 72 n.; *Metamorphoses*, 69 n., 71 n., 87 n., 105 n., 222 n., 239 n., quoted: 37 n., 217, 224; trans. Dryden, quoted: 33 n., 39 n., 87 n., 187 n.; trans. Gay, 70 n.; *Remedia amoris*, 42 n., 43 n., 44 n.(2), quoted: 174 n.

Owen, John B., xiii n.
Oxford (city), 139 n.
Oxford English Dictionary, 21 n. (gaul), 23 n. (purchase), 32 n. (swelter), 43 n. (gin), 45 n. (general), 55 n. (bottle-ricks, not recorded), 77 n. (canton), 79 n. (require; *see also* 35 n.), 120 n. (converse), 138 n. (mechanic), 153 n. (depravity), 154 n. (predicament), 158 n. (glavering), 179 n. (stick at nothing), 203 n. (scrutores), 221 n. (scrivener, annuity), 242 n. (privilege). *See also* the following, not glossed from *O.E.D.*: 15 n., 139 n. (ach), 20 n. (cars), 25 n. (meditate), 31 n. (salvage), 33 n. (unprovided), 34 n. (promiscuous), 35 n. (perspective), 38 n. (rate), 40 n. (genial), 43 n. (the white), 49 n. (gadding), 51 n. (elves), 54 n. (shell), 91 n. (middle vein), 95 n. (blind harper), 97 n. (pattins), 97 n. (hip), 118 n. (influence), 126 n. (condescension), 140 n. (common), 143 n. (occult qualities), 150 n. (dab), 176 n. (philanthropy), 181 n. (immaterial substance), 202 n. (schystic, kleptistic, metabolic).
Oxfordshire, 53 n.
Ozell, John, miscellaneous writer, xxxiv.

Paeonia, in Demosthenes' oration, 208, 210.
Pagasae, in Demosthenes' oration, 207, 208, 210.
Pallas, *see* Athena.
Paphos, in Cyprus, 79, 79 n.; island of, 79 n.
Paris, Roman actor, in Juvenal, 94, *95 n.
Parker, Samuel, the younger, *Sylva*, 231 n., quoted: 121 n.
Parnassus, 69.
Parry, John, the Blind Harper, 95 n.
Passerati, Joannes, *Nihil*, xxxix, 179 n.
Patrick, Simon, *The Hearts Ease*, 212 n.
'Patriot' Opposition to Walpole, *see* Opposition.
Pausanias, *Descriptio Graeciae*, 19 n., 40 n.
Paxton, Mr., laceman, 54, 54 n.
Pelham, Henry, xiv; administration of, xiv, 69 n.
Peloponnese, *226 n.
Persia, 228 n.
Persius Flaccus, Aulus, *Satires*, quoted: 150; Delphin edition of, 84 n.; trans. Brewster, 119 n., quoted: 150; trans. Dryden, quoted: 31 n.
Peru, 19, 73.
Peterson, William, xlii n.
Phaedrus, Gaius Julius, *Fabellae*, *88 n.
Pharos, Egypt, 94, *94 n.
Phera, in Demosthenes' oration, 208.

Philip of Macedon, attacked by Demosthenes, xlii, 205 ff.; father of Alexander the Great, 226.

Philip V, king of Spain, xlii.

Philosophical Transactions, see Royal Society.

Phocis, in Demosthenes' oration, 211.

Piccadilly, 57 n.

Pierians, daughters of Pierus, 69, 69 n.

Pindus, mountain in Greece, 69 n.

Pitt, Lady Lucy, 105 n.

Pitt, Thomas, governor of Madras, 103 n.

Pitt, Thomas, *see* Londonderry.

Pitt, William (later 1st Earl of Chatham), 95, 95 n., 103 n.

Pitt Diamond, the, 103, 103 n.

Plato, xxii, 70 n., 142, 143(2), 231 n.; *Apology,* 184 n., 225, 225 n., 241 n.; *Crito,* 225, 225 n.; *Phaedo,* 143 n., 224 n., 225, 225 n.; *Phaedrus,* 143, 173 n.; *Republic,* 9 n., 30 n., 41 n., 143 n., 156 n., 184 n., 215 n.; *Symposium,* 143 n.

Plautus, Titus Maccus, *Rudens,* 118 n.

Plebeian games, in Juvenal, 92, *93 n.

Pliny the Elder (Gaius Plinius Secundus), 202; *Naturalis historia,* 20 n., quoted: 33 n.

Pliny the Younger (Gaius Plinius Caecilius Secundus), *Epistles,* 202 n.

Plumb, J. H., 57 n.

Plutarch, 36 n.; on consolation, xxxviii; *Bruta animalia ratione uti,* 120 n., 153 n.; *Consolatio ad Apollonium,* xxxviii n., 212 n., 216 n., 218 n., 220 n., 221 n., 222 n.(2), 224 n.; *Lives,* xxix, xxxiii n., *Alexander,* 226 n., 227 n., 228 n.(3), 235 n., *Romulus,* 26 n.

Plutus, 239, 239 n. *See also* F's trans. of Aristophanes' *Plutus.*

Polybius, 36 n., 176 n.; *Histories,* xxix n., 10 n.

Pope, Alexander, xi, xxviii n., xxxii n., xlviii, 19 n., 69 n., 78 n., 193 n.; compliment to, 69, 78, 136; F's exemplar in verse-essay, xxviii; *Twickenham Edition of the Poems:* Vol. I (ed. E. Audra and Aubrey Williams): *Essay on Criticism,* 52 n., 203 n., quoted: 36 n., 147 n., 185 n.; *Pastorals:* 'Summer', quoted: 118 n.; *Sapho to Phaon,* quoted: 62 n.; *Windsor Forest,* 41 n., 68 n., 118 n.; Vol. II (ed. Geoffrey Tillotson): *Elegy to the Memory of an Unfortunate Lady,* quoted: 58 n.; *Eloisa to Abelard,* quoted: 37 n.; *Rape of the Lock,* 70 n., 71 n., quoted: 74 n.; Vol. III. i (ed. Maynard Mack): *Essay on Man,* xxxii, xxxii n., 19 n., 52 n., 56 n., 141 n., quoted: 30 n.,

33 n.(2), 37 n., 39 n., 40 n., 230 n.; Vol. III. ii (ed. F. W. Bateson): *Epistle to a Lady,* xxxi, 43 n., 51 n., 70 n.; *Epistle to Bathurst,* 34 n., 103 n.; *Epistle to Burlington,* 19 n., quoted: 60 n.; *Epistle to Cobham,* xxxii, xxxii n., 31 n., 51 n.; Vol. IV (ed. John Butt): *Imitations of Horace: Epistles,* 36 n., 41 n., 51 n., quoted: 36 n., 57 n.; *Odes,* quoted: 25 n., 36 n.; *Satires,* xlv, 107 n., quoted: 19 n., 67 n., 82 n., 'Sober Advice from Horace', quoted: 33 n.; *Epilogue to the Satires,* 26 n., 199 n., quoted: 29 n.; *Epistle to Dr. Arbuthnot,* 29 n., 58 n.; *One Thousand Seven Hundred and Forty,* 53 n.; *Second Satire of Dr. John Donne,* quoted: 63 n., 237 n.; Vol. V (ed. James Sutherland): *The Dunciad,* 64 n.(3), 99 n., quoted: 25 n., 161, 179 n.; Vol. VI (ed. Norman Ault and John Butt): 'Bounce to Fop', quoted: 19 n.; 'Epigram from the French', 65 n.; 'Epigram, On the Toasts of the Kit-Kat Club', quoted: 77 n.; *Epistle to Mr. Jervas,* 52 n.; 'To Mr. John Moore', quoted: 33 n.; 'To the Author of a Poem, Intitled, *Successio*', 51 n.; 'The Universal Prayer', quoted: 31 n.; 'The Words of the King of Brobdingnag', quoted: 20 n.; Vols. VII–VIII (ed. Maynard Mack *et al.*): trans. Homer's *Iliad,* 22 n., 52 n. Prose: essay in *The Guardian,* quoted: 137 n.; *Letters,* xlv, 153 n., 176 n., quoted: 176; *Correspondence* (ed. George Sherburn), xlviii n., 176 n.

Porticos, the Roman, in Juvenal, 92, *93 n.

Porus, king of India, 228, 228 n., 233.

Postgate, J. P., 221 n.

Potidaea, in Demosthenes' oration, 207, 208.

Potter, George R., 159 n.

Potter, John, *Archaeologiae Graecae, or The Antiquities of Greece,* 91 n.

Powell, Thomas, *The Art of Thriving,* 154 n.

Prateus, Ludovicus, 84 n.

Preston Candover, Hampshire, 79 n.

Prior, Matthew, xi; influential on F's love-poetry, xxviii; *Literary Works* (ed. H. Bunker Wright and Monroe K. Spears): 'Adriani Morientis ad Animam Suam Imitated', quoted: 59 n.; *Alma,* 52 n.; *Carmen Seculare,* quoted: 36 n.; 'Cupid Mistaken', 72 n.; 'The Despairing Shepherd', quoted: 82 n.; 'The Dove', 72 n.; *Down-Hall,* quoted: 55 n.; 'Epigram' (Yes, every Poet is a Fool), 65 n.; *Henry and Emma,* quoted: 79 n.; 'Her Right

Name', quoted: 72 n.; 'The Ladle', quoted: 15 n., 51 n.; 'Love Disarm'd', 70 n.; 'A Lover's Anger', quoted: 74 n.; 'Paulo Purganti and His Wife', 70 n.; 'Predestination', quoted: 153 n.; 'Presented to the King', 68 n., quoted: 38 n.; 'Satyr on the Poets', quoted: 70 n.; *Solomon*, 56 n., 166 n., 224 n., quoted: 20 n., 32 n., 33 n., 44 n., 68 n.; 'To a Child of Quality', quoted: 82 n.; 'To Fleetwood Shephard', quoted: 57 n.; 'To Mr. Charles Montagu, on His Marriage', quoted: 82 n.; 'The Wedding-Night', quoted: 62 n. Prose: dedication to *Poems* (1709), 150 n.; *The Hind and the Panther Transvers'd* (with Charles Montagu), quoted: 45 n.

Priscus, Helvidius description of, by Tacitus, 29 n.

Propertius, Sextus, *Elegies*, xxviii, 69 n., 82 n., *84 n., 118 n.

Prussia, 93 n.

Publilius Syrus, *Sententiae*, quoted: 158 n.

Pufendorf, Samuel, *De jure naturae et gentium*, 32 n.

Pulteney, William (later Earl of Bath), xiv, 73, 73 n., 75 n., 248 n.; compliment to, 248; possibly F's false 'Patriot', 53 n.

Pulton, Ferdinando, *De pace regis et regni*, 167 n.

Pump Court, Middle Temple, xv.

Purney, Thomas, *The Ordinary of Newgate His Account*, 8 n.

Puttenham, Richard (attrib.), *Arte of English Poesie*, 95 n.

Pydna, in Demosthenes' oration, 206, 207, 208.

Pyrrho(n) of Elis, xxxii, xxxii n.

Pythagoras, *see* Dryden trans. Ovid's *Metamorphoses*.

Quadrille, card-game, 133.

Quin, James, actor, 53 n.; compliment to, 53, 136.

Quintilian (Marcus Fabius Quintilianus), 94, 114; *Institutio oratoria*, 147 n., 159 n.

Rabelais, François, xvii, xxxix, 42 n., 174 n.

Rackham, H., 20 n., 120 n.

Ralph, James, *The Touchstone*, quoted: 152 n.

Rawson, Claude J., vii.

Ray, John, *The Wisdom of God Manifested*, 175 n.

Réaumur, René Antoine Ferchault de, *Mémoires pour servir à l'histoire des insectes*, 195 n.

Rehearsal, The, see Buckingham.

Rhodes, island of, 23 n., 116.

Rich, John, manager of Covent-Garden Theatre, 5, 5 n.

Richards, John, *Hoglandiae descriptio*, 54 n.

Richardson, Samuel, xlvii n., xlviii; *Pamela*, xliv n., 85 n., 99, 99 n.; and F's *Shamela*, xiii.

Richmond, Charles Lennox, 2nd Duke of, 30 n.; F's *Of Good-Nature* addressed to, 30 ff.

Richmond, Sarah Lennox, Duchess of, 30 n., 35 n., 79 n.; compliment to, 35, 79.

Ring, the, in Hyde Park, 63, 63 n.

Roberts, Edgar V., vii.

Robertson, D. W., Jr., vii.

Robertson, J. Logie, 31 n., 34 n., 38 n., 40 n., 41 n., 53 n., 118 n.

Robinson, Sir Thomas, 103 n.

Rochester, John Wilmot, Earl of, 30 n.; *Satyr against Mankind*, 33 n., 153 n., quoted: 33 n., 153; 'Upon Nothing', xxxix, 179, 179 n.

Rollins, Charles, *Histoire ancienne*, 36 n.

Rome (Romans), xxxi, 36 n., 40, 40 n., 54, 54 n., *84 n., *101 n., *103 n., *107 n., *109 n., 177, 177 n.(2), 188, 188 n. *See also* Latin language.

Roscommon, Wentworth Dillon, Earl of, 'On Mr. Dryden's *Religio Laici*', 33 n.

Rothschild, Ferdinand, Baron, 131 n.

Royal College of Physicians, 111 n.

Royal Exchange, 177, 177 n.

Royal Society, xxi n., xl, xl n., 191 ff.; *Philosophical Transactions* of, xxxix, xl, xlv, 191 ff., 193 n., *195 n., *198 n., *199 n., *200 n., *202 n., quoted: 197 ff., 253–9 (Appendix D). *See also* F's *Some Papers Proper to be Read before the R—l Society*.

Sabine maidens, in Juvenal, 104.

Sailor's Opera, The, 67 n.

St. Augustine, *De civitate dei*, 37 n., 175 n., 230 n.

St. Bartholomew's Day, 93 n.

St. James's Evening Post, xlvii n.

St. James's Park, 58 n.

St. John Chrysostom, 159 n.

St. Paul, xviii n., 168. *See also* Bible.

St. Peter, 60, *60 n., 251.

Sale, William M., xlvii n.

Salisbury, Wiltshire, 68–70, 68 n., 69 n., 71 n., 79, 79 n.

Sallust (Gaius Sallustius Crispus), 64 n.

Salmasius, Claudius, Latin scholar, *94 n.

Samos, island of, associated with Juno, 40, 40 n.

Sandwich, Countess of, 78 n.

Saturn, 84, *84 n., *85 n., *86 n.

Sayre, Farrand, 231 n., 234 n.

Scipio Africanus Major, Publius Cornelius, *105 n.

Scotland, 19, 195 n.

Scott, Daniel, *A New Version of St. Matthew's Gospel*, 168 n.

Scouten, Arthur H., 7 n., 8 n., 67 n.

Scripture, *see* Bible.

Seagrim, Randolph, debtor to Fielding, xvi.

Seasonable Admonition to a Great Man, A, quoted: xxxi n.

Second Homeric Hymn to Aphrodite, 79 n.

Sedley, Sir Charles, *Bellamira*, 153 n.; 'On Fruition', quoted: 62 n.

Semele, and Jupiter, 237 n.

Seneca, Lucius Annaeus, 23, 213; on consolation, xxxviii, 212 n.; *De beneficiis*, 227 n.; *De brevitate vitae*, 10 n.; *De clementia*, 30 n.; *De consolatione ad Helviam matrem*, quoted: 137 n.; *De consolatione ad Marciam*, xxxviii n., 212 n., 216 n., 220 n., 221 n., 222 n.(2); *De consolatione ad Polybium*, xxxviii n., 212 n., 216 n., 218 n., 222 n., quoted: 159 n.; *De constantia sapientis*, 214 n., 216 n.; *De ira*, 120 n., 160 n., quoted: 212; *De otio*, 33 n.; *De tranquillitate animi*, 170 n., 213 n., 216 n.; *De vita beata*, 170 n., 213 n.(2); *Epistulae morales*, xxxviii n., 10 n., 33 n., 51 n., 56 n., 174 n., 188 n., 212 n.(2), 213 n.(2), 214 n.(2), 216 n., 218 n.(2), 220 n., quoted: 124 n.; *Naturales quaestiones*, 228 n.; *Phoenissae*, 221 n.

Sergius, Roman gladiator, in Juvenal, *95 n., 96, *96 n., 97, *97 n., 98, 99.

Serpentine, the, in Hyde Park, 63 n.

Shaftesbury, Anthony Ashley Cooper, 3rd Earl of, 12 n., 220 n.; *Characteristicks: Inquiry Concerning Virtue and Merit*, 125 n., quoted: 30 n.; *Letter Concerning Enthusiasm*, quoted: 126, 157; *Miscellaneous Reflections*, quoted: 10 n., 33 n.; *The Moralists*, 33 n.; *Sensus Communis*, 119 n., 149 n.; *Soliloquy*, quoted: 25 n., 126 n., 181 n.

Shaftesbury, Dorset, 68 n.

Shaftesbury, Susannah Noel Cooper, Countess of, 35 n.; compliment to, 35.

Shakespeare, William, Theobald's edition, 69 n.; *All's Well That Ends Well*, quoted: 222 n.; *As You Like It*, 140 n.; *Hamlet*, 222 n., quoted: 127 n., 159, 222;

2 Henry IV, quoted: 81 n.; *Julius Caesar*, quoted: 151; *King Lear*, quoted: 33 n., 180; *Love's Labour's Lost*, 95 n.; *Merchant of Venice*, quoted: 38 n.; *Merry Wives of Windsor*, *89 n.; *Othello*, 48 n., quoted: 174; *Sonnets*, 61 n.; *Venus and Adonis*, 61 n.

Sheers, Sir Henry, 176 n.

Sherburn, George, vii. *See also* Pope.

Sheridan, Richard Brinsley, 6 n.

Sherlock, William, *Practical Discourse Concerning Death*, quoted: 225, 225 n.

Shilleto, A. R., 31 n., 45 n., 49 n., 60 n., 72 n., 141 n., 142 n., 155 n., 177 n., 242 n.

Sidney, Algernon, *Discourses Concerning Government*, 38 n., *113 n.

Sidney, Sir Philip, *Arcadia*, 99 n.

Silius Italicus, Tiberius Catius Asconius, *Punica*, xxvii, 81, 81 n. *See also* F's 'A Simile, from Silius Italicus'.

Silver Age, 86, 86 n., 87.

Simonides of Ceos, xxxii.

Simplicius of Cilicia, commentator on Epictetus, xxxiv n.

Simpson, Evelyn M., 159 n.

Sinope, birthplace of Diogenes, *226 n., 231 n.

Sirius, star, 118 n.

Sloane, Sir Hans, collector, 60, 60 n.

Sloper, William, and Mrs. Cibber, 89 n.

Smart, Christopher, *The Hilliad*, xlviii.

Smith, Alexander, *Memoirs of the Life and Times of Jonathan Wild*, 8 n.

Smith, John, *Select Discourses*, 143 n.

Smith, W. G., 64 n.

Socrates, xviii n., 12, 42 n., 123, 142, 143(2), 184, 184 n., 213, 223, 224 n., 225, 231 n.

Solomon, 168, 221, 223, 224 n.; Ecclesiastes, Proverbs, *see* Bible; apocryphal Book of Wisdom, 221 n.

Solon, 224, 224 n.

Soper, John, 79 n.

Soper, Patience, 79 n.; probable compliment to, 79.

South, Robert, *Sermons*, 157 n., 170 n.(2), quoted: 30 n., 33 n., 137 n., 158 n., 167 n., 168 n., 170, 171 n., 188 n., 204 n.

Spain (Iberia), 40, 40 n., 60, 68, 78, 97, *103 n., 115, 205 n., 251.

Spanish Succession, War of the, 40 n.

Sparta, 36 n., 177. *See also* Lacedaemon.

Spears, Monroe K., *see* Prior.

Spectator, The, 9 n., 28 n., 30 n., 42 n.(2), 52 n., 56 n., 60 n., 99 n., 113 n., 119 n., 130 n., 146 n., 147 n., 149 n., 158 n.,

159 n., 165 n., 175 n., 177 n., 220 n., quoted: xxxviii n., xli n., 24 n., 28 n., 43 n., 70 n., 77 n., 121 n., 125 n., 127 n., 145 n., 157 n., 164 n., 188 n., 214 n., 220 n. *See also* Addison, Steele.

Spence, Joseph, *Observations*, quoted: xxxii n.

Spencer, Floyd A., 70 n.

Spenser, Edmund, *Daphnaida*, quoted: 63 n.; *Faerie Queene*, 31 n., 46 n., 79 n.

Stair, John Dalrymple, 2nd Earl of, anecdote of, 131, 131 n.

Stanhope, George, trans. Epictetus, xxxiv n.

Steele, Sir Richard, *Guardian*, quoted: 31 n. (see *Guardian*); *The Lying Lover*, 160 n.; *Tatler*, quoted: 49 n., 57 n. (see *Tatler*); *The Tender Husband*, quoted: 35 n., 52 n.

Stephen, Leslie, edition of F's *Works*, xlix.

Stevens, John, trans. Mariana's *General History of Spain*, 4 n.

Stillingfleet, Edward, Bishop of Worcester, 181 n.

Stilpo, Megaran philosopher, 214, 214 n., 217.

Stimson, Dorothy, xl n.

Stoics, xxiii, 30 n., 31 n., 33 n., 154; F's attitude toward, xxiii n.

Stokes, Bob, prize-fighter, 111 n.

Stokes, Mrs. Elizabeth, prize-fighter, 111, 111 n.

Strabo, *Geographica*, 60 n.

Strachey, Sir Charles, 132 n.

Strafford, Earl(s) of, 63, 63 n.

Strahan, William, printer of Volume I of F's *Miscellanies*, xlvii n., liv.

Stratocles of Amphipolis, in Demosthenes' oration, 207.

Sturgess, H. A. C., 51 n.

Suetonius (Gaius Suetonius Tranquillus), xxix, xxxiii n.

Sulmo, Italy, in Juvenal, 106.

Sulpicius Rufus, Servius, epistle to Cicero, 224 n.

Susa, Persian winter capital, 228, 228 n.

Sutherland, James, vii. *See also* Pope.

Sutton, Ned, the Champion of Kent, 111 n.

Sutton, Mrs., prize-fighter, 111, 111 n.

Swift, Jonathan, xvii, 193 n.; marginal note on Hanover, quoted: 193 n.; *The Prose Writings* (gen. ed., Herbert Davis): *A Discourse Concerning the Mechanical Operation of the Spirit*, 183 n.; *Gulliver's Travels*, 119 n., 137 n., 143 n., 241 n., quoted: 44 n., 164 n. (*see also* F's poem to Celia, 'On Her Wishing to Have a Lilliputian'); 'Hints towards an Essay on Conversation', 149 n.; *Intelligencer*,

quoted: 204 n.; 'On Good-Manners and Good Breeding', quoted: xxxv n.; *Polite Conversation*, 195 n., quoted: 54 n.; *Tatler*, 153 n.; 'Thoughts on Various Subjects', quoted: xxxvii n.; *A Tale of a Tub*, xxxix, 179 n., 221 n., quoted: xxxix n., 188 n. Letters: *Journal to Stella* (ed. Sir Harold Williams), quoted: 91 n. *The Poems* (ed. Sir Harold Williams): '[Charles Carthy's] Modest Apology for Knocking Out a Newsboy's Teeth' (attrib.), quoted: 67 n.; 'A Quibbling Elegy on Judge Boat', quoted: 66 n.; 'The Run upon the Bankers', quoted: 57 n.; 'To Mr. Congreve', quoted: 19 n.

Sybaris, city of Italy, in Juvenal, 116.

Syphax, king of Numidia, 104.

Tacitus, Publius (?) Cornelius, 36 n., 64 n.; *Agricola*, 29 n., quoted: 177 n.; *Annals*, xxix n., 170 n.; *History*, 29 n.

Tallard, Marshal, captured at Blenheim, 47, 47 n.

Tarentum, city of Italy, in Juvenal, 116.

Tarpeian Rock, in Juvenal, 90.

Tarquin, the second (Tarquinius Superbus), 125.

Tatler, The, 30 n., 99 n., 130 n., 137 n., 153 n., 161 n., 195 n., quoted: 24 n., 42 n., 44 n., 49 n., 54 n., 57 n., 97 n., 126 n., 132 n.(2), 142 n., 157 n., 165 n., 177 n., 218 n. *See also* Addison, Steele, Swift.

Taylor, Robert, vii.

Teerink, H., 64 n.

Temple, Sir R., 52 n.

Temple, Sir William, *Essay upon the Original and Nature of Government*, 153 n.; *Observations upon the United Provinces*, 81 n.

Temple Bar, 130, 130 n.

Terence (Publius Terentius Afer), xvii; *Adelphi*, quoted: *114 n.

Test Act, 26 n.

Thales, 223, 224 n.

Thalia, muse of comedy, 240.

Thames River, 89.

Thebes, *105 n.; in Demosthenes' oration, 211.

Theobald, Lewis, 69 n.; mocked by F, 69. *See also* Shakespeare.

Theocritus, *Idylls*, 25 n., 118 n.

Theophrastus, xxxiv.

Thessaly, in Demosthenes' oration, 208, 210.

Thomas, Elizabeth (attrib.), *Codrus: or the Dunciad Dissected*, 51 n.

Thomas, W. Moy, 76 n., 81 n.

Thomson, James, xxviii, 19 n.; *Liberty*, xlv, 36 n.(2), 40 n.(2), 41 n., 52 n., quoted: 38 n., 41 n., 230 n.; *The Seasons*: 'Spring', quoted: 31 n., 34 n.; 'Summer', 41 n., quoted: 40 n.; 'Autumn', 23 n., 29 n., quoted: 53 n.; 'To Amanda', 118 n.

Thornton, Bonnell, *Drury-Lane Journal*, 231 n.

Thorpe, James, vii.

Thrace, in Demosthenes' oration, 208; Olynthus in, 205.

Tibullus, Albius, *Elegies*, xxviii, 29 n., 54 n., 82 n., 118 n.(2), quoted: 221.

Tillotson, Geoffrey, *see* Pope.

Tisiphone, 86, 87, *87 n.

Titian, 52, 52 n.

Titius, T. (?), Cicero's consolation to, 222 n., 224 n.

Trembley, Abraham, Swiss naturalist, xxxix, xxxix n., xl, 193 n., 202, 253 ff. *See also* F's *Some Papers Proper to be Read before the R—l Society*.

'Trifler, T.', 'The Elogy of Nothing', 179 n.

True Patriot, see Fielding.

Tullia, Cicero's grief at death of, 214 n.

Tully, *see* Cicero.

Tunbridge Wells, 91.

Turnebus, Adrianus, 89 n.

Tyrrhenian Sea, in Juvenal, 96.

Upton Grey, Hampshire, 53, 53 n., 79 n. *See also* F's 'A Description of U—n G—'.

Ustick, W. Lee, xxxiv n.

Valerius Maximus, *Dictorum factorumque memorabilium*, 226 n., 227 n.

Vandals, 40. *See also* Goths.

Vartanian, Aram, xxxix n.

Vejento, Fabricius, *95 n.

Venice, 36 n., 89 n.; Venetian school of painting, 52 n.

Venn, J. A., 51 n.

Venn, John, 51 n.

Venus, 39, 40, 40 n., 69, 71, 77–80, 79 n., 101, 236, 237, 239.

Vernon, Admiral Edward, xiii. *See also* F's *Vernoniad*.

Versailles, 55, 55 n.

Vertot, l'Abbé René Aubert de, *Histoire des révolutions de la république romaine*, 36 n.

Villars, Duc de, Marshal of France, defeated at Malplaquet, 47, 47 n.

Vince, Miss (of Salisbury ?), 71, 71 n.

Virgil (Publius Vergilius Maro), xxvii, xxviii, 24; *Aeneid*, 80 n., 81 n., 105, *105 n., quoted: 80, *86 n., 237 n.; trans. Dryden, 22 n., 37 n., quoted: 55 n., 80 n.; *Eclogues*, 64 n., 69 n., quoted: 25 n., 197; trans. Dryden, 34 n.; *Georgics*, 34 n.; trans. Dryden, 34 n., quoted: 24 n., 46 n.; trans. Addison, quoted: 55 n. *See also* F's 'A Parody, from the First Aeneid'.

Vogt, George M., 141 n.

Waller, Edmund, xxviii; poems: 'Of a War with Spain', 34 n.; 'On the Duke of Monmouth's Expedition', quoted: 28 n.; 'To a Fair Lady, Playing with a Snake', quoted: 60 n.

Waller, Edmund, political writer, *see* Chesterfield.

Walpole, Horace, 'The Praises of a Poet's Life', quoted: xii n.; *Yale Edition of the Correspondence* (gen. ed., Wilmarth S. Lewis): 57 n., 93 n.(2), 103 n., 185 n., quoted: 193 n.

Walpole, Sir Robert, xxvii, xxx, xxxi n., xlii, 30 n., 31 n., 56–9, 58 n., 64 n., 66 n., 73, 95 n., 111 n., 193 n., 248 n., 249, 251; and F's *Jonathan Wild*, xi, xxix, xliii, 9 n.; and F's *The Opposition*, xiii, xiii n.; appealed to by F for patronage, xiii n., 56 n., 59 n., 248 n.; attacked by F in: early plays, 56 n.; *Dialogue between Alexander and Diogenes*, 229 n.; *Essay on the Knowledge of the Characters of Men* (?), 176; *The First Olynthiac of Demosthenes* (?), xlii, 205 n.; *A Full Vindication of the Duchess of Marlborough*, xiv; *Liberty*, 37 n., 41 n.; *Of True Greatness*, 25 n., 26, 247 n.; *The Vernoniad*, xiii, 57 n.; created Earl of Orford, 56, 56 n.; fall of, xiii, xiv(2), 9 n., 53 n., 176 n., 190 n.; subscribed to F's *Miscellanies*, xlviii. *See also* F's epistles 'To the Right Honourable Sir Robert Walpole', and Opposition, above.

Walter, Peter, scrivener, 67, 67 n., 130, 193 n., 199 n.; as 'Petrus Gualterus' in F's *Some Papers*, xl, 191 ff.

Warburton, William, *Divine Legation of Moses Vindicated*, *90 n., *91 n.

Wars, *see* Austrian Succession, Jenkins's Ear, Spanish Succession. *See also* Battles.

Wasey, Dr. William, physician, 111, 111 n.

Watts, John, printer, 63, 63 n. *See also* F's 'J—n W—ts at a Play'.

Weekly Register, quoted: 73 n.

Wells, John Edwin, xlvii n., liv n., 57 n.

Wesley, Samuel, the elder, *Poems on Several Occasions*, 66 n., 231 n.

West Indies, 105. *See also* India.

Westminster Abbey, 66 n.

Westminster Hall, xii.

Wharncliffe, Lord, 76 n., 81 n.

Whichcote, Benjamin, *Select Sermons*, quoted: xxx.

Whisk, card-game, 133.

Whitby, Daniel, *A Paraphrase and Commentary on the New Testament*, 124 n.

Whole Art of Converse, The, by 'D. A. Gent.', xxxiv.

Wiggin, Lewis, M., xiv n.

Wild, Jonathan, xi, 8–9, 8 n.(2). *See also* F's *Jonathan Wild*.

Wilks, Robert, actor, 5, 5 n., 6.

Williams, Aubrey, *see* Pope.

Williams, Sir Charles Hanbury, 193 n.; 'A New Ode', quoted: 53 n.; 'To Sir Thomas Robinson', 103 n.; trans. Horace ode, quoted: 79 n.

Williams, Sir Harold, *see* Swift.

Wiltshire, 71 n.

Woffington, Margaret (Peg), actress, xlviii, 93, 93 n.

Wolfius, Hieronymus, Latin trans. of Demosthenes, 205 n.

Wolverhampton, Staffordshire, 51 n.

Woodfall, Henry, the elder, probable printer of Volume II of F's *Miscellanies*, xlvii n.

Woods, Charles B., vii, 15 n.

Worcester, David, xxix n.

Work, James A., xxx n.

Wright, Andrew, xvii n.

Wright, H. Bunker, *see* Prior.

Wycherley, William, *The Plain Dealer*, 166 n.

Wynne, Sir Watkin Williams, 95 n.

Xenophon, 216 n.

Yonge, Sir William, politician, 66 n.

Young, Edward, xxviii, 19 n., 78 n.; compliment to, 26, 78, 136; *Love of Fame, the Universal Passion*, xxxi, 12 n., 26 n., 134 n., 228 n., quoted: 28 n., 29 n., 32 n., 45 n., 79 n., 186 n.

Young, William, *see* F. trans. Aristophanes' *Plutus*.

Zeuxis, 80 n.

Zirker, Malvin R., Jr., xxxi n.

Zollman, Philip Henry, F.R.S., 195 n., 254.